Journey Towards
a Falling Sun

T0308553

Journey Towards a Falling Sun

A novel by N. Lombardi Jr.

Author of *The Plain of Jars*

Winchester, UK
Washington, USA

First published by Roundfire Books, 2014
Roundfire Books is an imprint of John Hunt Publishing Ltd., Laurel House, Station Approach, Alresford, Hants, SO24 9JH, UK
office1@jhpbooks.net
www.johnhuntpublishing.com
www.roundfire-books.com

For distributor details and how to order please visit the 'Ordering' section on our website.

Text copyright: N. Lombardi Jr. 2013

ISBN: 978 1 78279 494 3

Design: Stuart Davies

Printed in the USA by Edwards Brothers Malloy

We operate a distinctive and ethical publishing philosophy in all areas of our business, from our global network of authors to production and worldwide distribution.

In memory of Keith Harwood

PROLOGUE:

NEW YORK, MARCH 23, 1984.

The taxi dashed desperately into another lane, hoping to percolate through the bottleneck on First Avenue. A siren wailed somewhere behind.

"Traffic's murder today. Anytime it rains, it's like that. Never fails."

The woman in the back of the cab put her face to the window, and focusing her eyes through streaking beads of water, stared beyond them at the black sheen of a rainwashed street.

"I dunno what it is about New York drivers," the cabbie said in a louder voice, "but every time it rains, they seem to go nuts."

Tessa Thorpe remained quiet, still gazing vacantly out the window, ignoring the driver's comment, his words somehow lost amidst the squawk of wipers rubbing against the windshield, the hum of the engine, and the splash of tires through the puddles.

The taxi pulled over to the curb. "Here we are, Belleview. Ten-fifty please."

Belleview. A name more ironic would be hard to find. Belleview. A Beautiful Sight.

She paid the cabbie, got out, and slammed the door behind her, not bothering to wait for her change. Battling a pointless reluctance, she climbed the steps to the entrance door.

Thorpe made her living as a psychiatrist, specifically in the field of law enforcement. Officially attached to the NYPD, her services were also at times requested by the likes of the FBI, the CIA, and in one case, Defense Intelligence. This time it was Interpol. And although she relished the challenges her profession posed, she hated the atmosphere exuded by the institutions she invariably had to work in; like this place, Belleview, although it still fared better than Creedmore.

The lobby, illuminated by a sterile white neon florescence, its walls painted a pale sickly green, contained a murmuring of subdued despair. She cut quickly through the crowd in the waiting room and walked straight to the reception.

"Can I help you?" a nurse asked in a nasal voice, her face full of the authority the counter between them had given her.

"I have an appointment with Dr. Goldstein."

"I'll call him. Just take a seat over there."

She headed over to one of the empty chairs by the wall and sat down, looking at the others waiting in the lobby: old people moping with solemn faces; children, oblivious of the anguish around them, playing much too loudly; and men and women, their manner and gestures betraying the discomfort associated with an unpalatable duty.

Tessa herself was a bit uneasy. She didn't like starting a case in the dark; she had never done so before and didn't see the reason why she had to do it now. Most of her subjects were dangerous psychotics, some of them high profile, but she was told that this was not the situation here, except perhaps for the possibility that he posed a danger to himself. There was indeed some criminality in the background of this thing, but from the briefing she got, this guy was some unwitting bystander. Although it was made to appear as an act of terrorism, evidence was mounting that this was not so. In any case, she needed him to talk.

Tessa liked her job, despite the fact that it practically robbed her of any semblance of a social life. And while she was certainly good-looking – bright brown eyes, thin but nevertheless inviting ruby lips, and lustrous dark brown hair (one lover referred to her as a languorous brunette) – she found the dating game tiresome. As macabre as it sounded, she enjoyed working with the criminally insane, although this guy was not a criminal, and she suspected he wasn't insane either.

"Dr. Thorpe?"

She looked up at a light-haired, lab-coated doctor with a bulbous nose looming over her. "Oh, hello...Doctor Goldstein?"

"Yes, that's right. Can we go to my office?"

She jumped up to follow him and on the way to the elevator she asked, "How is he? Is he coherent? I need to talk to him."

"He goes in and out. Came in what you might describe as a hysterical state, straight from the emergency ward at Columbia."

"Medication?"

"Xanax, Prozac, Valium, whatever it takes to calm him."

The bell rang as the metal doors opened up in front of them. The small crowd in the elevator inhibited further conversation, and they rode up in silence to the third floor.

"He's a bit catatonic at times," Goldstein said as they left the elevator.

She walked by his side as they proceeded down a strip-lighted corridor, the walls covered with white tiles, almost like one big bathroom, but with an exaggerated smell of disinfectant.

"He's been writing something," he added, as he opened the door to his office. "They found him in his hotel room covered with a jumble of handwritten papers, along with some other stuff." He crossed the room to his desk by the window and pulled out a large manila envelope from one of the drawers and handed it to her.

She emptied the contents of the envelope, the bulkiest item being a stack of letters bound with a rubber band, as well as the aforementioned sheets of papers, many of them rendered illegible by blood stains. There were also two photographs: one with a group of African children posing with balloons, with the subject in the back row standing next to a pretty black woman who held one of the children in her arms. The other photo showed only a bunch of balloons in the sky. On the back of that photograph, someone had scrawled the word "Freedom!"

Then there were the newspaper clippings, four of them:

AMERICAN, TWO OTHERS, KILLED IN TURKANA DISTRICT
AMERICAN FOUND ALIVE!

BOMB BLAST ROCKS LONDON HOTEL – IRA SUSPECTED
KENYAN GOVERNMENT RELEASES AMERICAN DETAINEE

She returned the contents to the envelope, which she then stuffed inside her briefcase as they left the office. Goldstein led her down the same corridor as before and stopped at Room 304, a private room. Inside this room, a bed and a lamp-less night table were the only pieces of furniture. Sitting on the bed was a young man, knees drawn to his chest and hunched over with folded arms; his head, capped with shiny black curly hair, was cradled in his limbs as if he were exhausted. Both his wrists were heavily bandaged with gauze and cotton.

"Daryl? Daryl?" Goldstein said.

The slumped figure made no response.

"Daryl, how are you feeling?" A standard question that was met with silence.

"Dr. Thorpe has come a long way to see you. It seems you're special."

"My medicine," the stricken man moaned from the alcove of his groin.

"Not for another…" the doctor brought his arm up to look at his wristwatch, "…hour and a half."

The patient finally lifted his head, revealing a tawny complexion. He was young, in his early thirties, and his ethnicity was an ambiguous blend of Afro-European. Fairly good-looking, except that his face was bruised and puffed up.

"Self-inflicted," Goldstein explained, seeing that Thorpe had taken note. "He gets these fits and starts hitting himself, especially when he comes down off the medication. Had to put him in restraints a few times."

"Hello, Daryl," Tessa said.

"You're a policeman," the subject said. "I mean woman. Policewoman. They sent one yesterday, a policeman, a man police, but I really wasn't feeling well yesterday."

4

"I'm a doctor. A psychiatrist."

"I don't feel well today either. I'll never feel well," he said, not listening to her. Then he motioned to her to come closer, closer, closer, so he could whisper in her ear. "I have a confession", he confided softly. "I killed them, both of them."

It was then that Tessa slipped up, despite her eleven years at the job. She forgot to move her head away when she made her rebuttal. "No, Daryl, that's just your guilt making you feel that way."

"DON'T YOU DARE FUCKING CONTRADICT ME!" he screamed, too late for her to take her ear away in time. She covered it, and with a grimacing face, summoned her professional discipline to check her initial anger, as Goldstein placed his hands on the young man's shoulders, fearing he might become uncontrollable.

An orderly stepped into the room, in an automatic response to the screaming, which was not allowed, and stood ready to intervene.

"Where's my medication?" the young man repeated.

"I told you, another..."

"Alright, don't fucking give it to me. Let me suffer. I deserve to be tortured. I understand." Then he went sort of glassy-eyed. "It doesn't matter what you do, or don't do...because the stars...the stars...they don't sing for me anymore." He paused to jerk his head up, looking at the ceiling, his eyes roaming in search of imperceptible objects. "Nothing...nothing...they're silent..."

Then he went into a brief fit of uncontrollable sobbing before punching himself in the face, at which point the orderly swiftly approached to hold his arms down on the bed. The patient summarily calmed down, giving Tessa the chance to try again.

"The doctor tells me you've been writing something," she broke in. "What is it? Want to tell me about that?"

The patient stared blankly upwards, taking his time before answering, "It's a story," he finally said.

"What kind of story?"

"A love story."

"Are you in the story?" After getting no response, she asked another question. "Do you remember the man? Did you ever see him?"

Daryl Loomis just stared up.

"I want him off his medication by tomorrow," she promptly addressed Goldstein. "He's no use to me like this."

"WHERE'S MY MEDICATION?" he suddenly screamed at the mention of the word.

"And put him in restraints before I arrive," she instructed.

"Understood."

PART 1

ENCOUNTER

NAIROBI, AUGUST 15, 1979.

The sidewalks were crowded that day; a Monday morning, like any other Monday morning, the pavements stirring with a medley of bobbing pedestrians returning to routines they had abandoned on Friday afternoon.

On that day he casually sauntered along, finding himself immersed in a sea of ethnic diversity: African businessmen nattily dressed in three-piece suits and tasteful ties; circumspect Indians in drab-colored buttoned shirts and polyester slacks; Sikhs sporting their extravagant turbans and prominent beards; Somalis with Kushite faces of burnt copper marked by aquiline noses; Arabized-Indianized Swahili, an indigenous race from the coast of East Africa; and even more striking, quite incongruous in this urban setting, Masai warriors robed in their flashy red tunics and carrying their spears. All of them contributing to a potpourri of races and cultures jostling under a gentle August sun, in streets congested with horn-blaring traffic.

Nairobi, Green City in the Sun. A venue for international conferences. The Great Metropolis of Black Africa.

Daryl Loomis gave a casual glance to the cylindrical tower of the Nairobi Hilton, clear and prominent in the morning light, then, more attentively, to the office girls in tight skirts chattering loquaciously on their way to coffee houses for their mid-morning break. Their silky brown legs and softly swaying curves intoxicated him, filling him with the exuberant promises of a beautiful day.

Fuck, it's great to be alive.

In this diverse plethora of humanity, Loomis felt comfortable. Born from the union of a Nordic father and a Bahamian mother, he now lived in a place where he did not have to choose one heritage over the other. Here, he was neither white nor black, but an exotic blend. His curly black hair capped the square, long-jawed face of a northern European, which contrasted with the rounded features and milk-chocolate skin within it. His lips were full and sensual, his nose a bit broad but subdued, his facial appearance not distinctive enough to fully define his origin. His eyes, which he considered as his most valuable asset in his pursuit of women, were wide and bright and hazel-colored, changing from a golden-amber hue to an opalescent jade, depending on the light.

He hummed as he walked, lacking any sense of destination, but content in knowing that today he had money in his pocket; drinking and womanizing money enough for at least two weeks. Feeling just fine, he ambled along, sometimes rather haughtily, putting both hands in his trouser pockets, leaving his lips alone to support the cigarette dangling from his mouth. With no plan to fulfill, no place to be until his meeting with Barnes, he was just killing time, carrying himself at a relaxed pace down Moi Avenue, his oversize cashmere sport coat hanging loosely from his broad shoulders.

Let the good times roll. That was life's purpose for Daryl Loomis.

But as he reached the small plaza in front of Standbank House, a young African in a pinstripe suit ran past, bumping Loomis roughly and jolting him out of his short-lived rapture. The man ran on ahead, as if in pursuit of an escaping bus, and Loomis saw a small package drop from his hands onto the pavement. Another African, similarly attired in a suit, picked up the package, then called in vain at the unresponsive runner, who was apparently already out of earshot. The man with the package finally turned toward a young African woman who was walking alone in the same direction.

"*Huyu ame angusha bahasha yake*, that man has dropped his package," he told her, "but he didn't hear me. Now he has totally disappeared. *Nifanyeje*? What should I do?"

The woman, her slender figure revealed under a clinging pink dress, slowed her gait to a halt, tilted her sunglasses to the edge of her curly-kit, wet-look, permed afro, and accepted the parcel from the stranger who beckoned her to inspect it. It was a thick brown envelope, with a plastic window showing the face of a one-hundred-shilling note.

"There's a lot of money in here, but there's no name or address written on it anywhere," she remarked in good Kiswahili, still scrutinizing the envelope. Her face was delicate and attractive. "I'm sure he'll be right back looking for it. He can't have gone far before missing such a valuable package," she added.

"No, that man is gone... *kabisa*! Completely! I saw him getting into a car. Now, what are we going to do with this?"

Loomis, who had stopped just behind them to watch what was unfolding, decided that this girl was good-looking enough to make the effort. He threw his butt down and stepped forward, and then grabbed the shoulder of the man's suit jacket and dragged him towards a parked car by the curb. Shoving him against the car, he exploded with a barrage of insults and accusations.

"*Wewe wasumbua msichana wangu, eh*? You bothering my girl? Thought she was alone you piece of shit...you *mwizi*...fucking thief...I should..."

"Just what do you think you're doing?" the woman exclaimed, her eyes bulging with disbelief. "He's not a thief! He happens to be a Good Samaritan who is trying to return money to its rightful owner!"

Loomis wheeled around to face her. "Good Samaritan my..." He checked himself, "It's a con, this man is a crook!"

Though his accent sounded American, she still could not construe his exact origin. "I don't know where you come from," she said, just as the shaken guy pressed against the Toyota broke Loomis's grip and dashed across the street, "but here in Kenya people tend to help one another, even if they are strangers."

Her tone, sanctimonious and preachy, put him off. Perhaps he should have minded his own business. "Maybe upcountry, but not in Nairobi," he retorted with an equally holier-than-thou voice, shaking his head slightly from side to side in order to sound more forceful. His intervention, considering that its sole purpose was saving a damsel in distress and consequently being rewarded with a romantic rendezvous, was appearing to be for naught.

Some of the people walking by had already stopped and gathered to view this exchange.

"How would you know?" she said, in the manner of a mother castigating her child. "And acting like you know me... Who do you think you are to come barging in, manhandling people?"

The onlookers chuckled at that, and Loomis was beginning to feel stupid. "Wait a minute, I was only... "

"If I were you, I would leave this instant before that man brings a policeman here to arrest you for assault."

This advice brought forth another burst of laughter from the spectators.

"You're shaming me in front of these people," he protested

"You *should* be ashamed," she chided.

Again, a hearty round of chortles from the audience.

"I should?" He looked at her, making a strong effort at being angry, but failed. Her expression, harsh as it was, could not hide the beauty of a flawlessly oval face, set with an engaging, full-curved mouth, a flat button of a nose, and, above her high noble cheek-bones, almond-shaped eyes seductively hooded with an Oriental allure. It was the face of an African princess, covered in a skin of dark satin, the erotic camber of her jawline merging into a long and graceful neck. How could he get mad at that?

Distracted by desire, he embarked on his own patronizing lecture. "Listen, babe, that man was about to suggest to you a trip around the corner to share the loot, since obviously the owner cannot be traced, or perhaps he would convince you that it was stolen money anyway. He would argue against bringing it to the police by saying they would just pocket it and your loss would be their gain. Then this person leads you to a place known to him and – what do you know – an accomplice comes in claiming he's a policeman and is going to lock the both of you up. Now the first fellow starts getting panicky and urges you to pay the cop off with some 'chai' so that he'll let the two of you go free. If that ruse doesn't work, then the both of them will just take your money by force. Even the person who dropped the envelope was in on it. You'll see there's only that one note inside, the rest is just paper stuffing to make it look like it contains a fortune."

"That is a ridiculous story. Maybe it's you who wants to keep this money."

A fit of guffaws erupted from the crowd. The group had become larger by now, sidewalk diversions being of popular interest to Nairobi passers-by.

"Now you're the one being ridiculous. A hundred shillings couldn't last me fifteen minutes at the bar. I'm not that desperate. You keep it."

The crowd thought that one was hilarious, and their strident belly laughs confirmed this.

"I certainly will not!" And with that she replaced her sunglasses and briskly walked away.

"Where are you going?" he asked incredulously.

She turned. "To the police!"

The crowd applauded, cheered, and whistled, and Loomis walked away feeling like a jerk.

* * *

His morning peace shattered, he made his way towards Mama Ngina Street, then entered a coffee shop. He joined the queue to buy his coffee and samosas, then wove his way past business people and tourists to get the last empty table, which was still littered with cups from previous patrons. While arranging himself in his seat he watched one of the bus girls as she cleaned an adjacent table, taking in the voluptuous outline of her tight skirt as it wiggled with her laboring. His size exactly, he noted. His ego still bruising from the envelope incident, he sought to soothe it, so when she came to his table to clear the used cups, he greeted her. "*Habari*?"

"*Mzuri*. Fine."

"What's your name?" Loomis inquired nonchalantly, while

squeezing a lemon slice over his samosas.

"Evelyn."

"Hello, I'm Daryl."

"*Jambo*," she greeted in a happy tone.

"Evelyn who?"

"Evelyn Mbita."

"Oh, *wimuseo!*" Loomis exclaimed. Recognizing from her African name the girl's tribal origins, he began to converse with her in the Kamba language, her mother tongue, making Evelyn giggle in admiration, as it was designed to do, as it was also designed to get her address, phone number, marital status, her hours off, and a tentative date for Wednesday, all of which he obtained by the end of their conversation.

"We shall meet," she said afterwards, going back to her duties with a smile.

* * *

Pamela Amonee Emuria stopped at the curb just as the pedestrian signal flashed red, even though the way was clear. One could never be too cautious with these madmen drivers, especially the city buses. She stood fidgeting, waiting for the light to change, as she knew she risked being late for her choir practice. But better late than never; first she had to do her civic duty.

After crossing the street she continued hurriedly down Moi Avenue until it curved around and became University Way, and walked up to the Central Police Station. She entered inside and greeted the reporting officer. "*Habari.*"

"*Mzuri,*" he said gruffly, his eyes stern and probing, peering at her from the recesses of his puffy black face.

She took out the envelope from her *kikapu* basket and placed it on the counter. "This envelope was dropped by someone and it contains a great deal of money," she explained in her proper, grammatical Kiswahili.

"Let me have a look." As the policeman opened it, he grinned, then broke into full-fledged laughter, raising the envelope to show to his fellow officers behind the counter.

"There's nothing in here but paper," he told her, "and this one-hundred-shilling note. See?"

He showed her by pouring out its contents. "They were just crooks trying to cheat you. Did not one of them ask you to share the..." he paused to laugh, "ha...the loot?"

"Yes, but...he ran away."

"You want the hundred shillings?" he asked, bending his head forward and leering at her, before giving her a deriding wink.

"No...no, you keep it."

Hearty laughter followed her as she turned and walked towards the door. Swelling with shame, she made a hasty exit out of the station and walked quickly on towards the university, this time not paying any attention to the pedestrian signals.

* * *

Loomis found himself returning in the direction he had come from, cutting across Tom Mboya Street to leave behind the big-business affluence of the city center for the sleaziness of the River Roadi quarter: a bawdy area of ramshackle lodgings, merchant bazaars, and seedy bars, its streets full of people too numerous to be contained on the narrow sidewalks alone. Contrasting styles of music shouted from speakers hung outside bars and eateries, giving the place a carnival air, while out on the pavement, maize roasters turned their cobs over makeshift grills which they fanned incessantly. Miraa sellers, standing behind wooden stalls, continuously wrapped and unwrapped the banana leaves shrouding their herbaceous merchandise as they argued stridently with haggling clientele. In the tiny streets, big wooden handcarts, their sweat-soaked shirtless shunters huffing and panting from pulling their ponderous loads, vied with the motor traffic while Indian women in florid saris window-shopped with their unrestrained children. Rambling past all of them was a madman covered in rags, his buttocks partly exposed, singing fragments of traditional songs in between his litany of disjointed obscenities.

Appetizing aromas of *pilau* rice and *mikate wa mayai*, a meat-stuffed omelet, emanated from the doorways of Arab hoteli's, reminding Loomis that he was still hungry. He walked into the Yassin Hotel, greeting Abdullah, the manager, with the Islamic greeting, "*Salaam aleikum!*"

"*Wa alaikum assalaam*," returned the old Arab, chewing on a big wad of *miraa* stuffed in his left cheek. "You want to chew with me today, Mr. Daryl?"

"No, not today, Abdullah."

Abdullah popped a peppermint candy into his mouth to neutralize the bitterness of the masticated plant debris. He smiled showing green teeth. "Fresh from Meru, just now," he said, his jaws grinding non-stop.

"Some other time, *Bwana*," said Loomis, using the respectful Swahili form of address.

"So where you from? I not seeing you for many days," the Arab said, switching to his Pidgin English. "You hungry? You eat, I pay. On house."

Limping on his bad leg, he led Loomis over to one of the Formica-topped tables and sat him down in a steel chair which squawked vulgarly against the floor whenever it was moved.

"Chicken biriani very nice today."

"Sounds good to me, but just a half plate. And one samosa." He was practically addicted to samosas, and ate at least one at every opportunity.

"Wey, *kijana!*" yelled Abdullah at a black waiter in a white frock that looked like a lab coat. "Take his order. Me, I'm paying."

After Loomis told the waiter what he wanted, the young man screamed it out to the kitchen in the back and strode vigorously to another table. The Arab bent his head close to Loomis's ear and spoke in a low tone. "Mr. Daryl, I hear you in Tanzania."

"That's right. Came back on Saturday."

"Any gold?"

"No, Abdullah, no gold."

"Plenty gold in Tanzania. I have a friend...in Arusha...he does black market. Pays two hundred shillings one gram."

"I'll keep it in mind."

"What about red mercury? The Libyans paying a lot of money for that. They use it in jet planes."

"Never came across it."

"What? With all the digging you do?"

"I think it's a myth."

At this point, being called for more important business, the Arab said to Loomis, "We talk later, okay?" and hobbled off to his place behind the glass-fronted display counter that flaunted deep-fried Swahili snacks.

Tuning out the clamor of clanging chairs and yelled orders, he ate rapaciously.

Loomis then said goodbye to the Arab, who was on his way up to chew his miraa with a couple of cute Somali girls permanently residing in the second-floor lodgings. Grinning, Loomis turned and stepped back out onto the throng-filled streets.

* * *

Pamela was already late for her session with the university choir. When she arrived at the music hall she was dismayed to see the students milling about smoking cigarettes and laughing at their own private jokes. In her mind she admonished them. They could have been practicing the parts they had learned, or perhaps studying the next section of the score. She felt pressured, as the music festival was only three weeks away.

Music was the thread that wove Pamela's life; everything else she relegated to mundane necessity. For her, singing was aesthetically the highest of all human activities, fusing language and melody to express the supernal feelings of the soul; an act which acknowledged the wonder of creation.

Her teaching was driven by this conviction, so the attitude of her students naturally disheartened her. She reckoned that the next hour would be one of overly arduous labor, and not of shared exultation. It was so much easier with her children's choirs, she reflected, their artlessness leaving them uninhibited to discover the triumphant delight of their own voices.

The session was difficult, as she expected, but only in the beginning. She took each section separately, the tenors, the sopranos, the altos... While working with one group, the others got bored, even sleepy. But she continued undaunted, coaxing and nagging until each section was perfect. When, towards the end of the hour, they were all put together, they themselves were amazed with how their own diverse voices led to the creation of a unified and glorious sound, and they sang with smiles of revelation on their faces. But the biggest smile of all was Pamela's. *They have heard, they have realized.* She knew that from this point on the rest of the sessions would be easier.

Leaving the hall with a fresh exhilaration, Pamela went to her office to mark her first-year students' papers on elementary music theory. She was happy, so happy that she forgot all about the unpleasant events of her morning in town.

* * *

Eventually Loomis circled back to the city center as the hour of his appointment with Barnes was drawing near. At Kencom House, he looked on at a rather disorganized mob fighting to gain entrance into the *matatu* vans and city buses which had rolled in to haul them away, the size of the crowd constant as a steady flow replaced those who embarked. The matatu conductors, young Africans sloppily dressed in dirty cast-off clothes and an odd assortment of hats –

from balaclavas to berets – shouted out their routes above the noise of the main-street traffic and banged uproariously on the sides of their vehicles to signal the driver to move on whenever no more passengers were forthcoming. There seemed to be an unwritten law which prevented a conductor from getting into a stationary matatu, for they all without exception ran behind clinging to the doors of the vans as they sped away before clambering inside. The city buses were no less colorful. As the buses filled up with passengers, people tried to enter their narrow doorways three abreast, shoving and squeezing past each other, frantically determined to get a place inside, while many of them lost their wallets to pickpockets. The latecomers had to stand on the steps and hang tenaciously on to the doors as the buses made sharp turns at arrogant speeds, transforming a simple shuttle home into a commuter's equivalent of an amusement-park ride.

Loomis dodged across the busy thoroughfare and wove his way through the brimming sidewalks, heading towards Nairobi proper. While trying to stay within the shade of monolithic office blocks, his thoughts turned to the beggars huddled or standing at their stations. Many of them were lame or sick. The most tragic were the children: coughing, crying infants who slept through cold nights with their abandoned mothers, attracting sympathetic souls to the tin cans set out in front of them; young boys, when not foraging in the dustbins for food, offering to keep an eye on your car for a small fee, earning them the name of "parking boys"; and little girls who, by the age of ten or so, would start their careers in prostitution, begging shillings from passers-by. Loomis, after his seven years in East Africa, realized this phenomenon was not just a simple case of poverty, but also the result of a breakdown in traditional mores coming in the wake of so-called progress.

Entering Uni-Afric House, he crossed the marble-walled lobby to the elevator. Disembarking on the third floor, he glanced to his left and saw the offices of Hydro-drill Limited, guarded by thick glass doors that exposed a teak reception counter on the other side of them, and which required a strong effort to push them open.

"Hello, I'm Daryl Loomis. I believe Mr. Barnes is expecting me."

"One moment please." The receptionist, a young Indian girl, got on the intercom and spoke to it in a low, furtive voice – an office mannerism Loomis had come to hate. Looking up at him, she told him to have a seat.

He sat down and lit a cigarette to ease the nervousness he usually suffered before such meetings. Though not really caring about what other *wazungu*, Westerners, thought of him, he deemed it prudent to conceal his feelings about the Africans and the part they played in his social life. Most expatriates kept to themselves in exclusive clubs and fancy hotels, many of them money-minded professionals concerned with profits and getting the job done. The few Africans they did socialize with were generally highly placed wealthy elitist types. Uninterested in the lives of the local people, they were preoccupied with denouncing the inefficiency, indolence, and corruption which often marred the smooth running of their enterprises. Consequently, any discussions of the locals tended to be negative, and Loomis avoided such discussions, or else kept quiet while others talked. It made him feel awkward since most of his friends were mainstream black Africans, people whose company he enjoyed.

Still, his knowledge of the customs and languages of East Africa had gained him a reputation as a capable site administrator in addition to his skill as an engineer. He had an uncanny knack for uncovering and putting an end to such nuisances as petty theft, drunkenness, the pilfering of foodstuffs by the workers to seduce the village girls, and the clandestine selling off of valuable fuel. And although Loomis played around to the point of excess during his time off, he worked equally hard when under contract. As extreme as his vices were, he gave one hundred and ten percent when he was on the job. He took pride in his work and strived to instill this pride in his staff. His jobs kept him in the bush for months at a time, seven to eight months of the year, so naturally when he was released back into the city he wasted no time indulging in wine, women, and song.

"Mr. Loomis, you can go in now."

He entered the managing director's office, only to be met by the back of a swivel chair behind an enormous pinewood desk.

"I'm not interested in any excuses," said a voice behind the chair. "We agreed they would be ready by eleven o'clock tomorrow and that's when I expect them to be delivered. Look, instead of wasting time with me on the phone, you should be moving your arse to make sure it gets done. Tomorrow, eleven o'clock, understand?!"

The chair swung around revealing its occupant, a handsome European in his early forties with dignified gray hair and a pair of steel-blue eyes. He was dressed in the colonial fashion: white short-sleeved button shirt, khaki safari shorts, knee socks, and desert boots. Cecil Barnes put down the cordless phone and gestured towards the straight-backed chair in front of the desk. "Sit down...Loomis, is it?"

"Thanks."

"Has Haley explained this job to you?"

"A bit." Loomis heard from others that Barnes was the toughest boss they had ever worked for. A ruthless businessman, the owner of about ten companies he had started from scratch, he was a real ass-kicking tyrant.

"Thirty exploratory boreholes in northern Turkana district. The locations have already been picked out by the consultant. We have about three hundred days to do it, with mandatory breaks every ninety days. A realistic schedule of works must therefore be drawn up immediately and strictly followed in the field. We are employing you as our site agent, field supervisor, and resident geologist, and I expect you to submit a technical report on the works and findings within a month of demobilization. If you have any questions, shoot. I have a busy day today."

"Plant?"

Barnes removed a sheet of paper from a blue spring file on his desk and handed it to Loomis. "That is the preliminary list of what is available and earmarked for the contract. Check it, update it, and get the stuff mobilized."

"Hmmm, Dando 250, top drive," Loomis commented, studying the sheet. At that point a messenger came in with a pile of papers and telexes. Barnes received them with a more than typical aggression and went through them one by one, now ignoring his visitor.

"What's this?" Barnes demanded of the messenger, holding up a short slip.

The messenger, who had been fidgeting nervously, answered meekly, "Requisitions from Mustafa, sir."

"Bloody idiot! What use is this to me if he hasn't signed it yet?" He examined the next sheet. "And this? What the hell! Cypress doesn't cost this much! He's making a deal with sneaky relatives again. Alright, get out, I'll have to speak to him myself."

The messenger exited in a hurry, apparently relieved to get out of the office.

Barnes gave Loomis a conspiratorial glance. "Bloody Indians. Damn good employees, but if you don't watch them, they'll rob you blind," he said, assuming Loomis to be in total agreement. He then picked up the internal phone and berated his Asian purchasing officer.

When Barnes finally put down the receiver, Loomis asked him, "This rig is mounted on a Leyland, not a four-by-four?"

"So? What's the problem? It doesn't rain up there, it's a bloody desert. Are you expecting to get bogged down in mud? Forget it. You don't need a four-by-four lorry to carry the rig."

"What about the sand in the laagers?"

"Haven't you ever heard of sand traps? If you take the time to read the list I just gave you, you'll see that we have them. Listen, I don't have time to argue over the plant list right now. Go over it and then come back to me."

"I heard we're supposed to do double shifts. Am I supposed to work day and night?" Loomis asked.

"That shouldn't be necessary if you keep things under control. Are you worried? I heard you were bloody good with the *watu*." Watu, the Kiswahili word meaning 'people', was an expatriate term for the Africans.

Loomis remained cool at that last remark. But what really struck him about his comment was that this was not about color per se. After all, he himself could be considered a black man under other circumstances, yet Barnes did not treat him as such. That's probably because he was American. He didn't count as one of the 'watu'. In any case, he brushed this off and tried to resume a more professional air. "Has the consultant provided any maps yet?"

Sure enough, a map materialized from out of the spring file.

"As you can see, there are a lot of usable tracks," Barnes apprised him as Loomis studied the topo sheet.

"Lot of gullies and laagers too." He felt his professional air already waning.

"Look, Loomis," Barnes snapped. "I've been running operations in the bush myself for God's number of years, and not that, not rain, not tribal wars, not anything has ever stopped me from completing them on time. So let's get down to business. Do you agree to the conditions of employment we sent you?"

"Yeah, I've got the contract right here, signed and sealed."

"Fine. Now I'm sorry to rush you, but I have a meeting in fifteen minutes with a major client. We've got a big contract with them in Madagascar, and they've just increased the Bill of Quantities on very short notice. That's one reason why I'm in a very, bitchy, mood."

Loomis was put off by the slow emphatic drawl Barnes used in this last statement, and now he too wanted an end to this meeting. "Okay, look, I'll be back in about a month. That'll give me enough time to think about this, but I can tell you right now that I intend to mobilize a lot sooner than the tenth of October."

"Good. Go over those lists, draw up a schedule of works, and get in touch with me then. By that time I'll be in a better position to discuss this thing."

"Alright," Loomis said, getting up, "have a good day, Mr. Barnes."

"Good day," Barnes responded, but already his head was down, attending to some other matter on his desk.

* * *

Katy Hesland opened the office door without her hands it seemed, for when she entered, her arms were ladled with a load of textbooks. Stout, middle-aged, with short curly hair dyed a strawberry-blonde to hide the gray, she wore a smile that distended her huge, rosy-color cheeks. An American teacher brought to the university to bolster the instrumental section of the music department, she shared an office with Pamela, their desks facing each other from opposite sides of the room.

"Good morning, Pammy."

Pamela looked up and returned the smile. "Hi, Katy."

"Oh, what a day," the woman groaned, as she kicked the door shut with her foot, still fumbling with her books. Her face changed to one of exaggerated, mock weariness. "How I hate Mondays!"

"Just console yourself that it's nearly half over."

Katy put on her wide smile again. "Pammy, you're a miracle worker. Would you believe I was in the foulest mood all morning until I saw you just now? You seem to have a knack for always brightening my day."

Pamela bowed her head to avoid her friend's gaze. Any sort of praise like that, even in jest, made her feel slightly uncomfortable.

And Katy herself knew this, for how many times did Pamela tell her to please stop it, but she couldn't help being so effusive. *Darn,* she said to herself, *I put my foot in it again.* Of course, she didn't really understand the reason for Pamela's needless and burdening humility, but sensed it was deep-rooted. Some psychological thing.

"How's the choir doing?" she asked to dispel the moment of awkwardness.

"Very well, I think they'll be ready in time," said Pamela, with a hint of satisfaction.

"Wish I could say that about the band. We might have to scratch them."

"No, don't say that. After all the hard work you put in? It's been only three months since you got them going. And you started with nothing. Look how far you've come with them."

"Oh, ignore me, Pammy. I'm just singing the Monday blues. We'll see how it goes in the next few weeks," Katy said as she replaced the books into the shelves above her desk. "Jon has left already, hasn't he?" she said, trying to make small talk.

"Yes," Pamela told her. "On Saturday."

"Where to this time?"

"Back to Holland. He'll be staying for quite a long time. Eight months. He wants to make sure all his business matters are settled and to use the time to finish up the house."

"You mean 'palace' from the way he describes it." Katy had a loathing for Jon, but adroitly managed to hide this from Pamela. "So how has your day been?" she asked, changing the subject.

"It started out poorly but went well afterwards. I took a trip to town this morning to buy guitar strings, and somebody tried to rob me."

"You're kidding! In broad daylight? Was it a purse-snatcher?"

"No, those people who drop packages that look like they're full of money."

"Oh, those creeps! You know Roger, right? That Swedish fella? About one week after he arrived here they pulled that stunt on him and poor Roger, what did he know? He went with them and they took everything from him. He said he was almost arrested by a policeman. But of course you know that trick."

"Of course, yes." She knew now, anyway.

"So then what happened?"

"They ran away and I took the package to the police," she recounted simply, leaving out what she felt were irrelevant details.

"Good!"

"Aren't you going to ask me about the good part of my day?"

"No, it will only make me envious. The choir, right?"

"No, something else. I really need to go home and see my grand-mother, she is not feeling well these days. So, I asked Dr. Otundo for three days off and he agreed, as long as I get someone to take over my classes."

"Someone?" Katy asked, raising her eyebrows.

"Pleased, Katy, I'll prepare the notes."

"There's a devil behind that angel face of yours. You know very well how many days I owe you."

Both women laughed.

* * *

Kenyatta Avenue, the widest street in Nairobi. A pair of elongated concrete islands runs along the middle of the avenue, dividing it into four lanes, ostentatiously adorned with trees. Nandi Flames ablaze with their red blossoms, tall, heavy-leafed palm trees, and Jacarandas foaming with clusters of lilac flowers, shade the busy city traffic. On the flanks of the street, behemoth buildings inter-mingle with the single-story remnants of an incongruous past. Kenyatta Avenue, the subject of picture postcards.

But Loomis continued straight on Koinage Street without turning on to the Avenue, in order to avoid the annoying catcalls of the shoe shiners, the bracelet hawkers, the conmen, and the black-market money changers who sought out their daily bread from the human multitude which streamed past. He followed instead his usual route through the backstreets, ducking through the cave-like passageways of the arcades underneath the buildings until he reached the Arch, the pub of the Ambassador Hotel.

Entering, he found that some of the rush-hour madness outside had already preceded him in, as evidenced by the noisy chatter. His eyes searched for the friends who had promised to meet him, finally spotting Okova and fellow instructors from the Kingozi Language and Cultural Center.

"*Ham jambo wote!*" He greeted each by hand, and then solicited an unclaimed chair from a neighboring table.

"Daryl Loomis, the supreme *mjanja*, the rogue of rogues, back from the wild bush of Tanzania. Watch out Nairobi!"

"*Wacha!* Leave it, Omondi."

"You're late," Okova complained. "You're a *mzungu*. You're not allowed to follow African time."

Just as Barnes's reference to the watu made him ponder, he realized that his friends often referred to him as a mzungu, or a white man.

"Wacha! Leave it, Okova."

"Hey chief!" Omondi called to a passing waiter. Then, to Loomis, "Still cold Tusker, Daryl?"

"Yeah."

"Tusker *moja baridi.*" Omondi placed a ten-shilling note on the waiter's tray.

"Daryl, we were just discussing a great idea we got coming up," said Mathenge, another of the group of four that founded Kingozi, a cross-cultural consulting firm. "Cultural tours. We can still take clients to the game parks, but along the way we stop in the local villages and arrange for them to stay with a typical rural family for a couple of days. The younger tourists will go for it. Could be money, what do you think?"

"Sounds great. Why not? You already got Europeans acting out Swahili plays at Kingozi. You might have something."

"So, Daryl, what trouble did you get up to south of the border?" asked Omondi, with a breezy grin, a grin that was perpetually fixed on his soft boyish features.

"Who me? Just work, as usual."

"You didn't write," complained Okova.

Loomis swiveled to face him, and gave him an accusing stare. "I thought you were going to take some time off and visit me."

"I was busy."

Loomis took a swig from his beer bottle, not bothering with the glass that came with it. "Did you pay the rent?"

"We're drinking it."

"Damn it, Okova! Now I have to go back to the bank again. We shouldn't piss Kipkoech off like this."

"Don't worry, he's an understanding man."

"Well, if we're going to drink the rent money, I'd prefer to do it somewhere else."

"Don't you like this place, Daryl?" Omondi asked.

"This is part of a tourist hotel, the beer is too expensive," Loomis complained.

"There's no jukebox," added Okova. "And no available women. Just Sugar Daddies and Sugar Mommies out with their young things."

"But it's a good meeting place," said Omondi.

"Yeah, if you have appointments with ladies who are coming to meet you," Loomis pointed out. "Which I know, without a doubt, that you, Elvis Omondi, could never be lacking. But I am, so I say *kwaherini*, goodbye to you all. Let's go, Okova, let these guys drink their own rent money."

After leaving the Arch, while walking to Okova's Morris-Mini, Loomis narrated the story of the conmen and their would-be woman victim.

"What a silly bitch. You should have left her alone man," said Okova. He spoke with an African version of a black American accent, his pronunciation of English a product of three years as a foreign student in Jersey City. Even Okova's physical characteristics had become Americanized: he was tall, but he walked hunching his lanky body over in a pronounced slouch; a Van Dyke beard made his triangular face even pointier; and on his head, without fail, was some type of hat, usually a bizarre one, to conceal his prematurely receding forehead. Of late, Okova had taken a fancy to tweed peaked caps.

"Where should we go, Okova? I'm on safari to Kisumu tomorrow, so I want to get thoroughly pissed falling-down drunk. That way I can fall asleep on the bus. And ladies, bwana. God, I need a woman tonight." He broke his stride and paused, as if having a revelation. "Let's go to Outer Ring, it's close to home."

"Good. We'll pay Kipkoech tomorrow. Or maybe the day after."

Outer Ring was a residential estate for the white-collar working classes located at the eastern edge of town. At its core was a shopping center consisting of a long, two-storied, terraced building with apartments above a row of *dukas*, bars, and butcheries. By the time Loomis and Okova arrived, there was a flurry of activity within its glare of lights as wives and daughters hurried to finish their errands before dim twilight faded into total darkness.

Contained within the shopping center, gaudily visible and obtrusively loud, was the Delux Bar, where the pulsating din of Congolese music competed with the shrill laughter of drunken patrons. Inside the bar, gathered like faithful devotees in front of a shrine, a group of people stood around feeding coins into a glittering, stentorian jukebox. Large, languid waitresses, their ample busts and buttocks stuffed tightly into white uniforms, casually shuffled to and fro serving the customers, that is, whenever they weren't sitting down drinking with them. The atmosphere was one of raucous mirth, where stories were traded, plans made, politics discussed, and contacts exchanged. Alcoholic happiness led to strangers becoming friends, even kindred, in a transient moment of celebration at the end of the day.

Loomis and Okova slithered into a table, and after the mandatory teasing and flirting with the waitress, made their order: two Tuskers, one warm, one cold, and a whole roasted chicken. During the third round of drinks, Okova abruptly cut off Loomis in their conversation and said, "I think I know that girl."

Loomis turned his head around while Okova got up and wandered off. He returned shortly with two girls.

"This is Ziporah," he announced with an inebriated smile,

nodding his head towards an athletic-looking girl in a beige Punjabi Suit, "a switchboard operator at KCC, and this..." he put his arm around the shoulders of the girl on his right, "is Helen, her cousin, who is looking for a job." The second girl, Helen, was short and plump, but coquettish in a frilly red dress. "I'll find work for you, don't you worry," Okova said, staring deeply into her face. "Think you can teach wazungu to speak Kiswahili?"

"Maybe," she cackled, embarrassed.

"Girls, please join us," Loomis offered, making a sweeping gesture of welcome with his arm. "You must know the problem when two young guys like us go into a bar alone. So many girls coming up to you and annoying you. Just sit here for a while so they don't bother us. We'll buy the drinks."

The girls took their seats giggling, and more drinks were brought. Loomis was fond of African ladies. They were uncomplicated. No elaborate game-playing, none of this flirting without anything behind it; they were easy to approach, and if they agreed to your company, it was a sure bet you were going to get laid. As with most Africans, they appreciated joking around and having a good laugh. Like now for instance, when coy introductions gradually became playful banter.

"So, Ziporah," addressed Loomis with a disarming smile, "there is a question I always wanted to ask a telephone operator. May I ask it?"

"What is that?"

"Do you operators listen in on people's conversations?"

"I got a PhD in economics," Okova bullshitted to Helen. "Ten years I was in the States..."

"You know, as soon as I saw you," Loomis said, "my heart was pounding like a drum."

Ziporah snickered. "Stop it!" she said, genially.

"You have a car?" Helen asked Okova.

"Yeah...this car I got tonight is only my emergency backup vehicle," he fibbed. "My Mercedes is being serviced."

"Did anyone ever tell you that you have beautiful teeth?"

Then the chicken arrived.

"Is this really a whole chicken?" Okova asked incredulously. His question was directed to no one in particular, since the waiter had already hurried off. "Every time, never fails, these people always gotta taste some of it. But this one was a glutton."

Loomis called the waiter over. Gesturing with his index finger, he made the waiter bend down as if to accept a secret. "You have given us a deformed chicken."

"Eh? *Nini*? What?"

"This was a lame chicken, a cripple."

"What are you saying? This chicken is good."

"Is this a whole chicken?"

"Of course."

"Why does it only have one leg?"

Guffaws from everyone, including the waiter who took that opportunity to make a timely exit.

Finishing the meal, they raised their glasses in a toast. First, the men toasted the ladies. The ladies toasted back. All four of them toasted the waiters and waitresses, excluding the one that had served the chicken; then, a toast to the crippled chicken itself. People from the neighboring tables joined in and additional rounds were brought for more toasts: to life, booze, and the sweet difference between men and women. As a result of all this toasting, countless half-liters of beer were slapped down on their table while the jukebox blared on and on and the night became a continuous blur.

At around midnight, the pair roused themselves to leave and stumbled on their way to the Morris-Mini, accompanied by the two willing and eager ladies. They were drunk and happy, comforted with the thought of warm beds that night.

Fuck, it's great to be alive.

* * *

Pamela closed the windows of her bedroom and drew the curtains. There were a lot of mosquitoes about, born from the Long Rains just passed, but she had been too preoccupied to let her mosquito net down. Now it was too late, for those on the wing would sneak in. Instead, she let the pyrethrum coil sitting on her night table repel the troublesome insects. She was tired, having stayed up late preparing the notes for the classes Katy was to take, but gratified that she would be able to make her trip and reach her upcountry home by Saturday. Switching on her portable radio-cassette to play Tchaikovsky's 'Concerto No. 1 in B flat minor,' her favorite music to sleep to, she quickly undressed and got into bed, turned off the night lamp, and soon fell into a peaceful slumber.

August 15, 1979, the day Daryl Loomis first met Pamela Amonee Emuria, was drawing to a close.

IN THE BEGINNING

Loomis's father had come from a long line of bakers of Swedish descent who had settled in Minnesota in the nineteenth century. Shortly after graduating high school, however, Lars Sudstrom left the area of his forebears and moved to New York City in order to ply his trade in the big hotels, reasoning that his specialty, cakes and pastries, could fetch big bucks in the Big Apple. Unfortunately, his long hours at the oven resulted in a salary that was less than he had anticipated. Adding to his disenchantment was that for someone like him, the glamour of New York just wasn't accessible. A shy Midwestern man who generally kept to himself, he made few friends there, and his love life was a disaster, marked by heartbreak after heartbreak. At thirty-two, still a virgin, Lars decided to take a cruise to the Bahamas, his first vacation, hoping to find the girl of his dreams. And lo and behold, his dreams came true in the form of a sweet, pretty Caribbean hairdresser who ran a salon just outside his hotel in Nassau. After several more trips to visit her, he finally brought her to New York, where they got married, rented an apartment in the Bronx, and where Carmela, his wife, became pregnant. Lars was ecstatic.

But his happiness was short-lived. Carmela died while giving birth, leaving Lars distraught. Knowing that he could never look at his son without reviving his grief over his wife's death, he felt he was terminally tainted for the rest of his life. His despair was so overwhelming that he hung himself in the closet before his son even received his name.

Being a newborn whose parents were dead, Lars's son would have been a prime candidate for adoption, had it not been for his mixed race. Luckily, however, even back in 1949, there were liberal-minded couples eager to give their love to a child of any color, regardless of the unspoken social prejudice against colored or mixed-race children. When Bob and Marcia Loomis looked at the week-old, tawny infant named Baby X, sleeping peacefully in his crib, they knew he was meant for them. Plus, the timing was perfect: Marcia just had a miscarriage and was overcome with a desire to suckle.

Despite the love, attention, and guidance his adopted parents offered, Little Daryl reached an age where these things began to pale in importance compared to peer acceptance. Growing up as a kid was tough for him, and his troubles began at about the age of six. As he lived in a predominantly white neighborhood, his appearance was definitely different. The other kids on the block referred to him as the "Doody Boy," apparently associating his skin color with feces.

"Look, here comes the Doody Boy! Doody, doody, doody!"

Kids can be cruel. Who hasn't heard of that before? On one occasion, they cornered him in a park. "Hey, Doody Boy, you look like *Little Black Sambo*. Ever read that book?"

Little Loomis shook his head to signal that he hadn't, his fear mounting.

"Yeah, he runs around a tree real fast. Can you do that?"

Darryl nodded a yes.

"Except Little Black Sambo doesn't have any clothes on."

At this, they ganged up on him and stripped him naked, and when he refused to run around the tree, they tied him to it and whipped him with a stick.

Later on, his peers were old enough to realize that Bob and Marcia were not his real parents. "You're adopted, you're an orphan!" One little girl had the linguistic sophistication to call him a bastard.

When he was in Junior High school, girls became the problem. Ironically, one of his crushes at age fourteen was a blonde, blue-eyed Swedish American, but on his first date, after presenting himself to her parents, he could sense their disapproval, and even though they reluctantly allowed him to take her to the movies, she told him at the end of the night that she could not see him anymore because he was colored.

So then he began to hang out with the black boys, hoping to get access to black girls. At first they treated him just as badly, calling him names such as Uncle Tom and Sidney (after Sidney Poitier), names which he did not understand. Easier to figure out was 'whigger'. But such abuse did not last long, as if it were merely an initiation, a rite of passage, to make sure that he went through what they went through, because after some time they accepted him, although it was similar to the adoption of his parents, but more like a mascot. He did reach his objective, though, which was to meet black girls, but they too played with his head, only teasing and flirting, since just about all of them already had boyfriends.

Apparently his new companions were a bad influence, because they did things that were considered bad, like drink cheap wine and smoke marijuana, get into fights, and steal things: first bicycles, then even cars. After he got arrested on one of these escapades, his parents decided to take action. They enrolled him in a private, boys only, prep school.

A wise decision on their part, for, notwithstanding his naughty behavior, Daryl had always come home with a good report card.

As expected, he did well in his studies, particularly in the natural sciences like biology and earth science. The revelations he received from the knowledge that the existence of things transcended the stupid behavior of his peers was like a release for him, a release from prison.

But things were to get better. He'd decided on the Colorado School of Mines for his tertiary education. Situated within the foothills of the Rockies, with Clear Creek, the water source of Coors beer, running through the center of it, it was a far cry from urban New York. And here also were girls who, being no longer under parental supervision, were easy to meet and date. And all of them were white girls. By now, the late 60s, thanks to the civil rights movement, racism was no longer politically correct. In fact, the opposite was true; having a black lover became fashionable.

While at first he thought that the tide was turning in a good way, it soon became apparent that these girls wanted more than just his penis. They wanted fidelity and commitment, and on their terms...or else. And they wanted this and that as well. Marriage even. He himself was not capable of offering any more than superficial company and hearty sex; risking his heart was out of the question, as he had made it his first rule in life never to get hurt, having had his feelings brutalized enough during his painful rise to adolescence.

So, in order to escape his entanglements with these women, some of them older ones divorced with kids, he joined the Peace Corps to help poor villagers dig water wells.

They sent him to Kenya, and they could not have picked a better place. His release from prison was really complete. He fucked black women for the first time; fucked without any obligation, without responsibility, without any implicit demand for commitment, or even the mention of fidelity.

And the men were good company as well, tremendously affable, jovial as could be, with no care in the world, living life from day to day. So easy to get close to, with no hangups to spoil a good time. Loomis had never before found himself in a place as ardently sociable as Kenya, and it spurred him to learn not only Kiswahili, the national language, fluently, but other local indigenous languages as well. His life there filled a longstanding vacuum inside himself, remedying the dilemma of his nebulous identity. In short, he became Africanized.

After his stint as a volunteer, Loomis began to get jobs in the drilling business, mainly water-well drilling, sometimes with international consultants, but more often than not with local drilling contractors. He made good money by Kenyan standards, more than enough to fund his recreational pursuits, and consequently never considered career advancement, turning down good opportunities that would nevertheless have taken him out of East Africa, a place that he had already decided he would never leave.

Fuck, it's great to be alive.

* * *

Her Christian name was Pamela. But her Teso name was Amonee, which some people, particularly her beloved grandmother, whom in fact she had been named after, claimed to mean Black Diamond. She was the seventh of eight children, but for some reason, her father loved her more than all of them.

Her home was situated five kilometers from the roadside market of Malakisi, and the way to it was a zigzagging path that ran up and down sunlit ridges of a fertile area where rich red earth sustained a luxuriant cover of vegetation.

In her early childhood, she felt cozy and warm, immersed in the relaxed atmosphere of her village. She felt that no place could be more beautiful. She would walk through *shambas* of rustling maize stalks, their tops higher than a man's head, foretokening a harvest time which lay only a few weeks away, while the floppy fronds of banana trees would wave a reposeful welcome. She was continually captivated by the sunlight winking at her through the canopy of gum trees whenever she fetched water from the small stream near her house. She would cross it by hopping from stone to stone, and always found Etok, the small boy on the other side, forever waiting as if he had never left his station, chewing on a stick of sugarcane while watching his family's herd of cows browsing the grass.

Most people knew each other, even if only casually, and this in some ways extended her feeling of family. In her own home, it was an indescribable contentment to be in the company of her siblings, to be surrounded by a familial love that begins as soon as an African child is born. And her dear mother, always toiling but never without her bright contented smile, singing all the time as if her labors were the very source of her happiness. But Amonee was actually Daddy's little girl, who showered her with more than her fair share of his affection compared to the rest of his children. Competing with her father's love for her was the special relationship she had with her grandmother, the older Amonee, who at the age of eighty-two, could still sing as sweetly as anyone the old folk songs that were recited at all the major feasts.

Old Amonee would cup the younger Amonee's face within her gnarled hands, and say to her, "You are special, the most beautiful child in all of Malakisi, you are our very own Black Diamond." The old woman would say this with such conviction, that, despite Amonee's difficulty in accepting this, it must have been true. And indeed, the manner in which others in the village would treat her seemed to evoke the same sentiments, with lavish praises about her beauty and spirit. Rather than feeling pleased by that, it scared her.

Her serene existence terminated abruptly at the age of eleven, on the day that Etok was replaced by his father in the tendering of the cows on the opposite bank of the stream. On that day she learned that being special, being a black diamond, was a curse, a curse that elicited desire and envy. And for Etok's father, it was a desire he struggled daily to control, a desire that was driving him mad, that made him surreptitiously spy on her from a different vantage point than his son's whenever she did her family's laundry by the stream.

"Ajok, Amonee."

"Hello, Uncle," using the kinship term out of respect for an older man.

"I have seen some beautiful fish upstream. Special fish. Come, let me show you."

She followed him as he led her through the stream, for a distance that seemed a bit far and that should have aroused her suspicions.

He stopped. "Come," he entreated.

As soon as she was within reach, he pounced on her like a wild animal with a ferocity that struck a terror in her that she had never known. He covered her mouth with his hand and pulled up her cotton frock. Then came a searing pain in the middle of her body, like she was being stabbed, pain so intense she had to scream, but she couldn't with his hand on her mouth. She could not even breathe, and eventually passed out. She had lain in the shallow water for what must have been hours before a neighbor found her and brought her home.

The first person she remembered seeing at her home was her grandmother, who looked at her with a tragic face and tear-filled eyes. Amonee collapsed in her embrace, crying in the warmth of her safety.

"Oh, precious thing, no one can take the Black Diamond by force, and those that try will be cursed with a horrible fate. Don't despair. You will heal. Remember always that your love is reserved for that special one who will come to claim you. He will restore you and protect you."

In the village, there were few secrets. Although Amonee would not talk about what happened because of her shock and shame, it wasn't long before the identity of the perpetrator was known. Her father became possessed with hysterical rage. He sought and found his *panga*, the long, extra sharp machete that he always used to cut down the sugar cane, and ran out of the compound followed by a group of vigilantes eager to reap vengeance upon Etok's father.

But at his home, they were met with news that he had not come home. It was two hours later that they found his dead body in the forest behind the maize fields at the end of the village, apparently the victim of a bite from the tree-dwelling black mamba. It seemed that vengeance had already been reaped.

After the rape of his daughter, Amonee's father was obsessed with protecting her, so he gathered up all his savings, and arranged a village ceremony whereby friends, extended family members, and other concerned villagers collected money to put into a fund to send young Amonee off to the sisters within the shielding confines of Loreto Convent High School in Nairobi. The Black Diamond needed to be kept safe.

* * *

Her time at Loreto Convent School she considered to be her second life, a full seven years completed within its walls, a time that blended seamlessly with her third life after graduation, since it melded those qualities that would complete her as a person, and define her as an adult.

The new world she found herself in would introduce her not only to the Queen's English, but more importantly to the sounds, stories, and passions of Western music.

It started after only her second day, when she saw the piano in the assembly room on the third floor. She pawed at it, trying to remember her grandmother's songs. She could only recall the funeral songs, and quickly found the keys to produce the melody. Within an hour she had gotten the whole thing down from start to finish, and played it over and over, each time more emphatically. It resounded throughout the third floor and above, and soon attracted much of the faculty, who stood transfixed by the notes that she played.

For the next few years she was groomed in classical music, and it did not take long before she became the school's premier protégé, who annually represented them at the Music Festival as a concert pianist. Further to this, Pamela also turned to vocal music, as she felt that the magic of voices surpassed the sounds of any manufactured instrument. Despite being a student, she first assisted and then completely took over from ailing Sister Rosemary as the conductor of the choir. It soon became apparent that this was her true genius.

Pamela did indeed enjoy what she was doing, but she grew wary at the price. The price was the praise and profuse compliments she had to endure. It brought back old fears and made her uneasy.

The other, somewhat related consternation she had to grapple with was her aversion to visiting home. Once a month, her parents and some of her siblings would come to see how she was doing, but she herself could not bring herself to reciprocate these trips. She had already embarked on a new path in order to flee from the memory of that painful day, which posed as a tenuous and dangerous bridge between her old life and new. But eventually, the anguish of not seeing her grandmother, who was too old and fragile to journey to

Nairobi, instilled in her a determination to face her demons and make the safari back to her village. The first occasion was difficult and awkward, as she struggled to fend off thinking about what she had expressly forbidden herself to think about.

Thereafter, she forced herself to go home once a year, though it was never without some distress, and her time there was always plagued by the desire to rush back to the comfort and protection of her life at the convent school. There, in the artificial bounds of that insular institution, she felt she was able to control the things that went on around her, to construct a safety net that secured her from external sources of harm. Her regimented efficiency and pragmatism could only be abandoned in those moments of spiritual release that she found in her music.

As the school's music program flourished, the faculty and students were invited to perform at various government functions, which never failed to delight the high-profile audience. At one of these affairs, just a few months before her graduation, and shortly after her eighteenth birthday, something happened that would be a further milestone in her life. She met a man.

It was the Assistant Minister of Health who brought him over after her recital and introduced him. He was a tall white man, with silvery hair that made him look distinguished rather than old, since his smooth, youthful face suggested he was in his early thirties. He impressed her with his air of graciousness and manners. From their first meeting he was infatuated with her. Soon afterwards they were to have lunches on the weekends, walks in Uhuru Park, and even dinners at fancy European restaurants. He gave her money to send to her parents. He sponsored her university education in England, and even paid for her graduation present, a backpacking tour of Europe, entrusting his niece to accompany her for protection, as he himself was too busy to take the time off.

And upon obtaining her degree, his influence, and those of the government officials he kept as company, landed her a teaching position at Nairobi University.

Eventually, of course she had to pay back the attention and devotion he showered on her. At first soft kisses, which she could endure, then the more difficult, passionate ones. Sex itself remained the frightening monster she had to do battle with. The first time was a terrible ordeal, bracing herself against the pain that was predictably made worse by the memory of her rape. Because of her resistance, both emotionally and physically, he never questioned her virginity. During subsequent episodes, her discomfort subsided, but the act itself remained joyless.

His company in general, however, was quite comfortable. They had common ground as regards to their pragmatic approach to life. And although outwardly he showed congenial warmth, his emotions were subdued and composed, which suited her just fine, as she was just as reluctant to open herself up.

He was a businessman, though she never asked him about his business. But whatever it was, it must have been a lucrative enterprise. From her visit to his home in Holland, and his buying behavior in Nairobi, she recognized an acquisitive nature that went along with his wealth, insisting on the best quality in the things that he purchased, in addition to a penchant for collecting beautiful works of art. This did not bother her in and of itself, but the way he flaunted her in front of others troubled her. A renewed sense of fear emerged, the cause of which she could not fathom. A recurrent fear. The fear of being the Black Diamond.

KISUMU, WESTERN KENYA, AUGUST 17, 1979.

He was the third person to get aboard the matatu, this one a Peugeot pickup with a cabin built onto the bed, making it look like a meat truck, which in a sense it was. Being the third passenger meant that he had just missed his chance to sit in the front cab, leaving him no choice but to enter the back compartment. Sitting alone, he bent over and put his head in his lap, trying to reclaim the sleep he had lost the previous night. It had been a Friday night, and he and Godfrey, a local Luo friend, had decided upon a rousing farewell in the town. But even considering that, he might have been a bit more restrained if he hadn't run into his former sexy squeeze, Penny Atieno. He vaguely recalled ordering more and more rounds until he had become stupid and Penny had become wild. Godfrey, not being much of a drinker, had by that time already turned out to be quite useless, sleeping with his head on the table after having broken his personal record of seven bottles of beer. In bed, Penny was insatiable. Now, at seven o'clock in the morning, he was suffering from a considerable hangover.

Kisumu bus stand, adjacent to the Municipal Market, was not a pleasant place for one who was unwell. The market stalls, alive with the buzzing chatter of traders and shoppers, smelled of lake fish and rotting vegetables. The overflowing public latrines reeked of excrement. Vociferous vendors, with wooden trays strapped to their shoulders, screamed out their wares, swarming over the passenger vehicles peddling anything from watches and socks to medicines and screwdrivers. Unruly turnboys noisily loaded, arranged, and unloaded the luggage on top of the vehicles, arguing obstreperously. In order to attract potential customers, all the drivers had to repeatedly blare their horns while relentless *manambas* (ticket sellers) solicited aggressively, calling and whistling at anyone who passed. Sometimes, when fighting over a customer, rival manambas would have a tug of war with a human rope, and often luggage would end up on a different matatu than the one its owner was travelling in. Saturday morning was particularly hectic as many arrivals from Nairobi struggled to get means to their upcountry destinations.

Loomis sat half delirious, making a substantial effort at blocking out the offensive sounds and smells that were plaguing him when he heard two voices reverberating in his head.

"But this is only going to Kakamega," a woman protested in Kiswahili.

"Yes, *ndio*!" replied a male voice.

"But I want one direct to Bungoma."

"You missed the one for Bungoma. It just left. You take this one to Kakamega. There are so many vehicles leaving from Kakamega for Bungoma. If you wait here for one you will wait a long time. Get in quickly, we are in a hurry."

"Well, I don't know. You see, this is the first time I came by train to Kisumu, but usually I take a bus directly to Bungoma..."

"Too loud," protested a hung-over Loomis in English, but not loud enough for any of them to hear him.

"When is this one leaving?" she asked.

"Right now, right this instant, sasa hivi!"

She entered the matatu and sat down on the opposite end of the opposite bench away from Loomis.

"Hah, that's a laugh," Loomis said dreamily, without looking up. "This thing is still empty; it'll be at least a goddamned hour."

The woman either did not hear his comment, or decided not to consider it. Instead she merely looked at Loomis with disdain. Wrinkled shirt, trousers stained at the bottoms, and he smelled of stale beer, obviously drunk. Then he belched.

"Ahh-oipp."

How appalling!

Loomis raised his head and scratched at the two-day-old growth of stubble on his cheek before burying his head in his lap again.

Pamela was taken aback. Could this be the man who tried to help her that day? "Excuse me," she said.

He looked up, startled at being addressed.

There was no doubt, it was definitely him. Pamela was reluctant, but she knew she owed him, at the least, an apology. "Aren't you the person who saved me from those conmen in Nairobi?"

Loomis opened his eyes wider, even though it hurt, and put all his efforts into focusing them. A black seraph's face, crowned with an appealing curly-kit afro, slowly crystallized into view. Her body was practically lost inside a massively-flowing *kitenge* gown. "Well, whaddya know. Hello, how are you? Did you ever bring that package to the police?"

"Yes, I did, and I was ashamed to find out that you were right. I did act like a fool and I'm sorry. I apologize for the way I behaved."

The sincerity in her voice surprised him, even made him feel a bit guilty. "Oh well, that's okay, no need to apologize," he shrugged. "I guess you never saw that trick."

"No, it never happened to me before."

"You're heading up to Bungoma, is that right?" He began to wonder if he was being given a second chance.

She changed her position on the bench to sit across from him in order to reply him face to face. "Yes, I hope what the conductor said is true. About getting matatus from Kakamega."

"Well, I would tend to doubt anything he says – you're just a fare to him. But one thing I do know, this thing won't leave until it's full."

A vendor thrust his heavily laden arm through the rear door. "FLASHLIGHTS, KEY CHAINS, PHOTO FRAMES?"

"And you, where are you going?" she asked Loomis, ignoring the hawker.

"Not far. Oluti, a small village before you get to Kakamega."

Three men climbed into the matatu and noisily found places along the benches, creating a hiatus in the couple's conversation. Meanwhile Loomis searched for something to say.

"So you are a Bukusu, then?" he asked her.

"No, I'm not. I'm a Teso."

"Oh wonderful, I..."

"*Omolo, ja-Koguta! Ere wach!*" A Luo from the town, upon entering, had recognized Loomis and decided to initiate conversation in the local vernacular. "Are you well, Omolo?" he asked in DhoLuo.

Omolo was the name that Godfrey, his resident drinking associate, had given him, and the name that was used whenever he was introduced to people in Kisumu.

"I am well."

"Are you from Koguta?"

"Yes, yesterday."

"Where to now?"

"Kakamega." Saying that he was only going to Oluti would require too much explanation. Loomis was only following a typical African habit. He turned his head to look at Pamela, who was now staring aimlessly through the glass panel which looked into the front cab. He faced the Luo again. "Listen, Owiti, I want to talk to this girl before she gets a chance to escape," he implored, hoping Pamela did not understand DhoLuo. "You don't mind, do you?"

"No, you go ahead. She's very beautiful."

A woman with a sleeping infant and two young boys scrambled inside.

"So you said you're a Teso?"

Pamela turned to face him. "Yes, that's right."

"*Nawi kon alaway ealo Bungoma?*" (Where in Bungoma is your home?)

"My goodness, you know our language!" she cried, a wide smile indicating her pleasant surprise. It was a beautiful smile, filled with artless enchantment, and the brightness of her lovely white teeth seemed to illuminate the inside of the matatu.

"Not really, it's Kiturkana. But it's almost the same language as yours."

"How interesting. You have lived up in Turkana then?"

"Yes, on a couple of occasions."

"And you must have lived here as well. I heard you speak DhoLuo."

"Yes."

"You seem to be very good at languages."

"Thanks."

"Actually, we are from Malakisi," she disclosed, getting back to his original question.

Four more passengers, including a rather broad-bottomed woman, squeezed into the last remaining places on the benches. Pamela started to feel an uncomfortable pressure on her hips and legs. "We should be leaving soon. This matatu is already full."

"A matatu is never full," Loomis reminded her. As if on cue, an old man entered and surprisingly enough managed to nudge his small posterior into a hitherto nonexistent space between two other passengers.

"You work in Nairobi?" Loomis inquired, determined to be persistent.

"Yes, I'm just up for a few days' visit to my home."

"Oh, that's nice," he commented out of politeness. "So what type of work do you do?"

"I'm a lecturer at Nairobi University."

"Ho ho, I see. What do you lecture in?"

"Music."

"Really? My interest too. Say, would you know if there's any truth to the rumor that Petite Lovy will leave Super Mazembe?"

She laughed. A heavenly laugh, as mellifluous as oriental wind chimes.

"No, just kidding," he chuckled. "Music. A professor of music. Glad to meet you, Professor."

She laughed again. "I'm not a full professor yet."

Another man entered, and, with no space left on the benches, found a standing position in front of them, eclipsing their view of one another.

"I'm sorry, I didn't catch your name," Loomis said from behind the man.

Pamela moved her head left and right attempting to get a glimpse of Loomis's face. "Pamela," she told him, giving her name's Kenyan version, with the emphasis on the middle syllable. Pa-MEL-a. "Pamela Emuria. And yours?"

His face suddenly materialized from under the man's crotch. "Loomis, Daryl Loomis," he said, with the most enchanting smile he could muster under the circumstances.

She lowered her head so that it was level with his. "And what do you do, Mr. Loomis?"

"I'm a geologist. Civil works and water drilling."

"Oh, that sounds interesting."

"Yeah, usually. As a matter of fact, I'll be going back to Turkana in a few weeks. Have a big job up there."

"I wish you a lot of luck, Mr. Loomis. It must be a difficult occupation, always moving around in the bush."

"I'm used to it."

A young couple with a little girl joined them in the matatu, filling a space near the rear of the compartment where they stood half bent, their hands behind their necks gripping the suspended handrail. They were almost immediately followed by another family, and an aged woman in a floral, floor-length dress. By now the matatu was really full: full meaning about twenty people, sitting and standing, in a space comparable to an elevator. Loomis's head was pounding, reminding him of the previous day's excesses. It was difficult to chat up a girl in a matatu, particularly between a man's crotch, so he momentarily gave up, hoping for a later chance. The vehicle finally moved out of the bus stand, but only to a nearby petrol station to fuel up while the people inside sweated and gasped for air. Within a few minutes a baby began to wail with discomfort, forcing the mother to remove one of her large breasts from her brassiere and stick it in its mouth. She then discreetly covered the whole operation with a shawl. After what seemed like ages, the vehicle moved on once more.

From the petrol station, the Peugeot took the north road out of town and began its ascent up the steep, green-covered slopes of the Nandi Escarpment, leaving Kisumu below on the valley floor. About a half hour out of town the matatu pulled over and the conductor made an urgent announcement.

"Those people who are standing up, get out."

Traffic police. They were up ahead, and if the matatu was found stuffed as it was, (its usual condition), the driver, conductor, and even the standing passengers would all be charged with the crime of overloading. The matatus and the traffic police played a cat-and-mouse game which often involved nothing more complicated than a simple bribe, but sometimes the charade entailed more sophisticated strategies such as this.

"Meet us past the police check, just behind the curve in the road. There's a shortcut here," the conductor revealed, pointing to the right side of the road.

The bent-over passengers who were made to suffer these further iniquities were fairly convivial about it, for the most part laughing it off with a philosophical patience. But the aged, rheumatic-looking old woman in the long dress was exceptionally distressed. Loomis rose and offered her his seat and turned to get out in her stead. "See you later," he said, in the general direction of Pamela.

As he followed the others dashing across the maize fields, he wondered why he was acting so chivalrously on the day of what could possibly be the worst hangover of his life. Surely, if he had not offered, someone else would have volunteered to spare that old mama this cross-country sprint, a jaunt which was certainly not doing him any good. His head felt like it was trapped inside a cathedral bell ringing the congregation in for prayers while his stomach flipped and flopped. He stopped in mid-stride, doubled over, and vomited. Why was he doing this? Obviously to impress Pamela.

The passengers found the matatu at the designated meeting place. Loomis was the last to arrive and was therefore stuck at the back with his backside protruding out the doorway while the conductor hung outside on the freely swinging door. Chances of further conversation with Pamela were now nil.

On the way once more, the driver shortly stopped the vehicle for the second time, taking the opportunity to reprimand a herds-boy whose cows were blocking the road. That aside, they made good progress, owing to a rare decision not to stop for any more passengers. At Oluti, Loomis disentangled himself from a human web of limbs and got off while the conductor groped inside for his brown shoulder bag. After accepting his luggage, Loomis went over to the window where Pamela was seated and tapped on it, making her turn around.

"Bye!" was all he could muster as the vehicle hastily sped off. He stood staring after it as it receded quickly down the road. "Shit!" he swore. Anyway, he at least knew her name and where to contact her. Pamela Emuria, Nairobi University. Music.

NAIROBI, SEPTEMBER 7

He wandered around the campus, giddily excited in the pursuit of his quarry, following the directions leading to the Music Department, which he obtained from the guards at the entrance gate. As he approached a one-story building consisting of rows of offices, his heart rate accelerated just a bit. He strolled along the facade in as casual a manner as he could feign, trying to figure out just which office was hers by reading the white lettering on the black nameplates just to the left of each door. He stopped when he saw 'Dr. K. Hesland /Assistant Prof. P. Emuria'. He gave this door a light rap.

"Come in, it's open," beckoned a husky female voice, not hers, certainly.

He swung the door open, and upon seeing a plump dyed blonde in her forties roosting behind a white metal desk, entered warily.

"Hi," the tubby white woman greeted, with an expression of mild curiosity, thinking that the dark, attractive man in the cashmere sport coat was lost.

Unique-looking. Indian? Swahili? Half-caste?

"Oh, hello," he replied, looking slightly disoriented. "I was looking for Pa-MEL-la Emuria."

"Came to the right place," she affirmed in a rising pitch that Loomis interpreted to be a defensive tone. Like a "yeah so what's your business here?" sort of tone, or maybe that impression was a product of his own guilt reminding him that he was being mischievous.

"Is she in?" he asked.

"Well, do you see her?"

He looked stupidly at Pamela's empty desk and was convinced that this woman was being hostile.

"Oh, I'm sorry, just joking with ya," she burst out with a chuckle, much to his relief.

"Pammy, uh, Ms. Emuria went into town for a few things. Should be back by lunchtime. Are you a friend of hers?"

Loomis, now off his guard, went into charm mode, giving her a rakish grin. "Hope to be."

She smiled coyly. "I bet you do." She looked at him with puckish eyes.

It was working. Definitely receptive now.

"So, how do you two know each other," she asked with a cheeky interest.

"We share a common fascination for music," he fibbed. "Do you know exactly where she might have gone to in town? I mean, favorite places to shop, stuff like that?"

"You're an American, yeah?"

"That's right. From the Big Apple. And you, I'm guessing...Nebraska?"

"Close. Kansas. You might try Ebrahim's Record Store on Kimathi Street, it's a sure bet she'll stop in there, she's always got things on order."

"Thanks." He made to leave.

"Wait, aren't you going to leave a name and message in case she comes back?"

He opened the door, trying to pre-empt further inquiry. "Daryl Loomis. Tell her the guy who helped her with the package."

"Package?"

But he was already out the door.

About ten minutes later, the door opened again. It was Pamela. "I forgot my list," she hurriedly explained, going over to her desk sifting through her papers.

"Oh too bad, you just missed him."

"Who?"

Katy raised her eyebrows naughtily. "Some cute guy looking for you."

Pamela scrunched up her face in puzzlement.

"Light-skinned black man, reminded me of Michael Jackson on the album cover of *Off the Wall*...young, about your age, late twenties, early thirties..."

Pamela shook her head, still befuddled, indicating that it didn't ring any bells.

"The man who helped you with the package."

Her face expanded into one of incredulous amazement. "How did he find me?" she asked herself.

"Who's the guy, Pammy?"

Pamela did not answer immediately. She grabbed the piece of paper she had been searching for and headed for the door. "I'll tell you about it later," she promised, closing the door with an uncharacteristic briskness.

* * *

Loomis was patrolling the sidewalk in front of Ebrahim's Record Store like an obsessed man, walking back and forth, chain-smoking the time away. Sooner or later, she was bound to come. It suddenly occurred to him that she shouldn't be seeing him like this; she might get the impression that he was stalking her. He would have to go inside and appear to be browsing innocently, so that their meeting would seem accidental. He threw his butt away and walked inside the shop.

A sale on European classical records was announced on a cardboard sign by the cashier. He thought about his forthcoming sequestration in Turkanaland; he would need something livelier than that to brighten up his nights in a tent. He went straight to the section labeled *Zilozopendwa* (beloved oldies) to pick out an old Tabu Ley tape and a few classics by Daudi Kabaka. He walked around the shop with these items in his hand, for almost a half hour, trying his best to act the part of an earnest shopper, keeping one eye on the entrance. Every time the little bell that was set against the top of the door would tinkle, he would take extra notice. One false alarm after another, until finally the bell rang true, announcing her arrival.

She stopped at the counter. "I have an order, they told me it was ready. Emuria is the name."

The young Gikuyu behind the counter told her in Swahili to wait a few minutes.

"Oh, you have a sale today," she said, upon reading the sign. She turned to go down one of the two only aisles in the shop.

Loomis, in the second aisle, looped around so that he could bump into her.

"Oh, fancy meeting you here!" he exclaimed with showy exuberance.

She looked at him, but not with the delightful expression of surprise that he had expected, but with a cold hard stare and a deprecating frown. "Yes, fancy."

Unflustered, he continued the opening gambit. "What a coincidence! Must be fate making us bump into each other all the time."

She turned away from him to peruse the stack of record albums in front of her. "Is it? Coincidence? Fate?"

His opening was a flop, and he wasn't sure why. So he waited.

"You came to my office early this morning."

She knew. How did she know?

"Yeah, well. Just came by to say hello."

"Katy told you I would come here."

He tried to stall his reply. "Yeah, well, maybe she might have mentioned that, I'm not sure." He took the time to study her. Her slender legs and her shapely rounded bottom delightfully filled her tight jeans. She was wearing a white blouse with flaring sleeves, the kind that turned him on, and on her head, a large blue headkerchief. Looking at her, he wanted her more than ever. But, as she flipped through the record albums with an exaggerated brusqueness, it seemed obvious that she was not a happy camper. Not sure of what to do, he went into emergency-recovery mode. Time to throw in some honesty.

"Okay, I confess I was waiting for you here. But you have to admit that on the two previous occasions it was purely chance."

No response.

"Do you realize that before that scene with those crooks we could have been passing each other on the street hundreds of times without noticing each other? We might have been in the same bus, the same bar, even in the same elevator, and never had known it."

"I suppose that is possible," she finally answered, "not in a bar, however."

"So?"

"So what?"

God, she was a tough nut, and his frustration at the thought that he was going to lose her was beginning to rattle him.

She picked out a record, probably one she didn't even want, he reckoned, just to get away from him, then practically stomped to the front of the shop.

At the counter, she demanded to know if her order was ready. It was, she paid, and exited hurriedly. Loomis put the cassette tapes he was holding down on the counter and desperately followed her out.

"Anyway, the point is, through fate or destiny, or whatever force, we now know one another by face and even by name, and I think we should take that opportunity to elaborate on that."

"And how do you propose we do that?" she asked sardonically.

He decided to pull out all the stops. He put on what he called, his 'Robert Redford smile'. "By having dinner with me Friday evening."

"I'm sorry, but I'm busy on Friday."

"What about Saturday?"

She didn't answer, but instead puffed air between slack lips, a gesture of agitated impatience, and started to quicken her pace down the street. She was walking so fast he had to make an effort to keep up with her.

"Well?"

"Saturday as well."

"Sunday afternoon?"

"No!"

"But we should get to know each other."

He was grasping at straws. He stumbled as he tried to stay with her, for she was almost trotting to escape his attentions. He was losing her.

"Ah now, Pamela, you're not even giving me a chance."

"A chance for what?"

"To conquer your heart," he blurted stupidly.

"I don't want my heart conquered, thank you." She stopped short and wheeled around to face him. "You think you are the first man to want me?" Her face was now tightened in a grimace. Her eyes were brimming, on the verge of tears.

Something in his brain was telling him, *Abort! Abort!*

But what was about to happen next would divert the course of their exchange.

"Leave me..." she cried, then broke off in mid-sentence as shouting screaming people ran by from every direction, converging towards a noisy commotion taking place across the street. A ring of angry, swearing men were striking at something in the middle of their circle. Off to the side, a European girl, possibly a tourist, stood staring at them, eyes wide with terror, her hands gripping her hair in fright. She screamed. "No, no, oh my God, no!" A white male grabbed her by the waist and dragged her away.

"It's a thief," Loomis explained. "They're beating him. Probably nicked something from that mzungu girl."

This was one of the few things that Loomis had to endure with agony in his life in East Africa. It reminded him of the abuses he suffered as a child. A thing that revolted him, but yet he had the coolness of mind to realize that this was their way, and as an outsider he should not interfere. Still, the pain it caused him was excruciating and the only thing he could think of was to get away.

He took her arm and led her away. "C'mon, let's go."

"But they're going to kill him!"

"That's almost a certainty," he said with artificial glibness.

"That's murder!" she shouted. "Nothing he could have stolen could be worth more than his life." She broke his grip to run towards the scene, but he nearly tackled her as she stepped off the curb. He put his hands firmly on her shoulders, then commanded her. "STAY...HERE."

For a brief moment, she saw the panic in his eyes, and dutifully obeyed.

He scurried across the street with apprehension, knowing he was going against his better judgment.

He joined the circle of vindicators and studied the thief. Dressed in a ragged denim vest and a dirty pair of jeans, he was being kicked and punched from one side of the circle to another, bleeding profusely but still conscious. In addition to the weapons of fists and feet, one of the avengers struck and stabbed at him with an umbrella. Loomis timed his entrance as the thief fell on the far side of the ring, jumping in the middle and trying to avoid the blows which were intended for the person at his feet."Wachana naye, leave him be!" he yelled at the crowd. He was frightened; they had already seen blood and it was going to be difficult to restrain them. In the frenzy of this violent melee, a boot heel from a flying kick caught him in the head and he fell on top of the bloodstained thief. "Shit!" he spat out. Some members of the mob came in and jerked Loomis off their prey, but he struggled with them, inviting more blows, until Loomis collapsed to the ground.

The crowd, momentarily checked by their embarrassment at causing him injury, pulled back as he struggled to his feet. For a split-second they stood still, poised but hesitant, though he knew they would not stay that way for long. An Indian storekeeper who was viewing the scene from his doorway came forward and helped Loomis drag the thief into his shop, as Loomis still fought off the attackers before crossing the shop's threshold and slamming shut the grilled iron gates. The enraged mob surged towards the gates and clanged on them furiously demanding their victim back, while Loomis and the shopkeeper sat the battered thief on a chair behind the counter, the Indian giving the youth a handkerchief to wipe his bloody, puffed-up face.

"You should thank this man," the shopkeeper told him, referring to Loomis, "he risked his life to save yours."

The pack of vigilantes continued to throng outside shouting threats, their anger and violence not yet dissipated.

"You better call the police quickly," Loomis told the Indian, "or else you may not have a shop anymore."

While the shopkeeper dialed the phone, Loomis stood, conscious of something warm and sticky on the side of his head, and realized he was bleeding. There was blood all over his cashmere sport coat. "Shit."

Then he heard someone calling his name.

"Daryl! Daryl!"

He turned around and saw Pamela's concerned face pressed against the bars of the grating, in the middle of the melee.

"Oh no, you're hurt," she sadly observed.

"It's nothing, just a scratch." Keeping his gaze on her, he boldly asked through the iron barrier, "How about that date Friday night? I think I earned it, don't you?"

"I...I have a meeting with my children's group Friday night."

"Well, can't I come and sit in? Afterwards we can go somewhere."

"Alright. It's at seven, in the music hall of the university, Chiromo Campus."

"Good. You better get going. I'll have to stay until the police arrive. See you then."

"Please be careful." She squirmed her way past the now-thinning crowd, turned around to vainly wave goodbye, and disappeared down the street, still trying to comprehend just what exactly had taken place.

* * *

Loomis stepped off the number 23 bus at the stop outside Chiromo campus and lit a cigarette. It had taken him quite a while to get there – considerable time waiting for two buses, and an additional forty-five minutes for the rides – and now he was glad he had left early.

He didn't want to blow this one. After this children's thing he would suggest coffee at her place. She seemed the hard-shelled sort, tough to crack but, he figured, all the more sweeter for it; yet it wouldn't do for her to sack out at his place, especially with his housemate Okova around, who would, as sure as the Pope was Catholic, be rip-roaring drunk on a Friday night. No, it would have to be her place. She was just that type.

In spite of his attempts at self-assurance, he was actually a bit edgy. *Don't worry, just be yourself. No, on second thought don't be yourself, at least not your usual self.* This bird had more class than his usual prey, and he would have to adapt his tactics.

Nearing the music hall he heard a loud racket coming from within: drums banging, horns tooting, and bells rattling. He peeked inside and saw about thirty children, jumping and dancing, each in possession of some kind of instrument. But no Pamela. He decided to try her office.

Pamela was inside, busy behind her desk. She was wearing a bright yellow blouse with a gray skirt, her curly-kit afro now gone and in its place, a plaited hairdo with 'cornrows' converging upwards to the apex of her head, where a tasseled bun sat adorned with a red ribbon. It was a pretty schoolmistress look, and Loomis liked it.

He removed the butt from his mouth and threw it down. "*Hodi,*" he called, requesting permission to enter.

She looked up. "Oh, hello, Mr. Loomis, I'll be right with you."

Mr. Loomis? What happened to Daryl? He felt deflated.

She stood up gathering some of the articles on her desk. "I'm just trying to get a few things together," she apologized. Actually, she was so caught up in her preparations, she had forgotten about his visit. Maybe she had wanted to.

"It seems your students have started without you," Loomis noted.

"Oh, I always give them some instruments to experiment with before class. Freedom of expression is so important. Lets them explore the world for themselves."

Loomis got out of her way as she headed for the doorway with papers in hand whence she proceeded to lock up the office. That completed, they walked into the hall.

"That's enough, children!" she screamed above the din. To Loomis's surprise, the activity ceased at once, except for a few tardy toots and clangs. "This is Mr. Loomis, our guest for the evening, so I want you to show him your best singing. Okay, everyone, sit down." She waited for the children to sit. "Clarence, please find your own chair," she admonished one boy who was apparently trying to take a girl's seat by force.

"Now, how many of you remember the new song we learned last week?"

Hands jerked and wavered in the air, accompanied by shouts of "I do, I do, Miss Emuria!"

So far, so good, thought Loomis. *She's a Miss.* Not that it mattered all that much. It was nice to catch one on the stray sometimes.

"Well, let's go over it now and see how well we do," she said as she handed out sheets with the words printed on them. After they all received a sheet, she grabbed a guitar from the corner of the hall and sat on a stool in front of the class.

"You forgot to give Mr. Loomis a sheet," pointed out a cute little girl in the front row.

"No, that's alright," responded Loomis with an awkward smile, "the words are in my head."

"And that's exactly where I want you to put them," Pamela told the class. With those words she began strumming the guitar, and when she cued the children to start singing, she sang along with them, a Madonna-like smile on her face. Her clear, honeyed voice rose distinctly above those of the children, and pulled him in like the call of a siren. She alternately closed and opened her sparkling eyes, swaying her head and shoulders to the music, and when she threw a warm glance in his direction, it sent a shudder through his body.

It could have been then, in that instant, that something started to happen to Loomis. Or, on the other hand, perhaps this something was always there, hidden underneath layers of false nonchalance; a desire waiting to be stirred; a longing for someone. He was sure of one thing: no one that he could remember had ever made him feel what he was feeling at this moment. It didn't seem he had any choice but to surrender to the rapture of her spell.

The song ended, too soon for Loomis, and Pamela became engaged in teaching them a new one. As she wrote the lyrics on the blackboard, explaining their meaning, and sang to illustrate the melodies, it became obvious that she had had a lot of experience with children; the kids were eating up every minute. They practiced this new song for half an hour more and then Pamela announced it was time to go, resulting in a chorale of crestfallen pleads and protests:

"No, please, Miss Emuria..."

"Let's stay..."

"A little longer...please!"

They didn't want to leave; they were enjoying her as much as he was.

A captive of his joyfulness, he suddenly shouted, "Okay, wait, I have one song that I would like to sing for you." He took the guitar from a pleasantly surprised Pamela, picked at it in an explorative manner, and moments later began to sing:

"There's a hole in the bottom of the sea

There's a hole in the bottom of the sea

There's a hole, There's a hole,

There's a hole in the bottom of the sea

There's a log in the hole in the bottom of the sea..."

He continued on until the end in which there was a germ on the flea on the fly on the frog on the bump on the log in the hole in the bottom of the sea. The kids cheered, and at their insistence Miss Emuria promised she would write down the words and teach it to them next week. She instructed them to hand in their instruments and reminded them of their extra lesson on Monday afternoon. They asked her if they could come to her house as they usually did after class.

"Not today, I have a visitor," she explained, meaning Loomis.

This made him feel proud and important for some stupid reason, but also, oddly enough, guilty, and in empathy with the children who would be denied her company on his account. "It's alright," he said, "let them come for a little while."

She looked at him with that angelic smile. "Alright."

He didn't know what they were in for until he saw her car and the number of children who wanted to get in it. It was a Fiat 500, the smallest car he had ever seen, like a toy, its roof barely reaching his chest.

Seven of the kids managed to squeeze into the back and Pamela declared that that was enough.

"Get in," she told Daryl, "the others will follow."

And follow they did, running and singing all the way to her house at the faculty residence, about a half mile from the hall.

It was like a child's birthday party, Pamela serving tea and cakes while the children danced and sang. A full hour went by and Loomis, with a soft spot in his heart for kids, participated in their games, performing tongue-twisters in English to their gleeful amazement. At nine o'clock Pamela began clearing up with the help of some of the older children and shortly afterwards forced her young pupils to a reluctant departure. When the last child was out the door, she told Loomis to relax in the sitting room while she went to the kitchen to boil more tea.

The furniture was still in minor disarray from the evening's entertainment and he set out to straighten things up. As he put back the chairs, Pamela called out from the kitchen, "You don't have to do that, please, sit."

"No, it's alright, I'm finished." He sat down on a lengthy colonial-style sofa which was positioned along one of the walls. The sitting room was rather large, big enough to be occupied by two ample bookcases, a piano, and a moderate-sized dining set. Loomis could hear Pamela humming to herself in the kitchen and shortly she came in with a tray bearing cups, sugar, and a kettle covered with a tea cozy.

"You're very good with children," Loomis told her as she poured the tea.

"And so are you, Daryl."

Daryl again, a good sign.

She looked at him as she handed him his cup and noticed the bruise on his head. "That was more than just a scratch," she commented. "It has swollen up. You should put some ice on it. Do you want some ice?"

"No, that's alright. It's too late now, it'll heal."

"It's just that I feel like it's my fault. It seems whenever you run into me I get you involved in some kind of trouble. I wouldn't blame you if the next time you see me you walk away and ignore me," she said teasingly. But perhaps that was just wishful thinking on her part.

"No, I won't do that, I can assure you." He spoke nothing further but watched her sit down on the chair directly opposite the sofa. Then, "So with all your duties here as university lecturer, you still find time for these kids?"

"Oh it's a lot of fun; it isn't really work at all. They're the children of faculty and staff here, so I couldn't resist."

"You do really enjoy teaching children, I can see that."

"Yes, they are very open to learning, if you can manage to hold their attention."

"Which I noticed you do quite well."

She closed her eyes and smiled guardedly, her usual insecure reaction to compliments. Except that it wasn't really her usual reaction. Strange, coming from him, it didn't scare her – she even liked it. Strange. Her expression became restrained in thought.

"Is there something wrong?"

She gave out a self-conscious chuckle. "No, I was just thinking...it's nothing to do with you." She tried to convince herself that it wasn't.

"You have a very nice voice," he continued.

He did it again. And again, it seemed that she even enjoyed it. Strange. She chose the strategy of turning the compliment back on him. "And you also. You would make a very good baritone in a choir. Do you do much singing?"

"No, just fooling around." After a pause, he continued, "You're very serious about music, aren't you? It's a lovely profession, a teacher of music."

"I'm also a student; one never stops learning. I'm convinced it's unfathomable. I mean, can you explain just how a person enjoys music? A biophysicist would say it was all a matter of vibrational waves tickling the sensory system – but it's certainly more than that! It's a mystery explained only by the existence of the soul. Why does certain music appeal to some and not to others? Each one of us has tastes peculiar to that person."

"Precisely. You, for instance."

"Excuse me?"

"I see you lean towards Western tastes...the classical albums you bought?"

"Oh yes, well, I have to. It's in the syllabus."

"And traditional stuff?"

"Yes, I used to be quite involved with traditional music and dance. In fact, some years ago I was working on thesis material concerning the songs of the Kuria people. But I have yet to finish. Someday." With that she became silent and reflective.

"You went to university here?" Loomis asked, hoping to get off the subject of music.

"No, in the UK."

"And after that you started teaching here?"

"No, the first thing I did after graduating was to tour Europe with a backpack for six months; then I went to Israel and worked on a kibbutz for another six."

"A kibbutz? Are there many Africans who do that?"

"I wouldn't imagine so. In the beginning, the children used to stare at me and call me 'Kaffir,' but after a while they grew accustomed to me and we became good friends. In the end I must say it was a wonderful experience."

He was fascinated. She was different, unique, in a class by herself. "I bet you've seen more of the Western world than I have." Loomis himself had never been to Europe. Or anywhere else for that matter outside of East Africa.

She sighed wistfully. "There are even times when I feel I know more about Western culture than I do my own."

"What culture?" he challenged. "McDonald's? Harrod's? Club Med? It's just consumerism. Nothing to say about how to lead one's life or live with one's neighbor, just listen to what the television says and buy, buy, buy!" He surprised himself, lashing out at memories of his pre-existing world. "American culture died a long time ago. As for me, I'll take a mud hut and some land to till any day."

"Maybe you're right. Sometimes I think back to when I was a little girl fetching firewood from the forest and it makes me feel that somehow I've lost something over the years."

The image of her as a little peasant girl appealed to him; someone who was intimate with both worlds, old and new. "So how was your visit home?" he asked her.

"Very nice. I hadn't seen my family for so long. And where is your home, Daryl?"

"Buru-Buru," he answered teasingly, as Buru-Buru was a suburb of Nairobi.

"Oh stop," she exclaimed laughing, going so far as to reach out and slap his knee like he was a naughty child. She checked herself. Why did she do that? It was way too forward and familiar. Her face went sober. "Oh, I'm sorry," she apologized.

Loomis was pleased. *Now we're getting somewhere.* Appropriate time for his shy, 'Montgomery Clift' smile. "That's okay, I deserved that. Actually I don't have a home as such, except here in Kenya, but I'm an American if that's what you mean."

There followed a pause in their conversation. Pamela smiled and slowly shook her head, amused by some private thought. "Omolo," she mumbled, almost to herself.

"What?"

"That Luo in the matatu called you Omolo."

"Oh that, yeah, just kidding around. A friend of mine gave me that name. He used to introduce me as Omolo, his long-lost brother returned from overseas. The name stuck. Actually, he did have a brother named Omolo, but he died at an early age."

"And what were you doing in Oluti?"

"Visiting friends."

"In a small village?"

"Well, we had a job there a few years ago. Lived in the village for about a month, and, you know how it is, made a lot of friends."

"You're funny," she said.

"What do you mean?"

"You don't act anything like other Americans I know."

"Oh yes, well, that has been pointed out to me before. Maybe it's just that I can't muster that false feeling of superiority over peoples of another culture."

He was holding up pretty well, he thought. The intellectual, informed, sensitive type; that should hook her in.

And it did, for they found themselves engaged in an enthusiastic discourse concerning culture and history and a comparative analysis of European and African viewpoints, and other such heady stuff.

Loomis actually shocked himself. He could not remember how long it had been when he had talked so much, about such serious things, and so eloquently. At least not when he was this sober anyway. She just seemed to be drawing it out of him. Whatever the reason for it, he could see that he was captivating her by his opinions on things.

They continued to talk, converse, chat; about the nature of his job, the educational system in Africa, the Palestinian issue, the precepts of Buddhism... He was still a bit awestruck that he could have such conversations with a Kenyan woman.

As the night grew late, he, quite unexpectedly, grew restless and uneasy.

"What time is it?" he blurted.

She glanced at the wall clock above the piano. "Eleven-fifteen," she replied, then continued with the point she was making.

Twenty minutes later, his uneasiness had increased to anxiety. "Excuse me," he said, interrupting her again, "but do you know what time the last bus leaves?"

"I don't know. We can go out and check. But you're welcome to stay here if it's too late to travel." Pamela's own words took her by surprise. What was she saying? Of course, she meant he could sleep in the living room, but even that could be construed as inappropriate. If the neighbors were aware he had stayed the night, it would prove most embarrassing and difficult to explain. But what if there was no bus? Maybe better to give him a lift, even if it was far.

"No, I should get back tonight." Loomis could not believe he said that. What was wrong with him? Even if he made it to town it was doubtful whether he would be able to reach the suburb where he lived. He'd probably end up sleeping in a run-down lodging. But he was afraid of the decision she would have to make if he stayed – he would not be able to bear it if she were to assign him to the sofa – that could forever doom him to a platonic relationship. Or perhaps it was the other alternative which frightened him. Whatever the case, it was clear that his battle plan had to be forsaken, for he had not been prepared enough for someone like her, and now all he wanted to do was to leave and regroup his thoughts.

"Alright," she answered, greatly relieved, unaware of the conflict in his own head. "Let me drive you to the bus stop."

She collected her keys and they exited together. A soft rain was falling, unusual for that time of the year. They hurried into the car, and after it was warmed up, drove to the bus stop. There, they sat waiting, the rain beating gently on the roof of the car, exaggerating an already awkward silence. Loomis wanted to say so many things to her, but he wasn't sure what. It was difficult to translate his feelings into words.

"There's a certain magic about you, that's why those children adore you," he said, regretting it as soon as it spilled from his mouth. It sounded so, so...stilted.

This time, his compliment did scare her, reminding her of what she was trying to run away from her whole life.

"Please don't say things like that."

"I'm sorry. Actually, I knew it was not the right thing to say, but... I just couldn't help it."

"No, it was a nice thing to say. I can't explain why I don't like to hear things like that."

"I promise I won't do it again," he apologized, except he did not really understand exactly what wrong he had just committed.

The rain came harder now, and again they were wordless. Loomis was nervous, as if anything she said or did could determine the course of his life. Finally, the bus, probably the last one, arrived. If he wanted to reach town, he would have to get on it.

"Well, I guess I better go. Can I see you again?"

"Yes," she answered.

"When?" Just then the bus began to pull out. "I have to go." He opened the door and leapt out into the rain.

"Wait!" she cried. But he had already run to the bus which had stopped for him, and reaching it, he clambered inside.

* * *

Pamela found it hard to sleep, tossing and turning, trying to figure out what was happening to her. She had already tried her best to forget about the incident with the thief, attempting to file it away in a low-priority section of her mind, which was her normal approach to unpleasant events. And of course she did not tell Katy, that would have made it more difficult to efface the memory and brush it aside. But still it persisted and she knew the reason for this. It was him.

Because of him. The whole incident was about him, not about the poor desperate wretch who tried to snatch someone's purse so he could survive another day.

She had witnessed for a small fraction of a moment his vulnerability, his fear and revulsion. He had wanted to run away. Instead, he overcame his weakness and by doing so, saved that man's life. But what disturbed her further was that she knew he would not have done it if she wasn't with him. It was some sort of symbiotic bond, a burden which she did not want to bear.

She did have to admit, however, that he seemed a nice person, not as shallow as the impression she had first had of him. Warm and affectionate with the children; intelligent and perceptive; sensitive...but there were many nice men in the world, that didn't mean she should have relationships with all of them.

And how could she manage to enjoy his compliments? Except of course for that last one, but even that one that did not frighten her in the usual way. It was more like alarm over an unwarranted personal invasion, an unsolicited intimacy, as if he had seen her naked, for what she was, her secret revealed. This was a familiarity she did not welcome.

And why did she agree that he could visit her again? *No, this cannot go on.* The last thing she needed was for him to complicate her life. Her world had been very neatly arranged and already kept in order by another man, one that she had grown used to for several years, and all that time she hadn't involved herself in any relations outside of casual acquaintances, her sexual fidelity unfailing.

If Daryl should come back, she would have to be cold to him, even discourteous, and make it clear to him that she didn't want him in her life. She would tell him to go away and not see her again.

* * *

The next morning, Loomis, with only a towel around his waist, exited the concrete shower cubicle somewhat vexed after discovering the taps were dry, and went back to his shabby guest-house room. He felt confused.

The little devil on his left shoulder kept telling him he was a dope, and that it was his own fault there was no water to bathe with, that he deserved being kept awake all night by merciless mosquitoes and the loud creakings of the spring bed occupied by the amorous couple next door. If he had stayed at her place he would have woken up to a good-looking chick who would have served him breakfast in bed, grateful for the services rendered during the night. Instead he had acted like a schoolboy on his first date.

The little angel on his right shoulder countered that argument, saying that he had made the right decision, that lust should take a back seat with this woman, for she attracted him in other ways besides physical desire. And not to discount the possibility that he had been so nervous last night, had he attempted, he might have failed to prove his manhood. Anyway, a man was more than just his loins. *Pole pole ndio ni mwendo*, slow and steady was true speed.

But when could he see her again? To go back after only one day would seem a bit pushy. Next Saturday, very early, would be his best bet. Until then, could he endure a whole week without seeing her? Fully dressed, but still feeling grubby and bedraggled, he went downstairs and departed from the decrepit lodging impertinently named the Heavenly Night Guest House.

* * *

The week seemed to plod along in slow motion. Loomis found it difficult to go out with his friends. He was too embarrassed to talk about Pamela. They probably wouldn't understand and even make light of it. On the first two nights out with them his behavior was subdued, and when asked what the matter was, he replied that he thought he might be coming down with something. And indeed, for the past three days he had been faking a mild case of malaria in order to stay at home. Meanwhile, his anticipation of seeing her grew until it became oppressive.

Saturday eventually came, and walking to her house he felt short of breath, as if he were hyperventilating.

For Pamela, it was just the opposite. With each day that passed since that Friday night, her relief increased, and she could calm herself with the thought that he would not visit her again. The memory of him was fading into an amusing but emotionless recollection, exactly what she wanted.

She wiped the perspiration off her face with a handkerchief as she looked up at the sun. From its position, she could tell it was *saa nne*, the fourth hour. Two more hours to go until noon and it was already hot, and she was getting weary. She had been weeding her garden since seven-thirty, and couldn't comprehend where people got the stamina to work in their big *shambas* from dawn to dusk.

She heard the sound of someone knocking on her front door, and thinking it was the woman who brought her fresh eggs on the weekends, she yelled out, "Hello, I'm in the backyard!"

Loomis appeared at the side gate. "Good morning."

Her face all but dropped.

Loomis stood there, a bit terrified. It was evident that she was not happy to see him, and he felt all his self-confidence draining out of him. What was it with this woman, cold, hot, then cold again? She was making him feel like an ass.

"Did I come at a bad time?" he asked apologetically. In his head, he was saying, *I'm sorry, sorry for wanting you, don't be angry with me, but what do you expect, it's only natural.*

"Well, it would have been better if you had called first."

"You never gave me your number," he stated in his defense, again in a repentant tone.

She felt a bit stupid, of course he was right, and it was a lame excuse to justify her irritation.

Loomis thought fast. *Make small talk quick, diffuse the awkwardness.* "Doing a bit of garden work I see... Hmm, you've got a big *bustani* here." The backyard he looked into was treeless but capacious, and besides the pink-blossomed bougainvillea, her vegetable garden took up most of the space.

"Just some weeding," she told him, somewhat resigned, "but it's turning out to be quite a chore." She was wearing a cheap cotton dress, torn at the shoulder, and an old faded head-kerchief, her appearance like that of a peasant girl, making her seem more feminine, more earthy, and needless to say, more desirable.

He had an idea. He needed time to delay conversation until she could at least warm up a bit to his presence. He removed his cashmere sport coat and hung it on the picket fence before entering her yard. "Here, let me have that *jembe*."

She gave him a wide-eyed look and handed him the hoe, watching him as he skillfully uprooted the invading weeds without injuring her tomato plants.

"I see you know how to use a jembe quite well," she said, in spite of herself.

"I learned on a farm in Central Province. A guy I used to work with has a home there. Some time later, when I was unemployed, I stayed there for three months. Had to earn my keep, so you might say."

"Let me get another jembe." She ran into the house, and when she returned with the other hoe, joined him in his labors.

Loomis looked longingly at her sleek figure, bobbing as she bent down weeding. Maybe a man was more than just his loins, he told himself, but that was no reason to deny their existence. Without sexual intimacy, he could not truly claim her as his woman, could not possess her, and the way he felt now, he wasn't going to settle for anything less than total possession. This woman was a prize waiting to be taken.

After half an hour, she stood up and said, "That's enough for now, you can go and relax while I make lunch." It was the polite thing to do, she decided. She could not just order him to leave; at least, not until after lunch.

Loomis gave her his hoe and collected his jacket, and they

entered the house together.

"If you want to wash up, I think you already know where the bathroom is."

"Yes, I remember. Oh, by the way, I have something for you." He took out a white envelope from one of his jacket pockets.

"A letter?"

"The words to the song, the one I played for the kids."

"Oh yes, thank you." She accepted the envelope with some ambivalence, as it threatened to reverse-engineer her efforts to keep him away from her.

Loomis, after washing his hands, went into the sitting room where he found an unopened bottle of beer and a glass on one of the end tables.

"I assumed that you drink beer," Pamela said with a slight hint of disparagement, walking in with an opener in her hand. "I thought you might like one. I keep them around for visitors."

"Sure, that would be great." From her tone, he suspected this could be some sort of a test, since it was still early, before noon. Maybe he should have declined, but he could not resist the relaxing effects of alcohol. He needed to ease his tension.

She opened the bottle and poured its contents into the glass. Before returning to the kitchen, she turned on the stereo, which began to play Puccini's *Madame Butterfly*.

Loomis removed a cigarette from the breast pocket of his shirt. "Do you have an ashtray?"

"Yes, of course."

"You don't mind?" he asked as an afterthought.

"No, go ahead."

But from the affected manner of her voice he could tell that she did mind. "Nah, it's okay, forget it. It's a dirty habit anyway."

"Yes, it is."

In the kitchen she began cutting the onions and tomatoes she intended to use for frying. As she busied herself with her task, she thought about her predicament. She would not be rude to him, but firmly explain how it could not work between them. She liked him, and perhaps under different circumstances she could have committed herself to him. But, as the way things were, the most they should hope for was a platonic friendship, and if he had more ambitious plans than that he should abandon them.

"Do you have any other music besides this?" he asked in a mild shout from the sitting room.

Loomis's verbal intrusion scattered her thoughts. She put her knife down and went to her guest. "What would you like to hear? I have some Stevie Wonder if you prefer."

"You have anything like 'Vijana Jazz'? Something local?"

"I've got an old Franco tape?"

"Great. Could you put it on for me?"

"Yes." She searched for the cassette and, upon finding it, inserted it into the player, then returned to her work. She was cutting the meat when she heard Loomis sing out along with the music.

"*Cheri bondowe, nakaka bondo we...*"

"You know Lingala too?" she inquired loudly from the kitchen, surprised.

Loomis, who had been wandering around looking at the pictures on the walls and studying the photographs displayed on her furniture, was suddenly made aware of his singing out loud, having gotten carried away with the bouncy, elaborate melody of the vocalist, and now was acutely embarrassed.

"No...I uh, just mimic the sounds," he called out in reply. "I don't know the meanings of the words." Lingala was the lingua franca of Zaire, a strange mixture of French and Bantu. The Zarois were famous for their skillful musicians whose songs were popular in Kenya, where no one actually knew Lingala, but would sing along in the fashion that Loomis had done.

"You have a quick ear. You would make a good musician," she told him, hollering above the music.

"I enjoy music, except for the kind you put on first," he shouted back.

"The opera by Puccini? To really enjoy something like that it makes a difference when you do know the meanings of the words. It's a beautiful story."

He continued circling the room, viewing various photos of Pamela graduating from high school, walking the streets of what appeared to be a city in Europe, standing with some other girls in front of the Kenyatta Conference Center, and one of when she was a young girl posing with her family at their village home. God, she was beautiful even then. Loomis, realizing that perhaps she was expecting a further comment from him, asked, "So you know Italian then?"

"Only a little, but enough to understand my favorite operas."

When he came to the piano on the side of the room, he noticed a picture taken of her standing next to a tall, middle-aged white man with longish, silver-white hair. *Must be a fellow professor,* he figured. He crossed to the far wall to one of the bookcases. Kiswahili dictionaries, music books, coffee-table photo books on African wildlife... Elementary Russian? *And what's this? Tolstoy, Dickens, James Joyce, T.S. Elliot, Milton? Better avoid a conversation about literature,* he told himself. The only classic he could remember reading was 'The Legend of Sleepy Hollow,' where this Ichabod Crane fellow was having some to-do with a village schoolteacher, and another guy, who liked carrying his head around like a bowling ball, ended up chasing him on a horse. After that, this Ichabod Crane was never heard from again.

"Do you like Sukuma-wiki?" Pamela asked, popping her head through the archway. Sukuma-wiki, known in the States as collard greens, was the most commonly eaten green vegetable in Kenya. Its Kiswahili name meant 'to push the week', presumably until you scrounged up enough money to buy some meat.

Loomis stood erect and faced her, a little shamefaced at being caught nosing around. "Er...yes, I do. I hope you're cooking *ugali* with it."

Ugali was the staple food of most East Africans. Pour cornflour into a pot of boiling water, and when it gets mushy, stir it arduously until it becomes a semi-dry doughy mound.

"I didn't intend to, but if you want..."

"Please," he entreated.

She went back to the kitchen and returned the English potatoes she had originally thought to cook, and filled a pot with water.

Loomis continued to browse through her bookshelves. That's when he noticed she had two copies of *Anna Karenina*, and this gave him a sneaky idea.

"I see you have two copies of *Anna Karenina*," he yelled out to her.

"Yes, one is in Russian."

"Good book. I read it a long time ago," he lied. "I'd like to read it again. Could I borrow one of them? The English copy, I mean." Loomis had no intention of improving his literary knowledge, but instead the lending of the book provided an assurance of seeing her again.

"It's a classic, available in any library," she shouted back, nipping his plot in the bud. "And I don't like lending my books out," she added. "Try the British Council."

It didn't take long to prepare the ugali and vegetables, and by that time the meat was also done. "Lunch is ready," she announced, cuing Loomis to go to the bathroom to wash his hands for the second time. Finished with that, he walked back to the sitting room and sat himself at the dining table which was at the far end. As she set down the silverware at his place, he pushed the knife and fork aside saying, "I don't need these. Ugali tastes better with my hands."

"Well, leave them there anyway." She did not want him to upset the order that a dining table should have. She went back to get the food, bringing the steaming mound of ugali last, then cut a piece of it and put it on a small plate which she placed in front of him, then cut a piece for herself. Obviously, she did not approve of the traditional way of grabbing from a communal portion.

Loomis seized a handful of the maize meal and began kneading it in his hand. Pamela watched him intently, and was fascinated when she saw him using his thumb to make a small depression in the doughy ball. Sensing he was being watched, he looked up. "Just making my '*tonge*'," he explained with a childlike grin.

She smiled.

She was warming. That made him feel a whole lot better, and his sense of control was returning, so much so that he took the gamble of being a bit bold.

"You know, your face looks more natural when you smile."

Her smile abruptly vanished. She hadn't been aware she was smiling.

"How about you? Can you make one?" he playfully challenged, scooping the vegetables with his 'African spoon' and popping the whole thing in his mouth.

His frisky mood was infectious, undermining her willpower. "I can make a better one than yours. You don't forget what you learn as a child." To prove her point, she put down her knife and fork and began eating the ugali with her hands. "You see," she vaunted, showing him her effort. The ball of ugali had a deep depression which made it look like a tiny basket.

"You win, yours can hold twice as many vegetables as mine," he conceded smiling. They continued eating, with Pamela's silverware lying idle for the rest of the meal.

After clearing the table, she took a chair and sat in her customary place opposite the sofa, which Loomis had all to himself.

"Pamela, I'm sorry, but I forgot your other names."

"Emuria," she responded.

"That's your father's name, isn't it?"

"Yes."

"What about your traditional name, your own name I mean."

"Amonee."

"Do you mind if I call you Amonee?"

"Well, I don't mind, although nobody calls me by that name except my family."

Good, thought Loomis, *I will be the one person outside your family to call you that. That will help to make me closer to you than the others,* he told her in his mind.

"Would you like to hear some more music?" she asked.

Now she's mine, he reveled to himself. He knew exactly which direction to take, a place where she would not be able to escape him. "How about playing guitar and singing a little?"

"Fine." She rose and left the room, then came back with a guitar which she began to tune. "Do you know any songs by Leonard Cohen?" she asked.

"'Suzanne' is my favorite," he told her.

She strummed the guitar, playing the appropriate chords, and after a few bars, began to sing the first verse. He joined her, and this made her stop her voice in order to listen to his. She liked his voice; it was strong and smooth. Her own voice returned, but this time in high harmony. It was a pleasant sound, with her part tucked neatly under his:

"...and you touch her perfect body with your mind..."

Blissful minutes went by while they sang together, and Loomis felt he had achieved a small, but important victory. When, they finished, they sat for a few moments in satisfied serenity.

"Very nice," she commented with a smile of genuine happiness.

"Do you know this one?" Loomis asked, begging the guitar from her. He knew she would and again they sang together:

"Mailaika, nakupenda malaika, Angel I love you...*nashindwa na mali sina wey,* I am defeated by the wealth I don't have... Otherwise I would marry you"

Much of the afternoon went by in the same manner, playing the guitar and conjuring up old songs. After a while, she got up to play the piano. First a selection by Brahms, then one of her own compositions.

"Do you like it?" she asked, after finishing her piece. By now, her strategy of keeping him at bay had waned.

"Yes, you're quite a composer."

"Do you know how to play piano, Daryl?"

"Just a little."

"Let me hear." She rose, but Loomis objected.

"There's enough room for both of us," he assured her.

She slid over on the bench to give Loomis space to sit down beside her. Actually, the only music he knew how to play on the piano was a few things he saw Chico do in a Marx Brothers' movie. As he played with the keys, she laughed. He'd do anything to hear her laugh, to hear those sweetly resonant vibrations coming from her beautiful throat; he'd even walk down Kenyatta Avenue with maize cobs sticking in his ears.

Soon dusk approached with the promise of night. Had she begun to think he was overstaying his welcome? But if she did, she gave no indication of it.

"It's nearing six-thirty, I better prepare supper. I have some fish that a neighbor gave me this morning. Would that be okay with you?" To her wonder, she actually didn't want him to leave.

"I love fish!" he exclaimed, greatly relieved. He didn't feel like leaving either. He didn't know whether he would ever feel like leaving.

During their meal, there was light conversation, with Loomis steering it towards his work and his upcoming project in Turkanaland, with the aim of impressing her. Then he helped her carry the dishes to the sink and convinced her to wash them later, that they should take this time to relax.

In the room that was both a living and dining room, Loomis took his seat on the sofa while Amonee sat on her usual chair across from him. No one said anything, and the silent seconds nagged at him with the message that it was now or never.

"Amonee, I...I...think you're very beautiful...no, I mean...not just good to look at but...really beautiful inside too...I mean you're intelligent and polite, sincere..."

Oh god, she thought, *here it comes, the moment I've been dreading.*

"Look, what I'm trying to say – what I'm trying to say is that...I think I'm crazy about you."

She looked down silently at her lap with a grave expression on her face, and folded her arms. She did not answer, just sat there, and Loomis was starting to panic.

"I'm sorry if I upset you." He now regretted revealing his feelings.

"It's...not that, it's just..." Amonee could not say the words that she had originally planned to say in the morning. She felt confused. It was her fault. She had been receptive to him, the opposite of what she intended. She had done everything she had told herself not to do. Why? Because of him. He made her act this way. How did he do that? In her befuddlement, she was possessed with a wish to surrender. To raise the white flag and say, *Okay you won, you conquered my heart.* To leap into the chaos of unrestrained feeling.

She heard herself blurting out words that she could not believe she was saying, "I feel the same way about you." Did she? Did she really? Yes, and it was a relief to take down her defenses and admit it.

She got up and sat next to him on the sofa, the close proximity of her body to his, and the feminine fragrance it exuded, electrifying him. He had to contain himself to prevent taking her in his arms.

Looking deeply into his eyes, she said, "But I already have a friend, a European. We've known each other for almost ten years..."

Loomis was finally struck with the realization that a woman as wonderful as her could never be unclaimed. He was sure that other people who knew her must have felt the same way about her as he did, and out of these people, there was one who managed to squeeze his way past the crowd and into her heart, the lucky bastard... He should have known that what was happening to him was too good to be true. He should have known.

"...and he's overseas at the moment," she continued, "He wants me to marry him and live in Europe. But I'm not sure if I want to leave my country." A heavy pause. "Perhaps there are some things about our relationship that I'm not satisfied with. I don't know. I had never thought about that before."

Loomis was seized with a sick sensation in his gut. If it was defeat, he wanted it to be quick and merciful. He wanted to run out of the house and get away. He almost tuned out what she was saying.

"You know, I've never been with another man all this time that I've known Jon."

Jon, so that was his name.

"I remember," she continued," there was one man who sat next to me once, in a cafe. We started a conversation, and when I excused myself, he got up and followed me. He was very friendly and intelligent, and he came from my home area, but when he asked me for a date, I didn't know how to answer him, I started running down the street. I didn't want to stop, I ran for a full ten minutes. That was the closest I ever came to being unfaithful."

"Well, I should have known that you weren't free. I can see the way you attract people. There's just something special about you. So I hope you understand if I got a little out of line. I won't bother you anymore." Loomis got up to leave.

"No, please...sit down." *Look, you came into my life and did this to me,* she wanted to say, *don't abandon me now.*

He returned to his seat, curious to know what was next. Amonee put her chin in her hand but said nothing. Loomis grew impatient. "Are we going to see each other again?"

"Yes."

"When?"

"I don't know."

At this point, Loomis intuited that she was handing control of the situation over to him. "How about next Saturday?"

"Yes."

He kissed her. Only a little peck, closed lips quickly alighting on closed lips, keeping his arms to himself.

She sat upright. "But next Saturday I promised to take the children to the *Bomas of Kenya*," she remembered. "They've already paid for the tickets."

"Great, we can go together. I don't mind the children." He gave her another small kiss, this time putting his right arm over her shoulder, giving her a mild squeeze. "Can I stay tonight?" He wanted very much for her to submit her body to him, to give herself to him as a woman gives herself to her man. Then it would be a lot harder for her to walk away from him, and he'd have a running chance against Mr. Mysterious.

"No, not tonight, I'm confused. Let's slow it down a bit. I have to be sure of what I'm doing."

He was disappointed, he wanted her so badly, but the fact that she agreed to see him again still elated him. At least he wasn't being condemned to the sofa. "Alright, whatever you want. In that case, I better leave now, it's getting late." *And suppressing my carnal desire is becoming a torture*, he wanted to add. "I can meet you in town on Saturday."

"Where?"

"How about the parking lot of the Railway Club, it's on the way. Say, eleven o'clock?"

"Eleven o'clock is fine. The dancers start at noon."

Loomis, once again rose to leave, asking for his sport coat. Amonee went into the closet to fetch it, then helped him to put it on.

"Oh, I forgot...the book."

"What book?"

"*Anna Karenina*. You wanted to borrow it, didn't you?"

"Oh," he laughed. At first his instinct was to make up some cockamamie story, but instead he told her the truth, "I really didn't want to read it. I wanted it as an excuse to see you again."

She giggled. The heaviness was now gone. "Are you always such a tricky person?"

"I was, but I think you're going to reform me."

She smiled her wonderful sunshine smile. That was how Loomis would always picture her, smiling.

"Let me escort you," she said.

* * *

Loomis, dressed in a maroon polyester suit, sat at the bar of the Railway Club, sipping from a bottle of bitter lemon. On the adjacent barstool sat Geoffrey Wanyoni. Geoffrey was Okova's brother, but you wouldn't think so by looking at him. He had a big square head perched on broad shoulders that belonged to a thickset rugby player's body, in total contrast to Okova's ant-like head on a gangly frame. Geoff was a lawyer, a high-powered one, the majority of his clients being politicians who had gotten into some sort of trouble. Hence his interest in the *Kenya Weekly* magazine that he was currently absorbed in, trying to stay abreast of all the latest government shenanigans.

"How's my wild baby brother doing?" he asked from the side of his mouth without removing his face from what he was reading.

"Okay, you know, same as always."

"He could have done a lot better than this Kingozi nonsense," he adjudged from the confines of his magazine. "Three years of education in America, and all he comes back with is an accent that makes him sound like some drug-dealing street nigger." He turned the page.

"Give it a chance, Geoff. Kingozi's got potential."

"Fly-by-night operation. It won't last."

Sometimes Geoff got in these high and mighty moods, but he wasn't a bad chap. Whenever Loomis's funds were low, and Okova was flat broke, he never failed to make a donation to their merry-making enterprises, and sometimes would even join them. He was a rich man to be sure, with three wives in three separate houses in Nairobi, multiple concubines, two latest-model Citroens, and a big farm in Naivasha.

"Hey, not everyone can be high-flying lawyers," Loomis told him. "Or maybe you expected him to join the medical profession?"

Geoff threw his head back to let out a hearty laugh. "Ha, yeah right." He swiveled towards Loomis. "So, who you waiting for? A chick?"

"Well, yeah, what else."

Geoff snorted. "I don't know who's the worse influence on who," he said, smirking.

"Let's face it, Geoff, you're the same as us, except you got more money. Shit, it's ten-thirty, I better get my ass to the parking lot."

"Okay, have a good one."

Loomis paced the parking lot, lighting up a cigarette. For the rest of the day he would abstain, as smoking in the company of kids seemed incongruous, and besides, she didn't like it. He was in an extremely euphoric mood, and as he walked and puffed, he waited with keen expectation.

Then he saw a white van pull in. She had told him she was going to borrow a van from the university, so he knew it was her.

She veered it around to pick him up. It was jam-packed with the kids, but the front seat was empty, waiting for him. She swung her head to him, and he was nearly bowled over by how gorgeous she looked – her hair was done up in braids all around her head, like refined dreadlocks, complete with bangs hanging over her bright eyes, the braids adorned with multicolored beads in the manner of the Samburu girls on the picture postcards. To add to her beauty, she was dressed in white – a flowing lacy blouse that highlighted her gleaming dark face, and white cotton slacks that showed off her womanly curves. He had never seen her, or anybody else for that matter, so beautiful, and even more so with that magnificent smile. "Get in!" she giggled exuberantly.

He climbed in and she turned the vehicle around and pulled out the way she had entered.

"I think we're going to have a good time today," she promised him.

"Oh I know so," he said. "Hey, I know you don't exactly appreciate compliments, but I just have to tell you that you look really stunning. Great hairstyle! Did you do that for me?"

"I've decided that you're the only one allowed to compliment me. And yes, I think that I did do it for you, but don't get a big head about it."

"Who, me? With my modest nature?"

Hearty laughter from the both of them, joined by the kids who did not fully understand, but needed no explanation to emulate the adults. It was becoming a ride laced with collective delight.

Fuck, it's great to be alive.

When they got to the stadium, it was only eleven-twenty, still early. Amonee alighted and slid the side door open, making sure that the children did not wander too far after disembarking. Loomis noted that a small infant was among them, certainly less than a year old, carried by her six-year-old sister.

"Isn't she a bit young to appreciate the show?" Loomis asked.

"Dottie was allowed to go under her parents' condition that she take her baby sister," Amonee explained.

"Oh."

When all of them were gathered up, they marched in two lines towards the gate under Amonee's instructions. The kids had some sort of self-imposed discipline that emanated from her authority, and Loomis was very much impressed.

Once inside the stadium, they managed to find enough space on contiguous benches to keep the group together in one place, a fortuitous occurrence mainly due to their prompt arrival. The children bantered, argued, and joked together, and all the while Loomis and Amonee shot joyful glances at each other and made small talk.

The Bomas of Kenya was a visual treat: two hours of nonstop performances of traditional dances from all the major ethnic groups of Kenya, a must-see for tourists from around the world, not to mention the thousands of African families that flocked there every weekend. Amonee brought out her camera and snapped abundant photos, while the children ooo'd and aah'd.

During an interval in the performance, Loomis asked, "What is it with you and these kids?"

"I love their innocence."

"Well, I think everyone does."

"Yes, but perhaps me more than most. I lost mine too early."

It sounded as if they were entering some serious territory, so Loomis did not inquire further. Instead, he questioned how innocent they really were. "Yeah, but they can be very cruel to each other too," he said, remembering his own horrible childhood.

"Yes," she said, "but even though they can be bad for a short while, I believe that a lot of their persistent wickedness is learned from adults. They are very impressionable, and more observant and even better learners than you or I. They pick up everything. Adults are extremely inattentive compared to children."

She sounded like a child psychologist. So he just had to ask, "Did you ever study child psychology?"

She laughed. What a beautiful sound. If he had known this question was so funny, he would have asked it earlier, just to hear her laugh.

"Well, I did take one course in it, but that hardly makes me an expert."

"But you are," he said smiling, knowing that it would make her laugh again.

She did, but this time shaking her head in exaggerated embarrassment.

When the show was over they filed out, and Loomis asked her what was next on the program.

"I told the parents to pick them up at the office at five, and some of the others I'll drop home, so we still have a couple of hours with them. I thought of going to Uhuru Park."

"Sounds great!" He was happy to hear that their day together would continue.

Once in Uhuru Park, they strolled around, keeping an eye on their group of kids like two sheepdogs tending their flock, taking the opportunity to converse with each other, which was actually the main purpose of their rendezvous.

"So, I leave the day after tomorrow," he told her.

"And how long will you be gone?"

"It will be three months before my first break. Can I write to you?" he asked, expecting nothing but the affirmative.

"Yes, of course." She stopped walking and went into her bag to give him her card. It included office address and home address, and both telephone numbers as well.

One of the kids skipped past, yelling, "Uhuru Park, Uhuru Park!"

Amonee turned her attention to the children. "Yes, children, this is Uhuru Park. Does anyone know what Uhuru means?"

"Freedom!" a few of them chorused.

Loomis chimed in, "Yeah, so what does freedom mean?"

Silence.

"So nobody can tell me?"

"It means we are free," said one of the older ones.

Loomis spotted a vendor selling helium-filled balloons.

"Hello!" he shouted, waving him over.

The man approached briskly, eager to make a sale. "*Ngapi*? How many?"

"*Zote*. All of them."

"Zote?"

"Zote. Shilingi ngapi?"

"Two hundred shillings."

Loomis paid the man, and took possession of all the balloons, more than enough for the children, while the vendor looked on in curiosity.

Amonee as well watched him quizzically.

"Okay, everyone, take a balloon," he requested, handing them out. He had four left over, so he kept two and gave Amonee two.

Loomis turned to the vendor. "Oh, hello. *Unaweza kupiga picha kwetu*? Can you take our picture?"

The man ran over, grateful to pay back his good fortune in selling all his balloons. Amonee handed him her camera, then joined the group that Loomis was organizing for the pose. She scooped up the infant from Dottie's grasp.

"Press the button on the top," Amonee instructed.

The man did so and then looked up to show he had accomplished this task.

"Okay, now kids, when I count to three, let go of the balloons," Loomis instructed.

"But they'll float away!" someone protested.

"I want to teach you the meaning of freedom. I can buy you more balloons later."

They looked at him unflinchingly, determined to keep their prizes. No, not good enough, they weren't going to lose their balloons which they just got.

Without forewarning, Amonee released her two balloons, then proceeded to jump up and down, laughing like a crazed kid.

Loomis followed suit, throwing his up in the air. "Look at them go!" he shouted, looking upward. "That's freedom!"

When the children, now persuaded that letting the balloons go was more fun than holding on to them, finally released their captives, Amonee grabbed the camera from the vendor, pointed to the sky and clicked the shutter.

To compensate for their lost balloons, Loomis bought samosas for all of them from another enormously pleased vendor.

* * *

They walked back to the van. Amonee packed the kids in, and made sure all the windows were open, because they would not be departing for at least a few minutes more. Then she walked up to Daryl.

"Well, I guess that's it for today."

"Just for today?" he asked.

She looked at him silently.

He turned his gaze down, putting both hands in his pockets and began to shuffle his feet sheepishly. "I know you're confused. Well, if it makes you happy, you should know that I'm confused too. My main interest has always been in getting..." he was about to say 'laid'..."a woman in bed...even, well you probably know, even when

I started coming on to you." He looked up at her, as if to emphasize his sincerity.

She smiled.

God, he was becoming addicted to her smiles.

"I know," she said.

"Well, it's more than that now."

"I know," she repeated, still beaming as if pleased about it.

He looked down again, and blew out a puff of air like he had just sprinted a hundred meters. "Oh boy," he muttered, akin to someone stiffening to endure great pain. Once more he shot his gaze up at her. "So I can write to you, and maybe give you a call sometime?"

"Of course, I already told you. You have my address and my telephone numbers – both of them."

"Yeah, right, just wanted to make sure. Anyway, you know, I won't be back for three months and maybe then we'll have had enough time to come to our senses, and just be friends," he said, as if assuring her.

She approached him closely. "I'm glad we met."

"I am too, Amonee."

They stared into each other's eyes, embraced tightly, and brought their faces together, their mouths meeting in a kiss, a real kiss this time, tasting each other's joy, their tongues fluttering around each other, an oral communication in a language without words, and which must have lasted at least a full five minutes. When they finally got tired, they released each other, and Loomis noticed all the children with their faces plastered against the windows of the van, their eyes stretched wide to the point of popping out, wondering what Miss Emuria and Mr. Loomis were doing. Kissing!

"Boo!" he shouted at them, and they all drew back giggling hysterically.

He turned to Amonee, and gave a forlorn wave of goodbye. "Goodbye, Amonee."

"Goodbye, Daryl."

Then, as hard as it was, he turned and walked away.

PART II
THE TURKANA JOB

NAIROBI, SEPTEMBER 26 – 28

She was sleek yet well-mounted. A real beauty. Clean and made up, she was just itching to be turned on. Penetration would be quick and deep with this baby, Loomis knew, as long as there was enough fluid to lubricate the hole. But she was big, too damn big for his taste. Her needs were great, requiring constant attention, and the thought of lugging her around the desert wilderness negated all her charms. In his opinion, the Dando 250 was just too cumbersome for this job. Her folded mast extended a full sixty feet from cab to tail; together with the V-8 Detroit diesel, the heavy-duty mud pump, and the 350 psi compressor all bolted down on the platform, the rig-lorry unit must have weighed close to thirty tons. All this to be carried over rough country with only a single-diff, back-axle-drive Leyland.

"Sand traps my ass," Loomis muttered bitterly. He turned to the other lorry, a Bedford ten tonner. This one was a four-by-four, but looked so old he suspected it was ex-British army from World War II. A 'Hiab' crane sat between the cab and the bed. Underneath this rust-eaten hulk, a dark figure was busy disemboweling its belly with a set of spanners.

"Jambo!" Loomis called.

An African in greasy blue overalls crawled out from under the truck. "Jambo."

"*Kuna shida gani*? What's the problem?"

"Rear prop shaft is broken," the black man answered flatly. He had a small, handsome dark-brown face; a pencil-thin mustache bordered his upper lip.

"Shit! So this has only front-wheel drive now?"

"Ndio. Yes."

"What's your name?"

"Wafula, Christopher."

"Are you the mechanic for Turkana?"

"Ndio."

"How long will it take to get another prop shaft?"

"*Si jui.* I don't know. I put in a requisition two months ago. Still waiting."

"Doesn't Mustafa do anything besides park his fat ass behind his desk all day?"

"Si jui. I don't know." Still with a deadpan face.

"*Kreni ina fanya kazi*? Does the crane work?" Loomis asked him.

"Sometimes."

"Well that's encouraging," Loomis quipped in English. "What about that lorry over there, is that assigned to Turkana as well?" he asked, resuming in Kiswahili and pointing to a spanking new, cherry-red Mercedes Benz transporter parked on the other side of the yard.

"Ndio."

"How come it doesn't have number plates?"

"Njoroge still hasn't registered it."

"Wonderful!" he cried out, once again in English, throwing his arms up in exasperation. "Who's Njoroge?"

"Admin Officer."

"Okay, finish what you were doing, I'll be right back." He sauntered moodily over to the other side of the Hydro-Drill plant yard, which on this particular morning appeared as a desolate graveyard of rusting scrap metal, bizarre-looking hulky shapes, and disordered piles of cables and pipes splayed out under a hot morning sun. He headed towards the huge go-down, wary of what he was getting into. If he complained, he knew the reply he would get. "But this is Africa," they would tell him.

At the entrance of the shed he found four Africans, also in overalls, sitting on wooden boxes conversing amongst themselves.

"*Ham jambo,*" he greeted.

"*Hatu jambo,*" they all replied, in a low, indifferent-sounding chorus.

"I'm looking for Onesmus Shigoli, the drilling foreman."

"I am he," claimed a broad, burly giant, still seated. He looked mean: an extraordinarily wide, bell-shaped nose squatted in the center of his oily black face; his eyes, in stark contrast to the rest of his proportions, were small and startlingly animal like; his teeth were pointy. All this conjured up allusions of King Kong.

His lack of respect annoyed Loomis. As a subordinate he should rise when being addressed.

"I am Daryl Loomis, the site engineer for Turkana."

The large African rose slowly, his height no less impressive than his girth, and the others followed suit.

"Are these our drillers?" Loomis asked, referring to the other three.

"Ndio."

Five of the staff present. Five out of twenty-three.

"Where are the others?"

"Si jui. I don't know. *Bado hawa ja fika.* They haven't come yet."

"Why aren't you getting the equipment ready to be loaded?"

"One lorry is broken down. The other still needs number plates."

"That doesn't prevent you from getting the equipment out and stacking it. And you don't have to wait for the plates to load the Mercedes."

"What, just us?" one of the other drillers asked in apparent disbelief.

"*TWENDE!*" Shigoli shouted, and the other drillers entered the go-down before Loomis had a chance to answer the question.

They were going to be a tough bunch, he feared. An arrogant crew, dubious lorries, and missing personnel. Great start. And he had hoped to get most of the heavy loading done today – the three-hundred odd meters of temporary casing, the three tons of drilling mud, and the camping equipment, among which was the heavy 6 KVA generator and a four-foot-long deep freezer. He returned to the Bedford feeling reluctant and fretful, and crawled underneath it to join Wafula examining the front end.

"These nipples haven't been greased for a long time," he noted angrily.

"This lorry just in from Kitui. The fault of the drivers."

"Where are the drivers now?"

"In the canteen."

Loomis got up and strode impatiently over to the canteen, a small wooden kiosk where two women cooked maize and beans and boiled porridge over charcoal *jikos*. Outside the shack were wooden benches where the diners sat.

"Who are the drivers for KTV-280 and the new Mercedes?"

A shabbily dressed young man stood up abruptly. "We are." His companion, an old guy in a faded safari suit that had that slept-in look, rose more sluggishly. His gaunt body was so feeble, it took many seconds for it to stand erect. A definite *chang'aa* drinker.

"Go and help Wafula. And make sure that Bedford is greased! That's all we need is to break down in the middle of the desert."

The two drivers slurped down the rest of their porridge, returned the empty calabashes, and left. Loomis went over to the Land Rover he was given in the morning and got in. It was time he had another chat with the people in the office.

* * *

The office was hectic, filled with, what seemed to Loomis, a superfluous haste and unjustified panic. Though Barnes's office was down the hall, his voice could be heard booming irately. He stepped up to reception.

"What's all this about," he inquired from Ushma, the Indian receptionist.

"Bad day today. Problems with Madagascar."

Loomis recalled hearing about that project the last time he was here. "Can you tell me where I could find Mustafa?"

She motioned with her arm down a corridor which ran at right angles to the main corridor, and which was dammed in the middle by a pair of fire doors.

"Thanks."

He proceeded in this direction, and as he neared the fire doors, they burst open vehemently with the panicked emergence of a very short, but stocky African with bundles of files in his arms and who ran past Loomis, nearly knocking him down. Loomis momentarily looked back at him as he ran down the hallway before resuming his hunt for Mustafa. He stopped at a door that was titled 'Purchasing Officer', and opened it.

If lard could take human form and sprout greasy black, combed-back hair, then it would have been Mustafa. Thick eyebrows overhung shifty black eyes, the flesh below them hung in brown pouches, his nose, a porky protuberance above fleshy lips that were forever fixed in a smile of ingratiating form devoid of any substance. Among his crooked teeth were patches of dull gold. His belly drooped into his lap. He sat on a small swivel chair, the kind best suited for a petite secretary, and upon which his bounteous thighs and buttocks were overflowing and practically dripping from the undersized seat.

"So you're the famous Mustafa?"

Mustafa's smile persisted unfazed in the face of Loomis's acerbic greeting. "Yes, I help you?"

"I'm Loomis, with the Turkana job. The prop shaft for the Bedford, KTV-280, how come it hasn't been purchased? We need that thing today."

Mustafa put up his hands and wiggled them, as if he were adjusting the faucets in a shower. "No money."

"Oh, for Chrissakes."

"I make requisition, it get approved, and I issue Local Purchase Order. Waiting for money. Maybe will get later."

"Where is Njoroge's office?"

"Next door."

He exited and walked a few paces until he spotted a door that said 'Administrative Officer'. He opened it, but no one was inside. He really had no choice now but to see Barnes personally, and to that end he returned the way he came from. As if experiencing deja vu, the fire doors banged open again, the same African holding the same bundle of files exploding through them.

"Fucking madhouse here," Loomis mumbled.

When he got to the Managing Director's office, he opened it.

"Don't you knock?" Barnes bellowed.

"Don't have time," Loomis retorted. He had learned as a kid that submission to intimidation was not a good strategy. He wasn't going to play that game. "I got an ancient lorry missing a rear prop shaft that was supposed to be purchased last week."

Barnes leaned over to his intercom. "Mustafa, get in here!"

A sharp knock vibrated the door .

"Come in!" Barnes shouted.

And who should enter but none other than the short African with his wad of files. "I found it," he announced to his boss, and placed the pile on Barnes's desk.

"Is this all of it?"

"Yes."

"Hmmph."

The little stocky guy left as speedily as he had entered.

"I also need to see Njoroge."

Barnes looked at him. "He was just in here!" he barked incredulously, pointing at the door as if Loomis should have known.

So that was Njoroge.

Another knock, this one a fearful little tap, barely audible.

"Mustafa, get in here!"

The fat Pakistani entered and stood cowering in front of Barnes's desk.

"What's the holdup with the prop shaft for KTV 280?"

"I don't get money for it."

Barnes screamed, "Don't those bloody idiots know we have an account there?"

Mustafa fearfully explained that it hadn't been paid up for six months.

The affair ended with a calm "Oh I see" by Barnes, and, more importantly, a check.

Leaving the office, Loomis finally cornered Njoroge as he was making yet another dash through the corridors, to ask about the registration of the Mercedes. Njoroge just shrugged it off, saying he would attend to that tomorrow.

* * *

By the time Loomis had returned to the yard, there were six new arrivals. Only twelve men now missing. Outside the go-down were piles of various drill bits, tool boxes, and some "fishing" attachments. The size of the heaps indicated there wasn't much done while he was gone.

"Everybody listen up. I'm called Daryl Loomis. I am the operations manager for this job, the *Bwana Mkubwa*, the Big Boss, and the sooner we get to know each other, the better. So I think it's time I know your names." He approached them, an individual at a time, requesting names and inquiring after the places where each was from: a bald-headed Ugandan with a scruffy beard, called Ben; Kariuki from Central Province; Ocholla from Nyanza; Obasi from Kisii; A Nandi named Kiprop; and a short coastal African called Kadogo, Kadogo a nickname for someone small. The young driver was a Masai who gave his name as Joseph, and the old guy in the wrinkled safari suit was known as Ezekiel. After the introductions, Loomis ordered everyone back to work, leaving instructions to bring out the casings, and then went with Wafula to check out the Bedford's crane.

Nothing happened when Wafula switched on the ignition.

"I guess this is one of the times it doesn't work," Loomis wryly commented.

"I think it's the katouti," opined Wafula.

"The katouti? What's that?"

"The katouti, the katouti," Wafula repeated, for lack of a better word.

"Oh! The cutout!" Loomis realized, now enlightened. "Well, fix it, we got eighteen-inch pipe to load."

"Excuse me, suh," said someone behind him in thickly accented English. Loomis turned around to see a youthful-looking African in crisp shirt and shorts, knee socks, and loafers. "I am Mutua, the camp manager, suh."

Loomis gave him an appraising glance. A large head with comically wide eyes perched precariously on a skinny, narrow-framed, long-limbed body, his legs two sticks of ebony with knobby knees. He looked like a fugitive from a Bugs Bunny cartoon. "The camp manager?"

"Yes suh."

"I see. Have you made a list of what we need?"

"Not yet, suh. I onry now alived." He had that common Bantu affliction of switching r's and l's when speaking English.

"Well, let's get to it, Mutua. I want that stuff on the lorries by tomorrow morning, latest."

"Yes suh."

"And don't keep saying 'yes sir'."

"No, suh," he promised, bounding away.

No matter what Wafula did to coax the crane, he could not get it to respond, and as the minutes went by Loomis could feel his stomach tighten. Six-meter sections of steel casing, each weighing a quarter of a ton, now had to be loaded by hand. "Remember, this is Africa," they would tell him. Well that was just the answer he would have for them if he failed to mobilize before the end of the month.

The men did not welcome this suggestion of manual loading; they muttered protests when Shigoli gave the order. Loomis, with an aim of inspiring his staff, took off his shirt and joined them on top of the Mercedes as they began to load the heaviest pipe. With the supervision of Shigoli the men soon fell into a rhythm, chanting and singing their way through the chore. In a short time it became apparent that their zeal and strength was simply too much for Loomis. He found himself stumbling awkwardly about and generally getting in the way, and soon retired on the side.

By six o'clock all the casing was loaded and Loomis called them all together and addressed them.

"I see we have accomplished something today. Now, tomorrow, the prop shaft for the Bedford will be ready and Njoroge will register the Merc, and if we hustle, we can get on the road the day after that."

This announcement elicited a chorus of complaints. The schedule did not really give them enough time to do all the things one does before embarking on a long safari. Some had to arrange for money to be sent to their upcountry homes, one driller had a sick child in the hospital, and another had a funeral to go to. Obviously, since they had just returned from their leave, the stories were but pretexts to indulge in a few more nights in Nairobi. Loomis ignored their protestations and climbed into his Land Rover.

"Tomorrow, seven o'clock," he reminded sternly before driving away.

The next morning, two turnboys, each assigned to one or the other of the lorries, two more drillers, and a gum-chewing welder appeared along with those accrued on the first day. That left six personnel still outstanding. The men worked slowly and with much lethargy, presumably bitter at what they felt was an unnecessary haste for departure.

Then the prop shaft arrived and Wafula and another guy became engaged in installing it in the venerable lorry. He looked at his watch. Almost ten and no sign of Njoroge. So when was the Mercedes going to be registered? He walked past the lorry in question where some of the men were loading sacks of drilling mud, and went into the go-down to help Mutua to organize the camping gear. After lunch two more of the missing staff showed up. But no Njoroge. He telephoned the Hydro-Drill office only to be told that Njoroge had been out all day. By four o'clock both lorries and a Land Cruiser pick-up were fully loaded and ready to go. Loomis dismissed the men, telling them to prepare themselves for tomorrow's departure, in any event. Before going home, he stopped into the office where Ushma, the receptionist, informed him that Njoroge had just come in and just as quickly gone out again, probably home. Fuck it. Something was telling Loomis it was time for a cold Tusker.

Another morning later, there was more confusion as three new men arrived, including Juma the cook, and they had to be sent home to collect their personal things, surprised that the safari was tentatively scheduled to begin that very day. Loomis checked the camping equipment and found some things lacking, and Mutua ran frantically here and there while the American Negro, as the men referred to him behind his back, voiced his disapproval. Then Njoroge turned up.

"Where the hell have you been, Njoroge? We were ready to leave today but now we have to be delayed because of your negligence."

"Take it easy, Mr. Loomis. You can still leave today if you like. It has not reached noon yet, still early now. I'm going this very instant to the Motor Vehicle Department."

"That will take all day. I'm not going to set out at night."

"If it takes ten minutes, even that would be too long a time. *Twende*. Let's go"

It seemed Njoroge was well-known down at Motor Vehicles. He jumped to the front of the queue and chatted with the clerk in a manner so informal as to suggest more than casual acquaintance. The registration, necessary permits, inspection stickers, and plates were all obtained in exactly six and a half minutes.

"I have to admit, bwana, you sure made it look easy," Loomis conceded.

"Ah, I just slip him something. I treat him good, he treats me good. Besides, he's my brother-in-law. This is Africa, bwana."

* * *

Ushma smiled prettily and told him to go straight in, Mr. Barnes was expecting him.

Barnes swung his chair around. "Good morning, Daryl. I hear you're all set to go."

"Yeah, just a final chat with you, then collect the impress money, and we're off."

"We'll send up a lorry to Lodwar in a week or so with more fuel and the first of the linings. You've calculated about three thousand liters of diesel a week and one drum of petrol per month for the Land Rover. That sounds about right. Do the people in the stores have that written on paper?"

"In triplicate."

"Good. From time to time one of our directors will be visiting you to check the stock and see how you're doing. Most probably Reg Greenbottom, a crusty old bird, but you'll get used to him. So make sure you have a tent for him."

"Yes, we took some extras."

"Now, the impress money for the site. We can give you forty thousand to start off with. That should hold you for a few weeks. We'll try to arrange it so that in the future you'll be able to pick up further funds in Lodwar."

"Fine. I'll call the radio room every evening by telephone to give a report of our progress. After Kitale I'll start using the radio."

"Good." Barnes stood up and extended his hand to Loomis and gave him a firm handshake. "Good luck, Daryl. Let's get this thing done without a hitch."

"Right." Loomis left the MD's office and went back to see the receptionist.

"Ushma, be an angel and get me through to the University of Nairobi, Miss Emuria's office."

"Sure."

After a few minutes, the connection was made. "Hello?"

"Hello, Amonee, how are you?"

"I'm very fine, Daryl. I'm so glad you called. I was wondering if I would hear from you again before you left."

"I couldn't go without telling you. The lorries are loaded. We'll be leaving today."

"But it's already noon, how can you leave now?"

"Well, I think we can make it to Nakuru before dark."

"Isn't it true that lorries have to be off the road by six?"

"We have special permits. They're not hard to get as long as you're not transporting food."

"Oh, I see."

"You must be very busy, Amonee, your voice sounds a bit anxious."

"The music festival is this week and I feel tense somewhat."

"I wish you luck. I know your choir will do well."

"Thanks, I hope so."

"I'll be thinking of you, Amonee."

"I'll be thinking of you too. Isn't there some way I can write to you?"

"You'll have to wait until I send you a letter. We'll take a post box in Lodwar, but I don't know the number yet. Probably care of the Catholic Mission, but I have to confirm that."

"Please be careful and have a safe journey."

"Don't worry. And the first leave I get, at the end of December, I'll be coming to see you. Is that alright with you?"

"I'll be waiting."

"Bye for now, Amonee."

"Goodbye, Daryl. Take care and I'll see you when you get back."

"Bye."

"Bye."

Click.

Something unsatisfying about that conversation on the telephone. Restrained, would describe it. Perhaps they were already coming to their senses. He wanted to say such stupid things as "I love you", "I'm gonna miss you so much" etcetera. But she was in the office, so he figured that gushy stuff like that would be inappropriate.

* * *

She put down the phone, but still kept staring at it.

"If you don't want to talk about it, I won't ask," Katy remarked.

"I'm a bit confounded about what I'm getting into," Amonee confessed.

"Look, Pammy, you're young and beautiful, and these situations are unavoidable. If your relationship with Jon is good, then there's nothing to worry about, in fact you should be grateful because it's like an opportunity to test it before you get married. Anyway, that's how I see it, but never mind me; I'm certainly not the expert, having been through two divorces." Actually Katy did not believe her own advice, but she figured, what the heck, people in love didn't follow anyone's advice; they only hear what they want to hear.

"I'm comfortable with Jon."

"Yes, I'll grant you that."

"He's going to be away for three months," she said wistfully, referring to Daryl.

"And that's a good thing. Time enough to think about it."

"I never told you about how he saved the life of a purse snatcher."

"He did?"

Amonee told her the story.

"Well," Katy said, "when I first saw him I thought he was a bit of a rascal, but a nice one. It doesn't surprise me."

Then she told him of their three occasions together following that.

"Wow, yeah, you're starting to have a relationship. Just take it slow, Pammy, take it slow and things will work out."

"Yes," Amonee agreed, but with some uncertainty in her voice.

ON THE ROAD

Some minutes past one, after lunch had been taken, they were ready to go, even though one driller was still unaccounted for.

"Who is this driller who hasn't reported yet?" Loomis asked Shigoli.

"Sikhendu. Cooper Sikhendu."

"Do you think he's going to make it on this trip of ours?"

"He'll show up. He's like that sometimes."

They were to travel in convoy with Nakuru as the day's destination: the Leyland-mounted rig driven by Wafula; the old Bedford piloted by Joseph; Ezekiel behind the wheel of the new Merc with the water bowser in tow; a Toyota Land Cruiser with an office caravan hitched behind; and Loomis's Land Rover bringing up the rear. Loomis was not in a hurry. Being the one responsible for the group, he had to travel behind the rest in case any of them ran into trouble along the way; that way he would be able to find them and take the appropriate action. But he couldn't remain too far behind; he would not want them to reach Nakuru a considerable time before he did. They would get lost in the town without him getting a chance to instruct them about the following day's departure. He thought about the lorries struggling down the winding escarpment road, knowing they would have to go down in first gear. Maybe there was enough time for a visit to Chiromo campus.

When reaching the Westlands roundabout, Loomis, driving the Land Rover, went around it in full circle to reverse his direction, and Mutua, his travel mate, was bewildered.

"Suh, the way to Nakulu is the other dilection," he stated with unrequited concern.

"I know that, Mutua, and stop calling me sir."

"What should I core you then?"

"Try Daryl."

Mutua did so, but preferred 'sir', since it was easier to

pronounce. His enunciation of the American's name was something akin to Dalir. Loomis recognized the problem and quickly sought to rectify it.

"How about Loomis?"

"Oh yes, Roomis, that is much easier to say."

"Fantastic."

"Bwana Roomis?"

"Yes?"

"Why do you have that lubber tube in your mouth?"

"I'm trying to quit smoking. Chewing on this helps."

Loomis passed Chiromo Campus without entering, and once more circumnavigated another roundabout to return to his original direction. "I wanted to see someone," he explained to Mutua, "but there isn't enough time."

They drove through Westlands, then past Kangemi and into Kiambu district, a patchwork of farms green with maize stalks and other ripening crops. Occasionally, depending on the position of the road, they could see in the distance the silvery clouds shrouding Mount Kenya, the largest mountain in Kenya, and second only to Kilimanjaro in height in the whole of Africa. Cultivated landscape eventually gave way to forests of wattle, tall cedars, and evergreens as they approached the rim of the eastern escarpment. After that was the tricky descent down a snaking two-lane blacktop, the traffic of which was fairly considerable, it being the only road linking western Kenya with Nairobi and Mombasa. To overtake around the numerous blind turns was like playing Russian roulette, but many made the attempt and one had to be on the lookout for those reckless fools. The road was an old one, built by Italian POWs captured in Ethiopia during the Second World War. The Italians had even erected a small chapel at an overlook alongside the road to enshrine their labors.

But the road, before falling away to the lowlands, offered a spectacular view of the Great Rift Valley, with the Mau escarpment bordering the western horizon. Down below, between the two mountain ranges, was flat, golden grassland. A satellite tracking dish stood out like a white pimple in the yellow plains. Ancient volcanoes, among them the bowl-like caldera of Longonot and the spiny ridge of Suswa, formed a line resembling a caravan of huge beasts plodding through the valley, while Lake Naivasha, its blue surface splotched with the pink patches of countless flamingos, could be seen to the north. Above, fluffy, cotton-like clouds floated in a sky of ardent blue, their shadows mottling the valley floor below them.

Upon reaching the bottom of the escarpment, the Land Rover entered the plains and soon caught up with the lorries. Following slowly behind them, Loomis gazed at the scenery, which was now of intermittent golden-barked acacias populating a sea of tall brown grass. Candelabra Euphorbias contrived to appear as giant hands thrusting out of the ashy soil, their thick-fleshed, cactus-shaped branches like prickly fingers grasping at the air. From time to time they passed herds of Grant's Gazelle and an occasional giraffe browsing close to the road.

The convoy stopped in Naivasha, a small town about five kilometers from the lake of the same name. Loomis found only the three lorries present, Shigoli and Ben apparently using the Land Cruiser to race ahead to Nakuru for a headstart on its beer and women. Loomis told the lorry drivers to go on and not to stop until they had reached the day's final terminus. Once in Nakuru, they were to meet at the lorry park next to the bus stand. Thus instructed, the vehicles trundled off while he and Mutua remained behind to nurse a couple of sodas.

On their way once more, Loomis soon sighted the bleak portals of Mlango wa Mungu, "God's Door", polished, eroded pillars of rock which stood at the southern end of Lake Elmentaita. Further north, the desolate look of the country began to dissipate with the appearance of cattle ranches and wheat farms. Signs of civilization increased as the Land Rover drew closer to Nakuru, the hub of the Central Rift Valley.

It was seven o'clock when Loomis was reunited with the lorries in Nakuru, but the Land Cruiser with its occupants, Shigoli and Ben, was nowhere to be seen. He told the men present to be back at the lorries at saa moja, the first hour (seven a.m.) the following morning.

After a quiet night of exhausted slumber, he left the Stag's Head Hotel and drove to the lorry park at precisely seven. Besides the turnboys, there was no one. But by ten-past almost everyone was there, everyone except Shigoli and Ben, who forced them all to wait until they arrived at eleven-thirty. Loomis knew it would be considered improper to reprimand Shigoli in front of the men, but he was indignant at losing face. If one of them was to be publicly shamed, better it be Shigoli rather than him. Without calling the two latecomers aside, he began to shout his warning.

"Where the hell have you two been? Are you such lords that we leave only when you yourselves are ready? Is that how it is?"

"We were just around," Shigoli answered curtly.

"If any of you pulls a stunt like that again, I will make out a written complaint and send it to the head office. What is the point of travelling in convoy if we end up going our separate ways? This isn't the Safari Rally goddammit! It is for you to wait for me and not the other way around!"

"You should have told us the plan when we were leaving Nairobi," protested Shigoli.

Loomis was on the verge of losing his temper. "Next time stay with the convoy." He turned to face the rest of the men. "We should be able to make it to Kitale before nightfall. We shall stop in Eldoret for lunch, and later in Kitale town we will meet in front of the Bongo Hotel." He about-faced to shout at Shigoli and Ben. "You understand my Kiswahili? If you arrive early you will wait for us. Haya, twende!"

Loomis watched his motley crew clambering in and on top of the vehicles, the men talking loudly and sniggering with laughter, making Loomis aware of a mistake he'd just made: Never show your anger. A nagging suspicion that the reins of authority were starting to slip through his fingers was growing ever so stronger.

The cortege was once again on its way. The road, upon leaving Nakuru, cut diagonally across the Rift Valley to the Timboroa highlands up on top of the opposite escarpment. Although not as winding or steep as the mountain road they had descended the day before, the distance uphill was long and progress would be slow. Yet with tarmac all the way to Kitale, it would be the last easy day they would have.

They drove for five tedious hours, first through the dark forests of Timboroa, then coming out into rolling farmland dotted with island coppices of blue gum and fig, until they arrived at Eldoret, a quaint, rustic little town whose narrow streets and miniature round-abouts reflected its colonial past. The drivers parked their vehicles in a line and the men went off in search of their ugali. Loomis ate at the big tourist hotel. Everyone was punctual in returning and they embarked having spent less than forty minutes for the stop-over.

Loomis was amused by the fact that hoary Ezekiel, using his seniority, had claimed the spanking new Mercedes while youthful Joseph was stuck with the ancient decrepit Bedford. This funny juxtaposition of the men and their lorries seemed complementary, and the way the lorries kept together illustrated the merits of the arrangement.

But it wasn't long before Loomis spotted the Mercedes parked quite a distance from the road, next to a group of low-slung mud huts. When he went up to investigate he found the turnboy lying in the cab with his legs dangling out the window.

"Where is Ezekiel?"

The lad quickly withdrew his legs and sat up. "In there," the boy answered, pointing to one of the huts.

"Go in and get him." Loomis himself did not want to go in. He knew what he would find. Ezekiel lumbered out in his usual slow-motion way, practically reeking of the stench of 'Kill-Me-Quick'. Without so much as a glance to the American standing with folded arms, he climbed into the cab, almost in the manner of a guilty dog slinking away from its master.

"Ezekiel!"

"Ndio, Bwana."

"After Kitale I'm sending you back. I don't want a drunkard for a lorry driver."

"But..."

Loomis turned away, not interested in any mitigation.

Atop the Uasin Gishu plateau, they had passed some of the highest and coldest areas in Kenya. By tomorrow or the next day they would be in the hottest. The lush, fertile countryside reminded Loomis of another contrast. Nakuru, Eldoret, and Kitale were all agriculturally oriented towns, surrounded by Kenya's richest farmlands. The land around Kitale, the Trans Nzoia, was especially productive and accredited as the breadbasket of the nation. But after Kitale the road would turn and drop into the Rift Valley for the second time, further north, and enter the dusty scrubland of Pokot and Turkana. Within a distance of only forty miles the land would change from a verdant quilt of plantations into a barren thorn-bush environment where often the hardiest grass failed to grow.

Tomorrow the going would be laborious, and they would have to leave at daybreak if there was to be any chance of making it through the Cherenganyi Mountains to Marich Pass. Loomis, anticipating the difficulties, had a plan that would ensure that the men showed up on time in the morning. When they were all assembled outside of the Bongo Hotel he revealed it to them.

"Each person can stay in any lodging he wants, but must inform Shigoli of which one it is. Shigoli, I want a list from you of where each man is staying. That way, in the morning, if any of you are not able to get out of bed quick enough, I can come and help you. We should be ready to go at six o'clock."

Some of the men laughed in disbelief. Others just shook their heads.

"Suppose I decide not to stay in any lodging tonight?" Ben brought up, obviously peeved. His bloodshot eyes accentuated the scragginess of his mottled gray and black beard, and together with his vastly receded forehead, gave him an old and tired look. He was an old-timer, apparently accustomed to having his own way. But that was just too bad.

"*Shauri yako*, your affair."

The group broke up amidst low grumblings as Loomis walked towards the hotel entrance. Ezekiel attempted to follow him in his slow pained gait, then, realizing the futility of his efforts, called out to him. "Bwana Daryl."

"We have nothing to talk about, Ezekiel," Loomis said without looking back. "Tomorrow you go back by bus. We don't need you. One of us will drive the Merc."

The old man stopped and stood still, watching Loomis enter the hotel lobby.

* * *

"Radio room," announced the deep raspy voice on the other end.

"Hello, is that Josek? This is Loomis here."

"Oh hello, Bwana Loomis. This is Benson. Are you traveling well?"

"Yes, I'm reporting that we have reached Kitale. I am at the Bongo Hotel, room 13 and we have no major problems, though we do have a minor one. Take a message. From me to Barnes. Message reads: Ezekiel, the Mercedes driver, is drinking while driving. Returning him tomorrow. Please send another driver alpha sierra alpha papa. Regards, end of message."

About a half hour later the phone rang. It was Barnes. "Listen, Daryl, this message about the lorry driver. Ezekiel has been with us for over twenty years. He's always been reliable. Hasn't had an accident yet, not even a fender bender. I can't believe he would be reckless with the lorry."

"Well, it's true. I caught him drinking chang'aa."

"We don't have another driver available at this time."

"You'll have to find one. I'm sending him back."

"Look, if you get another driver he may be worse than the one you already have. This is Africa. Just give him a warning and tell him the next time you catch him he's had it. Tell him I said so."

"Roger," Loomis answered, now resigned. He knew he would hear those three words from Barnes sooner or later.

* * *

"Ezekiel, I'm giving you a second chance. If I catch you again, you're fired, do you hear?"

"It won't happen again."

Loomis wondered at that. Drinking while driving, or getting caught? "Alright everyone, let's move."

First light had already signaled the beginning of a new day when Loomis turned in his driver's seat and glanced behind him. Enormous and clad with forest, Mount Elgon loomed over the extensive maize fields at its feet, and the iron roofs of Kitale town shone faintly through the misty morning air just in front of it. Returning his face forward, he looked at the mountains ahead with apprehension. Dark and foreboding, their sharp peaks formed the backbone of the escarpment, and the exit out through the Marich Pass was a tortuous fifty kilometers, a trek that could take two days or more.

The road led up, and up, and up, making the vehicles grunt in first gear. Vegetation became thicker and wilder with clumps of short trees amidst lush undergrowth soon turning into forest. Grey-barked cedars, with fluted, twisted trunks, gave way to a regimen of pines as they climbed higher still. The air was crisp and clean, as refreshing as an iced drink on a hot afternoon. Loomis knew that ahead, after coming down the western wall of the Gregory Rift and reaching its sun-scorched arid floor, the heat would rush at them in a cruel assault.

The road leveled off onto a mountain valley, passing a few

sequestered villages sheltered amidst groves of trees, the inhabitants clothed in the typical cast-off clothes of the African peasant. Farms were few and far between, for cultivation was a discouraging endeavor in the rocky, forested mountains. It was the land of the Pokot, a people who depended on livestock for their daily sustenance. From now on, the rest of the journey would be through the lands of pastoralists who spend all their lives moving from place to place with their herds.

Routinely, the young males of such tribes, much to the chagrin of the authorities, would go off to participate in the traditional pastime of raiding their neighbors for animals. Battles which were fought for hundreds of years still went on in that part of Kenya, with arrows and spears being replaced by automatic guns and grenade launchers, merchandise which flooded the black market as Amin's soldiers fled Uganda following the Tanzanian invasion. Armed bandits, called Ngoroko, had come into being, and the ruthless bands which took refuge in the Cherenganyis were especially notorious, known to rob shops and even hijack matatus. This was why Loomis wanted to make haste and spend as little time as possible in these remote mountains: news of the convoy's passage might start giving these bandits some nasty ideas.

It was now ten-thirty. Over four hours and only twelve kilometers covered. Ahead, the road worsened as villages grew scarcer, becoming narrower as the motorized procession ascended once again. Each driver checked his clearance of the green schist rock wall to their right, hugging it as much as they could; to their left was a steep cliff dropping off into perched thorn thickets and rocky crags. At one tricky curve, the office trailer almost tipped, threatening to take the Land Cruiser with it.

Descending, however, was more difficult. Even with the lorries engaged in first gear, they still had to ride their air brakes, which complained by hissing and sneezing, and, together with the screeching and creaking of the trucks, bounced eerie hollow echoes off the canyon walls. They were forced to stop countless times whenever the wheels became too hot with friction. In some places the track was gutted by ruts and furrows, over which the lorries crawled trembling and shaking, making their heavy cargo jump against their metal beds with thunderous noise. By nightfall they were nowhere near Marich Pass.

They stopped for the night and dug out the mattresses from the load on the Bedford, finding appropriate places for them atop the vehicles. Loomis connected the radio to the Land Rover's battery and, with Mutua's help, set up the aerial, even though he knew it was futile: reception was as dead as expected, the signals being blocked by the mountains. The men ate grudgingly from cold tins as Loomis had forbidden a fire and Mutua had buried the cooking utensils under heaps of tents. Tired and still hungry, they slept uneasily under a starry sky.

Loomis felt the soothing night breeze on his face, while images of Amonee flooded his mind. He was in the bush once more, only a day or two, but longed for her already, conjuring up her face; her entrancing smile and those big, amber eyes.

He turned over on his mattress onto his back and faced a velvet black cloth of sky studded with myriad dazzling stars. An incandescent Milky Way arched across the heavens. Crickets chanted a mellow mantra while frogs raucously serenaded mates. The barking call of a lone hyena, a sound somewhere between a yelp and a bellow, was answered by the haunting hoot of an owl. Before long he was relaxed, purged of worries. Bush life did have its moments.

The next day's progress was even slower than that of the day before. There was one bad section where boulders and trees had to be removed from the track. Then the inevitable happened: the rig got stuck. The back wheels were caught in a ditch of cobbles and gravelly sand, and all of Wafula's attempts to drive her out only resulted in the thirty-ton rig getting further entrenched. They jacked up the rig, dug under the tires, and placed the sand traps, iron strips vented with round holes, on the ground underneath the rear wheels. With the tires gripping the metal, the Leyland managed to budge itself forward, but only up to the end of the sand traps, at which point the wheels would slip again. One of the sand traps, propelled by the spinning rubber, flew out from under the right wheel with the speed and trajectory of a deadly projectile, and the men ducked bellowing with laughter. Eventually, Ezekiel had to tow her out with the Merc.

The rest of the day's trip was relatively uneventful, and by dusk they had reached the Marich Pass, the back door of the Cherenganyis. There they entered the Kerio Valley where they halted to sleep at a small settlement just outside of the mountains.

* * *

They woke up in a vast flat scrubland which looked limitless in the clear grey light of dawn: an expanse of alluvial sand, with a sparse cover of low bushes and shrubs, and a scattering of gnarled and spindly trees. The vehicles roared off in clouds of dust, the feathery smell of which nearly choked Loomis and Mutua whose Land Rover was the last in position. By eight, the heat was already sufficient to make them sweat heavily, and, the dust began to cake to their skins. The air was hot and thick and soon became oppressive.

The Pokots that were seen straggling along the sides of the road were dressed in traditional shukas and skins, in marked contrast to their kin in the mountainous areas the convoy had just gone through. Although they looked very much like their Turkana neighbors, who were beginning to appear in increasing numbers as the party proceeded north, to the discerning eye these two peoples could be distinguished by their facial features and the styles of the ornaments which they wore. All of the local denizens, but particularly the Turkana, reflected the wildness of the country in both their dress and habits. The men had blankets knotted over one shoulder which hung loosely over their otherwise naked bodies. Many exhibited mud skullcaps at the back of their heads, in which an ostrich feather was usually planted. Each of them, regardless, walked with two items: a long wooden stick, and. the *ekicholong,* a wooden T-shaped object which served as both a headrest and a stool. Around their wrists were circular razor-sharp knives, the *abarait* in Turkana language, but amusingly referred to as 'roundabouts', which were worn for defense as well as utility.

Turkana women were even more colorful. Their heads were shaven except for a row of stringy braids which ran down the middle of their scalps, the effect somewhat like a Mohawk haircut. Their necks were totally concealed by the *akiromwa,* necklaces of colored beads piled on top of each other from shoulder to chin. Although some of these ladies wrapped themselves in a goatskin cape, most were bare-chested, exposing saggy, overused breasts. V-shaped cowskin aprons hung from their curvaceous hips, covering their loins and buttocks, but baring their long lean legs. Their walk was stately, sensual, their natural step more elegant than the bearing of a fashion model on a catwalk. Iron bracelets, worn around their ankles, clanged in rhythm to the flap-flap of their aprons, making a Turkana woman a walking musical instrument. Their black skins glistened from the animal fat they smeared on it, a protection against the drying power of the sun.

At ten o'clock they were in Kainuk, a trading settlement with a row of shops on each flank of the road and surrounded by numerous dome-like dwellings made of sticks and grass. The vehicles all pulled over in a line, allowing Loomis to precede them to the police roadblock up ahead, in case explanations of their passage were required. The roadblock, along with the single-story mud structure which served as the police station, was set up only a few years before in the hope of curbing the banditry in the area. After Loomis delivered a few cursory greetings to the guards on duty, the convoy was let through to cross into Turkana district.

It was barely a hundred years before when the first Europeans entered Turkanaland. Throughout its colonial history, administration was all but lacking, and consisted chiefly of military patrols and expeditions attempting to pacify the belligerent Turkana and the external raiders coming from Abyssinia and the Sudan. The area was one of the last to come under British control, and prior to 1963, not even missionaries were allowed to travel through. In the meantime the place had become a refuge for ivory poachers, rebel guerillas from neighboring states, black marketeers, and outlaws of all kinds. Much of the administration had its hands full with border affairs and the operations that they had to conduct in response to the incessant raiding, which the peoples of the area considered as part of their cultural heritage. Even today semi-military forces and police patrols are constantly struggling to maintain an uneasy peace. Otherwise the Turkana have been left pretty much to themselves, resistant to the influences of both colonial, and subsequently, national authority.

They did not stop at Kainuk, but continued on under Loomis's insistence. The terrain became drier and more desert-like. Soon, everything seemed to quiver in the midday heat, while an intolerable glare, reflected from the white sandy soil, assaulted their eyes. But at least the terrain was flat and the going relatively good; the sun was only going to get stronger, and it was best to keep moving. Laagers – rivers of sand – now began to cut across the road more frequently, and surprisingly the Leyland-borne rig made it through all but two without requiring any outside assistance.

Eventually the Bedford overheated, and Loomis parked his Land Rover a short distance behind it. He got out and, walking up to small overlook, viewed the scene in front of him. Spidery, flat-topped acacia trees, their horizontal branches flattened by generations of wind, and tawny termite mounds the shape of uncircumcised phalluses, stood in well-spaced ranks like advancing armies frozen in time, while the lonely rust-colored funnel of a dust devil zigzagged its way among them. Beyond, etched against the distant skyline, the jagged silhouettes of ominous mountains. It was quiet, deathly quiet, and this disconcerting stillness imparted to the desert an ethereal dignity, harsh and impersonal, which made him feel like a lowly intruder, one as inconsequential as an ant on a picnic table, alarming and exciting him at the same time. He worried about its effects on the men; he knew they had no sense of adventure. To them this was a lousy contract full of hardship in a savage place a long, long way from home.

At Lokichar, another trading settlement, they stopped for food and drink. After shaking off the elderly Turkana beggars – half-starved outcasts who owned no livestock and were unable to survive the desert without cows and goats – they entered the settlement's only hoteli, a wide wood-and-mud shelter, where they all sat and ordered the same thing: *chapati* and goat meat. The fact that they ate the same food was not a coincidence. It was all the menu had to offer.

Returning to their vehicles, the Hydro-Drill staff were careful not to step on the handicrafts lined up on the ground by the Turkana women selling them. Loomis, after a quick perusal, bought a female doll in the guise of a Turkana girl and made out of goatskin – a present for Amonee.

The last leg took nearly four more hours. The rig got bogged down again in three of the many laagers they had to cross, and the sand traps were already becoming bent with usage. Towards dusk the men spotted a cluster of small buildings nestled in the bosom of several tit-shaped hills. Shortly afterwards they crossed the bridge spanning the dry chasm of the Turkwel River and entered Lodwar.

Lodwar was not just another outpost, but a frontier town. It was the site of the district's headquarters and administrative center of Turkanaland. The district commissioner and his government officers – involved in, among other things, law and order, health, education, and livestock management – were based there. A large police station, with a fleet of lorries and Land Rovers, sat on top of a hill overlooking the entrance to the town. A sizeable Catholic mission, which included a school and the only petrol station in Turkana, coordinated the activities of the district diocese. Water was supplied by a single well sunk in the laager of the Turkwel channel. Electricity from three diesel generators not only provided lighting, but also enabled one to sip a cold drink in a bar cooled by large ceiling fans.

There were two "main streets" in Lodwar: rectangular strips of sand separating two rows of shops intersecting at right angles at the town's only roundabout, a ring of whitewashed stones. The town had expanded radially from this center, and seen from the air Lodwar looked pretty much like a circumscribed 'T'. To the southeast of this 'T' was a tarmac airstrip to accommodate the numerous private and government planes flying to and from the district. Lately, there had been some talk of bringing phone lines there. For Loomis and his men, Lodwar was to be their main link to the outside world, the only town in 25,000 square miles of desert scrub.

TURKANALAND, OCTOBER TO DECEMBER 1979

Chemunga's Bar, situated near the roundabout, was the largest bar around. It had four ceiling fans, of which two actually worked, and the floor space was so ample that the twenty-three crew members of Hydro-Drill Ltd. took up hardly a third of it. Loomis had called a meeting. He hoped his relationship with the men would improve because from that point on they would all be living in much closer quarters. He bought a round of drinks in an attempt to assuage them, and announced that they would stay in Lodwar for one day, enough time for him to organize the casual labor.

Later on, Loomis found it difficult to fall asleep. Almost all of the lodgings were linked to bars, and strident laughter and scratchy music from a cheap phonograph kept him awake. Shigoli, Ben, Kariuki, and Kiprop had taken neighboring rooms in the same place. Loomis would now find it harder to separate himself from the crew. He wished he didn't have to. He would rather be drinking with them, telling jokes and swapping stories. But he knew from experience that if he socialized with them too early in the contract, they would lose respect for him. Circumstances forced him to play the part of the mzungu, a role that was in conflict with his lifestyle and the one aspect of the job he hated most. He tried to imagine Okova as one of his crew and shook his head grinning.

At one o'clock in the morning, after the bars had closed, Loomis was still awake. Squadrons of mosquitoes whined in the air, darting in and out of his ears, and alighting on every part of his body to feast, making him continually scratch and slap himself. The nights in Lodwar were unbearably hot, and when he tried to cover himself for protection, he felt like he was inside an oven basting in his own sweat. At some point in the night weariness overtook his discomfort, and the next thing he knew he was listening to the recorded cry of a Mohammedan muezzin shouting from a cassette player. The Muslim proprietors of the hoteli across the street were calling the town, faithful and heathen alike, to wake up.

Swathed in his towel, Loomis procured a metal bucket, drew his own water from an outside tap, and bathed inside a small shed which had 'bafu' written on the door. After a cup of thin tea at the Muslim hoteli, he drove to the diocese offices opposite the airstrip and asked to see the bishop.

The Turkana job had been known by the local government authorities and the Catholic mission for some time now, as such an activity, a well-drilling project that covered almost the entire province, was not a trivial endeavor. It was a long-awaited event that many hoped they could profit by. One potential gain arising out of this was employment for the locals.

The bishop was away, he was told, but perhaps Father Tom could help him.

He was directed to a concrete house with a long veranda screened with mosquito netting. Seated inside the veranda, at a small table, having his morning tea, was a big white man wearing a green shirt and black shorts, his blocky head capped with bristles of red hair, the lower half of his beefy pink face covered with a closely-cropped beard of burnt orange. His pale blue eyes, despite their deep sockets, twinkled whenever he spoke, or rather sang, in his heavy Irish brogue.

"Ah, Mista Loomis, top of te murnin ta ya," he said without getting up.

"Father Tom?"

"Yes, tis mey. Sit down. Have ya had yur tey yet?" He poured a cup of tea for his visitor. "Wey was tinken ye met bey cummin any day now, but wey decided ta kep quiet till ya arrived."

"Thank you," Loomis said, taking the seat next to the priest and accepting his cup of tea.

"No use gettin thum excited beforehand. Wey have plenty of workers fo ya. By tamara murnin I'm sure tell bey morenuf ta chose from."

Loomis was not happy with that suggestion. "Is there any way we can get this thing out of the way today?"

"Believe mey, tamara early in te murnin would be best. What time would ya wanten ta bey off ten?"

"I was hoping for six o'clock."

"Ya bey hare a bit beyfor. Shouldn't take long. So, have ya ever bey in Turkana beyfor?"

"What? Oh yes, twice. Once in Kitilo on a road investigation, and..."

"So ya bey knowen it ten?"

"Huh? Oh, yeah, a bit. Excuse me, Father, I'm having a bit of trouble hearing you."

Father Tom chuckled. "Neva ta worry. Ya not te furst ta complain. Tirteen years hare and I have not ta lose mey brogue."

Father Tom was a character. He had been over just about every square inch of the desert; seen droughts, floods, Ngoroko battles, and intimate tribal ceremonies. He walked miles through the desert on foot to see his parishioners – no motorcar for him. He needed to relate to the "Turks", not only for conversion purposes, but also to facilitate the mission's programs of health and social welfare.

Three cups of tea later, Loomis found himself daydreaming of Amonee and not quite capable of following Father Tom's funny story about Sister Ursula demonstrating a pit latrine and nearly falling to the bottom when the termite-rotted wooden platform collapsed. "Can ya believe tat now?" Father Tom asked him, laughing himself hysterically into a coughing fit.

Loomis had a growing urge to leave and write a letter to Nairobi as he waited impatiently for a chance to hint at departure.

"Lucky fer her one of te poles bey stoppen her fall," the priest chortled.

"Yes, indeed, lucky...sorry, Father, I hate to leave you, but we have some preparations to make and..."

"Sure, sure. Sorry fer keppin ya sa long. I tend ta bey getten carried away wit te new visitors. Okay, tamara."

"Thank you very much, Father."

"I'll bey tanken you, Mista Loomis."

At nine-thirty in the morning the sun, radiating white heat, had already become something to avoid. Loomis put on a pair of sunglasses but still could not keep from squinting. He parked the Land Rover, got out, and as he strolled along a sandy avenue, took in glimpses of the local denizens. Most of the citizens of Lodwar were down-country people, many of them businessmen, from transporters to shop owners, and even proprietors of such unlikely commercial ventures as makeshift photo studios and beauty salons, or 'saloons' as they were written on their crude signs. Outside the shops were tailors with pedal-driven sewing machines and at one spot under a shady tree were the artisans who made sandals out of discarded tires. The ubiquitous Somali were present with their tea houses and little hotelis, and some Luos remained trading in the fish from nearby Lake Turkana despite the dwindling profits. A surprising amount of traffic shuttled in and out of town stirring up the dust; the bulk of it was made up of government Land Rovers and vehicles belonging to the numerous European aid agencies concerned with food relief and health care. Intermingled with these aliens were the indigenous Turkanas, some dressed in a curious mixture of Western and traditional fashion. The majority of the Turkanas lived in native dwellings on the outskirts of town, while beggars, poor and herdless, slept on the verandas of shops.

Loomis entered Chemunga's Bar and sat down at a corner table while the barmaids busily swept the debris of the previous night. He asked for a soda but was told to wait a bit, that they weren't open yet. In the meantime he took out some folded sheets of blank paper and began to write, becoming so engrossed he didn't even look up when the soda was finally brought. After a while, he became considerably disturbed when someone else came over and sat at his table. Loomis ignored him, even though he sensed the stranger was staring at him.

"*Alawaye ilosi iyong?*" the intruder asked in the Turkana

language. "So, where are you heading to?"

Loomis stopped writing and gave him a glance. The face he looked into was square and chocolate brown, with features that seemed to have been sculptured: an abruptly pointed nose, thin neat lips, prominent chin and cheekbones, and heavily slanted eyes, the last a trademark of a Turkana. Perhaps it was an illusion, but Loomis thought he could detect a hint of glittering in those eyes, giving him the distinct impression that this was a wise guy intent on annoying him. The stranger was clad in fatigues, military in color. His manner of dress revealed that he was not a bush Turkana, and that he should know Kiswahili, and not be speaking in Kiturkana.

Although he desperately wanted to be rid of this unasked-for company, Loomis could not resist the temptation of answering him back in the same language, a move that would inevitably delay reaching that objective. "*Alosi ayong Lorogumu.*"

"And what are you going to do in Lorogumu?" the Turkana asked, showing no surprise that the foreigner could comprehend and speak his native language. Loomis took that as a challenge.

"*Kalosete sua etich*, we are going to work."

"Can you take me with you?" the stranger continued in his mother tongue.

"You want a lift?"

"No, I want a job."

Figures, he thought; the bush telegraph had already alerted the whole populace about their arrival.

"Do you know Kiswahili?"

"Yes."

"Can we converse in it please?"

"*Sawa sawa*, Okay, no problem," the African agreed, switching to the national language. And then, "I am a driver."

"I'm only hiring casual labor, and they're being provided by the Catholic Mission. Go and see Father Tom, tell him I sent you. But the pay is in food, not money."

"Oh no, not good. I need money."

"A driver, eh?" Loomis milled this over. Five vehicles, but only two full-time drivers. And vehicular transport was to be the only connection to Lodwar once they were out in the bush.

"What kind of license do you have?" Loomis asked him.

"Class C." The Turkana took out a small red booklet from his shirt pocket and handed it over.

"Peter, Ekal, Lokimat, Imana," read Loomis from the license. "So you can drive a lorry then, isn't that so?" he asked, returning the booklet.

"Ndio."

"How many years have you been driving, Peter, or should I call you..."

"McKracken. I have been driving for eleven years."

"McKracken?"

"That was my nickname in the police."

"You were a policeman?"

"Ndio." To emphasize his former status, McKracken pulled a beret from his back pocket and ceremoniously stretched it over his short kinky hair.

"Why did you leave the police?"

"I was fired."

"For what reason?"

"I crashed a vehicle."

"I see, now you want a chance to crash one of mine."

"Not my fault."

"I see, it was the vehicle's fault."

"Ah, no, no," the Turkana laughed. "My commanding officer's fault. He got me drunk."

"You like to drink while driving, do you?"

"No, that was the only time."

"What was so special on that occasion?"

"I was with my commanding officer. He bought the rounds. You don't refuse your C.O."

"That seems to me to be a stupid reason." Loomis paused.

"Anyway, you didn't have to tell me that."

"But you asked. Do you want me to tell lies? Me, I am a very trustworthy person, I don't lie, I don't steal, I don't cheat..."

"You only get drunk."

"Ah, no more."

"You no longer drink *pombe*?"

No answer.

Loomis looked at him. There was something charming about the guy. "Do you know English?"

"Perry well, thank you," McKracken answered in his English.

"Very well," Loomis repeated, emphasising the 'v' sound, knowing that the Turkana people had no 'f' or 'v' sounds in their own language.

"Very well," McKracken said, correcting himself.

Loomis took some time to ponder this opportunity. All of his staff were down-country people who knew nothing of Turkana, let alone the language. He knew from experience that negotiations with the locals were inevitable. The chap could also help out supervising the casual labor – they probably knew fuck-all Kiswahili as well, and Loomis's knowledge of the Turkana tongue was limited, and shaky at best. "Wait for me outside until I finish what I'm writing."

The Turkana promptly got up and exited.

It was hard for Loomis to compose the letter, even though he had thought it through beforehand. He had become distracted by the interruption, and it took him some time before he was able to transport his frame of mind back to the romantic exploits he had had in Nairobi.

When his letter was completed, Loomis tucked it into an envelope and addressed it to Amonee care of the university. He paid for the soda and departed, finding the Turkana waiting for him in the shade of the storefront veranda.

"Okay, Bwana McKracken, let's go make a call."

"No telepoans here."

"We have a radio. C'mon."

When they got to the Land Rover, parked in a clearing some fifty meters in front of the bar, Loomis opened the rear door and showed McKracken the radio. "Set it up," he told him. "If you really were a policeman, it shouldn't be a problem." Then he went inside the cab and wrote on a standard form message sheet while the Turkana brought out the components.

"Ready," McKracken announced.

That was quick. Loomis had only just finished writing the message. He studied the aerial which was cleverly set up between the vehicle door and a moderately large growth of desert palm. He handed the African the message sheet. "Transmit it. The call sign for the office is 'Hotel Quebec'. Ours is 'Tango Charley'."

McKracken took the microphone in his hand. "Calling Hotel Quebec, Hotel Quebec, this is Tango Charley, come in."

No reply came. The Turkana cocked his head and repeated the signal.

"Tango Charley, Tango Charely," crackled the radio. "This is Hotel Quebec, how do you read? Over."

"Not perry bad, about strength three. How do you read me? Opa."

"Roger, strength three. Is this Bwana Loomis? Over."

"No, this is McKracken. Opa."

"Come back, I didn't copy."

"McKracken. I hap a message po you. Are you ready to coffee?"

"Mind your p's and f's," Loomis reminded, interrupting him.

"Roger, go ahead," the radio requested.

"Prum, a – Delta Lima to Charley Brapo, uh, Bravo. Number Tango Charley oblique zero zero oblique zero one. Friority, uh, priority normal. Coffee? Uh, copy?"

"Copy."

"Message reads: 'now in Lodwar'..."

"Copy."

"...organizing casuals..."

"Come back. First word."

"Organizing. Oscar, Romeo, Gulp, Alpa, Nopember, India, Zebra, India, Nopember, Gulp. Casuals.Opa."

"Roger, go ahead."

"Exfect to leap po pirst drill site tomorrow. Opa."

"Copy."

"Number two. Hiring one casual on wage terms as driper, uh, driver, radio oferator. Coffee?"

A pause. "I copy, go ahead."

"Regards, end op message."

"Are you this new driver and radio operator? Over."

McKracken looked at Loomis who gave a nod of agreement, then pressed the sending button again. "Roger, that is appermatip."

"McKracken. Is that a roger?"

"Ndio."

"Welcome, Bwana McKracken. This is Josek. Do you have anything else? Over."

"Negatip."

"Thank you, Bwana McKracken. Hotel Quebec, over and out."

"Not bad," Loomis said.

* * *

Loomis dismissed McKracken, informing him of the meeting in the evening at Chemunga's. The site boss himself went off in search of Mutua, who was to help him in the purchasing of supplies. Once united, the pair bought some live goats, a quantity of tinned food, cooking oil, and slightly stale cabbages that came from Kitale. Potatoes, cassava, and onions were grown locally in a few patches on the riverbank, and sacks of these vegetables were squeezed in the back of the Land Rover. As they shopped, Loomis at times noticed his own crew members walking idly by, not bothering to greet him. What was their problem? Such coldness in Africans was extremely rare, and a sign that things were not as they should be.

In the afternoon, when the heat became intolerable and forced everyone to seek shelter, Loomis stayed in his room with the door open studying the maps, trying to prevent his excessive sweat from dripping on them. According to the schedule of works he had drawn up in Nairobi and had presented to Barnes, they would first strike due west of Lodwar to the Lorogumu area, then work their way northwards along the western flanks of the Loima Hills, up to the valley of Kakuma and beyond. After that they would return to Kakuma and proceed along the eastern flanks of the hills until they were back in the Lodwar area. It was an awful lot of ground to cover, and Loomis worried over the maps. They didn't look too accurate.

Later, before attending the evening meeting, Loomis checked the petrol in the Land Rover and found it to be unexpectedly low. He had added twenty liters between Kainuk and Lokichar, and he was hard put to explain the loss. It shouldn't have been that low, something was not right. *Wafula had better check the carburetor before we go,* Loomis decided. He opened the back door to get at the jerry cans and grabbed what he thought was a full one. But its lightness made him question the amount it contained, and upon opening the cap, a glance confirmed his suspicions. Checking the other cans, he found that they too were about a quarter short, too much to be missing from spilling or evaporation during the ride.

It dawned on him that he should have been more cautious. The doors of the vehicle were locked but the windows were not. Even a small oversight extracted its due. The petrol thief, he surmised, was not a stranger, otherwise why would they take only a little from each jerrycan and a bit from the tank? To try and hide the fact that any theft had occurred at all, that's why. Shigoli, Ben, Kariuki, and Kiprop were all staying in that same lodging, and the Land Rover was parked in its courtyard. It must have been one of them.

The meeting at Chemunga's was brief. McKracken was introduced, instructions for departure were given out. The men sat at the table sullen and silent. Loomis did not order any beer, having remembered the bill of the previous night for twenty-two Tuskers. After the meeting he told Shigoli, Ben, Karuiki, and Kiprop he wanted to speak with them outside.

Once out on the sandy street Loomis summoned up enough courage to confront them about the petrol theft, insinuating his ideas about who might have taken it. They immediately got defensive.

"Are you saying we are thieves?" Shigoli indignantly asked. "It is your fault you left the vehicle open. It could have been anyone." And with that, the big black man strode off, demonstrating hurt and anger, while the others followed behind him. Loomis stood alone feeling impotent.

He went back to his room and quietly drank three beers while taking another apprehensive glance at the topos. But all he kept thinking about was the missing petrol and how they stole it from his own vehicle. At this moment they would be partying with the money they got from its sale. A fourth beer helped to calm him. A pyrethrum coil he bought earlier in the day kept the mosquitoes away and when he turned in he fell soundly asleep reviewing the words he had written to Amonee, intentionally blocking out any thoughts concerning drillers and petrol.

* * *

At six o'clock in the morning, with the sluggishness of sleep still stuffed inside his head, Loomis drove to the mission office, a small, square building constructed of concrete blocks. There he was met by a mob of skinny Turkana males of various ages, from kids to old men, who immediately descended upon the Land Rover as soon as it pulled in. Loomis struggled with some difficulty to open the door and get out, and after succeeding, regretted he had bothered to. They swarmed around him, pleading with voices and gestures for a chance at employment, and he had to practically fight his way through to get to the office door, where Father Tom, today dressed in his black priestly robes, had suddenly appeared to give the operations manager a timely rescue.

"Maybe you better handle this, Father," Loomis suggested.

"I was tinken tat ta beyin te easiest way. God knows I dunt fancy it neither. Te drought of seventy-tree is still wit some of tem. *Akoro nakalan*, much hunger," he said, patting his stomach, "even up ta now. How many would yer bey wanten ten?"

"Twenty-five I think is sufficient. That's as much as I can take without asking for problems. There really isn't that much work."

"Neva ta worry. I'll find jobs fer te utters. Just sit in te shade and I'll pick ya twenty-five. Are ya sure tat all you bey wanten ten? Some of tem are bound ta bey runnen away."

"Out there, in the middle of the desert?" Loomis asked, incredulous, extending his arm in a northerly direction.

"And why not now? Tis ter home. Oh well, ya can always come back fer more."

As soon as it was apparent that Father Tom was about to begin his selection, the Turkanas quieted down and arranged themselves in as orderly a fashion as they could muster, standing still and erect as if at attention. Sometimes he exchanged a few words with an individual before choosing or rejecting him. He seemed to be picking some from each age group, and when two elderly, bearded men were picked, Loomis came forward to object.

"Father, I don't really think that the work we have to offer is suitable for them. It requires a bit of muscle and those guys look like they're standing on their last legs."

The burly, bearded priest tilted his head and gave Loomis a funny glance before he spoke. "I tink yull bey finden men such as teese a help ta ya. Tair elders, ya know. Tey'd bey knowen some useful tings out tair where yer goan. Not only where ta find water and wild fruits, but tair's sights and smells out tair tat only tey'd bey knowen. And yuv some jobs tat taren't too laborsome, da ya not? Teese men would be maken fine 'askaris', would ya bey knowen tat now? Tey dunt fall asleep like te younger ones."

Askari was the Kiswahili word for guards. "I really don't envision watchmen as a priority once we're out of town."

"Ya neva bey knowen who or what yull be meeten out tair. I'd

129

bey consideren good watchmen. And anutter ting, believe it tor not, would ya bey aware tat tey can forecast trouble?"

Loomis eventually gave in. If a priest believed all that, maybe there was some truth to it. Thirteen years in Turkanaland, this man of the cloth must have picked something up.

Loomis instructed his twenty-five laborers to proceed to the roundabout in town and wait there for the vehicles. He himself drove to the police station where he was to meet the crew. As he arrived the Mercedes was just coming back from its chore of filling the water bowser; Loomis had decided the night before that, as much trouble as it was to haul around five tons of water on what promised to be a brutal track, it was infinitely better than to barge off into the desert without it.

The Bedford, meanwhile, had gone to the mission go-down to collect the sacks of maize and beans that were to be used to feed the casuals, and was now apparently waiting in town. When Loomis and the other vehicles got to the roundabout of whitewashed stones, they found Joseph and his turnboy busy fighting off a horde of Turkanas attempting to board the lorry. No wonder Father Tom had wanted to delay the conscription of workers until the last moment.

"Only twenty-five are ours!" Loomis cried out. "And no 'lifty'! We're not carrying passengers."

It took some time to sort out who was who, but in the end the original twenty-five laborers found places amidst the loads of the lorries. Some of them had climbed onto the rig where the excess Hydro-Drill crew had perched themselves. Loomis chased them off. "No casuals on the rig!" he shouted. "McKracken, you come with me in the Land Rover."

The vehicles, once more in a line, started up and rumbled onto the road that led west out of Lodwar. The Turkana laborers cheered and waved to their comrades in the sandy street below who were responding with equal enthusiasm. They were off. Or were they? At the edge of town, a shirtless, lone figure, clad only in shorts and sandals and wearing a large, goofy hat with an exaggerated brim, stood waving down the convoy. And to Loomis's astonishment, all the vehicles in front came to an abrupt halt.

He slammed the steering wheel with his open palm. "What the fuck is it now?!" He opened the Land Rover door with a roughness that displayed his anger, and stormed over to the stranger, who was now conversing and laughing with the crew members that had climbed down to greet him.

"Shigoli, what the hell is going on here?" he demanded. "Why are we stopping here? Who is this idiot?"

"Sir!" the stranger said sharply, whipping off his hat, snapping to attention, and giving Loomis a mock salute. "My names are many. Kasongo, Pambamoto, Earl of Kakamega. But, in truth, I am called Professor Asha-sha-tay."

The tall African had a loony smile full of brown-stained teeth, and protuberant bug-like eyes. His kinky hair was cropped in a ridiculous pyramidal shape. A madman, Loomis realized.

Shigoli, fearing Loomis was about to lose his temper, broke in. "This is Sikhendu, Bwana Loomis. Cooper Sikhendu, the driller that was missing."

Oh great, Loomis thought to himself. *Just what I need, a clown.* "What is wrong with your mind? You think we're going on a picnic? Get on board one of the lorries. Quick!"

The half-naked African grabbed his duffle bag and procured a place atop the Dando 250 and they started off again: the Land Cruiser jeep pulling the aluminum office caravan, the monstrous-looking drill rig, the Mercedes lorry towing the rusty water bowser like an elephant leading its baby, the weary coughing Bedford with the Turkanas on top clapping and chanting, and the Land Rover, all of the vehicles posing as a somewhat ludicrous parade riding off on a cushion of dust, looking inapt against the backdrop of the immense, stark, desert.

* * *

As expected, the track was bad, but passable in the dry season. Any downpour, even one of moderate duration, could have effectively cut them off from Lodwar for hours or even days, so fierce would be the struggle between water and the hard-baked soil. The rough road limited their speed to under thirty kilometers an hour, too slow to generate any substantial breeze to cool their sweltering bodies. Even the Turkana casuals had become quiet with weariness. Time as well as motion seemed also to have slowed down to a ponderous pace. Loomis felt his rump burning with salty perspiration in addition to the aching soreness that came with sitting in a bouncing Land Rover for hours at a time. The scenery itself was tiring and depressing: parched and yellow, Turkanaland was scorched by the sun, scourged by the wind, and the little rain which visited during the year came all at once, resulting in short-lived torrents clawing into the land until they left gullies, ravines, and gorges. The monotonous vegetation, thorn trees and just-as-thorny bushes, possessed a stern and embittered look, appearing as resentful outcasts of the plant kingdom sentenced to a harsh exile. The land exuded emptiness, devoid of any signs of animal life, save for the yellow-necks and sand grouse which they startled whenever the convoy entered a laager. On one occasion, however, Loomis spotted four camels browsing snobbishly in the distance, apparently unconcerned with the whereabouts of their human owners.

Physical discomfort was spiced by the usual traumas of a safari in rugged country. Some of these had been anticipated, such as the Bedford overheating and the Dando 250 getting stuck in the laagers, which happened so often that it was becoming routine. Others, however, arose unexpectedly, such as the water bowser busting its back axle.

While the gum-chewing welder, whose name was O.T., busied himself welding the bowser axle, Loomis sat down with his back against the bowser and stared out at the desolate, lunar-like landscape. Brown, pockmarked lava boulders were scattered over yellow crumbly soil, a soil that could offer no better than wind-tormented trees and withered bushes. And the wind, a constant, relentless, hot brushing against your face that, when it stopped, you felt a certain relief. That's how it would be from now on.

He sighed. *Forty-eight men. Seventy tons of plant. Out here in this God-forsaken place.* And he was the one responsible for all and sundry. It was certainly not the biggest job he had ever been on, and he had worked in remote areas before, including Turkana, but in all those other instances there were other expatriate staff to divide the responsibility. On this contract he was the geologist, the site agent, the accounts clerk, the drill technician, the chief mechanic, and surrogate father. He dreaded it.

After an hour O.T. was finished and Loomis crawled underneath to examine the welder's labors. He didn't know too much about welding but he could recognize a good seal when he saw one. The axle was as straight as if it came right out of a machine works. If it broke again, it wouldn't be at the seal.

"Damn good job," Loomis said. "Tell me, what does O.T. stand for?"

"One...Time," the welder replied, popping his bubble gum.

It wasn't until midday that they began to see some form of human habitation – *manyattas*: rings of thorn brush encircling semi-spherical huts made out of sticks and palm leaves. The caravan was approaching Lorogumu, the last permanent settlement west of Lodwar – just a line of shops magically appearing in the middle of nowhere. Shigoli stopped the Land Cruiser in front of one of the larger thatched structures which advertised itself as a hoteli, bringing the procession to a halt. There they had another meal of chapati and goat meat.

Loomis made McKracken drive while he himself made attempts at catching some shuteye in the passenger seat. The desert scenery was becoming monotonous and the land was strangely devoid of people. Some time later they reached that part of the day he considered the most uncomfortable: when the late-evening sun hung low in the sky blasting its horizontal rays through the windows. At once Loomis was taken with panic. While driving he had been marking their progress on the map by clocking the kilometers and noting topographical landmarks. But as a sleepy passenger, he had forgotten all about this exercise, his mind wandering in daydreams of Amonee.

"Stop the car and honk the horn," he abruptly ordered McKracken.

When this was done the caravan grounded to a standstill.

"Pull out of line and draw up to the Land Cruiser."

As the Land Rover drew up even to Shigoli's vehicle, Loomis stuck his head out and shouted, "I'm going on alone to look for the benchmark. Everyone else wait here."

"Why?" Shigoli asked, surly. "We should stay together."

"Just do as I say."

Loomis knew that the best way to locate the convoy on the map was to go back to Lorogumu and retrace their path. But he couldn't let the men know he was lost. He went on ahead with McKracken and hoped to God they hadn't passed the benchmark miles back.

Three hours later the beam of Land Rover headlamps told the crew that Loomis was returning. He had found the benchmark and they would make camp by it. According to the map, he explained, the borehole, which he would locate tomorrow, was very near to the benchmark. The weary group followed him and by the time they reached TP13, it was almost midnight. Tents were haphazardly pitched and a fire made. The rest of the camp would be set up in the morning. The Hydro-Drill crew ate a hurriedly prepared dish of ugali and dried fish, simply but tastefully prepared by Juma the cook. The Turkana laborers ate raw maize.

Later on that night, Loomis peeked out of his tent flap and watched the ring of men sitting around the campfire. Their arms and faces shone coppery in the light of the flames, and their teeth glowed white whenever they were bared in laughter, which was quite often. There were snickers and chuckles, and sometimes not very restrained guffaws. Sikhendu was hamming it up, re-enacting their encounter on the road. Loomis had suspected that this fellow was going to be bad news; already he was fuelling a mood of rebellion. The clowns were always the most treacherous.

* * *

A cool dawn washed the land with light, leaving a crystal-clear vista of dun-colored earth and austere, weather-beaten vegetation. Morning was beginning and it now remained for the men to set up the camp properly: the generator, refrigerator-freezer and lights to be connected, a makeshift kitchen and a latrine to be constructed, and an iron uniport to be erected as a store. The tents, made out of heavy-duty canvas, were large enough to place three cots inside of them for the junior workers, whereas the senior staff such as Shigoli and Ben, Sikhendu and Wafula, and Mutua and O.T., shared space with only each other. Inside Loomis's tent was a table and chair in case he wanted to work, though most of the work would be done inside the office caravan which contained two desks and housed the radio.

Loomis left the men to their tasks and set off with McKracken and two casual laborers to hunt for the borehole. After ambling around in the Land Rover for an hour or so, trying to make sense of the map he was studying, he was sure they must be in the right vicinity, and they all disembarked to search for their objective on foot. "Useless maps," he muttered to himself.

Twenty minutes later, McKracken and the casual laborers had found it. They brought Loomis to a rise where they saw, about three hundred meters away, a bright red flag waving loudly against the drab colors of the landscape. The borehole was a good two miles away from where the crew was putting up camp.

"Have you found the borehole?" Shigoli asked when the site engineer returned.

"Yes, I found it. It's a bit far." Loomis looked at the camp. It was just about complete. Even the latrine looked ready. The men would certainly bitch when they were to be told.

"How far?"

"I think we'll have to drive to work."

The men were not exactly pleased, but they were at least accepting when Loomis explained that the rig and lorries could not make it there without first clearing a decent track, and the camp would have to stay put anyway for the time being. Still, Loomis could not help but feel a fool. He outlined the plan whereby he would go with the two lorry drivers, McKracken, and all the casuals to make the road. The drillers were to go to the borehole site and start digging the mud pits.

There were a lot of detailed decisions to be made when making an access road in the bush. Did you go this way and fill in that gully, or that way and dig out that mound and clear its thick brush? Loomis and the lorry drivers were rarely in agreement in these matters and to compound their difficulties further, the Turkana laborers did not seem to be very familiar with pickaxes and shovels, although they weren't too bad with a panga, the African version of a machete. The organization of the road team resembled more like unbridled chaos than systematic effort, and regardless of the three hours spent toiling in the sun, not much was accomplished.

That evening, Loomis, through McCracken's mispronounced English, transmitted a radio message which read: SET UP CAMP AT TP13. ACCESS ROAD STARTED. DRILL SITE CLEARED AND MUD PITS DUG. EXPECT TO SPUD IN DAY AFTER TOMORROW.

* * *

Where the sky touched the land, a red glow burned itself orange, then amber, consuming an oyster-blue sky. Slowly, almost impercep-tibly, the horizon flamed into a celestial crown of golden rays, as shadows dripped off the backs of things and spilled along the ground. Scorpions crawled out from their burrows, francolins fluffed their feathers, and baboons yawned in the shelter of a rocky overhang, while the scarce vegetation present readied itself for its daily dose of sun. The desert had awoken.

And so had Daryl Loomis. He stepped out of his tent and into the virgin daylight, shading his eyes with his hands. He saw the smoldering campfire being re-fed by the elderly pair of watchmen who had been tending it during the night. Juma was scrubbing a pot with sand and water. Here and there, members of his crew, most of them half-naked, stood cleaning their teeth with the 'chewing sticks' they had picked up along the way. Others were crowded around the faucet of the water bowser washing their hands and faces. Tinny music squeaked from a radio in someone's tent. Everything seemed normal enough, yet he could still detect that something was amiss. Then he saw McKracken loping towards him with a handful of the casuals following closely behind.

"I have some bad news," he announced in Kiswahili. "The laborers have all gone, except for these."

Six. Plus the two old askaris. Seventeen of them had taken off during the night. Loomis could have kicked himself. He should have known, even without Father Tom's warning, that most Turkanas were not accustomed to any labor harder than walking with their animals or digging a shallow well, and the taste of work they got yesterday was sufficient for them to decide that they could do without it.

Plans for the day had to be modified. The crew alone now had to finish the task of road clearing, while Loomis and McKracken went back to Lodwar in the Merc to obtain more workers.

Upon arrival at the mission, Loomis was relieved that Father Tom was gracious enough not to mention any 'I told you so's'. On the contrary, the Irish priest was so sympathetic as to lend out his most reliable workers who had already been given jobs in the mission. On this occasion Loomis took along thirty-two men and supplementary bags of food. They returned in the middle of the night and were met with both a report that the road was three quarters complete, and a radio message that claimed the linings and fuel from Nairobi would be in Lodwar within the next two days.

It wasn't until the fourth day at site that the rig, lorries, and camp were moved close to the borehole, with the Mercedes proceeding to Lodwar to meet the lorry coming from Nairobi. McKracken and the two old Turkana watchmen, scouting around in the Land Rover, managed to locate water underneath the sand of a laager about three miles away, which was a bit of luck, since they needed it not only for their own sustenance, but for the drilling operations as well. At last everything appeared ready for the drilling to commence, and Loomis could now answer Barnes's sarcastically worded message of the previous day that questioned the efficiency of the site manager's planning. The spudding in of the borehole was already two days later than Loomis had predicted.

* * *

"Here's your mail, Pammy. You must have been pretty busy not to stop in the mail room this morning. It's already close to noon," Katy declared handing over the small bundle.

Shuffling the envelopes, Amonee saw that one of them was postmarked Lodwar, and not bothering to get her silver letter-opener, tore at it impatiently with her fingers to get the contents out.

Dear Amonee,

Hi! I hope you are well. Our trip to Lodwar was a bit rougher than expected but we have arrived safely. I have a lot of work ahead of me and I'm keeping fairly busy. Met a very amusing Catholic priest here. Tell you more about him when I see you.

So how are the kids? Tell them I said hello.

Well, have you come to your senses yet? I don't think I have. Even though the logistics of work keep my mind pretty much occupied, I find my thoughts running off to join you every chance I get. At the risk of upsetting you, I have to say that I miss you already, and it is bringing a kind of loneliness to my job which I never experienced before I met you. I think you are the most beautiful woman I ever met, and yet you are not vain or even aware of your beauty. You are highly educated and independent, no small thing for an African woman, but you possess a humble nature, modest and gentle. And you are such a happy person, always with a smile. It is all these things which attract me to you. Please don't take my words as the insincere and calculated flattery of a flirtatious letter. I've never told you how I feel about you because when I'm with you I just clam up with nervousness. Maybe it's because the effect of your company upon me feels so good I'm scared to upset it with a few bold words. I hope this doesn't alarm you, but I wish to be more than just a friend.

Yours,

Daryl

P.S. How did the music festival go?

"It's from him, isn't it?"

"Who?"

"You can't hide it, Pammy," Katy said with a sly smile. "Sitting there with your eyes all ga-ga and that dopey smile on your face."

Amonee picked up the letter and stared at it. "It's such a lovely letter." She read it again while her plump companion became discreetly quiet behind her desk. Then she pushed aside the pile of papers she was involved in, searched for her prettiest stationary, and began to write.

* * *

The men had been disturbingly quiet all morning. They jacked up the rig, raised the mast, greased all the nipples, and secured the sub and lead rod into the drill head, all without a word to the site boss. Loomis felt redundant, almost useless. They didn't seem to need him.

Turkana people came out of nowhere to view them with curiosity. The men, some with a blanket drooped over their shoulders, others wrapped in sarongs, stood leaning on their walking sticks while the women in their cow-skin garb stood stock still, holding their various gourds of milk to their chest, all of them watching the Hydro-Drill crew dispassionately. Even with the drill rig and other strange machines, the Turkana were not easily impressed.

"Shigoli, we'll first make a pilot hole using a 5 and 3/4 inch drag bit," he instructed, attempting to regain his role as the engineer in charge. But the burly African merely pointed to the 5 and 3/4 inch drag bit which was already attached. It was a silent rebuff, a reminder that they knew what to do without any orders from him.

Someone started the mud pump and Loomis headed over to the water-filled pits. Kadogo and Obasi had by now dumped a full bag of bentonite into the circulating water and were continuing to throw in handfuls more of the powdered clay.

"Hey, that's enough! Don't add any more."

"*Weka*! Put it in!" came a shout from behind.

Loomis turned to face Shigoli. "You're going to make the mud too thick."

Shigoli did something he hadn't done before. He spoke to Loomis in English. "Don't want borehole collapse. Heavy mud no problem. We ream after with light mud. I do this many years, I know."

"Do you realize how far we are from Nairobi? We have to make the bentonite last as long as possible, we don't know when we're going to get any more. So don't tell me about my work!"

Shigoli's response to this was to walk huffily away.

In addition to the uncooperative attitude of his chief driller, and the fact that he was being ignored by all, the increasing jolly mood of the men further unnerved him. He interpreted their excessive joking and laughter to be mocking his authority. And once again Sikhendu appeared to be in the center of it all. Loomis was beginning to hate the bloody buffoon.

And all the while the Turkana bystanders stood staring with expressionless faces.

The Bedford honked its horn, signaling its readiness to embark, and off went Loomis, McKracken, and twenty laborers in search of gravel, which they had no problem finding in the numerous dry stream beds that coursed through the cracked and broken terrain. But explaining to the Turkana casuals the method of sifting gravel through the various mesh-sized sieves proved to be a bit more difficult, requiring nearly two hours of instructing, correcting, debating and cajoling before the process seemed to be understood. In the end the laborers were given food and told to remain there until the he returned some time in the days ahead to look at what had been done.

Returning to the well site, Loomis noted that the mud pump was connected and all other preliminaries had been completed. With a nod from Loomis, Ben turned the big diesel over, which came alive with a roar that hammered the motionless desert air. The Turkanas who had been standing around them jumped away with amused alarm accompanied by laughing, whooping and some fleeting screams from the womenfolk. They resumed their positions with renewed interest as the hydraulics were engaged adding a whine of its own, and the jagged steel bit spun rapidly as it pierced the sun-hardened sand. The crew impressed Loomis, performing as a well-trained team, handling and adding sections of pipe to feed the drill string as it penetrated deeper into the soil. The exhilarating momentum of the work, and the adept, professional manner of the crew, gave him a sense of optimism. Perhaps, once the work got underway, they could manage some sort of reconciliation.

Unfortunately, this optimism was soon extinguished with an argument over the stopping of the borehole, Shigoli wanting to end it, while Loomis insisted on its continuation. In the end, Loomis got his way, but the bickering only added more friction between the two men. The blinding sun and the insufferable heat further shortened tempers. All in all, it was a miserable day, and the last thing the site engineer needed was a scolding from Barnes that he was behind schedule. And this was precisely the message McKracken handed him as the nightshift came on duty.

The next morning he was reluctant to get out of bed, so great was his anxiety over what new madness the day would bring. He left the drillers reaming and went to check the casuals sifting the gravel. He almost wept when he discovered only nine of them present, eleven having disappeared two nights ago with what they claimed was their rightful share of maize and beans. Worse still, some misunderstanding led the laborers to believe that what was bigger was better, and a large collection of useless cobbles had been amassed, ridiculously unsuitable for a well-screen filter pack. McKracken charitably volunteered to remain and direct the operation, which would now have to start again from scratch.

Two more days passed, and the Mercedes still did not appear. The borehole was finally reamed wide enough to accommodate the linings, except that there were no linings, forcing the crew to ream again and place temporary casings to keep the hole open.

Where was the bloody Mercedes? Did Ezekiel go on a drinking spree and forget the job he had to do? Even worse, did he crash the lorry? Loomis was forced to take another drive to Lodwar to investigate. There he found that the lorry from Nairobi had just arrived, only an hour before he himself did. The Nairobi driver, when asked why he was so late, unnecessarily informed Loomis that the *bara bara*, the road, was *mbaya*, bad. Three days wasted, and because of stupidity. He thought of making a formal complaint, but he knew what Barnes's response would be, and he had no need to repeatedly hear those three notorious words. He already knew enough geography to realize which continent he was on.

In due course the galvanized linings, screen, and gravel pack were placed inside while the temporary casings were removed, but, as it turned out, despite all the efforts they had put in, the well was dry, bone dry. When Loomis went back to the office caravan in disgust, he received another message from Barnes, once again reprimanding him on the unsatisfactory progress and reminding him that according to the original schedule, they should have already been set up on the second site by now. Would he please explain?

That evening, McKracken went to see Loomis to confirm the message to be transmitted, and yes it was exactly as the site boss had written it. McKracken, still a bit confused, returned to the mobile office, grabbed the microphone, and pressed the sending button.

"Yes, Josek, I hap conpirmed. Message stands as is. Once more I refeat. Reads: THIS IS APRIKA, REGARDS, end op message."

"Roger."

The first borehole was completed. Only twenty-nine left to go.

* * *

The equipment loaded and prepared for transport, the camp broken, they embarked, north this time, to their second site with Loomis leading the way. It was a trek as wearisome as the ones they had undertaken since Kitale and as the ones in the future promised to be. Flat country was interrupted by biscuit-brown hogbacks of sandstone and boulders, and ahead they saw Moruapolon, the Great Mountain, known also as the Loima Hills, a huge plateau which spread for over forty square miles. The immense massif stood before them, haughty and defiant, its red face creased with shadowed ravines, and it grew larger in height and menace as they drew closer. Along the way the procession passed a few scattered manyattas and herds of cattle tended to by their Turkana masters, slowly making their way to the grazing lands on top of the mountain. The adults never showed any reaction to their passage other than to stand and stare at them impassively, but some of the children were bold enough to run a short distance towards the rumbling caravan, waving and shouting, acknowledging the novelty of such a bizarre spectacle.

By mid-morning they reached a junction, which bewildered Loomis since he did not recall seeing it on the map. The convoy stopped and waited while he consulted his large folded sheets. The map only showed a road leading to the northwest, curving back to the northeast further on. The other track was not indicated at all.

"We go left," he announced, stretching his arm and pointing to the desired direction.

At this point, one of the Turkana casuals stood up from his place on top of the Bedford. "That is a bad way!" he hollered in his native language.

"He says that road is bad," McKracken translated in Kiswahili.

"I heard what he said!" Loomis barked back. "But that eastern road is not on the map. I can't go by what he says, he doesn't even know where we're going to." He turned and shouted, "Twende! Let's go!"

For seven hours they travelled, and the road was one of the best tracks they had been on since leaving the tarmac two weeks ago.

"Look, there she is!" Loomis exclaimed, referring to the red flag standing off in a distant patch of bare, rocky desert. "We don't even need the benchmark. Nothing wrong with this road."

They continued farther on and then he saw something he hoped was a mirage. He rubbed his eyes but it was still there, appearing to be the top of a wall. "Oh shit," he mumbled under his breath.

McKracken stopped the Land Rover at the edge of a small gorge cut out of the land, apparently by one of the many ephemeral but violent streams which drained the mountains. The red flag waved tauntingly on the other side. The rest of the vehicles halted behind as Loomis got out and once again tussled frantically with the maps.

"This streambed isn't even marked!" he cried out defensively. He turned to find the elderly Turkana by his side, the old man's sunken eyes staring sagaciously down into the defile.

"*Erono nege*, bad place," the Turkana remarked.

Loomis crouched down on his knees and peered over the edge to study the ravine. He wasn't defeated yet. It was about thirty meters deep, but the canyon walls were not that declivitous. There would be no trouble crossing by foot, so the camp could be set up on the side that they presently found themselves. Even the water bowser could remain – they would pump the water over. It was only the rig and the casings that had to go across. Then the answer hit him. A cableway! They had enough one-inch steel cable, they had rock bolts, and they had a jackhammer drill. It could work.

"Shigoli!"

The big African came to his side, all the while gazing at the obstacle in front of them. "We turn back?" he asked, not expecting any answer but the affirmative.

"No. We make a cableway to get the rig over."

"But the rig weighs over thirty tons! It's not possible!"

"Yes it is. We shall dismantle it. Remove the mud pump and compressor. We have two monkey winches, and each can pull ten tons or more. We'll use two lengths of cable to span the gorge, but even one could do it."

"It is going to require much work."

"Easier than going back all the way around in a circle just to get over there, isn't it."

"Ndio."

"Tell the men. Have some of them start drilling holes for the rock bolts. The others can begin taking off the mud pump and compressor."

"I'm still worried."

"So am I, Shigoli. If I drop that rig you may find me selling neckties on the streets of Nairobi. I just hope the rock bolts are enough."

The crew accepted the orders with a lighthearted enthusiasm, tempted by the challenge and curious of the outcome. They broke into groups, laying out the cables, stripping the rig of everything which could reasonably come off and lifting them out with the Hiab crane, and drilling the rock-bolt holes in the places picked out by Shigoli. They worked with the same alacrity Loomis had witnessed before, Sikhendu again particularly animated. But this jovial manner of working did not bother the site boss, for he too, although he hated to admit it, was captured by their happy spirit. After all, the cableway was his idea and he was proud of it.

Evening came and all was just about ready. Two lines of cable stretched the breadth of the chasm, each end anchored into rock by four rock bolts so securely placed they would eventually have to be abandoned there. A metal harness made of drill rods and cable, with six pulleys, like a hollow cable-car, was fabricated by O.T., the welder, and the two monkey winches – each with their own length of cable for pulling the object to be conveyed – were also bolted into rock. There was also a brake cable, to be wrapped around the trunk of the one and only tree in the area, and which was to be held by twenty men to prevent any dangerous acceleration of the transported load. Launching and landing sites were cleared and prepared. Now there was nothing to do but await the following day to try out their invention.

In the morning, underneath a pale blue sky, a strange and unusually chilly wind rustled the bushes and swept up the sand. The great mountain loomed over them as arrogant as ever. Loomis was tense, his stomach jumping like it used to before a big game. The time had come.

First, the casings, wired together in bundles weighing two tons apiece. They used only one winch with two men jacking, the large pipes going across in less than ten minutes – a piece of cake. The mud pump was next and it too arrived with no problem. Then the compressor – approximately twice as heavy, it needed four men on the winch and took double the time to reach the other side, but once again without a hitch. The system was working perfectly.

Then came the real test. Ezekiel eased the Leyland onto the 'launching pad', and the harness was being attached with steel cables running through the cab and under the chassis. Loomis called out to the men on the brake line. "*Tayari*? Are we ready?"

"Ndio, yes, tayari!" they chorused in reply.

Loomis signed to the lorry driver. "Okay, Ezekiel."

The old man released the handbrake, shifted into neutral, then swiftly alighted from the cab. With a signal from Shigoli, the eight men on the other side of the ravine, four to each winch, started working the handles up and down pulling the winch cables taut. The rig shuddered, then moved, its motion only detectable by a slight movement of the tires. Inch by bloody slow inch it progressed to the cliff verge with a pace that froze all of their hearts. The men caught their breaths as the front wheels began to leave the ground. Those on the brake line braced themselves. Loomis was sweating, his jaws working non-stop on the chewing gum he had bummed from O.T. God, he wished he had a cigarette.

After what seemed like ages, all four wheels were off the ground – the rig was airborne! There was a short burst of cheers and whistles, and then when their acclamation had died down, only the creaking of the winch handles could be heard. But then there was another noise, a grunt of metal.

"What's that noise, Shigoli?"

"Si Jui. Don't know."

The fifteen tons of metal hulk swayed ponderously as it shimmied along the cables, and the coils of the brake line eased their way around the tree trunk as the gang of brakemen let out the slack. Loomis heard that noise again, a metallic cry of protest, but brushed it aside.

Twenty long minutes passed and the rig was one third of the way across. Loomis paced nervously up and down the edge of the ravine, muttering, "C'mon, baby, you can make it." Suddenly he stopped short and stared disbelievingly into the streambed below. "What the fuck!" He saw a figure, almost directly below the suspended rig, leaping and waving as if encouraging the inanimate mass above him to continue on.

"Shigoli, who the fuck is that down there?" Loomis screamed. But rather than wait for a reply, Loomis scrambled down the steep bank and ran towards whoever it was that was insane enough to be down there. It was Sikhendu.

"Sikhendu, you idiot! What the hell is wrong with you!" But on closer inspection, Loomis already gathered what was wrong with him. It was chang'aa.

Chang'aa was home-made corn whiskey, where anything like quality control was lacking, and it often ended up being ninety percent ethanol. Drinking that stuff in the desert heat could easily render one temporarily insane.

What happened next took place with amazing rapidity. One of the support cables broke free and whipped upwards, hurling rock bolts into the air before falling down the canyon side. The rig jerked free, slipping along the cableway under its own momentum, and the men holding the brake line screamed and shouted as the brake cable raced through their hands ripping flesh and imbedding steel splinters before they had a chance to let go. The cable unwrapped itself from the tree with a zizzing sound. The rig recoiled, tilting to one side, and a steel plate, the one the compressor had been mounted to and subsequently forgotten by the men who had dismantled it, rattled loose. It slid off the rig bed and hurtled down, revolving in the air as it fell. In a split-second Loomis tackled Sikhendu and knocked him to the ground as the plate crashed with a heavy thud only a few meters away. For one immeasurable moment there was a startled silence while Loomis, his eyes inflamed with frightened rage, stared into Sikhendu's terrified face. And then he lost control. With a crazed banshee yell, he slapped and flailed at the black man below him, Sikhendu protecting his face by covering it with his hands. Loomis eventually got off him and began to direct his assault on the dry stream bed, flinging handfuls of sand into the air. When he regained himself, he looked up and noticed that all activity had ceased, the men having stopped to look at what was happening below. The rig still hung precariously on the single remaining cable.

"WINCH THAT FUCKING RIG ACROSS!" he screamed in English, punching the air in the forward direction

The men leapt back to their duties as Sikhendu got up and ran away into the bush.

Loomis shuddered. He had freaked out, totally lost it. He was aware of a novel feeling inside him, one he had never experienced before. It was an awesome fear. A fear of death.

* * *

The rig did make it across. A path had been cleared and the huge machine set up at the borehole, the compressor and mud pump placed back upon it. Sikhendu was nowhere to be seen. All in all, an exhausting day.

Loomis signaled off the radio and leaned back in his chair with a sigh. Jesus, he could sure do with a beer. And a whole pack of cigarettes.

There was a knock on the office caravan door. "*Ingia,* come in."

The door opened and in stepped Shigoli, the big man stooping as he entered to avoid knocking his head. "*Hu jambo, bwana.*"

"*Si jambo,* Shigoli."

"I hope I'm not disturbing you."

"No, I'm finished for the day. Just to eat and sleep. Tell the men, no nightshift tonight. Let everyone rest. Have you seen Sikhendu?"

"Yes, he is here in the camp. He wants to know if he can talk to you."

"The only thing I have to say to him is that he's fired. McKracken will take him to Lodwar and he can jump on a lorry from there. I don't want to see his face again."

"To speak the truth," continued Shigoli, still standing, rubbing his hands nervously on the sides of his overalls, "he knew you would not talk to him, so he has sent me to plead his case."

Loomis toyed thoughtfully with the pen in his hands. He must tread carefully here. If he refused such a request, Shigoli, as the leader of the men, would lose face. This could very well be a chance to make amends with his burly foreman. All he had to do was listen. "Okay, sit down."

Shigoli did so but did not speak, waiting for a further cue from his site boss.

"Tell me what he wants to say."

"He wants forgiveness. He was drunk and won't do it again. He will work hard, I will see to it that he does."

"That's not easy for me to do. What he did warrants immediate dismissal. I don't think I have any other choice. We both could have been killed."

"His mother is very aged. He is helping her. And he is putting his brother through school. They will suffer if he has no job."

"That's not my problem."

"Do you not know that we Africans have extended family? Not just mother, father, wife, and children, but brothers, sisters, in-laws, aunts, uncles, nephews, cousins, all their children..."

"Yes, yes, I know all that, Shigoli."

"If any one of them is in difficulty, and you are employed, they can come to you and you are expected to help them. The little money we get is barely enough, but at least it is better than not working."

"Is that why you stole my petrol, because your salary isn't enough?"

Shigoli did not answer.

"You did take that petrol, didn't you?"

"*Hapana*. No."

"Then who did?"

"Si jui. I don't know."

"One of the men, it must have been."

"Yes, I think so."

Shigoli knew who the thief was alright, but Loomis also knew he would never say. "So I should forgive that too, forgive that theft, forgive all mistakes and blame them on extended family?" Loomis asked facetiously.

"Hapana. No."

"Listen, this is what I want. I want cooperation, hard work, and no more petty theft. When this job is finished I'll insist on a healthy bonus for everyone." Loomis indulged in a deliberate pause, enjoying the superior advantage and the sense of control he was experiencing for the first time since they left Nairobi. Cementing his relationship with Shigoli could lead to an alliance which would help keep the men in line. It was worth a try. "Alright, tell Sikhendu that

I forgive him, but only because you have spoken to me on his behalf."

"Ndio, thank you, bwana Daryl."

"And if there are any other incidents of any kind by anyone, I will hold you responsible. Let's do our job, Shigoli, and get the hell out of here. Control the men, and we won't have any more misunderstandings."

"Ndio." Shigoli rose to his feet in eager relief.

"And no more chang'aa!" Loomis yelled as Shigoli exited. "I swear I'll sack the next man I find drunk on the job!"

Loomis arched back in his chair and put his hands behind his head to support it. He was content, the matter was finished. Or was it?

The next morning, as Loomis arose and stepped outside, he found four one-gallon plastic containers placed in front of his tent, all of them filled with chang'aa. He smiled and got the feeling the day was going to be a good one.

* * *

From that point on Loomis did not have any more problems with his crew. They began to work concertedly rather than against each other. Before making any critical decisions, Loomis would have a consultation with Shigoli and Ben, even if he was convinced of his own opinion on the matter. In this way the second borehole was completed and the rig successively brought back to the other side in just three days. By the time they were setting up on the third site, an incipient camaraderie had developed that Loomis knew would remain for the duration of the contract. Perhaps, he reflected, he had been too distant and overbearing; perhaps he had been slightly paranoid about his position; or perhaps they were just too new to each other.

He laughed with his men. At night he would sit around the campfire telling gags and anecdotes relating to his past exploits. He got personal with them, greeting them in their own vernaculars; ribbing them about any amusing incidents which sometimes occurred during the day; and inquiring after their homes and families with genuine interest. The lingua franca among them was Kiswahili, with the exception of Mutua, who was predisposed to speak in English.

Loomis was now of the opinion that the men made up the best crew he had ever had. But things were to take a new course with the arrival of Reginald Greenbottom.

They were setting up on the fourth well-site when they got the message that Greenbottom would be coming with salaries and impress money. Loomis took the Land Rover to Lodwar, the Merc following behind with the mission of picking up more linings and food supplies.

The company plane was a two-engine Aztec, a six-seater. It taxied to a halt on the runway just beside the Land Rover as Loomis went over to receive the person climbing out: a tall, thin, rangy man with a balding head and skin that was blotched and excessively freckled, a skin never meant to be exposed to a tropical sun. The flesh on his face fell in folds like deflated bags and contrasted sharply with his long thin lips.

"Reginald Greenbottom," he announced, offering his hand.

"Daryl Loomis."

Hands met in a limp handshake. "Yes, I presumed so. Is this our vehicle?"

"Yes, as you may have already presumed."

Greenbottom was not impressed with his witticism. "Shall we be off then, before it gets too hot?"

"Sure, just a short stop at the mission. I have some men there picking up a few things. I want to leave instructions."

The pilot came around the nose of the plane and approached the pair. "Hi there!" he greeted. "Sean Macintyre." He gave Loomis a firm handshake. He had a pleasant face, about forty years of age, and his manner was one of imperturbability, suggesting a guy who was cool under any circumstances.

"Daryl Loomis."

"Nice knowing you, Daryl."

"You coming with us?"

"No, I gotta bring this baby back to Nairobi. Maybe next time."

"Well, you're more than welcome."

"Okay, see you."

After stopping at the mission and checking the matter of loading the Merc, they were off. During the entire ride back to site, Greenbottom was constantly rubbing his face with a handkerchief. "Bloody hot, isn't it?"

"Yeah, today and every day."

"We're a bit concerned, you know, about the slow start and the rate of progress," Greenbottom said, giving himself another wiping.

"Conditions are tough out here," Loomis replied.

"We had considered that and it was taken into account when the deadline was discussed. You were highly recommended, not only because of your past performance, but because you had some previous experience in Turkana. Surely, this shouldn't be new to you, the problems of working in such a place."

"Well then, you should have called me in when everyone was discussing the deadline."

"More likely as not, the watu need to be prodded a bit, don't you think? Lazy buggers wogs are. If it was up to them they'd sit under a tree and drink pombe all day. They're not drinking themselves to death I hope?"

"Not much to drink up here," Loomis said, taking a hole in the road particularly hard, bouncing Greenbottom off his seat.

"Easy, man! That's why these vehicles are always breaking down. Good machines, Land Rovers, but only if they're well looked after."

Loomis already decided that he didn't like the guy.

Greenbottom stayed for three days. He had many suggestions and just as many complaints. The accounts were an abominable mess. Too many casual laborers – "get rid of some, they get in the way." The staff was consuming too much maize meal, it should be monitored, they always made pigs of themselves when food was freely provided. He got angry when he saw the men using diesel to get the grease off their hands. Get them some liquid soap he told Loomis. "Look at that equipment scattered all over the place, that's how they lose things, have them line it up neatly, they should take pride in their work. You should show them, you should know better."

When asked about the salaries and impress money, Greenbottom calmly explained that the cashier had not prepared it in time, and that he himself had not been able to wait. Loomis did not have such an easy time explaining that to the men. He promised them he would fix them up with something after Greenbottom was gone.

On the day of Greenbottom's departure, Loomis did not exactly lament. "Don't hurry back!" he cried, certain that the whine of the plane's props drowned out his words.

After the fifth borehole, their fuel ran out, with no provisions made by the office to send more. "Buy it from the mission," they told him. He did and then the money was finished. "Borrow some from the mission," they told him. The bishop admonished Loomis, saying that they didn't mind providing fuel on credit, but money was another matter. What kind of firm was he working for? he asked. The site manager couldn't answer that one, so instead he continued pleading. He had to practically swear on the Bible to make good all debts before they gave him ten thousand.

But a timely receipt of a letter from Nairobi assuaged all his frustrations.

Dear Daryl,

I am happy that you finally were able to write to me. I am doing very well, and guess what? Our choir came in first place in the Music Festival! Katy's band also did well. It was a tremendous experience.

Not to fret about all those things you wrote about me, however if it was someone else I would have torn up the letter! As I told you, you are the only one allowed to compliment me.

And I guess I haven't come to my senses yet either, because like you, my backload of work cannot prevent me from daydreaming about the times we had together. I am looking forward to meeting you again so we can get to know each other better.

I feel for you when I think of the difficult job you are doing so many miles far from anyone. I hope this letter makes you feel less lonely. And despite your swaggering and show of nonchalance, I know now you are really a caring and gentle person.

All the children greet you and I am enclosing two snapshots which I think will help you to remember them. I wrote something on the back of one of the photos to make doubly sure you don't forget! Please take care of yourself and try not to work too hard. Until then, I remain, Your dearest friend,
Amonee

He gazed with delight at the photos she had slipped into the envelope. He flipped over the picture of the balloons floating up in the sky to see that she had written 'Freedom' on the back of it and it made him smile with poignant reminiscence. He must have read the letter five times before he went to sleep, keeping the photos under his pillow.

* * *

The sixth borehole was somewhere near Nomoropus. The deeper they trekked into the desert, and the closer they came within the fringes of the Great Mountain, the more they found themselves in country which was dominated by broad laagers, some of these huge dormant riverbeds greater than a quarter of a mile in width, with well-developed banks on each side shelving riverine forests of bushes and trees. Below the banks, the laager beds themselves were strewn with coarse ash-colored gravel, cobbles and large boulders of various hues, and in some places, even dead trees and heavy debris

– the very picture of desolation.

A laager was often a main center of Turkana activity because of the accessibility of water a few feet below the sand and gravel. Each family dug its own wells: a wide one for watering livestock and a narrower one for human consumption. Loomis and company, whenever they happened to be in a laager, either moving or getting stuck, would invariably see the Turkana and their goats, sheep, camels, and donkeys crowded around their waterholes. In the presence of these congregations the mid-day air would dance to the beat of hooves, the lowing and bleating of the herds, the ringing of cowbells, and the whoops and whistles of the herdsmen. The wells were deep enough to stand a person in, accounting for the periodic emergence of hands which came up out of them delivering bowlfuls of water, and pouring them into the long troughs of hollowed-out tree trunks that lay at the feet of the thirsty beasts.

The Hydro-Drill team eventually reached the borehole site and work proceeded so well that a slight boredom supplanted the previous stress. The days passed by, with the time for their first break plodding inexorably closer until it finally arrived. Loomis felt a warm relief, looking forward to being with Amonee in Nairobi in less than a week's time.

* * *

The Merc kicked up a cloud of dust as they raced towards Lodwar. Loomis, rather than occupying his own Land Rover, chose to stand in the lorry bed with his gang of men, banging the roof of the cab in time to the dirty song they were all singing. It was break time. Loomis, to celebrate the occasion, had broken open one of the gallons of chang'aa which he had been keeping since the day they were forfeited to him, saving it for just such an occasion. By now they were all feeling real good, and best of all, they had money. The most determined of them would try to make their way down-country to their village homes. The rest would blow their money in town.

Loomis himself would catch the company plane and fly to Nairobi.

The lorry screeched to a stop at the town's crude roundabout. Loomis jumped down from the bed, and along with Shigoli, Ben, and Wafula, headed over to Ngonda Bar, going through to the back courtyard and entering one of the thatched booths they had outside. A skinny Somali seated in the adjacent booth, chewed on his *miraa*, and studied them keenly as they came in. The Somali, despite the stiffling heat, was dressed in a suit.

"Habari Mzungu," he said to Loomis as the latter took his seat.

"Mzuri Mwafrika," Loomis returned. He didn't like being addressed as mzungu, certainly not in the smug tone the stranger had used. He ordered four beers from an expectant waiter and fell into conversation with his comrades, ignoring the fellow.

The Somali rose from his place and walked towards Loomis. He spoke up again. "You use this?" he asked, offering some miraa sticks.

"Sometimes." Loomis accepted a couple and put them in his mouth.

"Nice, eh? It is the beer of Muslims." He had a long, horse-shaped face, which was made to look even longer by his hawk-like nose. His eyes were needle slits, his curly jet-black hair cut in the style of a policeman. His presence was unnerving. "Are you the people drilling for water?"

"Ndio," Loomis answered.

"Find any?"

"One well so far looks good. But this is mostly test work."

"Buy me a soda," the Somali abruptly requested.

"You're sitting here and you can't afford a soda?"

"Pay is late. Life is very hard here for a civil servant."

"Oh, really? What do you do?"

"Police. CID." CID was the Criminal Investigation Department. "My name is Rashid." The Somali placed his hand in the inside of his suit jacket and produced his identification.

The waiter reappeared with the beers.

"And one Coke," Loomis added, as the waiter opened his bottle.

"Sprite," interjected Rashid.

"Catch any crooks lately?" Loomis asked facetiously when the waiter left.

"I'm on a case now. There's a Ugandan woman staying here in one of the rooms. Doesn't have an entry permit. I'm about to arrest her."

"Oh good, I feel safe already, knowing you guys are on the job."

The waiter came back with the Sprite, placed it on the table, and violently popped the cap off.

"I have a nephew here with me," Rashid said. "He's looking for work. You give him a job?"

"Sorry. We get our casual labor from the Catholic mission, and they're paid with food. And they're only taking destitute Turkana. If he wants permanent work, tell him to see the office in Nairobi. I'll give you the address if you like."

"No, I thought you could..."

"Sorry."

Rashid went back to his booth and sat quietly after that, drinking his soda until he finished it, at which point he got up, taking his miraa. "If you'll excuse me."

"Certainly. Go ahead and do your duty."

"We shall meet again another day," he said. Was that a cloaked threat?

"No doubt."

When the Somali was gone, Shigoli bent his head close to Loomis's ear. "Be careful of him. I hear he's a bad one. Always looking for 'chai.'"

"Ah, fuck him. Let's make a toast. To two weeks of rest and relaxation!"

They clinked bottles.

NAIROBI, JANUARY 1979

He knocked and the door swung open.

She stood in the doorway, her amber eyes dazzling, her lips opened to reveal her ivory-white teeth. Her black downy hair was brushed back into a frizzy ball-like bun at the back of her head. She was wearing a white sleeveless blouse that bared her charcoal-colored arms and a pink skirt that ended just above her knees. "Hi!"

"Hello," he said, holding something behind his back. He turned away from her as he entered so she couldn't see it.

"What are you holding there?"

"A present. For you." He presented it to her. It was a doll made out of goatskin, dressed as a Turkana female.

"It's lovely!" she declared, taking it with both hands and closing the door with her backside. She looked at him, beaming. "I'm sorry I don't have any gift for you." She was fibbing. She did, but now was not the time to give it to him. Besides, it was a surprise.

"Dinner would be appropriate enough."

"Oh, before I forget, I better turn the oven off." Putting the doll on the kitchen counter, she did just that, and then went over to the sink to run the taps. "This place is a mess. I didn't expect you to come quite so early," she apologized. Her voice was shaky, exposing her excitement. As if seeking refuge, she involved herself with the dirty dishes, commencing to wash a plate as the sink filled up with water.

Loomis stood close behind her. "I couldn't wait," he said in a low tone that was deliberately seductive. He drew nearer to her until he was close enough to smell the scent of shampoo on her hair.

"How is the job going?" she asked, still involved with her dish, the sink filling up quickly.

"I don't want to talk about work right now."

Amonee could feel his breath on the nape of her neck, and her hands, originally active in scrubbing, moved slower and slower about the plate until she was simply holding it. She began to tremble.

Loomis spun her around and kissed her, his body pressing hers against the sink. She opened her mouth and put her arms around him, her right hand still in possession of the plate she had been washing. Her tongue greeted his and she could taste the hot soft wetness of his mouth. Her head swam, her pulse raced, and she got the feeling she was soaring out of her body. She felt light, she felt airborne, then she felt...wet.

"Oh my goodness!" she cried, dropping the plate which fell to the floor with a crash of porcelain. She whirred around to shut off the faucets but it was too late, the overflowing water from the sink had already begun spilling onto the floor.

"The only room I haven't seen in this house is the bedroom," he whispered, undaunted by the minor chaos that had taken place. "Don't you think it's time you showed it to me? We can eat later."

She agreed.

* * *

No, it was never like this before.

Not for him, not for her.

He took his time, relishing the ecstasy of just being inside her. Then came the delicious frustration of not being able to get close enough, deep enough; being filled with a powerful urge to envelope her in his desire and to be enveloped in hers. He gazed at her face, now even more beautiful in the act of love-giving. "You're so..." he murmured, "...so...oh..." his mouth worked upon hers, their bodies in harmonic motion, "...lovely."

"Oh, Daryl..." she sighed. She was enjoying it. Actually enjoying it.

Before long, muffled moans and cries of delight were replaced by sharp grunts and gasps of surrender.

Afterwards, both of them were unable to move. He remained lying upon her, their legs entwined, their bodies tingling all over, and they soon fell into a dreamy sleep as she stroked his back. They never got to eat the roast chicken she had made.

Morning. Sunlight, through yellow curtains, lit up the room. Next to him in the bed, Amonee was sleeping on her side, her right hand by her mouth, her left arm extended toward the bedpost, legs poised like a runner in mid-stride, and which peeked out like polished ebony from under the coverlet that was rumpled chaotically across the bed. The soft sable curve of her hip rose sensually from under a pink sheet. She really was lovely.

She stirred, then turned and opened her eyes. "Good morning," she whispered.

"The best. The best morning of my life."

She smiled and ran her hands through the little nubs of hair on his chest.

"I can't believe it," Loomis declared.

"Believe what?"

"That I'm here with you."

"Neither can I."

"No, I mean someone like me with someone like you."

"Why do you say that?" Her voice was soothing, consoling, like a mother with a troubled child.

"Well, I just don't...well...seem like the type of person you would ordinarily be with."

"Why do you say that?" she repeated louder, this time showing genuine surprise.

"Amonee, what do you really think of me?"

"Oh, I think you are a warm, friendly person, open with people, happy, compassionate, good with children, you're handsome, you have beautiful green eyes, and..." She paused, and her mouth formed a demure smile.

"And what?"

She closed her eyes in modesty. "You know how to make love very nicely," she whispered.

"I can't take credit for that. It takes two to tango. You inspired me."

"What do you think of me?" she asked, with deep curiosity.

"I think you're the greatest cure for lung cancer ever discovered."

"What?"

"I haven't had a cigarette since I left Nairobi."

She laughed. "You know, we never got to eat the special dinner I made last night."

"You give me more than enough nourishment," he said, slipping his arms around her.

She placed her fingertip on his mouth, letting him nibble it.

"You're so beautiful, I can't stand it," he told her. Then, after more nibbling of her finger, he said, "You know, it's funny how we met."

"It doesn't matter. We met and I'm glad."

"I mean, I didn't have to interfere that day. Knowing you, there wasn't much chance of you following that rogue, you would have given him a lecture like you did me and told him to bring the money to the police. But you'd be surprised how many people fall victim to their own greed. How was I to know you were all that virtuous?"

"Mmmm," she purred, once again playing with his chest hair. "I'm not all that virtuous."

Loomis was in a mood for baring all. "I stepped in because I thought I could get a chance to seduce you."

"And you've succeeded. Aren't you clever," she added in a playful tone.

"You know what I'm saying. If you were a man I wouldn't have bothered. I was on the make."

"I knew that."

"You did?"

"Of course. I'm not that naive. Men flirt with me all the time. They use the flimsiest excuses."

"So then, you also figured out why I gave my seat up to that old lady in the matatu?"

"That too!" she exclaimed with an expression that reproached him. "I'm disappointed. And the thief as well, I suppose?"

"It was definitely his good fortune that you were there with me. It's you that makes me do all these crazy things. You have a positive effect on me."

But she already knew that. "Mmmm, I don't have to tell you what effect you have on me." She slithered underneath him and kissed him. Then they made morning love.

* * *

She rubbed her cheek against his, feeling the bristle scratching her.

"Where are your parents from?"

"Were from," he corrected her. "They're dead now."

"Sorry."

"Actually, I'm adopted."

She raised her head, looking at him, somewhat taken aback.

"The people who adopted me, were, and still are, very good people, but I was a bit of a bad boy."

"I can believe that."

"Even now, I only call them a few times a year. They're very disappointed that I spend my time in Africa. They want me to come back." A deliberate pause. "I have to confess, I'm not very good at reciprocating love."

"Only when you want to. You're just afraid."

"I see. So what makes you the expert?"

"I understand, because I'm also afraid."

A pregnant pause.

"I've already told you enough for one morning," he complained lightheartedly. "What about you? I know nothing about you except that you're the most wonderful person I've ever met."

"Well, I was born on a shamba in Malakisi, the seventh of eight children, two sisters and five brothers. I did very well in primary school, so well that my father sent me to Loreto Convent High School..." She stopped and suddenly put on a grave face. "I was raped when I was eleven."

Another heavy silence.

"I'm sorry." The thought that someone could have hurt her in that way was overwhelming, and he found his eyes becoming moist.

"I've never told anyone. Only my family knows."

Her admission made him reveal his own ghosts.

"My father killed himself after my mother died giving birth to me."

"Oh, Daryl."

"I guess everyone has a few skeletons in the closet. Anyway, we shouldn't let the past rule our future." He paused, wanting to change the subject. "Amonee is such a beautiful name."

"Thank you. I was named after my grandmother, on my mother's side. She was a very special person, kind of a...I don't know, like a prophet. She was highly respected in the village and everyone used to go to her for advice."

"The name suits you. You're also special."

"Thank you again." She loved it when he complimented her, though she still didn't know why. She kissed him lightly on the lips. "Oooh, it's ten o'clock already," she announced, glancing above him at her alarm clock.

"So?"

"I feel so guilty and lazy lying in bed for so long."

"It's Saturday today!" he suddenly declared. "Let's go to the football match."

"Oh, Daryl, I can't go to the stadium."

"Why not?"

"In all my years in Nairobi I've never entered inside."

"What kind of reason is that? There's always a first time for anything."

"You know what I mean. I don't like being with rowdy crowds."

"There won't be any rowdiness today, it's an international match, Kenya versus Zambia. Everybody will be rooting for the same team."

"If you say so. I'm in your hands," she said, smiling compliantly. "What time is the match?"

"In the afternoon, plenty of time yet. Time enough to eat that chicken!"

* * *

They attended the match, an exciting one right down to the wire, and when Kenya's Harambee Stars scored the winning goal in the final minutes, the crowd danced in triumphant jubilation, Loomis and Amonee leaping among them. She thanked him for taking her, it was truly a good idea, for she had had a wonderful time.

The day was still young, he insisted, why not make a night of it and go dancing?

She protested, saying that she had made it a rule to avoid such dubious places.

There's always a first time for anything.

Rowdy crowds?

"Trust me," he assured her.

* * *

The Garden Square was packed. Les Mangelepa was the band for the evening, and the music they played was spicy jumping hot, with a rhythm that rocked relentlessly. The music was translated into motion by the bubbling crowd on the dance floor, where cares and worries were, for the moment, obliterated with every beat. Youths pranced the latest steps in between bobbing couples; all and sundry bouncing with uninhibited felicity, united in their revelry. A stout middle-aged man, his bulk threatening to burst the seams of his suit, amazed Loomis with the skillful movements of his portliness, while his fat mama of a partner shook her pelvis like a nimble maiden at a fertility rite. Another woman, not quite as large, danced zealously with a baby shawled onto her back, and from the look on the infant's face, seemed as if he was enjoying himself just as much his mother. A group of kids, girls and boys from five to ten years old, jerked rhythmically in the corner as Loomis stared incredulously at a paraplegic who rocked and spun his wheelchair in time to the music.

But the person that gave him the most pleasure to watch was Amonee, who, with her eyes closed in rapture and mouth wide with joy, gyrated, rotated, grinded, and made other moves Loomis had never seen before. He was so distracted by her sexy writhing that he forgot about his own steps, and consequently often stumbled into neighboring dancers.

There was to be a short break, the crowd was told, and Loomis and Amonee retired to their table. The band was replaced by recorded music coming over the loudspeakers.

"First time in such a place, huh? The way you dance, my dear, I find that hard to believe."

"It's natural for us," she quipped. "Mind you, you're not bad for an American."

It wasn't long before a slow number was playing over the loudspeakers, a romantic ballad sung by Kenny Rogers.

"Will you dance this one with me?" he asked, putting on an overly fawning face.

"Yes".

They danced in each other's arms, slowly revolving like the glimmering mirror ball suspended above them, their faces snuggled into each other's shoulders. It was a Kenny Rogers love song, 'Crazy.' Never before had the words to a love song have any relevance for him, but now they did.

'Crazy, crazy in love with you'.

Was he crazy? Was he in love? Or maybe it was the beers? In any case he was ripe for making a bold statement. He lifted his head to look at her. "I think I'm in love with you, Amonee."

"Don't say anything," she whispered.

* * *

Loomis woke up, surprised at the lack of hangover, and noticed he was alone in the bed.

"Hey, sleepy head! Are you awake yet?" came Amonee's voice from the hall. She followed her question into the bedroom dressed in her robe and carrying a silver tray covered by a gleaming silver dome. "I lied," she confessed. "I do have a gift for you."

He sat up, and when Amonee placed the tray on his lap, he lifted the cover, revealing a neat pile of fried samosas. "How did you? ...When did you? ..."

"They were already made. I had them in the freezer. The children made them for you. They remembered the time in Uhuru Park when you bought them all samosas, and they felt they should reciprocate. And they know how you love samosas."

"I bet it was your idea."

Her response to that was a grin and a wink. Then she went into her bureau and pulled out a parcel from one of its drawers.

"Here's your gift."

"Not the samosas?"

"Another gift."

It was a heavy gift-wrapped package that she handed to him. Tearing the paper away, he saw that it was a book.

"Ah, *Anna Karenina*! Thank you."

She leaned her head towards him and their lips met in a wet smack. "Hurry up and eat your samosas," she abruptly ordered. "We have to get dressed."

"For what? Today is Sunday."

"Precisely. Time for church."

"Church?"

"That's right."

"You can't be serious."

"Why not?"

"I haven't been in a church since I was a kid."

"That's not a good reason. Yesterday I went with you to places that you wanted to go to. Now you have to do the same for me."

"But you enjoyed it!"

"Yes, but I didn't think I would before I went."

"Believe me, Amonee, the last place you'll find me in is inside a church."

* * *

The worst part of it all was that she was a Pentecostal. When the whole congregation began their passionate babbling in 'tongues', Loomis felt so awkward that he wanted to excuse himself and leave. Other than that, it wasn't too bad.

"So, how was it?" she asked him as they left the church.

"Interesting. Very interesting."

"I knew you would like it. We'll make a practicing Christian out of you yet."

"Let's not get carried away now." He looked at his watch. "It's one o'clock. Let's say we go somewhere for a bite of roasted meat and a few beers. It's what Sunday afternoons were made for."

"No, we can't. We have choir practice."

"We?"

"Yes, the church choir."

"You're not suggesting..."

"You know, I could really use another baritone."

"Oh no! Just because you got me into church, don't think for a minute I'm ready to sing hymns with a religious choir. Sorry to disappoint you."

* * *

She had a dulcet lilting voice. She sang the lead to their refrain and Loomis, in the middle of the back row, stood out like a coco-colored cookie on top of a chocolate sundae, his mouth wide open singing 'Lord Cleanse my Soul' in Kiswahili. At times she would glance at him and grin happily, and he would grin back. He himself was actually enjoying it; her happiness was his. Besides, the tune wasn't half bad for a religious song.

On the way home they squeezed hands and exchanged quick kisses when no one was around to catch them.

* * *

They were in love, and despite the enchanting clichés surrounding romance, it was no small matter. Being in love is a mind-altering experience, involving biochemical changes in the brain. In a sense, being in love is similar to being intoxicated by drugs. Except for the fact that romantic love is more resilient than the effects of any externally administered drug.

The power of being in love should not be underestimated. Millions of lives have been lost through its potency, from jealous rage, suicidal despondency, to valiant sacrifice. Its intensity, like hunger and thirst, is proportional to the need.

And Loomis and Amonee desperately needed each other.

In Loomis's lovestruck eyes she was a perfect being. She carried her beauty with an uncommon grace, born from an exceptional humility. Her demeanor was breezy and blithesome, with a vibrant flame inside her that emanated outward and transfigured anyone in her presence. He wanted to spend every minute with her, and so he would sit in on her classes, feeling proud of her. At home they would play guitar and sing along, or just listen to music. She enjoyed explaining the relationship of the flute to the strings in a Schubert quartet, while he in turn would elucidate upon the fluidity of rhythm in a song by Bokelo.

When he commented about the place she had put the Turkana doll, on top of the piano, she had told him that it was so she could play and sing to her. And that touched him in a way he could not explain.

There were walks in the afternoons, sessions with the kids, evening meals by candlelight, and best of all, blissful moments in bed when he felt he was about to burst with the feeling that he had the whole of the world in his arms; feeling her warmth next to him throughout the night; the erotic murmurings of her delicate breath playing on his arm as she slumbered; and her sweet odor of feminine musk upon a skin as soft as brushed velvet. He delighted in her body and he became intimate with every inch of it. Firm, yet pliant, gently molded, it gave out a host of pleasures ranging from exquisite tenderness to feral lust.

But the most precious gift she gave to him was his own self-worth. Her vision of him was the very image he had always aspired to be. With her, he found himself.

* * *

Amonee felt as if she had been sleeping away her entire twenty-eight years of life, and had just woken up to discover the wonder of being alive. The euphoria she felt colored her every action, and it was impossible to hide this exquisite feeling from Katy, who told her on more than one occasion that she was acting like a giggly schoolgirl.

"I can't help it, and I don't care, it's wonderful. What do you think I should do about it?" she asked her friend as she sat down at her desk one morning.

"I guess, for now, just go with it, sweetie. But remember, you're seeing him through rose-colored glasses. Try to remember your impressions when you first met him, that might be a more realistic picture."

"But I didn't know him then."

"You still don't." Katy was playing devil's advocate, not only because of her own experience with romance, which had long since proven to her just how deceptive it could be, but also because, in Amonee's case, of the risks involved. And although Katy could not help feeling happy for her friend, she felt it was also her duty to tether her back to the reality of her situation.

"So, what are you going to do about Jon?" she reminded Amonee. "He's not going to take it well at all." Her last comment had an ominous ring to it.

Amonee momentarily came down from her romantic muzziness. "No, he's not," she agreed, taking a seat. "Well, anyway, he won't be here for another five months."

"Well, you do realize that you have to tell him before he arrives."

"Yes, I know," she concurred with a fretful sigh.

* * *

It was the time of *vuli*, the short rains, and for the past week, like clockwork, showers would burst from the sky almost every afternoon. He ushered her quickly into her little red Fiat. They were already soaked.

"Where are we going?" she demanded to know as he shut the door.

"You'll see," he told her, and started the ignition.

He drove along until he found Ngong Road. At Adam's Arcade he made a left turn and drove to the end of the side street, where he pulled into the driveway of a moderately sized, ranch-style house. Just in front of the house, planted about a foot off the ground, was a small sign which read 'Kingozi Language and Cultural Center'.

"I want you to meet some friends of mine," he explained as they got out of the car.

Through the front door they entered the carpeted sitting room, which had been converted to a main office and reception area. At the far end of the room, by the draped terrace windows, was a desk. The young black man occupying it was speaking on the telephone.

"No, baby, don't say that...I told you my father just arrived from upcountry...couldn't get away...maybe Friday...listen, some people have just come in, I'll call you back later...okay?...bye!" Elvis Omondi put the phone down and got up chuckling. "Hey, here he is, Che Guevara...how are you, Che?" He turned towards Amonee. "Did you know that this guy is a revolutionary?"

Loomis put his hand on Amonee's shoulder. "Just another

nickname," he assured her.

"No, really, he likes overthrowing governments. You know, stealing other people's ladies."

"You're never going to forget about that, are you? That girl caught you with another woman, I was just picking up the pieces."

"Just teasing," Omondi explained to Amonee. "We often share ladies, no big deal."

At that moment, the phone rang again. "Excuse me, please," Omondi begged, hurrying back to the phone. He then began to talk in low whispers, leading Loomis to suspect it was another woman.

Okova, with his cap on as usual, entered the room. "Hey, man, what's wrong with you? You come in from the bush, sleep one night, and split. Almost two weeks now."

"Okova, meet Amonee, that lady I told you about."

"Ah, that explains it. Hello sister, Okova Wanyoni, Daryl's roomate."

"Hi," Amonee replied courteously. "Wanyoni, I've heard of that name."

"Maybe you're thinking of my brother, he's a big-shot Nairobi lawyer," Okova said.

"Yes, perhaps." A look of puzzlement crossed her face. "You two live together?"

"We share a place in Buru Buru," Loomis explained.

"I'd like to see it someday."

From behind his desk, Omondi let out a mischievous laugh. "No, really, that girl was only my relative..."

"You're welcome anytime," Okova told her. "I've got another class, I gotta go now. See you later," he said, going back into the corridor he had come out of.

"...listen, I have some people here...huh?...Kenya Cinema, seven o'clock?...right...see you then." Omondi hung up for the second time.

"Omondi, it looks like you still need somebody like me to help you out with all these ladies," Loomis said.

"No, I'm tough, bwana, I can handle them. So how've you been?

When did you get into town and who's this charming girl you brought? You haven't introduced us yet. Maybe you're afraid of us getting to know each other."

"This is my good friend Amonee. Amonee Emuria."

"Hello, Amonee. What's a woman as beautiful as you doing with this revolutionary? Just wait till he goes out of town." He proffered his hand for shaking. "My name is Elvis Omondi. I'm the managing director of this humble, but distinguished institution."

"Hi."

"I brought her," Loomis told him, "because I thought you might have a need for her."

"Daryl!" Amonee exclaimed, not knowing if she should be shocked.

"We already have enough Kiswahili teachers," Omondi stated.

"Not language, music. She's a music teacher. Don't you have some students who would like to learn some traditional song and dance?"

"Not a bad idea. It's good, a good idea actually. I like it."

"Daryl, really, you should have consulted me first," she complained. "Doesn't anyone want to know if I'm at least interested?"

"You're interested, aren't you?"

"I'm not sure if I'll be able to fit it in my schedule."

"You'll fit it in. You're good at that."

"The only thing is," broke in Omondi, "I'm not sure how much we could pay you. We've only just recently started this place."

"Well, if I decide to do it", she asserted, "I wouldn't do it for money. It would be a novel challenge getting outsiders involved in our culture. It would be fun."

"So you're interested?" Omondi asked, pressing for confirmation.

"Again, I have to see if I have the time."

"Here's my card."

She took the card as the phone trilled once more, and Omondi ran to retrieve the receiver.

"Hello...oh hi, Rachel..."

Loomis headed for the door, cuing Amonee to do the same. Then, in a loud voice, he announced their departure. "WE'RE GOING NOW ELVIS! BYE!"

Omondi cupped the receiver. "So when do we meet?"

"How about tonight, seven o'clock, Kenya Cinema?" That was one thing he and Amonee hadn't done together yet – take in a movie.

"I won't be there."

"But you just made a date with...you told her..."

"That was just to keep her from making any appointments with someone else. I have another date for this evening. Really classy. I'll be at the Six Eighty Hotel at nine."

"Let's go, Che," Amonee, tugging on his arm, said with a giggle. "I have another class at four."

* * *

They were in bed together. It was the same day they had visited Kingozi and the last night before he would go away again.

"Daryl, do you have other girlfriends?" she asked him while he was massaging her back.

"You mean now?" he asked incredulously. "No, only you. Why do you ask?"

She turned her body to lie on her back, so she could face him, her lovely-shaped breasts in full view.

"I know you're a bit of a playboy."

He laughed at the term. "Playboy?"

"A womanizer."

"I was."

"You're not still?"

"Look at me, in the eyes." He stared at her. "What do you think?"

She shook her head 'no', smiling silently.

Then he switched off the night table lamp.

TURKANALAND,
DECEMBER - JANUARY 1980

Images of Turkana.

Open yawning land, dotted with spots of vegetation, watched over by solemn, isolated hills.

Black men sitting, clad in brightly colored blankets, sharing the shade of a single tree with their cattle.

Bare-chested Turkana women in dark leather aprons, their bodies swiveling as they balance the loads on their heads.

Orange sunset light creating a landscape of soft pastels, in earth colors, red, buff, and grey.

Happy dancers, frolicking amidst round grass huts, steeped in a silver moonglow.

Images of Turkana.

For Daryl Loomis, the Hydro-Drill Contract was his third venture into Turkanaland, and these images were coming back to him.

The next stage of the project found them circling around the southwest corner of Moruapolon, the hilly plateau in their company at all times, perpetually in view to their right. Ahead, the shimmering blue shadow of Mount Moroto welled up out of the western horizon from across the Ugandan border. Two weeks had passed since they had come back from their break, and once again they were wandering the landscape of Turkana district, an open, yawning land dotted with spots of vegetation, watched over by solemn, isolated hills.

The country here afforded a greater human population than where they had journeyed previously, the tableland atop the hills offering pasture for their cattle, while the trees and bushes flanking the numerous laagers down below offered browsing prospects for the smaller livestock and wild fruits for the people. Closer contact with the local inhabitants would soon be inevitable.

The work had fallen into an orderly routine; from past experience they could now anticipate potential problems in advance; the flow of supplies from Nairobi became more dependable, mainly due to the chat Loomis had had with the office during his stay in Nairobi, and Ezekiel, along with the Mercedes, turned out to be a godsend – their shuttling between Lodwar and the sites proved to be a more than reliable supply line. Also, the Turkana laborers grew more proficient in their tasks – Loomis could even detect a sense of pride in their work – and better yet, the ones they now had were there to stay and had no intentions of running away. Even the machines had become more cooperative, for there were no major breakdowns. But the country was rough, and the construction of access roads took up most of their time and slowed their progress. Loomis accepted this and expected the office to do so as well.

When the troop arrived at the site of borehole number seven they were tired, hot, and grimy. The spot was located quite close to a homestead that sat on the opposite banks of a laager, and a group of Turkanas stood inquisitively watching as the strangers set up their camp. Loomis sent McKracken over to explain the presence of many men with big lorries.

"They want to know why we need such a large machine to dig a well when we have enough people here to dig ten wells," McKracken said when he returned.

"Never mind that. Did you tell them about the generator and drilling at night?" Loomis asked as he banged in a tent peg.

"No, I didn't tell them."

"You better. The noise tonight might upset them. Here, hold this," Loomis requested, holding out the corner of a flysheet.

McKracken took hold of the canvas. "They are already upset."

"What do you mean upset? Upset about what?"

"You have to beg permission. A family uses this part of the laager."

Loomis ceased his activity with the flysheet. "Huh? I didn't think that the Turkana owned any land except as a tribe. It's communal, isn't it? Everyone here is free to roam wherever they like. Is that not so?"

"Not on a laager during dry season. Everyone has their own piece, only enough for their own needs. Not owning, but we call it 'ekwar'."

"So I have to ask permission to drill a borehole here?"

"Ndio."

"Oh well, when in Rome," Loomis wistfully reflected in English. "Alright, help me finish setting up my tent, and later we'll pay them a visit."

In the early evening the pair set out to see the caretaker of the *ekwar* in the company of two young local men who, as they walked, held their thin herding sticks braced behind their necks, their right hands simultaneously clutching their *ekicholongs*. Their wrists were encircled by their razor-sharp *abaraits*, their forearms and biceps bedecked by arm rings of iron and colored plastic. One had his hair done up in the traditional coiffure – threaded hair weaved in intricate patterns, and plastered with blue-dyed mud in two patches, front and rear, forming a parting which ran across his head from ear to ear. The other wore a floppy, green safari hat. Their lean, charcoal-black legs moved in long hasty strides underneath the garb of their blankets.

They climbed up the bank and onto a stony promontory where the Turkana home had been made: a circular fence of piled thorn brush enclosing several huts – squat round bubbles of meshed branches in various sizes covered with animal hides; one, only an open ring without a roof. As they approached the largest hut, an old man emerged from within, holding a walking stick that was more for prestige than use, and beckoned the visitors to enter. Loomis had to stoop to enter, and was relieved they didn't have to go into one of the smaller dwellings, as he would have had to crawl in. The inside of this one was airy and dappled with the sunlight filtering through the framework of branches. Several cow-skin mats covered most of the dirt floor. Back along the stick walls sat ornamented Turkana women with their tonsured children, while above them hung vessels of goatskin, gourd shells, and hollowed-out wood in assorted shapes and sizes. A musky odor of meat and untanned leather, pungent but not too unpleasant, flavored the air. It was a smell Loomis would get used to; it was the very smell of Turkana life.

The old man toothed a smile that lacked the lower front teeth as he clasped Loomis's right hand. "*Ejok!*"

"*Ejok!* Good!" reciprocated Loomis.

"*Naa?*" the Turkana asked with a jerk of the foreigner's hand.

Loomis, familiar with this routine, made the appropriate response. "*Payaa!*"

"*Naa?*"

"*Payaa!*"

"*Naa?*"

"*Payaa!*"

"*Mata?* How is it?"

Instead of replying to the man's question, Loomis asked his own. "*Mata abero?* How are the wives?"

"*Mata ibaren?* How are your animals?"

"*Mata nawi?* How is the home?"

"*Mata ide?* How are the children?"

They continued this interrogation of one another, answering questions with other questions, until the old man broke off with a chuckle. It was a common greeting game, played among mature Turkana men, and it helped to bring their meeting to an amiable start, the aged tribesman showing amusement at this peculiar outsider who knew how to play it.

The guests found places on the cowhide while the two youths who had escorted them sat by the doorway on their ekicholongs. McKracken produced a large lump of tobacco and handed it to the old man, the act a symbol of respect and good manners. After that, the discussion commenced as the old man distributed a bit of the leaf to the two young warriors. McKracken did most of the talking with the help of a few interjections by Loomis, but it soon became obvious that the Turkana did not buy the story about digging a well.

"Your machine must do something terrible, not just make a hole in the ground. I have seen it to be many times the size of an *ekal*!" An ekal was what they were sitting inside of: the largest hut in a Turkana home where visitors were entertained.

"The hole it makes is very deep," McKracken explained.

"Drop a stone in it, count to three before it lands," Loomis added in broken Kiturkana, another of his useful interjections. McKracken repeated this statement, this time touching up on the grammar.

"Why so deep? The water here is less than the length of a man from the surface. Or do you think you will reach a place where the water does not finish, even in times of great drought? Enough to water all the animals of Turkana from this one well?"

"Don't know," Loomis answered. "Want to know. We look, we see."

"You must be clever. Perhaps I should be wary of your cleverness."

"He is not a person who will do you harm," vouched McKracken.

"Me friend," Loomis assured.

In the end the old man agreed to their request, finally convinced that they were only going to make a deep hole and then leave it. Leaving it unused was an important condition, for perhaps such a well would suck the land dry, and all the other shallow wells would be finished.

But after Loomis had reckoned the matter settled, McKracken and the Turkana patriarch became engaged in what sounded like a mild argument. The only words Loomis could pick out were 'emong', meaning a castrated bull, and 'aite', a mulch cow. The argument or debate or whatever it was, was punctuated by a lot of headshaking and exclamations such as lo! woi-ta-koit! awaa!

McKracken and the ekwar owner signaled the end of their discussion by getting up, and Loomis did likewise. The two visitors then departed amidst spirited farewells.

"It's all settled now," McKracken declared as they walked along the laager back to camp. "Only one ox. At first he also wanted two milking cows, but that is because he thinks you are very rich. Even an ox is too much. Usually it is only a goat or two."

"What? What are you saying?"

"You must give him an ox in return for using his ekwar."

"Where the hell am I going to get an ox from?" Loomis asked querulously in English.

McKracken, taking an example from Loomis, dropped his Kiswahili to answer in English. "He knows home not par away, and they hap an ox the old man want. They call the owner."

"How much does an ox cost around here?"

"Very cheef, it is dry season now. We get a good frice. Maybe pipe hundred shillings."

"Five hundred? I hope this doesn't occur too often. I didn't put things like this in the budget."

The next afternoon, after the completion of the pilot hole, they returned to the homestead responding to the summons that the ox and its owner had arrived and the presence of Loomis, together with his money, was needed to conclude the deal.

The naked boy who delivered the beast wanted two thousand shillings for it. McKracken protested indignantly. Loomis sighed in resignation. It appeared the eunuch bull wasn't the only one they had gotten by the balls. He couldn't help suspecting that he had been set up.

One hour went by, and despite a lot of heated babbling and theatrical body language, the price remained the same.

"Listen, McKracken, tell the old man that I have only eight hundred shillings to buy it with. Anything more than that, we'll forget the whole thing and move on. Then he'll be out of an ox. We won't drill here, that's all. Leave it up to him to bargain with the boy."

The old man needed only ten minutes to persuade the youth. Eight hundred shillings. Agreed.

"The old man is perry fleased," McKracken informed his boss.

"The old man has asked us to stay awhile. They are frefaring some milk."

"What sort of milk?" asked Loomis, knowing that the Turkana had about ten different ways of preparing it.

"*Echarakan.*"

They were made to wait in the ekal while the aged Turkana remained outside examining his new ox. Sitting in the hut, Loomis looked at the children. They were staring with wide curious eyes, their mouths agape, faces encrusted with mucous and flies. To get some reaction out of them, he pointed to things around them shouting the names of them in their language, which caused them to look at each other and giggle, before they repeated after him. Predictably, they imitated him in this game, choosing their own objects. The naked boys and their half-naked sisters shouted out words, inducing Loomis to repeat after them, causing the kids to laugh. The girls were their mothers in miniature with little goatskin aprons, and the row of stringy braids which ran down the middle of their otherwise bare scalps. The boys' heads were also shaven, save for a single isolated tuft of hair at the back. All of them were adorned with colored necklaces and bracelets, the older girls displaying the *akiromwa*, a heaping pile of beads that covered their necks.

The old man came in, sat on his ekicholong, and was followed by two teenage girls, each carrying an 'alapach', a traditional bowl made from a small, hollowed-out log. As they placed the bowls in front of him, Loomis found himself unintentionally distracted by their freely swinging breasts: full, firm, and with the largest nipples he had ever seen.

"*Tonyam!* Eat!" cried out an elderly woman sitting in the corner, her wizened face stretched tight in a maternal grin. A cascading array of arrow-shaped earrings ran down the length of her ears, from the top down to the lobe, and they swung like miniature wind chimes whenever she moved her head. Her deflated breasts were draped over a wrinkled pot belly; her bony legs jutted out from a cow-skin apron decorated with rectangular patches of gaily colored beads and bits of ostrich eggshell. She looked to be the senior wife.

Loomis returned the smile and looked down at his food: a pink, pasty mixture of curdled milk and blood, the blood obtained from a harmless incision the Turkana make on the neck of a cow. Using a stick whittled flat to serve as a spoon, he shoveled the stuff into his mouth, inciting profuse laughter, with the women and children making high-pitched sounds of glee.

"You are a Turkana!" the old man declared.

Loomis found it unnecessary to disclose that he had already sampled echarakan some years back.

The day was ending, the sun poised over a brown skyline ready to swallow it up, and shadows became long and stretched. Loomis had stayed longer than he had planned, and he felt slightly guilty about it, for he had never been away from site for such duration except when he had to make a trip to Lodwar. But everyone in the home had been in such a merry mood, and eager to know all about their visitor. The Turkanas liked to talk and banter and joke – it was their main recreational activity, and understandably so, since out here there were no bars, cinemas, discos, not even a radio to relax by, and conversation, along with dancing, was the only way to enjoy the time.

Standing outside, he watched the goat herd returning home from their daylong browsing, and listened to the bleating of the newly calved she-goats responding to the cries of their kids locked in the kraal. The Turkanas did not allow the offspring to go out with their mothers, apparently to ensure that the goats would not wander away on their own, and also to manage the milk production, which Loomis was about to witness. The baby goats, upon being let out, trotted anxiously among the adult animals, searching and calling forlornly for their mothers. This was the time for milking, a job for girls and small boys. As soon as a baby goat found its mother, it would begin suckling, poking and jabbing at the teats, providing the opportunity for the Turkana child to grab hold of another of the teats and milk into a tin can or a gourd shell. Each child had their own goats which he or she alone was supposed to milk, a rule Loomis soon discovered as he watched a little boy cry in complaint because another had attempted to milk his. The whole scene, children and animals in the subdued light of dusk, filled him with a strange tranquility.

McKracken appeared at his side. "We go back now?"

"Haya, twende. I have a lot of reports to write tonight."

That night, before turning in, Loomis picked up the copy of *Anna Karenina* that Amonee had given him, opened it to page one, and began to read.

* * *

They had just finished reaming and it was time to place the linings in. Loomis was having a short discussion with Shigoli concerning the depth at which to put the screens when McKracken interrupted them.

"The old man is sick," he reported. "He would like you to come."

"Wait for me by the tent," Loomis ordered.

Leaving instructions with his drill crew, Loomis, at mid-morning, let McKracken take him back to the home. Upon reaching the ekal, they found many people seated inside, who, surprisingly, were not paying any attention to the sick old man who was lying down behind them, but rather had their eyes fixed on another elderly, half-naked, hoary gentleman who was sitting at the head of their group. McKracken motioned to his comrade to sit down. "They've brought in an *emurun*," he explained.

An emuron was something akin to a seer in Turkanaland, and they were classed according to the particular method each employed to obtain their mysterious revelations. One could have dreams, toss sandals, or read dry tobacco leaves. The one present in the ekal at the moment was of the latter category, Loomis surmised, as he watched the stranger unwrap a small bundle of brown paper, the contents of which he subsequently let drop to the floor. The seer stared silently into the rust-colored heap at his feet, then he picked up a small twig and used it as a pointer as he spoke, much in the manner of a university lecturer pointing to the blackboard. The words out of his mouth came slowly, clearly, and Loomis was able to follow some of it, with McKracken filling in the rest.

"This is the home, do you see it?" he asked the gathering. "This is the ekal, that, the ekai..." He went on listing the various huts of the sick man's home, poking at some of the lumpier, darker leaves. "There is no bull in the middle of the compound, so it is not serious. He will not die."

Everyone looked up at the seer in silence, with one of the daughters heaving a sigh of relief.

The soothsayer wrinkled his brow in sapient concentration and went on. "But look here, do you see?"

They all craned their necks to get a better view at what he was pointing at.

"You see it?" he prompted. "Right here. See how the tobacco spreads out, that lighter spot here?"

"Yes, yes," answered some of the people sitting closest.

"That is the krall, the gate is open, and it is empty."

"Aaah," gasped a few of the women.

The emuron continued to look at the tobacco, and as he saw more things the participation of the group increased.

"This man has had these afflictions from time to time since the end of the last rains, and was soon thereafter taken to the white man's hospital. Is this not true?"

"Eeee, it is true, woi-ta-koit!" they exclaimed in turn. "How did you know?" asked one. They were surprised, for the emuron had come to this area only a few days ago.

"But before this sickness gripped him, he had quarreled with his brother-in-law. Is this not also true?"

"Awaa, that is also true," said the eldest wife.

"Look at this!" the seer commanded, excited, jabbing the twig in short bursts at the pile of tobacco. "Oih, oih...mmmm..." he paused, preparing the crowd for his latest disclosure, now making little circles in the air with his tiny stick. "The brother-in-law is named Lotethro, and last breeding season many of his she-goats aborted, and he became very bitter..."

This last statement precipitated a rousing discussion, and when Loomis asked McKracken to translate, the latter told him to wait, he would explain later. Loomis sat quietly and impatiently throughout the rest of the meeting, which by now had become incomprehensible to him. A half hour went by before the visiting pair got up, wished the old man a speedy recovery, and trooped back to borehole number seven.

After several minutes of walking in silence, Loomis eagerly demanded a summary of what had taken place.

"The old man has been cursed," McKracken told him. "His brother-in-law cursed him."

"I never heard of Turkanas practicing witchcraft."

"We don't."

"So then how could anybody put a curse on someone?"

"The brother-in-law was jealous because the old man's goats gave birth to many young that season. He blamed the old man for taking the best pasture, and in anger, wished bad things would happen to him."

"And that alone is enough to curse somebody, just to wish bad things on him?" Loomis asked in puzzlement.

"Yes."

* * *

The construction of the well completed, it was now time to test pump it. Many of the local Turkanas, as well as the crew, formed a ring around the well, and waited in anticipation as the compressor bellowed to a start. A spattering of drops was followed by a horizontal spout of water pissing out of the discharge tee, at first dirty brown, then glistening clear, and the local men fell into a lively discussion, apparently in praise of the cleverness of the outsiders. They stared disbelievingly at the water until eventually some of the braver ones ventured up to it and tasted it from their cupped hands, cackling in merry astonishment to the amusement of the down-country drillers. The well was pumped the rest of the day and throughout the night, the water never showing any signs of diminishing.

In the morning they broke camp in a hurry and Loomis, anxious to be on the way, did not return to the homestead to say goodbye, and consequently never did find out if the old man had recuperated.

It took a while to load the trucks, and by the time they had finished an early, rushed lunch, the sun was already high overhead. Climbing into his Land Rover, Loomis couldn't help but feel a strange affinity to the Turkana, some of whom lingered behind to wave goodbye. Here he was, in a land of roaming nomads whose history was comparatively timeless, and yet, they too, the Hydro-Drill team, with their wonderful machines of the technological age, had become wanderers themselves, drifting from borehole to borehole. He chuckled quietly to himself, amazed that he could have such lofty reflections after the hectic activity of the morning. "Haya, let's move out!" he shouted from the window.

Unbeknown to Loomis, he had already acquired a nickname in the village which would soon spread throughout the district.

The way to the ninth borehole was up the grade of the same laager they had been in, and they took a route just outside of the heavy vegetation on the banks. The Turkana and their herds were ubiquitous, and in the heat of the day they could be seen; black men sitting, clad in brightly colored blankets, sharing the shade of a single tree with their cattle. Camels, whenever the noisy convoy got too near, would cease their indolent browsing and lope panic-stricken down into the laager.

Not all of their time on the journey was spent driving and looking at the scenery. Much of it was taken up by bush clearing, maneuvering through trees, and towing the rig over rough sections. Two days, one night, and eleven miles later, they once again built up their mobile homes.

* * *

It was time for Greenbottom to make another visit and the Land Rover was sent to pick him up. When it returned in the evening, he jumped out to find Loomis by the working drill rig, stooping over and examining the rock cuttings. Daryl looked up, and wiping his hands on his trousers, rose to greet him. "Hello, Reg," he said smiling, his voice lost in the din the Dando was making.

"HOW DEEP?" shouted Greenbottom above the noise.

"SEVENTY-TWO METERS!" he shouted back.

Greenbottom, with arms folded, stood watching on as the site boss issued orders, conferred with Shigoli, and then peered through a pocket lens at handfuls of mud. At last Loomis signaled for the drill rods to be taken up, and turning, escorted Greenbottom to the tents.

"Doesn't look too bad," Greenbottom remarked. "You seem to be rather more organized now."

"Well, you know how it is, these things always get off to a slow start. It'll pick up from this point on."

"Not enough I fear. We'll never make the deadline at this rate. I'm going to suggest to Cecil that we request an extension of time. We don't have much choice. Abominable access, simply abominable."

"I'm glad you can appreciate the problems we're having," Loomis said, suddenly feeling a bit better about Greenbottom. Maybe he wasn't such a stuffy bastard after all. "You must be tired. I'll tell Mutua to prepare your tent and get you some grub. We're having goat meat *ala* Juma tonight." And then, before Greenbottom could make any comment, he quickly added, "Of course we don't eat meat every night, what with our limited budget. We slaughtered it on the occasion of your arrival." He chuckled naughtily under his breath.

That night Loomis stayed up late updating reports, sorting out the accounts, and all the other work that had been neglected over the previous few days. As he scribbled on and filed pieces of paper, he listened intermittently to a serenely haunting sound rising over the throb of the generator, and audible only when the rig was throttled back to pull out the drill rods: a chant that was rising and falling to a rhythmic clapping, supplemented by lots of laughing. Somewhere the Turkana were having a dance. This inspired Loomis to write a letter to Amonee. Even after he had finished writing, and gone to bed, the sound continued to travel through the night air, competing in time between the strident husky growls of the machines.

The next morning, after a six o'clock breakfast, Greenbottom entered the office caravan and found Loomis working on some sort of diagram. He sat down on the extra chair provided for visitors.

"Good morning, Reginald."

"Good morning."

"Sleep well?"

"How could I with all that racket going on."

"Yeah, the rig at night takes some getting used to."

"That wasn't what bothered me. It was all that bloody screaming and shouting, laughing and whooping, and all those clattering sounds and jingling bells."

"Oh. Just the Turkana dancing."

"Sounded like a bloody riot."

Loomis handed him the diagram. "According to this new schedule, which is based on our current rate of execution, we will need an extra sixty days to complete the contract."

"Hum. The client is going to put up a fight. That's a twenty-five percent increase."

"I've also written a report detailing the reasons."

"Well, we'll give it a try. The EEC have been known to attach stringent conditions and then ease up. At least they have shown some flexibility in the past. And Cecil can be pretty tough if he has to. Anyway, this is exactly the sort of thing we need to have any argument at all," Greenbottom said as he returned the diagram. "Let's have a look at your accounts now."

He pulled his chair over as Loomis handed him the books, receipts, and vouchers, then, putting on his reading glasses, proceeded to go through each entry one by one. Loomis retired to the other side of the mobile office, the radio side, and worked on a geological cross section on another small table, attempting to correlate the strata they had encountered in the boreholes thus far drilled.

A half hour later, Greenbottom asked loudly, "What is this? 'One ox for use of ekwar – eight hundred shillings'?" He held up a petty-cash voucher and waved it in the air.

"Oh that. Well, you see, the Turkana have this arrangement of sharing the dry season resources of a laager. A sort of traditional land-management scheme. It's called ekwar – some kind of user rights system. I had to pay to set up on the last borehole, to buy the rights you might say."

"That's uncalled for! Don't these people know we're here for their benefit? We'll have to charge the client for such things. It's one of our standard clauses, good thing we included it, but whoever thought we'd have needed it. It is the obligation of the client to obtain permission for access, but God knows they're going to laugh at this one. Hmmph! Dealing with people right out of the Stone Age."

Another half-hour later, while still working with their backs to each other, Loomis absentmindedly began a conversation.

"The other day I witnessed an interesting event. A man was ill in the village, and they sent for this guy who diagnosed the problem by reading tobacco leaves."

"Superstitious balderdash," retorted Greenbottom without looking up.

"To tell you the truth, I was impressed. He knew a lot of things about the people there, even though he was new to the place. Said the man was cursed."

"Ignorant savages," came the mumbled reply from behind. "Didn't they ever hear of doctors?"

Loomis turned in his chair only to be met by Greenbottom's back. "He was taken to a mission hospital in Lorogumu, and they couldn't help him," he continued. "But I don't think the idea of the thing is actually medical, at least not the way I see it. A curse to them is to have exceptionally ill feelings towards someone. These clairvoyants are like the keepers of morality so to speak. They're good at picking up local gossip, especially about people quarreling. They keep quiet about it until they're called in, then they expose it publicly. It reminds people not to be bitter or envious of one's neighbor, and I think it helps to maintain order in their society. I mean, for us, we have the Ten Commandments, heaven and hell, and a formal legal system, and the Turkana have these seers, who seem to be on top of things."

Greenbottom turned around with a disdainful face. "I think that's a lot of nonsense. Did you read that in a book some thesis-hungry fool wrote?"

Loomis gave up conversation and went back to his sketch.

The following day Greenbottom was due to catch the company plane and Loomis offered to drive him, hoping to accomplish a few errands in Lodwar and to re-read, review, and eventually post his letter to Amonee, but hoping even more that he would find a letter from her waiting for him at the mission. The drive was tiring and the pair did not converse much, but as they drew closer to Lodwar, Loomis brought up a subject he hadn't the confidence to bring up previously.

"What do you think of the crew? They work well, don't they?" he asked Greenbottom above the roar and the rattle of the Land Rover.

"From what I saw, they are performing as they are expected to."

"Well, they're a good bunch and they're living under tough conditions, tougher than most contracts. They've been pretty cooperative."

"Should they not be?"

"What I'm trying to say is that if they keep up this way, I'll recommend a generous bonus for them, something a bit above the usual."

"We shall see. By the way, Daryl, I feel I should mention something to you. I've observed the way you behave with the watu, and I think you're a bit too free with them – all this joking in Kiswahili. Don't get too close to an African, especially those you work with, otherwise they'll lose respect. Keep a distance from them, and for heaven's sake don't try and understand them. God knows I've lived here all my life and they still confound me. They look at things in a different way than we do. Remember, you're a foreigner, with European values. Just my advice to you."

"Thanks," Loomis muttered through clenched teeth. And he had just begun to think they might have been able to get along. Thank God he came only once a month.

Sometime after the plane had taken off, Loomis drove over to the mission with the dual purpose of clearing his debts and picking up his mail. At the reception, which was merely a wooden table set to one side of the entrance doorway and attended to by a Turkana girl wearing a gaudily printed dress, he ran into Father Tom.

"Tis Misturr Loomis kummen ta pay us a visit."

"Hello, Father."

The priest put his hand on Loomis's shoulder. "Oh, boy ta wey, te bishop told me tat if I should bey happenin ta see Misturr Loomis, I was ta tell him tat te bishop has gone on a long safari, and it wunt known when he would bey kummen back."

Loomis returned him an embarrassed smirk. "I didn't come for money this time. And anyway, does he think I like coming here to beg? I tell you, my knees are starting to get sore. But you'll be happy to hear that I've come to pay back everything I borrowed so far."

"Great *Akuj* in heaven!" he shouted, using the Turkana word for God. "I tink I can get ta bishop ta return early for tat. You just wait here."

"I thought he went on a long safari?" Loomis reminded, baiting him.

"Only ta his house. Tis a long enuf journey for him, mind ya, at tis age."

The priest departed with a chortle, and Loomis went into the mission's office to check on his mail. Flipping through the envelopes, he found a letter for him which was postmarked ten days before, tore it open, and began to read:

Dear Daryl,

I am missing you so very much and I fear I'll miss you more and more each time you return to Turkana. Since you've been gone I've felt so empty, that I'm lacking something, and this is the first time in my life that I ever felt this way. Of course, you have made me feel a lot of things I never felt before. I am beginning to discover a part of me that I buried some years ago and you are helping to bring it back. I appreciate that.

I've talked to Elvis Omondi and I think we will be able to work something out. I'm starting to get very excited about the Kingozi idea.

Katy says hello. She is sitting across from me now and she knows I'm writing to you even without telling her. She knows how my face looks whenever I think of you. Joyful of course!

I feel bad that you must work on Christmas Day. If there was a phone where you are I would call you so that at least my voice could keep you company. As for me, I won't be totally alone, for I will go home to Bungoma for the holidays. But some big part of me will be lost and pining for you.

I had better close before I say too much. But it's very difficult keeping my mind off you, and I'm strangled by the frustration at being apart. It's hard to work this way, you're very bad for my productivity. What shall I tell the department chairman? Just kidding my sweet!

Please write as soon as you can to let me know if you are alright. Know that I pray every night that you are safe and well. With all my undivided love,

I am yours,

Amonee

After seeing the bishop, Loomis sat in a small hoteli and updated the letter he had composed the other night.

Dear Amonee,

Hello darling.

I'm glad to hear you've missed me, but I apologize for the pain that it brings. You know I miss you just as badly, and this motivates me to work harder to finish this contract as soon as possible, so that afterwards we can have all the time in the world to be together. Even me, I don't feel like a whole person when you're not with me.

Unfortunately this is a tough place to work in and we're going too slow at present. One consolation, however, is the people who live here. The Turkana are very friendly once you get to know them and I find their company refreshing. They seem really laid back, and this is because they know who they are, they are Turkana, and their customs are still intact. They're not confused about their identity like most people down-country. They have yet to pay the price of material advancement. No thugs, prostitutes, nor drunks out here. (Only cattle thieves!) I guess that says a thing or two about the value of preserving one's culture.

Tell Katy I said hello. We had a few chats in the office but I didn't get a chance to know her as well as I should. She seems a nice person.

I have been reading Anna Karenina, *a little bit each night before I go to bed. I find the characters quite intriguing and the woman Anna very desirable (But not as much as you!). Do you think I am like Count Vronsky? I hope not!*

Sorry about your productivity. Try your best, my dear, I know it's hard. If need be, I can write to Dr. Otundo (that is the chairman's name isn't it?) and explain everything. Think he would understand?

I have to go. You should remember that you are always with me in my heart and mind and that helps to keep me going until I see you again.

All my love,

Daryl

P.S. Enjoy Christmas for the both of us

* * *

It was Christmas Day when they arrived at the tenth borehole. The Great Mountain was finally behind them but still present, now showing its northern face. To the northeast there was another, smaller set of hills, actually a serrated ridge with 'U'-shaped notches serially cut into the top, making it look like the jaw of a crocodile. Horizontal ledges of sandstone stuck out through the exiguous cover of vegetation, forming continuous lines which ran the whole length of the ridge.

"Nangolei Achop," McKracken announced, "the Hills of the Baboons."

At night he and the men celebrated their Christmas in the bush with a roasted goat, swallowed down with the second, and part of the third, gallon of chang'aa that Loomis had been keeping for such special occasions.

TURKANALAND,
JANUARY-FEBRUARY, 1980

For nearly a thousand years, the Turkana people lived in the northern Rift Valley, their culture and livelihoods virtually unchanged, rooted in a timelessness that had been practically intractable. It's not that the Turkana were averse to change, it's just that they did not have any cause to consider it. This is what the immutable desert had taught them: persistence – the ever-present wind, the repetitive cycles of day and night, birth and death, the appearance and disappearance of the grass on top of the hills...if there was any certainty to existence, it was that today is like yesterday, and tomorrow will be like today, and life flows on, with you, and without you.

The longer Loomis stayed in Turkanaland, the more familiar he became with the traditions of its people. He discerned just how complex Turkana social relations could be; how every type of social bond – parentage and kinship, friendship and marriage – was cemented and symbolized by complicated transactions of livestock. He discovered that a father, however old, owns all the stock in the home, and that a young man, to get married, must wander hundreds of miles to see scores of people in order to beg sufficient bride-wealth. In fact, begging was an admired art for Turkana men.

He learned the meanings in the subtle variations of garb and ornaments, and how a person's life story could be read in an article of clothing, a decoration, or a hairstyle; the loss of a family member, the birth of a child, the initiation of a son, all were recorded in the intricate details of one's manner of dress.

During his travels from site to site he witnessed many rituals. In one place, a woman who lost her property in a fire was anointed on the head and chest with the stomach contents of a bull calf, a remedy designed to rid her of bad luck. A week later he was present at a 'topunyare', a second burial, where the cattle of related families were symbolically corralled together. On another day he was privileged to be in attendance at the ceremony of 'akilokng' ikel – a rite of passage where pubescent children had their two lower front teeth ritually removed with a nail. Loomis recalled how the young girls and boys sat together, stoically enduring the pain, daring not to cry out lest they be shamed in front of their peers. It was a test of fortitude in a land where fortitude was a requisite for continued survival.

But however macabre these customs might have appeared to one of another culture, Loomis found the Turkana to be pretty much ordinary folk who spent a lot of their time carrying out their daily chores and duties, and discussing such mundane matters as the weather, or what happened to so and so, making polite inquiries about one's family, joking and teasing with one another, and generally acting out social roles that everyone everywhere seemed to play. However, they did exhibit what an outsider might consider peculiar behavior. Normally they were imperturbably unemotional, what Loomis would consider 'cool'. So cool, that the Turkana never apologized, not even when they accidentally spit on another, or inadvertently knocked someone down. Nevertheless there were violent arguments, some of which frightened Loomis until he became used to them. Emotional displays, such as screaming and crying, seemed exaggerated, to the point of being comical, as if they were actors in a play.

And despite the mutterings of his crew some nights around the campfire, in which they derided the Turkana, and whom they referred to as barbarians and savages, Loomis could find nothing about the Turkana that in his mind could qualify them as savage or barbaric.

* * *

One week before their break was due, while they were midway through the twelfth borehole, a demoralizing message came from the office:

FROM: CB PRIORITY: URGENT
TO: D.L.
1) NEGOTIATING W/CLIENT OVER DEADLINE EXTENSION
2) BREAK POSTPONED UNTIL FURTHER NOTICE
3) CLIENT'S CONSULTANT COMING TO SITE TO ASSESS
   SITUATION ETA LODWAR MORNING 29 JANUARY
ARRANGE TRANSPORT
REGARDS

Damn it! He had been counting the days till he would be back in Nairobi with Amonee again, and now this crap. Did they think they were machines, working seven days a week for two to three months straight and then to be denied their break? Even machines needed to rest. The men were going to be furious when they heard. He dreaded telling them.

When he did, they threatened to 'down tools' in protest. Loomis handled the situation diplomatically by telling them that he too had desperately needed to go to Nairobi and that he would insist upon their break after the consultant's visit. But the site boss said that last bit without conviction, for he knew that if the consultant was bearing down on Barnes, Barnes, being the cold-hearted aggressive businessman that he was, would demand that they continue working, the morale of the workers not even to be considered. There was only one way. It was all up to the consultant and Loomis would have to work on him when he arrived.

He sat in the office caravan and sulked. If there was only a phone, he could talk to Amonee, at least hear her voice. Maybe he would have been able to persuade her to come out there for a few days and see the place for herself. But there was only the radio. Then an idea struck him and he picked up the transmitting mike.

"Hotel Quebec, Hotel Quebec, Tango Charley, come in, over."

"Tango Charley, this is Hotel Quebec, go ahead." The metallic voice was very faint, and Loomis had to strain to hear it.

"Is that Benson, over?"

"No, this is Josek, over."

"Benson?"

Josek had to virtually yell into his mike. "NO, IT'S JOSEK,OVER!"

"How do you read me, Josek?"

"Very well, strength one, over."

"Well, I can hardly hear you, you're signal is very weak, there's a lot of static on this end. Listen, Josek, I want you to do me a favor. Over."

"Roger. What is it? Over."

"I want you to call the University of Nairobi and ask for Miss Emuria of the music department." He then passed on Pamela's telephone number and extension that he read from the card he had kept on his desk. "When you get her on the line, call me back. Do you copy?"

A pause, presumably while Josek was writing the numbers down. "Roger, that's a copy."

"What? Come back, I can't hear you! Do you copy?"

"I SAID I COPY, OVER!" screamed Josek

"Do it now, over."

"Roger."

Loomis waited, fidgeting with things on the small desk. A half-hour went by until the radio squawked again.

"Tango Charley, Tango Charley, this is Hotel Quebec, come in."

Loomis jumped at the radio with expectancy. "This is Tango Charley, go ahead Hotel Quebec."

"I have Miss Emuria on the telephone at this moment. What would you like to tell her, over."

"Did you manage to get through to Miss Emuria? Over."

"I HAVE MISS EMORIA ON THE LINE RIGHT NOW, OVER!" Even though Josek's voice sounded distant, Loomis could tell by the tone in his voice that indeed he was shouting.

"I can hardly hear you, Josek. Please tell her that my leave is postponed, over." He waited while Josek handled the phone.

"She says she is very disappointed. Over."

"Come back?"

"SHE IS VERY DISAPPOINTED, OVER!" Josek yelled over the airwaves.

"Ask her if she would like to come and visit me up here. There is a plane coming on the twenty-ninth which would stay for two days. Can she manage a couple of days off, over."

Again Loomis waited, all the time drumming his fingers anxiously on the tabletop. When Josek came back on the air, the signal was so weak, the words were unintelligible.

"What was that, I didn't read, come back, over," he pleaded, holding his breath until he could know her answer. He now put his ear flush with the speaker.

"SHE SAYS SHE CAN HEAR YOUR VOICE, OVER!"

He exhaled air in exasperation. "Tell her that's very nice but I can't hear hers. What is her answer, over?"

No response, reception was dying.

"Hotel Quebec, come back!" Again, his ear to the speaker.

"She says yes. Over."

"Couldn't copy that. Repeat!"

"SHE SAYS YES. OVER."

"Great!" Loomis cried out to himself. He pushed the sending button. "Josek, please get the details of the flight and then inform her of when and where it is leaving, it should be from Wilson Airport. I'll send a message to Barnes in the morning explaining her passage. Over."

"Roger."

"Thanks very much, Josek."

"Anytime, Bwana Loomis. Hotel Quebec over and out."

Loomis returned the mike and stood up. Then he thought he heard Josek transmitting again. He bent down to listen. There was a transmission but he could barely make out the words.

"Tango Charley, come back!"

Loomis took hold of the mike. "Yes, Josek, I'm here, go ahead."

"She says..." garbling static drowned out the radio operator's words.

"Come back, Josek, I didn't read!"

Josek had to shout again. "SHE SAYS SHE LOVES YOU, OVER!"

* * *

He could tell she had never stepped on the wing of an airplane before. She was crouching down, taking short little steps with her arms extended out to her sides to balance herself. He couldn't keep from laughing as he helped her down.

"Stop laughing!" she protested. "I've never been in a small airplane before. And climbing off the wing!" She was dressed in a khaki bush shirt and baggy safari trousers and had that beautiful blue head-kerchief, the one he now knew so well, tied around her hair.

The consultant stepped out, a middle-aged man with bushy brown hair traced with grey, blue eyes and sporting a grey goatee. He looked like a Frenchman, and Loomis would bet that he was. He jumped adroitly off the wing. "Jacques Madan, Fourchette Ingenuere."

He was. He extended a hand to Loomis.

"Daryl Loomis, geologist, site agent, Hydro-Drill Limited."

"Pleasure." He had a prominent accent and Loomis wondered about his command of English.

The pilot appeared from behind the tail of the plane. "Hello, Daryl."

"Hi, Sean. How was the flight?"

"Very pleasant," Amonee broke in. "The view was breathtaking."

"You should try flying in the hot afternoon with all those thermals," said Loomis cockily. "You'd turn green, right, Sean?"

"Ah, you just don't like flying, Daryl," the pilot remarked, with his usual unflappable expression.

Loomis faced the engineer. "Mr. Madan, I suggest we get

something to eat here before we start off. It's about a seven-hour drive."

"Ah, *oui*."

"Sean, are you coming with us?"

"No, just give me a lift to the AMREF office. There's a few of the Flying Doctors I want to say hello to. I'll be staying there if you need me."

After dropping the pilot off, McKracken drove them over to the Lucky Star Hotel, a small dingy restaurant run by Somalis. Outside were a number of men sitting and chewing miraa, one of which was Rashid, the CID man, who by now had met Loomis enough times to know his name.

"Bwana Loomis!" he called, getting out of his chair.

"Jambo, Rashid."

"You have visitors I see. Is this good lady your wife?" he asked, referring to Amonee.

Loomis suspected that Rashid knew she wasn't; it was just his way of prying. "No, just a friend from Nairobi."

The Somali shook her hand and then the Frenchman's. "Rashid Hemed."

"Pamela Emuria," she reciprocated.

"Madan," the Frenchman stated.

"We just stopped to get something to eat," Loomis said, lacking anything else to say.

"Yes, eat. Me, I have just eaten. Now time for miraa." And with that he released the trio to proceed inside.

After a few chapatis and tea, they started on their journey with McKracken at the wheel. During most of the way, Loomis was explaining to the consultant the difficulties of the terrain and pointing to the sections of the road which they had made, while the Frenchman nodded silently. Amonee, in the front seat so Loomis could be in the back with the engineer, stared out the window captivated by the scenery: a panoramic badlands of thorny scrub where a lone stone-faced mountain towered stolidly like a staid sentinel. At one point she exclaimed, "This really is the bush!"

"Do you like it?" Loomis asked.

"I think it's exciting...the empty wildness of it...the way it seems to stretch on forever...the fierce-looking mountains...the constant wind singing through the thorn trees...it makes one think deeply. This is a special place." She swiveled towards the French engineer. Since his bewildered hello in Nairobi just before boarding the plane, he had said nothing to her, and during the whole flight had gazed quietly out the window.

"Mr. Madan," she now addressed him. "I'm sure your work has taken you to many different parts of the world. Have you ever been in a place such as this?"

The engineer didn't answer her, but instead turned to Loomis. "Does Mr. Barnes know you are bringing a woman to the site?" His English wasn't bad but his accent put stresses on all the wrong syllables.

"Yes," Loomis answered, taken aback.

"You don't think it is improper, bringing a woman to a work camp full of men in a place that is a security risk?"

Loomis swallowed hard, and said with some guilt, "I didn't really consider that aspect. I guess I feel I can take care of her, just like I can take care of you, or any other visitor."

Amonee returned her face forward, feeling awkward and ashamed, like a tactless interloper, a cumbersome nuisance. Maybe it had been wrong for her to come.

Conversation stopped, and it was only after an hour or so that Loomis resumed with short bursts of technical chit chat to which the French engineer made less than little response. McKracken, isolated in his job, laconically drove on.

* * *

They reached camp by evening, Amonee being shown their tent and the bathing place, the latter being a small area partitioned on all sides by grass walls, and which had a bucket suspended on a rope that was used to tilt it. Inside the tent itself, Loomis's cot had been removed, and a mat with two sheets was laid out on the floor, the table and chair having been taken out and placed just outside under the shade of the flysheet. Around the tent were small trenches filled with a grey mulch.

Loomis and Madan went over to watch the drilling. It was nearly night when they returned.

"Boy, I tell you, the French are notoriously intransigent," Loomis complained as he reached the table set out in front of his tent, where a freshly bathed and newly attired Amonee was sitting. She had on a pair of blue jeans and a brightly colored tie-dyed blouse. Her kerchief removed, her natural kinky hair was exposed, crowning her sweet dark face.

"Be patient," she advised. "Europeans are more subtle than Americans. You can't be too direct."

"I don't have time to be subtle." He looked at her, sweat making tracks on his overalls. "You look very alluring. Is that being too direct?"

"Not from you." She paused. "Why do we have these trenches around the tent? What is that grey stuff?"

"To stop the soldier ants. And the scorpions. We save the campfire ashes in a bag and we use them as you can see. We wet the trenches with kerosene and water so the wind doesn't blow it all around."

"Ugh, scorpions!"

"Yeah, don't worry, they only come out at night."

"Yes, when we're sleeping. On the floor. That's comforting," she remarked sarcastically.

"You want to go home already?" he jokingly asked.

"I want to take a walk."

"Can I take a bath first?"

"Be quick."

The bath finished, they embarked together into the desert night.

Then, after they'd gone about two hundred meters away from the tent, Amonee abruptly plopped down. "Here is as good as any a place. It's far enough."

Loomis sat down beside her, and that's when he noticed something peculiar. "Hey, see that?"

All around them were little sparkles that seemed to be floating in the air.

"Fireflies!" she exclaimed with glee.

"Know what they're doing?" he asked cheekily.

"Of course I do."

"What?" Again, being cheeky.

"Mating. The ones in the air are the males, the ones on the ground are females. They signal to each other so they can join up and be together."

She leaned against him and he put his arm around her. Minutes went by until the sound of the generator, humming through the night air, reminded him of the camp's presence.

"We better go to the camp to check up on our guest. Dinner must be ready by now."

They got up and headed back where they found Madan sitting at the table in the makeshift dining area that Loomis had instructed Mutua to prepare that very afternoon. The table had been set quite nicely, Loomis noted. Madan was looking over the contract in the dull glare of the light bulb strung up on a pole over the table.

"Hello, Jacques. Everything okay?"

"Ah, *oui*."

Just then, Mutua brought them their dinner, goat meat and rice. Madan set aside his papers. As they dug into their food, Loomis asked with slight hesitancy, "How's the food, okay?" He wondered whether the crude fare would insult the fine culinary sensitivities of the French.

"Ah, *oui, bon*. Very nice."

"I noticed you were reviewing the contract."

"Ah, *oui*."

"Anyway, you saw today that the drilling is going well."

"Ah, *oui*, the drilling is satisfactory."

"Monsieur Madan," Amonee addressed, "would you like some more rice?"

"Ah, *oui, merci*," he replied, taking the plate of rice she offered, and scooping off a portion.

"Daryl?"

"No, I'm okay."

"Some meat?" Again she presented Madan with a plate.

"Ah, *oui*.

"Daryl?" she offered.

"No, I'm okay....the problem is one of access..." Loomis continued. "Otherwise we are doing good work here."

After a few more mouthfuls, Madan put the knife and fork down on his plate signaling he was finished eating.

"...twelve hours of air-lift development before we pump test..."

Mutua came with two hurricane lamps, hour-glass looking things with a kerosene wick inside. "Mr. Roomis, we shut generator now."

"Okay, Mutua, *sawa sawa*."

"Would you like some tea, Monsieur Madan?" Amonee asked, still retaining her air of natural courtesy.

"Oui, merci," he blurted. "Yes, please," he said again in English.

"You, Daryl?"

"...accurate logging – uh, what, tea? No thanks. We just need more time in such rough country..."

Amonee fetched a mug from the kitchen area then poured Madan's tea. "*Voulais Vous du sucre dans votre the?*" she asked him.

The Frenchman raised his eyebrows. "*Oui, deux. Parle vous Francais?*"

"Oui."

That started it. Off they went into a singsong of French. The engineer was smiling for the first time since his arrival, and Loomis couldn't tell whether the man was delighted at being chatted up by a beautiful woman or at hearing his noble mother tongue in a strange land. After fifteen minutes or so, Loomis grew impatient. Time was being wasted, and he needed every precious moment to convince him of their difficulties. He heard them mention the names of cities: Paree, Marseilles, Grenab, so Amonee was probably giving him an account of the places she had visited in France. Loomis was having trouble timing his entrance but fortunately Jacques helped him out with that one.

"She speaks perfect French!" he declared in English, turning to Loomis.

"Yes, I know, she's a linguistic genius. Now, Mr. Madan, certainly you saw how bad that road was coming in here. But before we worked on it, it was even worse, not even a track."

His face changed into cold severity. "That is the contractor's responsibility. You should have considered that when you bid the tender."

"But you must admit that none of the prospective contractors carried out any site survey. It would have been uneconomical in a remote place like this unless you were promised the contract."

"We provided topographical maps. Your estimation could have been based on that..."

"*Encore un peu de the, Monsieur?*"

Madan changed his expression from one of stone granite to one of obsequious compliance, "*Oui, s'ilvous plait.*"

"Those topo maps," Loomis frantically went on, "are based on air photos taken in '68. That's twelve years ago."

The Frenchman laughed condescendingly. "Certainly, Mr. Loomaas, you as a geologist don't expect the land to change geologically in twelve years?"

Asshole, Loomis thought.

Madan opened his briefcase and took out an aerial photo, and the two of them pored over it while Amonee cleared the table.

"You see these lines which look like tracks?" Loomis pointed out. "Well, they were tracks. Now they're gullies. Do you not remember seeing a gully paralleling the road as we came in?"

"Hmmmm." Madan stared at the photo. He looked up, apparently tired of scrutinizing the black-and-white print in the dull light of the hurricane lamp. Then he turned to Amonee who had just returned to her seat. "I am curious," he said to her, "what work do you do?"

"I'm a music lecturer at the university."

"*Sacre bleu!* And you play?"

"Piano, guitar, a bit of flute, but mostly I enjoy singing."

"A la!"

Wouldn't you know it? The engineer was a part-time musician as well. And guess what instrument he played – French Horn! There followed a long discussion about music: arias, concertos, and other things which Loomis knew nothing about, at which point he fell silent. But after a while the topic shifted into geology and Loomis found himself participating along with Madan in describing to Amonee the cycles of sedimentation and volcanism that took place as Africa and Arabia drifted apart during the formation of the Rift Valley, a topic that caused Amonee to express an almost canonical fascination. It was nearing midnight, but the subject of access roads and deadlines still didn't come up.

"I'm afraid," Amonee interrupted, "despite the wonderful company, I must retire for the night. *Bon nuit, Monsieur.*"

"*Bon nuit, cheri.*"

Both of them watched her walking back to the tent.

"Fascinating woman," Madan declared.

"Yes, she is."

"At least we are in agreement on that," the Frenchman quipped with a surreptitious grin.

Now was his chance. "Uhm, Monsieur Madan, just a short chat. I know there's a contingency clause in the contract..."

"Ah, yes, but it doesn't cover access problems, only breakdowns and drilling problems like losing the tools in the hole..." He broke off and looked over Loomis's shoulder. "What is she doing?"

Loomis turned around to look at his tent. It was flashing. Apparently, Amonee was switching a flashlight on and off, on and off.

Loomis grinned broadly. "I think she's calling me."

"You better go then."

* * *

Alone in the tent, the lovers embraced.

"Cute," Loomis said. "The firefly thing."

Her response to that was to put her chin on his shoulder and purr.

"God, only one night," he lamented. "Tomorrow the plane will take you away from me. Well, better than nothing."

"I'm not leaving tomorrow," she told him flatly. "I asked for two weeks off."

"What do you mean? The plane is waiting. You won't be able to get on another for weeks."

"Exactly two weeks."

"How do you know the plane's schedule?"

"I asked Josek to find out for me."

"Why you sneaky little..." he hesitated slightly, then decided it was alright "...bitch."

Her response was a smile, a sassy one. "I know," she said wickedly, and then gave him a darting kiss.

"What about your job?"

"Katy and I have a system. It's all worked out. "

"Wait a minute, the plane's schedule is tentative. If we don't get that extension our break is postponed, and that will mean another month or two."

"I think it will return as planned. Maybe even earlier."

Loomis released her and put his hands on his hips. "What?"

"I think you managed to convince Mr. Madan about the extension, and your company will give you immediate leave. Before the week is over," she clarified.

"I've hardly had a chance to talk to him. How can you be so sure?"

"Monsieur Madan is not blind, he can see for himself. Besides, I have faith in you."

They returned to their embrace.

* * *

McKracken was to drive the engineer back alone. Madan understood; the site geologist's place was at the well site. When pressed about the extension, the French engineer merely replied that it would be considered after more discussion, and that they would get an answer soon. However, when it came time to bid Amonee adieu his attitude was much less indecisive, as after he shook her hand he took it and kissed the back of it. *"Au revoir, cheri."*

"Au revoir."

After his departure, Loomis decided to show Amonee just exactly what he and his crew were doing out here in the desert, so he took her to the well site on the condition she don the proper attire. She looked adorable in the white safety helmet and the baggy blue overalls he had given her. She stared at the large machine in fascination as Loomis talked shop with Shigoli. To her, the rig was an intimidating, extremely noisy bulk of steel that contained an imposing, even frightening power, and she was impressed by the gaunt bald-headed man who ostensibly had the beastly thing under his total control.

"Very hard!" the man at the controls shouted over the racket, referring to the rock formation they were drilling through.

"Okay, Ben, increase the rpm but don't push it past two-five," Loomis shouted back. He turned to his drill foreman. "What do you think, Shigoli?"

"We use the DTH."

"Yeah, but let's wait a bit. Mud drill it until the penetration rate falls below a meter every ten minutes. Then go with the DTH. That compressor eats a lot of diesel."

"What's a DTH?" Amonee asked. She had wrapped a kerchief around her mouth to block the odour and dust, and she had her hands pressed to her ears to try to staunch the din.

"Down-The-Hole hammer. It's driven by air," Loomis explained in a loud voice. He elucidated upon a few other things to her. How the sticky drilling mud stopped the walls from falling in, the placing of linings and gravel, and the pumping out of water using air from the compressor. Her admiration for him grew, and while sitting together in the office caravan that evening she made the following remark:

"You must be proud of what you are doing."

"What do you mean?" he asked, not quite knowing how to reply.

"I mean using your skills to get water for people. Being involved in the betterment of people's lives."

"Betterment. Not sure about that. To me, this is all about resettlement. They want to tame the Turkana. Put in a productive well, then get people to form a community around it, and hopefully the water is enough to encourage farming. Stop their wandering. Of course, the way it is now, during the droughts herds are nearly obliterated; the animals die first, and then people, especially children, dropping like flies, so I suppose it's six of one and half dozen of the other. "

"Then why are you doing this, if not to improve their lives?"

"Who, me? Personally, I'm in it for the money. This is how I earn my daily bread."

"No, I mean the agencies who are funding this."

"Well, this is what we expatriates call development. It's simple, actually. You take some experts from an industrialized nation and get them to tell the local people what is good for them and what they need, then you persuade the government of that country to take a loan from you so that they can pay you to do the job. Even if the loan is defaulted, it keeps foreign companies in business and Europeans employed."

"I didn't know you were this cynical."

"I didn't know either. But since I've been in this business I've heard aid workers banter the word 'development' around so many times it makes me sick. To me, colonialism was the laying of a rotten foundation for the building and now it's settling and the walls are cracking. Development is the plaster we put over the cracks and when the plaster starts to crack we slap on more plaster. If only we could have left the world alone, but no, we say everyone must learn to drink Coca Cola and dance to disco music."

She looked at him, trying to figure him out. "You're a complicated man, Daryl Loomis."

"C'mon, I'm tired. Let's say we bathe and get some grub."

* * *

The next morning the well was finished: linings in, cleaned and developed, and when it was pumped it yielded an abundance of water. Everybody cheered – the crew, the casuals, the local tribes people looking on, and most of all Amonee, who saw the water leaping out of the hole as if it were a divine miracle.

Well number thirteen finished. It was time to move on.

In the afternoon, Loomis came back from checking the road to the next location and found Amonee sweeping the tent.

"The new road is looking good. Maybe we'll be able to move tomorrow, we're just about wrapped up here...hey, what are you doing?"

"Cleaning the tent."

"Mutua!" Loomis yelled out.

The lanky camp manager trotted over. "Yes, Bwana Roomis?"

"Didn't you tell Ekwom to clean my tent today?" Ekwom was one of the Turkana casuals, assigned the duties of housekeeping and catering to the needs of the site boss.

"Yes."

"Then why is Miss Emuria cleaning it?"

"She want to do it herserf. I tulied to terr her, but she wouldn't rissen."

"Okay, go back to what you were doing."

Mutua departed.

"Amonee, only Ekwom is allowed to clean my tent."

She approached him, held his face in her hands, and gave him an unhurried, gentle kiss. "It's our tent now. It should be private. Our love is in here."

"But he knows where I keep things. And he doesn't touch my papers or my books."

"Don't you agree it looks much neater now?" she chaffed him, pointing to the neat piles on the table.

"Yes, but now I won't be able to find anything," he complained.

"Just ask me, and I'll get it for you. Or are they secrets I shouldn't see?" she teased with a frisky smile.

He looked at her in earnest. "I have no secrets from you." He kissed her. "Do you have any?"

"Yes," she replied, with a slack expression. She made an effort to smile wanly. "All men and women keep secrets from each other," she said in a tone meant to deflect the discomposure of her reply.

* * *

They moved on, continuing north, entering the region of Kakuma, Kakuma itself a small outpost on the other side of the Baboon Hills. To the west, perpetually shrouded in gloomy indigo clouds, was the awesome dark wall of the Dodoth Escarpment, which marked the edge of the Gregory Rift Valley, and which the Turkanas of this area looked upon with apprehension, for it was over the top of it where the enemies came down from.

At the campsite, Amonee joined with the Turkana laborers and busied herself with erecting the tent, much to Mutua's embarrassment.

"Amonee, you're making Mutua feel bad. You are our visitor, no need to do that," Loomis protested.

"Oh, Daryl, don't spoil my fun. I'm beginning to enjoy this outdoor life."

"All right. But don't try to enter the kitchen area. Juma might come at you with a knife."

He was amused, but even more so, contented. An idea that at first seemed downright stupid, even reckless and hazardous as Madan had pointed out, turned out to be a superb one. Taking her into his world, this extreme existence, brought the two of them much closer. She was totally unfazed by the ruggedness, and more than merely adapting to the situation, she was relishing it, and all that made him love her more.

The day itself started out as a rather boring one, with the heat, the wind, and the flies unchanged from the day before. Amonee sat reading at the table outside the tent in between taking naps on the mat she had laid out beside it, while Loomis and the crew spent the blistering hours by preparing the access road. For them, it was bush-clearing time again. Chopping and slashing, digging levels, filling ruts, and coaxing lorries.

In the second hour of this road-building, Loomis noticed a solitary Turkana who stood one-legged with his ankles crossed, leaning on his herding stick, studying them fastidiously, silent except when he spat out the juice from his chewing tobacco. Not long after, McKracken approached the fellow with enthusiastic greetings. The pair became garrulous with talk and laughter and Loomis put down his panga to go over and investigate.

"This is my brother Lokori," McKracken proclaimed.

Loomis was skeptical. A brother could be anyone, from your cousin twice removed to just another guy from the same village. In Africa they could all be called brothers.

"*Ejoka*?" the Turkana named Lokori asked.

"*Ejok*," Loomis responded.

"*Nyai*?"

"*Mum*?"

McKracken spoke to Lokori and Loomis heard his name

mentioned in the way of introduction.

"He has been looking for a lost camel for four days now," McKracken informed his boss. "He still hasn't found it. When camels get lost, you can search for them for a whole month and sometimes longer."

"Tell him I'm sorry about that."

"You tell him. He knows Kiswahili. He even reached Kitale once."

"*Pole*," consoled Loomis.

"*Asante*. Thank you," the man smiled. His hairdo was noticeably elaborate, and the mud caps on his head gave the illusion that he was wearing a helmet like that of a Roman centurion. Strikingly enough, even his features were somehow patrician: a sharp chin, handsome lips which like that of Loomis, were full but not too thick, and a bony, refined nose with flaring nostrils. In any case, the result was a countenance of aristocracy, except perhaps, for the big wooden plugs that stretched open his earlobes.

McKracken continued his parley with this prince of the desert before turning back to Loomis. "He would like you to visit his home. It's not very far away."

"*Wapi*? Where?" Loomis asked Lokori directly.

"This way," Lokori replied, pointing to the north. "Less than an hour's walk."

"That would be great," Loomis declared, thinking of Amonee and how she would appreciate it. "How about mid-afternoon?"

Lokori agreed.

And as promised, he came by the campsite at three o'clock.

"Well look who's here!" Loomis suddenly announced.

She looked up to see a very black man wearing a blanket like a tunic, with one end connected to the other end over the right shoulder, walking towards them holding a thin stick with both hands behind his neck and a wooden thing that looked like a capital 'T'. His head was covered with blue mud, out of which stuck a white ostrich feather. Other than that, he was quite handsome.

"Lokori, ejok."

"Ejok."

"Amonee, meet my friend Lokori."

She shook his hand, but when she wanted to let go of it, he interlocked his thumb with hers and they shook again, this time in the style of an Afro-American. A third shake in the usual manner concluded the formality.

"Amonee, would you like to visit a Turkana home?"

"Yes, lovely, it's what I've been looking forward to."

"C'mon, let's go."

It was a good twenty-minute walk. Lokori led them with a stately gait, together with McKracken dressed in his military camouflage fatigues.

Upon arrival they were greeted by the women of the home, with the children standing behind them full of cautious curiosity. As they were escorted to the main hut, Loomis glanced around the compound and was impressed with Lokori's wealth. In one kraal there were over twenty camels, and there were two other large kraals for his goats and sheep. No wonder about his lack of concern over one lost camel.

"Lokori, I knew you were a rich man. You have many animals," he said as they reached the the entrance to the ekal, the large hut for visitors.

Lokori laughed before saying in his broken Kiswahili, "No, these very few. So many goats are along Tarac River. And I have many many cattle on top of Songot Mountain. They are with my brother's herd. I leave tomorrow, go and see them. Now, go inside the ekal, I just coming back."

With bent backs, the couple entered while McKracken remained outside talking to the other family members.

"It's very cool in here," Amonee noted. "And bright too."

The dome of the roof was covered only partly with animal hides, leaving large empty patches that served as skylights.

Sitting in the hut, Loomis looked amusedly at the Turkana females who had just entered and took their places opposite them.

Their leather aprons were long in the back, but in the front, more so for the younger girls, there was only a small strip to hide their femaleness. But amazingly enough, no matter in what position they were in, standing, bending, sitting, you never got a glimpse of it. And it's not like he never tried. But despite all this near nudity, they were not easy to seduce – they saved it for marriage.

"You seem to be lost in thought. What are you thinking about?" she asked him, sitting cross-legged in her jeans by his side.

Loomis gave her a contemplative smile. "Men's secrets."

"I see...Oh...I love her earrings," she said, pointing to a woman who had what looked like a series of metal spear-points inserted along the length of each ear. She pointed again, this time at a woman's leather skirt. "And those white ornaments sewed on their aprons, I believe they look like eggshells."

"Yes, usually ostrich."

All this pointing by Amonee prompted some of the women to sit down around her. As she listened to them chattering to her, she was surprised at how similar their language was to her own mother tongue, for she could pick out many of the words. "I think I understand what they're saying."

Loomis explained. "Your people, the Teso, were once part of the Ateker cluster, along with the Turkana. When everybody split up, you guys went south and mingled with the agriculturalists. The Teso were the only Ateker peoples to change lifestyle. But the language is almost the same."

"Really? That's amazing. My grandmother used to tell me we came from the deserts of the north. And that Jesus taught us how to grow cotton."

"I doubt it was Jesus himself, maybe the missionaries."

And as the women continued with their tittering, she asked him, "Do you know what they are saying?"

"Well, I can't catch all of it."

"Well, let's see, they said I look like a Turkana but I dress like a mzungu...they want to know where you're from and how we met...oh, yes, and how many animals did you have to pay for me."

"What are you going to tell them?"

Amonee turned back to the women and spoke her mother tongue, and they all burst out with hilarious laughter.

"What's so funny?"

"I told them only one chicken, that you're very poor, but of course they don't believe me," she answered chuckling.

A goat was to be slaughtered for them, not a ritual roasting, but to be boiled in the home so that the women could partake of it as well. In the meantime, milk was brought in. It came in a squat vessel made of a strange gourd and that was bunged with a long, tall cap. The cap served as a huge cup, and the youthful girl with the pretty little tits who had brought the milk poured the contents into it and handed it to Amonee.

"This is delicious!" she cried after sipping it. "Tastes like feta cheese. How do they make it?" she asked Loomis.

"Well, they take some fresh milk straight from the teat, and mix it with milk that has gone sour." He neglected to mention that they used sheep's urine to sour the milk.

Lokori returned, along with McKracken, and sat next to them. "Is this your wife?" he asked, while McKracken made jokes with the women.

"Yes," Loomis lied, hoping Amonee didn't hear the Turkana's question.

"How many animals did you pay for her?"

"Not so many."

But evidently she did hear this last statement, for she blurted out, "One chicken!" she said snickering.

"Oh, be quiet!" he told her.

She then asked Lokori, "How many animals do you have, Lokori?"

"Very many!"

"It's not known exactly," Loomis broke in. "The Turkana don't count the heads of their stock. They believe that if you do, all of the animals will die. Maybe that helps to reduce jealousy and excessive pride."

"How do you know so many things?"

"By being with people."

"But you even know more about my own roots than I do."

"Yeah, we're a real pair aren't we? Me, a Westerner trying to be an African, and you an African trying to be a Westerner."

"What are those scars on his arm and chest?" she abruptly asked Loomis. "They look like decorations."

McKracken entered into the discussion. "You see these here?" He ran his hands over his companion's chest.

Lokori smiled. He didn't mind McKracken touching him.

"Each one is an enemy he's killed."

"Yes!" Lokori said with pride.

"Enemies? What enemies?" she wanted to know.

"The Turkana have a lot of enemies," Loomis explained. "The Toposa, Marille, Dodoth..."

"Aye, Dodoth!" Lokori exclaimed in agreement.

"Stock thieves," Loomis continued. "They raid each other for animals."

"Oh, like the Masai used to do. They still practice that sort of thing out here?"

"Yes. It's hard to believe, isn't it? Such good-natured, seemingly gentle, affectionate people. And yet, if the need arises, a Turkana man can be a fierce, merciless killer. It's the law of the land here. Kill and be killed in the noble venture of stealing the enemies' livestock."

McKracken tapped Loomis's shoulder to get him to hear what Lokori wanted to say.

"*Ebu Lakwan*."

"What?"

"Something white," Amonee answered.

"Yeah I got that part. White what?"

"White hyena," McKracken told him. "He say you are 'White Hyena', 'Ebu Lakwan'."

Lokori smiled.

"To speak the truth, I tell him," McKracken admitted.

"Told him what?"

"Your name. The old man that owned the ekwar, remember him? He give you that name. He call you the 'White Hyena', with the big machine that sucks water from the ground."

Amonee was amused. "My, you seem to pick up nicknames wherever you go."

"But why white, because of my light skin?" Loomis wanted to know.

"No, because the white hyena very special, most people live and die and never see one. Like magic. "

An albino probably, Loomis gathered.

"The old man say you are different, you are from outside but can sit with Turkana people. Not even people from Kenya can do that."

As far as the Turkana were concerned, Kenya was a neighboring foreign country.

"Ebu Lakwan, let us sit with men while women prepare the meat," Lokori suggested.

"You're on your own," Loomis told Amonee as he rose to his feet.

"Not to worry. I'm sure we'll have plenty to talk about," she said, referring to the other ladies in the hut.

Gathered in the etien, the small open ring of thorns, the men traded stories. Lokori was narrating a tale of how, as a young boy, he got separated from the other herds boys one day while out to pasture.

"...I had drunk so much milk, I became sleepy and I fell asleep under – an edepal tree. When I woke up, they were gone: no people, no cattle, nothing. So I got up and followed the cattle tracks. But they led to a river, and I could not cross because the river was too wide and too deep and too swift to cross without an animal to hang on to..."

Loomis stole a glance outside towards the other end of the home where Amonee and the Turkana women were sitting around a large fire, chatting amiably, busily tending the food.

"...but some of the tracks paralleled the river and I thought perhaps that some of the group went a separate way from the rest. I followed these new tracks; I followed them and I followed them and I followed them...until I was so tired I had to sit down and rest in the bushes..."

Loomis returned his eyes again to watch Amonee, who was now helping the young girls in whipping up the soup. This was done using sticks with wooden blades fashioned at the submerged end, while the other end was placed between flat palms and spun by making rubbing motions.

"...it was late in the evening that I saw my father, for some of the herds boys had gone to my home to report I was lost, and my father had tracked me now to where I was. He did not say anything but he motioned with his hand for me to stay down and keep quiet. That's when I saw the buffaloes. I had been following the spoor of buffaloes!"

"Woi-ta-koit!Awaa!" his audience gasped.

"But it was too late. One big buffalo saw me and charged. Before I could do anything my father threw his spear right into the buffalo's throat and the buffalo went down, booomph!" Lokori slapped his knee for emphasis.

"Woi-ta-koit!"

"Your father was very much known as a great man," praised one of the young men. "Did he not go to Ethiopia to fight together with the wazungu?"

"None of his sons will be as great," Lokori lamented. "He had eight wives and over six hundred head of cattle."

Loomis brought his head up to see Amonee and two other girls bringing the food in long wooden bowls typical of the Turkana. She placed her bowl down in front of him.

"*Tonyam ekile*! Eat young warrior!" she ordered with an affectionate grin. Then she winked and returned with the other two girls.

The men ate slowly while continuing their conversation. After the meat they drank the soup, thick, creamy, and extremely tasty despite the fact that nothing, except water, not even salt had been added to it. At the end of the meal, everyone wiped their greasy palms on their bodies – their arms, necks, faces, and in the case of the Turkanas, even their legs – which was the normal way of washing one's hands.

As they made ready to depart, with night beginning to fall, Loomis heard men clapping and singing.

"They're calling people to a dance. Would you like to go watch?"

"Does a cockerel crow in the morning?" she posed facetiously. She laughed with glee. "Of course, I wouldn't miss it for the world!"

It was a three-quarter moon, and the white orb gave out an ethereal luminescence, like natural neon, bright enough to cast sharp shadows. The Turkanas were standing in a circle clapping, and chanting a song that rose in a high pitch and fell in a bass timbre, men on one side of the ring, women on the other. Inside the circle were two lines facing each other, one composed entirely of male youths, the other of young maidens. All the dancers were jumping, the bells they wore around their calves and ankles jangling loudly as they capered, but the style of this leaping differed between the sexes. The men threw their chests out and sprung their legs with a vigorous force in order to reach high in the air, and they jumped in unison. When they landed, they bent their legs slightly at the knees to put more weight on them, causing them to come down with loud stamping thuds which shook the ground. They also grunted, adding more power to their movements. McKracken, in his soldier's garb, was jumping among them.

The girls on the other hand, held hands and took nimble little hops that reminded Amonee of an entrechat in ballet. Unlike the men, they did not jump simultaneously, but rather created a type of syncopation with alternating movements. When one girl was on her way up, the two on each side of her were going down, like pistons on a crankshaft, and their aprons fluttered and flew as a mist of dust languidly rose from the ground.

Lokori grabbed Loomis to make him join in while the girls got a hold of Amonee. Loomis wasn't too bad, for he had done this sort of thing before, but he was surprised at how quickly Amonee had caught on to the female part.

Later on, the Turkanas performed another type of choreography in which the required level of skill precluded Daryl and Amonee from participating. One man only was inside the ring with about six of the maidens, and he jumped and charged at them in the manner of a provoked bull, while they in turn stuck their legs out attempting to trip him up. One of the warriors who had taken a turn at this had to be carried off to the side as he went into a convulsive fit akin to epilepsy, and although Loomis quavered at the sight, Amonee calmly assured him that such a phenomenon was normal in these dances, attributable to nothing more serious than over-excitement.

During the whole time that the big dance was going on, there were smaller circles consisting of animated children imitating the adults. The children were particularly gleeful, hopping, laughing, shrieking, chasing each other, and gamboling playfully among the rings. For Amonee, this atmosphere of happy dancers frolicking amidst round grass huts, steeped in a silver moonglow, was an experience unmatched in her life. It was magical.

* * *

It was late. The moon had already sunk into the horizon, leaving a dark and breezy night, and it was now the stars' turn to inhabit the sky. They lay down on the mat outside their tent.

"Thank you, Daryl."

"For what?"

"For a wonderful time. And for giving myself back to me."

Loomis was a bit embarrassed at that last statement. "You're welcome."

She leaned over him and rewarded him with a kiss.

"Did you enjoy the dancing?" he asked unnecessarily.

"You know I did. Ever since I met you, I've been more in tune with traditional music and dance, and when we get to Nairobi I have a surprise in store for you."

"What surprise?"

"If I told you then it wouldn't be a surprise."

"Okay, okay."

They were quiet for a time, lying on their backs, gazing up at the sparkling night sky.

"Hey, look at those stars! You see Orion, the warrior, with his belt, and there's his sword, you see it?" he asked her, pointing to the heavens.

"No. They just look like stars. I've never bothered to learn the constellations. I think it's nice enough to look at them all scattered about. The longer you look, the more they come out. It's beautiful."

They were beautiful, so beautiful he didn't quite know how to describe them. They twinkled ebulliently, as if, as if...

"They're singing," she said. "Billions and billions of them singing the song of creation."

"Is everything that is beautiful to you singing?"

"Yes. You just have to listen."

That's how he would describe them then. The stars were singing.

* * *

Early the next morning the site received the following radio transmission:

FROM: CB PRIORITY: NORMAL
TO: DL
1) CONSULTANT SYMPATHETIC CLIENT HAS AGREED TO SIXTY-DAY EXTENSION
2) BREAK TO BEGIN DAY AFTER TOMORROW
3) PLANE ETA LODWAR FEB 26 1700 HRS
REGARDS

PART III

OMENS

NAIROBI, FEBRUARY 1980

It was approaching *masika*, the Long Rains, and every afternoon like clockwork, puffy sculptures of cumulus clouds would parade across the sky. She was practically dragging him to her little red Fiat.

"Where are you taking me?" he asked in protest.

"Just be quiet and get in." She was dressed in a formal African dress with a floral pattern and her hair was once again braided with beads.

She drove along until she found Ngong Road. At Adam's Arcade she made a left turn and drove to the end of the side street, where she pulled into the driveway of a moderate-sized, ranch-style house. Just in front of the house, planted about a foot off the ground, was a small sign which read 'Kingozi Language and Cultural Center'.

"It's the surprise I told you about," she finally explained, as they got out of the car.

Inside, the reception room was full of young white people, the type that would belong to one or the other volunteer organizations.

"Oh, here she is now," announced a tall, redheaded girl upon their entrance, prompting them all to crowd around Amonee, greeting her warmly with hugs and pecks on the cheek, as if they were old friends meeting after a long separation.

Omondi appeared in the room, walking past the little gathering and giving a brief but warm hello to Amonee before approaching Loomis. "Hello, Daryl. How's Turkana?"

"It's still there."

"You're in for a real surprise."

"So I was told. These people, they're Americans?"

"Yes, volunteers from the Lutheran World Federation."

Amonee broke off from the gab of the group and turned around. "Daryl, I want you to meet some friends of mine. This is Jenny...Tom and Sheila...Mick..." She introduced all of them, each one responding with a 'hi' or a nod. "And this, everyone, is my special friend, Daryl,

Daryl Loomis."

"Hello," he said shyly.

"Are we ready?" she asked the group.

"As ready as we'll ever be," answered a skinny guy with a thin wispy beard, whose name Loomis vaguely recollected was Dave. He opened the sliding glass door behind Omondi's desk that led into the backyard and they filed out along with Amonee, Loomis and Omondi and a group of language teachers following behind.

On a table outside lay an assortment of traditional instruments, mostly of a percussion type, along with a couple of whistles. The members of the group in turn picked up their assigned items and lined up on the grass with Amonee whispering some last-minute instructions.

"This is a Teso funeral song," she declared to the audience of fellow teachers and guests, "that I learned as a little girl, which was very fortunate, since it seems to be dying out in the memories of the old people who once danced to it. I'm one of the few young people who know it." Then, to her little troupe, "Together with all of you of course!" Her students chuckled. She continued her speech. "It is sung to mourn the passage of someone who was especially beloved in the village. So if it sounds a bit sad, you know why." With a cuing glance to the ensemble, she went into a singing chant, her resonant voice rippling the air with bell-like clarity. The group responded to her melancholy soliloquy with a repetitive chorus, a typical African arrangement, and proceeded to break into a dance. The women erotically (a few almost comically) rotated their hips, and formed a circle, advancing clockwise in lurching steps and shut off the men, who were busy in motion outside the ring. The instruments were going and the whistles blowing, and there was a lot of woeful wailing. The circle of girls dissolved and now there were two lines, male and female, weaving into each other. The tall redhead burst forth with a keening, fluttering ululation, something that Loomis had previously believed could only come out the throat of an African woman. Watching the performance, he was thoroughly spellbound.

"What do you think?" Omondi asked.

"Unbelievable."

"Really something, isn't it?" said another voice. Loomis found Okova standing to his left.

"She really took this thing seriously," Loomis said to him. "It's better than I could ever have imagined."

"Yeah," agreed Okova. "I never thought I would see wazungu doing something like this. I didn't think it was in them. Maybe you, but...you're different."

A few minutes later the dance ended with laughter and applause. Amonee turned around to face the spectators. "How was it?"

"Amazing," replied Loomis. It was the only word he could get in, for the group immediately descended upon her, buoyant and bubbly with the success of their achievement, and chatted away merrily, while Amonee herself gave out praises and criticisms. *Just like the kids,* he thought to himself, *they love her.*

As the small assembly started to break up, Loomis dogged Okova back inside to nag him over some domestic matters. "Okova, is the house clean? Remember we're cooking dinner for Amonee tomorrow."

"Don't worry, I'll get somebody to do it. Might have to go back to the Masaku bar and see what I can pick up."

Back in the office, refreshments had been laid out in one of the larger classrooms, and a little party began, with people forming small circles of discussion. Loomis was standing with Mathenge, politely listening to the progress of the latter's latest project, when he heard a voice behind him.

"Hi!" It was the tall redheaded girl.

"Hello."

"Holly's my name."

"Pleased to meet you."

"You're working in Turkana, aren't you?"

"Yes, that's right, how did..."

"That's a place I really have to see before I go back home. But to get a ride there, that's going to be the hard part. How do you like working there?"

"It's interesting. Certainly different. Hey, that ululation, how did you do that?"

"Throat muscles. It's funny, I never even knew I had muscles in my throat. But Amonee showed me how to control them. She really has a talent for working with people. I mean you get to like her so much, it's like you really want to get it right for her sake, like you want to give back what she's giving you. That's the mark of a good teacher... How long have you known her?"

"About six months."

"I almost feel like I know you already, she talks about you so much."

"She does?" Loomis asked, showing surprise.

"Well, sometimes we get together for lunch. You see, I'm also a music teacher, I teach at a primary school just outside of Nairobi. Anyway, we've become very close and a lot of times we talk about, well, you know, personal things. She's very easy to get close to, a truly lovely person."

"Yes, I know."

"I'm going to have to leave a bit early, to try and catch a matatu back to Ruiru, so if you'll excuse me. I just wanted to say hello to you before going. It was nice meeting you, Daryl. Hope to see you again."

"Yes, likewise." Even women fell for Amonee, Loomis realized, bewitched by that indefinable something she carried within her presence. He could feel the pride that he had for her slowly fomenting into guarded jealousy, and now he wasn't so sure he wanted to share her with others. Her attractiveness to everyone made him uneasy; it was threatening in a way, for he was afraid it increased his risks of losing her. Feeling somehow saddened by his dilemma, he exited the backyard and entered the house and sought an empty classroom to be alone.

"So where is my young man taking me this evening?"

He turned around to see that Amonee had discreetly followed him into the room. Looking at her braided hairdo brought back memories of Uhuru Park. She stood opposite him with arms clasped behind her back, her face beaming with her comely smile, her flower-patterned African dress giving her a demure yet stately appearance. Her large, teardrop-oval eyes were glowing. God she was beautiful!

He gazed at her silent and serious, feeling all warm and gushy inside, his throat tight. "I love you, Amonee Emuria. Too much for words."

Her smile faded, replaced by a thoughtful face acknowledging the gravity of their situation. "I love you too, Daryl Loomis."

"Let's say we spend a quiet evening at home tonight."

"Alright," she answered softly.

The sound of a toilet flushing was followed by Okova's emergence from the corridor. "So where do we go for a few drinks?" he asked, rubbing his hands together.

"Us, we're going straight home, Okova, to the campus."

"No, don't say that. I was counting on you. My pockets are empty."

Loomis took a couple of hundred shilling notes from his wallet and gave it to him. "Here, have a few for me."

"Thanks!"

"Don't forget about tomorrow!" Loomis warned as the couple made their way out.

* * *

"Hey! Watch out, Okova! You're burning them! You've got the flame too high!"

"No, man, it's you! You're rolling them too thick and you don't put enough oil on them. That's why they're burning!"

Loomis and Okova were cooking chapatis at their attached duplex house in Buru Buru. Loomis was rolling the balls of dough flat with an empty beer bottle while Okova fried the pan-shaped pieces in a wide pot, the household still in need of a frying pan. Every few minutes or so, each of them would take swigs from their respective beers which they had placed upon the kitchen counter. Cooking chapatis was thirsty work.

"Okay, that's enough! Out of the kitchen!" Amonee ordered, fanning the smoke that began to collect in the air.

"Not me," protested Okova, "it's him."

"The two of you. The flame is too high, and Daryl, you are not putting enough cooking fat in the dough. And what are you cooking them in? A 'sufuria'?"

"We don't have anything else," Okova said in his defense.

"Amonee, we were the ones who were supposed to give you a prepared dinner tonight," Loomis said.

"Dinner, yes, not indigestion. Besides you've already cooked the choroko stew and it's delicious. I tasted it. Just leave and give me twenty minutes."

They submitted with resigned voices, then washed the flour off their hands. As they entered the sitting room holding their beers, a knock came on the door. "*Hodi!*" a voice called out.

"*Karibu!*" Okova called back.

In stepped a tall, balding African dressed in a loose pinstripe suit with the buttons open; his collar, lacking a tie, also unbuttoned. Above his chunky lips was a small Hitler-type mustache and, although he was fairly thin, a developing paunch stretched taut his white tuxedo shirt.

"Hello, William."

"Hello, Mr. Loomis, Mr. Okova. I heard you people were in and I wanted to know when I can send in the painter."

Amonee walked in from the kitchen. "Oh, we have a visitor," she said, wiping her hands with a dishrag.

"Amonee, this is William Kipkoech, our landlord and neighbor. He lives right next door in 120."

"Hello," he said shyly.

"Pleased to meet you." She presented her wrist for shaking, her hands not yet clean. "Will you stay for dinner?"

"No, I just came in for a minute."

"How about a beer?" Loomis offered.

"Sawa, just one maybe."

Okova, tired of standing, led them over to the sofa set in the middle of the room. Amonee came out of the kitchen with an opened bottle of beer and a glass, after which a discussion on the painting work ensued. She walked in and out of the kitchen setting the table while they continued their small talk, sipping their beers. "Dinner is ready now," she presently announced.

The men rose to wash their hands, including Kipkoech who no longer put up any argument. In Africa it was rude to refuse a meal once the table had been laid.

Throughout the meal, Kipkoech found conversation with Amonee rather pleasant and he took the opportunity to get acquainted. The two of them exchanged information about each other, and it turned out she knew a relative of his who was a fellow lecturer at the university. The pair dominated the table talk while Loomis and Okova were busy wolfing down their food.

"We're having a barbeque party at my house on Saturday," she told Kipkoech. "Would you like to come?"

"William, please, *karibu*," Loomis said. "Bring your wife and kids. It's going to be in the afternoon."

"Well, I'll try, I can't promise."

"My house is in the faculty residence within Chiromo Campus," she disclosed, "on Gandhi Lane, number eleven."

Loomis peeled off the label from his beer bottle and wrote the address on the back of it. "Here, so you don't forget," he said, handing the damp piece of paper to Kipkoech.

"How is the food?" Okova inquired.

"Very good chapatis," acknowledged the visitor.

* * *

After that, Amonee began to spend more time at Daryl's house in Buru Buru, and met Kipkoech the landlord on more than one occasion. She also got to know Daryl's upstairs bedroom pretty well.

The sex was becoming more familiar, more intimate, more uninhibited. Amonee had truly been transformed, from being a shy, reserved young woman into a sensuously feline creature whose hunger was awesome, so much so that Loomis would call her his Little Panther. He would often find a number of other nicknames to call her. Like Velvet Mattress, Chocolate Baby, corny, ludicrous names intended to make her laugh.

And she would reciprocate, calling him Omolo, Ebu Lakwan, the White Hyena.

But there was one that he came up with that evoked a very emotional response.

"You are my black shining star," he said one day, thinking of the time they had lain together under a starry sky in the desert "No, black star is like a black hole, which sucks everything up. Not good. Oh, I know, you're my...Black Diamond!"

She clutched him, holding him tight, and whispered, "You've claimed me," in a voice so low that he did not hear it.

These were the good times, the 'fuck, it's great to be alive' times. Loomis and Amonee were in that phase of their relationship where there were no doubts, no arguments, no scenes. But that stage was nearing its end. The signs of this were beginning to emerge, as Loomis was to later remember two incidents which had upset him during the latter half of his stay in Nairobi. The first one occurred at Amonee's party.

The party was held in the yard at the back of her house, complete with its pink-blossomed bougainvillea and the little tomato garden. A lot more people turned up than they had expected; even Kipkoech and his family appeared. Amonee had invited her students, fellow lecturers, and even some of the children from her evening sessions came with their parents. Loomis had told all his friends in Nairobi about it, and among those milling in the crowd were Peter Njenga, his former colleague, Geoff, Okova's brother; and of course the whole gang from Kingozi. The partygoers, standing and sitting, entertained themselves by chatting, eating, and drinking, keeping Loomis busy ferrying drinks and glasses while Roberta Flack serenaded them from the stereo. As he hurried along one of his shuttles he was intercepted by Amonee.

"Daryl, I didn't realize it, but Geoffrey and I have met before," she said, referring to Geoff Wanyonyi who stood facing her. "Oh, and this is Dr. Otundo, the chairman of the music department," she added, pointing to a short plump, very black bespectacled man at her side.

"Hello, Dr. Otundo. I heard a lot about you. I hope you're having a good time."

"Excellent party!"

"Say, Amonee, do we have any more paper plates? We're running low out here."

"They're in the cupboard above the sink."

Katy Hesland joined the group. "Why don't you take a rest, Daryl?"

"Maybe a little later. Hosting a party is actually more fun than attending one. Excuse me, I'll be right back."

Before he made it to the terrace doors, Okova, busy manning the grill, called out to him to get him a beer.

Loomis went inside and after entering the kitchen, collected the plates and beer, and put them on his tray. Before he could get a chance to leave, Geoff came barging in.

He looked a bit upset. "Hey, Daryl, what are you doing?" he asked in an alarmed tone.

"I'm bringing more plates, and some beer for your thirsty brother. Say, would you do me a favor and open the door for me."

"No, no, no...I mean with this woman?"

His face went askew in puzzlement. "I'm not sure I'm getting you, Geoff."

"Do you know who she is?"

Now his face went into an expression of preposterousness. "Of course I do: PaMEla Amonee Emuria, music professor, Nairobi University. Can you open the door please."

"Look, you've been spearing her, fine; now offload her, like you usually do."

Loomis's face went serious. "No, I don't intend to do that. She's the real thing."

"She's out of your league, trust me."

"Out of my...what?"

Geoff drew close and put his hand on Loomis's shoulder. "Dump her, brother, and stay as far away from her as you can. That's my advice. Don't say I didn't warn you." He took back his hand and headed out of the kitchen, leaving his friend stunned and speechless.

Loomis didn't enjoy the rest of the party. He gave stomach ache as a convenient excuse to a slightly concerned Amonee.

* * *

The second incident happened only a couple of days before he was due back on site. It was in the evening, when he had just returned from town, and had entered her house on Gandhi Lane where he was met by a barren silence.

"Amonee?" he called out. "Amonee?"

Reaching the doorway of the living room, he saw her sitting in a chair by the corner window, the pale light of dusk spotlighting the vacant expression on her face.

He remained standing in the doorway, oddly afraid to approach any closer. "Hey, don't I even get a 'how was your day at the office dear'?" he kidded, hoping to dispel the morbid image this scene was presenting, her solemn figure eerie in the nebulous obscurity of an unlit room.

She didn't even flinch.

"Amonee, is something wrong?" He went over to a dining chair and drew it to where she was sitting. He sat down, looking at her nervously. "What's the matter?"

She faced him and her rigid expression collapsed into a downcast grimace. Closing her eyes, she wailed, "Why did you have to come into my life NOW!" Then she threw herself at him and buried her face in his shoulder, her body heaving with her sobbing. Tears soaked the bottom of his neck, as she continued to clutch him fiercely, repeating. "I'm sorry, I'm sorry," over and over again. Then, she abruptly left his embrace and went storming off to her bedroom. He got up to trail behind her, but she slammed the door in his face.

"Amonee! What's wrong?" Through the door he heard her crying. She seemed to have thrown herself upon the bed, as far as he could figure out. "What's wrong?" he repeated.

Then, silence.

He tried again to reach her, his voice now quavering with despondent desperation. "Amonee, please, don't do this to me."

Continued silence.

He returned to the living room, and sat down, wondering what the hell was going on. He rummaged his mind trying to find some grievous thing he might have done to upset her. After an hour or so, she emerged, with a diffident smile, making an obvious effort at concealing what was troubling her. "I'm okay now, I'm sorry."

"It's okay, baby, but if I did something..."

"No, no need to talk about it, I'm fine now."

A dense stillness ensued.

She clasped her hands in front of her. "I was thinking of making you some sukuma-wiki and and beef tonight, with ugali. How does that sound?" she asked with a fake smile.

"Sounds good."

"Put on some music for me to cook by."

"All right."

He put on a cassette by Les Wanyika. He was not going to ask, he told himself, an awesome dread preventing him from pressing her about it.

Eventually she became her usual self and made comments about the songs that were being played, and even made some attempt at jokes.

When they went to bed, she asked him again not to ask her about her outburst, and he agreed, relieved to let the matter drop. He figured it probably had something to do with her time of the month. He had never been around a woman long enough to experience such things, and concluded that this was the price a man had to pay for a long-term relationship.

TURKANALAND, MARCH 1980

He left Nairobi with some uncertainty, but he interpreted the situation with Amonee as a progression from being in love to actual love, where the honeymoon was over and now it was time to sort of work things through; a natural development in the relationship between a man and a woman. Their love was maturing, and that alone compelled them to face the test of coming back down to reality. But they would pass that test. He was confident enough of that.

And it was in this state of mind that Loomis returned to work in Turkanaland, in some ways relieved to get a bit of time to reflect on things, and to tread slowly and carefully in order to preserve the most glorious thing he had ever found in his life.

The Hydro-Drill team returned to the site of borehole thirteen. They had left the camp in the care of Lokori's people, and had found it intact. Since the road had already been completed, they were nearly ready to drill. And pleasantly enough, Lokori himself was present to receive them when they arrived.

Loomis greeted Lokori and another local fellow who was with him, both leaning on their herding sticks in the customary fashion, the both of them having begun a conversation with McKracken.

"Ebu Lakwan," Lokori said with a smile.

McKracken brought up a topic which they evidently had been discussing prior to Loomis's arrival. "Lokori has convinced his friend to slaughter a goat for you. Is tomorrow good?"

"That's an offer difficult to refuse. Tomorrow's fine."

"Okay," said Lokori, then, with a sharp, sibilant sound, shot out a tiny missile of saliva from the gap in his front teeth. "Ebu Lakwan," he repeated affectionately, just for fun, before uncrossing his ankles and departing with his comrade.

* * *

Loomis, together with McKracken, sat waiting in the *etien*, one of the semi-spherical structures without roofs where the men slept. They had been sitting for over an hour now, and all that time Lokori's friend had been involved in an emotionally heated argument with two other young men, Lokori making an impassioned effort to mediate. Once again he witnessed a rather stagey exhibition of begging, with the man at one time throwing himself at the feet of the other two, and repeatedly pointing to Loomis, who in turn was growing tired of the whole spectacle. In fact, it only made Loomis feel more ill at ease, realizing that the young man was trying to bolster his prestige by entertaining the famous White Hyena.

"It's getting late, McKracken. I don't want to be out too long. What are they arguing about? Are we going to roast a goat or not?"

"That man is not married. He doesn't have goats of his own yet. So he must ask the permission of his brothers."

As Loomis pondered this, the announcement came that the goat would be roasted after all. It was to be a formal slaughter, they were told, and it would require the presence of one of the old watchmen employed in the Hydro-Drill camp.

"Why do we have to go all the way back to fetch our askari?" Loomis asked, following McKracken back to the Land Rover.

"Because the old man is a good map reader."

"Map reader? We need a map to go and roast a goat? Where are we going anyway?"

"Wait here, I'll be right back," was all McKracken said as he jumped into the driver's seat.

When the vehicle returned with the old askari, the men, with the addition of a pubescent boy, departed from the home, Lokori and the goat-provider carrying spears. They walked along one of the laagers that were fed by the Baboon Hills, keeping to the shade of the banks. During the onset of their walk they spotted a few of the area's scarce human inhabitants: small girls driving grey, slow-moving donkeys, occasionally whacking the animals with long thin branches, and bare-chested Turkana women in dark leather aprons, their bodies swiveling as they balanced the loads on their heads; all of them blending into the distance as silent, solitary figures.

The laager grew narrower and they were forced to scramble down into it. Loomis sensed an increase in gradient as he stepped, and soon they were inside a tightly closed gorge, the stone ramparts on each side grooved and ribbed with jagged, ochre-colored ledges of sandstone and shale. For a good hour more they trudged on into the deeper depths of this defile, through dark shadows that were funneled in by slanting sunlight. Suddenly the chattering of the men ceased, and all was quiet save for the piercing cry of an adeke bird which rang against the rock walls, warning the canyon of approaching strangers. Minutes later, a baboon barked in the silence. A cloud of swifts swooshed by, startling Loomis.

Despite the supposed lightness of the occasion, he was somewhat ill at ease.

Eventually they came upon a small sand bar tenanted by a few stunted esekon trees and the little band abruptly halted.

"This is where we shall slaughter it," Lokori declared.

The men sat down in a semi-circle, except for the goat-owner who was holding the goat by its muzzle, and the elderly askari, who now held one of the spears and was beginning some type of speech. A few short words and he stabbed the goat with a quick prick of the spear. The goat made no sound, but stood for a few seconds, before flopping down on its side. Blood spouted like a little geyser from the hole in its flank until one last surge signaled the beast's expiration. It appeared the old man had pierced the goat directly in the heart.

Lokori took off his abarait, the round, razor-sharp knife he wore around his wrist, and sliced the goat's belly up the middle while McKracken and the sheet-clad boy placed rocks in a semi-circle to serve as their 'table'. Then they gathered piles of branches and lit a huge bonfire.

In the meantime, the old man held the entrails of the animal, examining the small intestines, and all of the party soon gathered around him.

"Map reading," McKracken whispered to Loomis.

The old man spoke while pointing to certain cysts and colored splotches that appeared on the convoluted viscera. McKracken recapped the aged askari's pronouncements in Kiswahili for the benefit of Loomis. The first of these proclamations generated anxious comments from the others.

"Tst, tst...very bad," McKracken announced. "He sees no rain in Turkana this year..."

The elderly askari continued to unfold the animal's insides, running an index finger lightly over the surface, before making the next prediction.

"Ho, ho, now he sees enemies...enemies from the west are preparing to attack..."

"Attack? Where?" Loomis asked.

"He did not see."

Loomis then heard the old guy mentioning something about a mzungu, something about...being killed. "What's he saying?"

"A white man will be killed in the east, near the lake..."

"How?"

"Enemies."

There was a short pause in the translating while McKracken listened.

"You see that black spot? The old man says that is the Kokolok area and it is a place which should be avoided. It is unhealthy."

"Unhealthy? In what way?"

"Doesn't say."

Loomis gave a wry smile. "Enemies?"

"Maybe."

The old man must have finished seeing things, for they proceeded to take all the organs and skewer them with sticks which they subsequently planted around the blazing fire. Then the boy was called over. He got down on his knees in front of the dead goat, stretched open the rent in the belly, and inserted his head inside the carcass, slurping up all the blood which had collected on the bottom.

His head emerged showing red-streaked, distended cheeks gorged with blood which he swallowed with a single jerk of his head. That sight made Loomis feel rather queasy. After that they carried the whole carcass, fur and skin still on it, and dumped it on the fire.

Twenty minutes later and the goat was cooked. Loomis was given the delicacies of honour – the small intestine, the liver, and something that looked like an appendix. Then they got down to the real meat-eating. Loomis ate ravenously, even the skin, at least the thin crispy parts; the thick rubbery parts he discarded when no one was looking. He noticed the goat-provider did not partake.

"How come he's not eating?"

"It is his goat," McKracken explained. "We do not eat a goat we have given to someone. It is yours now, the whole goat." McKracken smiled as he stuck a rib in his mouth.

More pieces were brought and Loomis continued, but slowly now, for he was stuffed.

"You are a great meat-eater, Ebu Lokwan, the White Hyena!" Lokori exclaimed, laughing merrily. "In your country, do you read intestines?"

"No, we don't."

"How do you know when and where it will rain and where the enemies are?"

"Did you ever look up at night and see a star moving slowly across the sky?"

"Yes! I have seen that!"

"We put them up there. They move around the whole world. They are like eyes. They see where the rain and enemies are."

"Woi-ta-koit!"

"Some are so powerful, they can even see you standing next to your animals."

"Awaa!"

"And we also have great weapons that could destroy the whole world, just like that!" Loomis snapped his fingers.

"Woi-ta-koit! The whole world? Even we here?"

"Yes," Loomis answered.

"Those are bad weapons. If you and your enemies have a battle, you will kill everybody, even us, and we are not involved in your quarrel. We, we kill only our enemies, and only our enemies kill us. It is not right, your way, where you kill everybody."

Loomis couldn't refute the man's logic.

When the entire goat was consumed, except for the head and hind leg, which were given to the old askari (somehow being the proper thing to do, perhaps a fee for his divinations), everyone got up and wiped the grease from their hands all over themselves, mostly on their legs and chest, as was the custom. Then they started their trek back while the sun was completing its fall from the sky, its orange, sunset light creating a landscape of soft pastels, in earth colors, red, buff, and grey.

* * *

The following week Loomis was in Lodwar, one of the few occasions where he actually accompanied the supply run. His first stop was the Catholic mission, where he had to arrange to get more maize and beans for the casual laborers, and of course to check the mail. Together with McKracken, outside the mission office, he met the bishop: a short, white-haired man with glasses who walked in slow, careful steps. His face was old and it carried an expression of reconciled weariness.

"Good morning, Mr. Loomis."

"Good morning, your highness."

"The correct address is 'My Lord'. But you can just call me bishop. Or John, if you like. Ejok," he said politely, turning to McKracken. "How is your water drilling going?" he asked them jointly.

"Not bad. A bit slow," Loomis replied. "I came to order more food."

"Well, you know where the stores are and who the clerk is." As if that was sufficient enough small talk for him, the bishop turned to walk away.

"Is Father Tom around?" Loomis inquired, calling after him.

The bishop looked back with a face even more tired than before. "He is with our Lord Jesus Christ."

"Huh?"

"I'm sorry, I thought you'd heard. Father Thomas O'Shaughnessy was killed a little over a week ago."

A cold shock preceded Loomis's response, while a lump simultaneously formed in his throat. "No, no...can't be! Killed? How?"

"He went up to Todenyang near the Ethiopian border to try and negotiate peace between the Turkana and Marille. The Marille murdered him before he got to the meeting place."

"Oh dear God," Loomis sighed, gripped with a murky consternation. Then, for some reason, it occurred to him to ask, "How do you know it was the Marille?"

"It is an old custom of theirs, the warriors always cut off the testicles of a man they've slain. Now, if you don't mind, I must go up to the school for an important board meeting about the budget. We who remain must tread on, however difficult. Good luck in your work." And with that he slowly lumbered off.

"You see," McKracken said, "it was in the map reading."

"See what?" he snapped angrily. "Father Tom died about a week ago, probably a few days before we slaughtered that goat. The old man heard that news from somewhere and announced it when he looked at the goat's guts. That's how these guys do it."

"Maybe," was McKracken's guarded response.

They walked a minute or two in silence.

"McKracken," Loomis suddenly addressed. "What was that bad place the old man said to avoid?"

"Kokolok."

"Shit," he said under his breath. They had to drill a borehole in Kokolok.

* * *

That night Loomis had trouble sleeping. Disturbing thoughts were badgering him: all that talk about enemies and map reading. These guys knew something. They had scouts and spies – a veritable information network. He reluctantly admitted there could be some truth behind the talk. Trouble could be just ahead.

Now the fear came back, that fear of death he never experienced before this contract.

He recalled that time he was doing seismic work in Stiegler's Gorge, descending sheer, two-hundred-foot cliffs hanging on to only a sisal rope tied to a tree. He had been carrying detonators in his shirt pocket, liable to blow a hole in his chest at the slightest impact. He had slipped, and slid a full thirty feet before he managed to grab hold of an isolated bush, and escaped unscathed, only having ripped his trousers. He remembered laughing and then telling the team leader that he owed him a new pair of jeans.

Or how about that time when they were repairing the foundations of the railroad bridges on the Central Tanzanian Line? They had a piling rig on a platform, just the allowable one and a half meters from the active track and a goods train came roaring by with a door to one of the wagons hanging open. The door had hit the rig and flew off, nearly decapitating him. He had picked it up and joked that he could use it for the shanty he was building in Mathare Valley, and everyone had split their sides with laughter.

Come to think of it, he had never worried about the possibility of not coming back from a job. That's because he never had anything to come back to. But now he did, or so he thought.

He slipped into a fitful sleep filled with plaguing dreams. Amonee was in one of them. He was walking along with her down a long, dark corridor that seemed to have no terminus, melting away into blackness. She was walking fast and he couldn't keep up with her. He begged her to slow down but she kept to her pace, walking faster and faster until eventually the darkness swallowed her up. He had lost her, and overcome with unbearable anguish, desperately called out her name over and over again, but to no avail. She was gone.

For the whole of the next day, his mind was not on his work, nagged by an unidentifiable disconcertment.

* * *

And the next night, reading in his tent, sleep did not come any easier.

He threw the book down, and it landed with a slap and a slide on the canvas floor. "Stupid book."

He lay on his cot feeling a bit ashamed at his reaction, the dancing flame of his hurricane lamp throwing shadows around.

It's just a book, he told himself.

But to be fair, he really didn't like that part. The part he had just read. Didn't like it at all.

He rose and picked up the copy of *Anna Karenina* that she had given him and put it on his table. Maybe he just didn't feel like reading something that was depressing, or maybe it was because he was irritable that he still hadn't received a letter from Amonee, even though it had been over a month since he had returned to work.

In any case, he had to admit that he was no longer interested in finishing the book, because he really didn't like that part. The part where Anna threw herself in front of a train.

* * *

Her letter finally arrived a week later, on just another hot, bright, dusty day when Ezekiel brought the mail in from one of his runs to Lodwar. Loomis took the envelope from the old driver's hand and opened it with the usual anticipation that possessed him whenever he received one of her letters. Unable to wait, he read it as he walked back to his tent, but soon slowed his stride and questioned whether walking and reading at the same time could be straining his mental faculties, for the words she wrote made no sense to him. They were incomprehensible. Or was it that he simply refused to grasp their meaning?

Inside his tent, he sat on the chair to read it again. During the second reading his vague fears gelled into a harsh and brutal reality.

My beloved Daryl...

Beloved? How could she use that word in such a letter?

I know this letter will upset you...

Upset me? Surely that's an understatement!

...but truly the pain you are feeling as you read this letter is matched by mine as I write it. I never wanted what we had to end...

No? Then why are you writing me this fucking letter?

...nor did I ever think ahead to this day when I would say goodbye to you...

Say? At least that would have been more decent of you. But you're writing it, writing me off!

...please don't believe it has anything to do with you, it is my secret burden, meant for me alone... I had the knowledge from the beginning that it could never be. But I lacked the courage to admit it, and now I have hurt you...

Jon has come back to Kenya...

Jon? I thought he was history. It was me you said you loved! Should I roll over just because he decided to pop back in the picture? Who the hell IS this sonafabitch?

...and it would not be wise to continue seeing each other...

She's saying I'm not good enough for her. The bitch! She was just using me, using me for a good time. I've been a sap! ... No, it can't be...

...you are a very special person and I know you will find someone else, someone who is better than I...

No, please, Amonee, please, give me another chance...

...it is your happiness I pray for, not mine. I know you will never understand this, but I am making this decision out of my love for you, which you should never ever doubt...

No, please...oh please.

...I beg you to accept my decision. Please don't try to see me. Forget me. Amonee.

He crumpled the letter into a little ball and threw it violently against the canvas wall of the tent. He put his head in his hands, on the verge of tears. Then he got angry.

"Shit!" He got up and stood staring at his littered desk. "Godammit!" he swore again, shoving his papers, books, and maps onto the floor. He continued to shout, overthrow his table, and noisily kick about his various articles of property until Mutua called to him from outside.

"Bwana Roomis, is there a ploblem?"

"Mutua, I don't want to be disturbed by anyone! No one! Not even Shigoli, do you hear?"

Mutua appropriately left him. Loomis paced back and forth in the small space of his tent like a caged animal, black with fury and burning with pain. For the whole day he did not come out of his tent. Although Shigoli did make an effort, Loomis yelled at him in no uncertain terms to go away.

He didn't come out at night either. A few of the concerned crew stood outside his tent, listening to him muttering English words inside, clueless as to what they should do.

At nine o'clock the next morning, Mutua, peeking in, saw Loomis, fully clothed, sprawled out on his cot dead asleep. A nearly empty plastic gallon container was on the floor nearby, as well as a balled-up piece of paper. Mutua sneaked in to pick up the paper, and once outside, unfolded it. Although his command of written English was not so good, he caught enough of the words to get a drift of what the situation was.

Loomis woke up shortly after, sick as a dog. He stumbled outside and vomited, and then the pain came back; a pain that never relented, ever present from one continuous moment to the next. A raw pain of emptiness.

She had defined him, formed him, she had entered inside him

filling him up, and now that she had left, she had left him nothing of himself; he was merely a vacuous shell, a nobody, a nothing, a dead carcass.

A bum. After thirty years of existence, that's what he was. A misfit who rejected his own society, because it had rejected him, he was at best only an honorary member of the one he was living in, nothing more than an orphan adopted in transit.

She's out of your league, Geoff had told him.

The Turkana contract now appeared in his mind to be a prison sentence, a punishment. He was helpless to do anything about his situation with Amonee, being physically separated from her by over a thousand kilometers. Nor could he convincingly request an emergency trip to Nairobi giving his faltering love-life as a reason.

He went back in his tent, sat on his cot, and poured some more chang'aa into a tin cup. He didn't know any other way he could stop the ache.

Shigoli came by. "Bwana Loomis."

"Don't bother me!" he shouted from inside his tent.

"We have to go to Lodwar and pick up Bwana Greenbottom."

"Ah fuck him."

"You stay here?"

"Yes, I stay here!"

And for the rest of the day, just like yesterday, he proceeded to get as drunk as he could get.

* * *

Greenbottom arrived when the evening did, and despite being told that Bwana Loomis was not feeling well with a very bad headache, he insisted upon visiting his tent.

"Daryl, how are you feeling now?"

No answer.

"Are you sleeping?"

Loomis lay in his cot pretty much ossified, seething at that last question. If he were sleeping could he answer that question, and if he could answer the question was he sleeping? The inane logic only intensified his anger. *Get the fuck away from me you idiot,* he wanted to say. But he knew his most effective tactic would be to say nothing, and that worked, for eventually Greenbottom went away.

But as the night crept over the camp, he grew restless, feeling the urge to vent his bitterness. He left his tent surreptitiously with the fourth gallon of chang'aa, and stole into the night. Of course, in the desert he could not get far enough away, for the openness of it, helped by the wind, would carry his voice like a carrier pigeon bringing a message from afar. In any case, when he felt he had walked a sufficient distance, he began to shout into the night. At one point, he stopped his sauntering, and stood staggering, looking at the sky. The stars were shining bright, looking at him, or so he imagined, in silent condescension. He thrust his arm upward and pointed accusingly at them. "YOU CHEATED ME!"

He kept walking, alternating his self-utterances with loud, nonsensical shouts. "Bitch!" he cried on more than one occasion. He didn't realize that he was ambling closer and closer to the camp.

A figure approached, and in the leaden glow of the heavens, he could see it was a man wearing, of all things, a bathrobe.

"Loomis, what's all this racket?"

Jon would be wearing a bathrobe at about this time, with a self-satisfied smirk on his face after fucking Amonee...

Loomis charged at him. "I'LL FUCKING KILL YOU!"

Fortunately for the both of them, Loomis was met with a mountain of human flesh in the form of Shigoli.

"Stop, Bwana Daryl, don't make it worse."

"I'M GOING TO RIP HIS THROAT OUT!"

Shigoli managed to wrench him away, and held him up as they paraded around the camp, while Loomis, in a drunken stream-of-consciousness, poured out his soul.

A morning later, Loomis woke up, his head aching as if some little creature inside it with a sledgehammer was striking at the sides of his skull. His mouth feeling like it was full of cotton, he picked up the radio message that was lying on his pillow. It was from Barnes. Loomis was wanted in Nairobi for immediate consultation.

NAIROBI, APRIL, 1980

The room was large, with a floor as wide as a gymnasium's, and a ceiling as high as a cathedral's. There must have been at least several hundred people inside it, a crowd of mostly Europeans with a slight peppering of Africans and Asians.

The room was elegant, with mahogany paneling, exquisitely patterned Turkish carpets, furnished with baldachin sofas and custom-crafted furniture of teak and ebony, with electric candles on the walls, and a huge, glittering chandelier which looked down on it all.

And the room was resonating, vibrating with the sounds of the string quartet playing a Viennese waltz in front of the wall-sized, royally-draped French windows.

The performers were young Europeans, around fifteen years of age, the three girls and one boy (the cello player) all dressed in their finest evening wear. They finished to an enthusiastic applause from the audience, and they took humble, dainty bows before they walked away with their instruments, leaving the stage area to a plump, grey-haired woman stuffed into an overly tight gold lame evening gown, who sauntered front and center.

"Weren't they lovely, ladies and gentlemen? So young, yet so gifted..." More clapping. "And now, what we all have been waiting for. Our last performer for this delightful evening, perhaps our last chance to see her before her European tour, Kenya's own, Pamela Emuria, who will honor us with compositions from Liszt, Tchaikovesky, and Grieg. A warm welcome please, Pamela Emuria."

She walked on stage with an uncanny grace, a lucent aura that seemed not of this earth and which was more than just the effect from the diaphanous white, floor-length gown she was wearing, but rather exuded from her very movements. The audience responded with a standing ovation as she approached the concert grand piano, then, as she sat down upon her stool, they abruptly ceased their clapping and fell back into their seats in silent, rapt anticipation.

"My first piece is the Piano Concerto in A minor, Opus 16, by Grieg."

The lights of the chandelier and the wall lamps waned, dimming the hall to darkness, and she was framed by the lambent glow of a single spotlight. She took a deep breath before placing her fingers to the keys, and touching them ever so lightly with an intimate caress, began to play. Dulcet notes danced in the air and her body rolled gently to the melody, her head nodding knowingly and assuredly, her eyes closed in contemplation. She did not use a music sheet, for her favorite pieces she kept in her heart, never playing them the same way twice, their feeling and tempo conducted by whatever spirit possessed her at the moment. There was a power of high drama in her forte that recalled the tragedies of an onerous life, and took the listener's breath away; her pianissimo sung a song of melancholy and bittersweet irony, and then wistfully laid you down upon a soothing, silken sea of unparalleled serenity. And although her playing electrified all who heard it, thrilled by the radiance of the Black Diamond, she herself was alone in her music, and it was only at the end of each piece, when the audience awoke from their trance to applaud and cheer, that she was aware of the presence of others.

Later, her performance over, she sipped a cup of tea on an out-of-the-way sofa and soon was accosted by scores of people coming up to congratulate her. Among the first of these was an eminent trio: a broad European in a tuxedo, greying at the temples, his face refined in appearance, in the company of a handsome, silver-haired white lady, grave and aristocratic upon the arm of a middle-aged African gentleman ebullient in a three-piece worsted suit. The African, even more so than the others, carried himself with a stately posture, and his smoothened features – the soft smile and the paternal eyes – were apt to put one at ease. The gold chain of a pocket watch dangled noticeably from a button on his vest, and his whole mien was highlighted by the monocle he put on to study the program he

was holding. As this little entourage drew nearer, Pamela respect-
fully rose.

The white woman spoke first. "You play so beautifully, Pamela,
doesn't she, Everret?" She turned to her husband.

The African in the three-piece suit held his hand out to Pamela.
"She does honor to all Kenyans. Simply superb playing, my dear,
superb," he said in impeccable Queen's English. "I must say, that
was a marvelously jaunty interpretation of Liszt's Liebelstraum."

Pamela accepted his hand. "Thank you, Your Honorable."

"Pamela, I believe you know Sir Stewart Montague, the Chairman
of the Kenyan Cultural Center," the African said, turning to the
tuxedoed white man.

Cultural Center. The phrase nettled her, bringing Kingozi to
mind.

Montague gave her a hearty handshake. "Of course we know
each other. Good to see you again, Pamela."

"Yes, likewise, Sir Stewart."

"It's a shame Jon couldn't be here," His Honorable said. "He had
to take care of some urgent business matters, as a favor to me. I'm
truly sorry he missed your wonderful performance."

I'm truly sorry too, she found herself thinking. *I'm truly sorry,
Daryl, but it's not what I had wanted for myself, believe me. If only you
could know...* "That's quite alright, sir, I understand," another part of
her was saying.

"I hope you can forgive his abrupt departure, now that you
realize that I'm somehow responsible. I would hate to be the cause of
a quarrel between you two," he chuckled good-naturedly.

"We're going to miss you, dear," lamented His Honorable's white
wife.

"She'll come back to visit us. Won't you, Pamela?" the Minister
said playfully.

"Yes," she answered. "I shall come back."

* * *

He squirmed self-consciously in his chair, not quite able to suppress feeling like a naughty kid who had been sent to the principal's office. Barnes was playing his role perfectly, swiveling around in his chair talking on the cordless phone, silently going over his files, summoning people to his office to discuss unrelated matters; in general, acting as if Loomis was not even present. Loomis was aware of Barnes's game – he was trying to make him feel like a piece of shit. It was working. He did.

Now, with no one else in the room, on the phone, nor over the intercom, the office became uncomfortably quiet. Barnes was staring so hard at a sheet in front of him Loomis half expected it to ignite. Then the managing director's head suddenly jerked up, with that same burning gaze now directed toward him. "Do you know how much it costs to send the Aztec to and from Lodwar? Twelve thousand shillings. I should bill you for that. And I should terminate your contract immediately. That's what I should do."

But you won't, thought Loomis. *It's too late in the contract to get a replacement.*

"And don't think it's too late to get someone else," Barnes barked, anticipating the thought. "Haley said he would go up if necessary. He's very disappointed in you. Don't expect any more recommendations from him. You've made him look very bad."

"I'm sorry."

"I'm not satisfied with that, damn you! Insulting, no, no attacking, attacking one of the directors, ranting like a madman! And in front of the watu!" Barnes paused his castigation, but his eyes continued with their hard stare. "If I should decide to let this pass, and should you be responsible for any further mess, I'll shut you out of East Africa so tight you won't be able to work anywhere from Somalia to Mozambique, that's how bad you'll be blacklisted."

Loomis reckoned he was capable of doing it too.

"And I'm capable of doing just that, so don't take that as an idle threat." The cold blue eyes switched off their stare while his voice changed and took on a paternal tone. "Listen, Daryl, I understand the rough conditions, the pressure of work, of being alone with the watu. I've been in this business long enough to recognize what can happen to a man in the bush. Now I think you've just had a slight attack of bush madness, that's why I'm going to forget this incident and give you a second chance. However, if you don't think you can handle the contract anymore, just tell me, tell me now, I'll respect you for that."

"I'll be alright from now on."

"Are you sure? Remember, my threat still holds."

"Yes, I'm sure."

"Look. Spend the night here, get drunk, get yourself a little dolly bird, hump her to death, anything to get whatever it is in your system out for good. Tomorrow you go back afresh, and you finish the contract without further trouble. Right?"

"Right. I'm sorry about this. It won't happen again."

"I'm sure it won't."

They shook hands and Loomis left the office.

* * *

Out on the streets, he went to a kiosk and bought a pack of cigarettes, and, while chain smoking, wandered aimlessly about until a poster plastered on the column of a streetlamp attracted his attention with the faces of performers, advertising some notable event.

SPECIAL CONCERT §§§§§§§§§§§§§§§§§§§§§§§§§§§§§ SPECIAL CONCERT
SATURDAY APRIL 2
MICHELE SIMONET – FLAUTIST
INTERNATIONAL SCHOOL STRING QUARTET
PAMELA EMURIA – CONCERT PIANIST

GUEST OF HONOR
THE HONORABLE EVERRET MUTHONGO, MINISTER OF

JUSTICE
ADULTS 200/- CHILDREN 50/-
CULTURAL HALL OF THE BRITISH COUNCIL
§§§§§§§§§§ IN AID OF DOCTOR BARNARDO'S CHILDREN'S
HOME §§§§§§§§§§§

He stared at her picture longingly, as other passers-by continued to file past, some brushing lightly against him with curt apologies. He stood rooted, her image haunting him. Perhaps, perhaps if she told him to his face, the shock of it would free him of this crazy hunger, this unbearable longing he had for her. He would have to see her, even though the notion intimidated him. He would start slowly, feel around a bit, and build himself up to it. He would go to Kingozi first. Maybe they could tell him something about what was going on.

No one at Kingozi knew anything, not even Omondi. She hadn't been seen for over a month. Just stopped coming. No explanations, no word why. In fact, they were about to get in touch with him to inquire of her whereabouts. The inevitable questions then followed, and Loomis had to leave brusquely, leaving his friends to wonder what was afoot.

He had no choice now. He boarded a bus and took the ride to the university, his heart thumping during the whole of the trip. He alighted and, impelled by the momentum of his resolve, strode straight to the office. When he got there he found only Katy Hesland, and in spite of his original aim, he was somehow relieved by this. Perhaps she could give him some moral support before he faced Amonee. As he entered she looked up, her face betraying what appeared to be a sense of dread.

"Oh, a...hello, Daryl." Her tone and mannerism clearly expressed a message akin to 'you shouldn't be here'.

He closed the door behind him and stood facing her. "Hello, Katy. Is Amonee here?"

"No, she's...not around."

257

He studied Amonee's desk. There were papers and books, files, pens and pencils. It looked as if she was still here at the university at any rate. "Where is she?"

Katy didn't answer.

"Where is she, Katy, I have to see her."

She got up in order to meet him.

"Daryl, listen," she said nervously, "it's important you leave her alone. You'll only make matters worse. She knows what she's doing."

"Does she? I didn't know she had such a sadistic streak in her."

"Daryl, you can't understand...if you love her you'll let her go, she's..."

"Katy, put yourself in my place," Loomis interrupted. "I want her to tell me to my face that she wants him and not me. If she can do that, then I'll walk away like a gentleman."

"You don't understand, she's doing this for you..."

"For me!" he shouted, feeling incredulous and insulted.

"The greatest sacrifice anyone could give..."

"What sacrifice?" he sneered with a face bordering on disgust. "Is she at her house?"

"Her life, Daryl," she beseeched desperately, "her life!"

His initial timidity was dissolving in a surge of testosterone. "What the fuck are you talking about?"

"I'll talk to her for you," Katy pleaded, "then, if she agrees to see you...Daryl?"

He was already out the door.

Katy put her hand to her forehead. She knew it would end up like this. But what could she have done? She was only a spectator.

He walked to the faculty residence, entering Gandhi Lane where her house was. As he got closer, his feet got colder, causing him to slow his step until he finally stopped a short distance from her house. He froze, making an effort to see through the windows. There she was, in the sitting room, and he could hear her singing the opera from the sheets of paper she held in her hand. There was someone else, a man, seated in the armchair in the corner, a spectral apparition with long silver hair. His head was supported with his left hand, resting on his thumb and fingers in the manner of someone watching television.

Loomis felt sick; he wasn't sure if he should confront her in his presence.

But maybe that would be best, all three of them, clear the air once and for all.

Or would she despise him for that?

Unsure, he paced up and down till he could find the answer. Then he found it. It was lying in the trash can by the curb. The Turkana doll.

He went over and solicitously picked it up. It looked at him glassily, making an irrefutable statement of finality.

Slowly he walked back up the lane holding the doll, too stunned, too overwhelmed with a plethora of different intense emotions to notice the two, well-dressed Africans coming towards him; not until they were almost upon him did he bother to look up.

"Excuse me," one of them said, stopping Loomis with an outstretched arm.

"Do you live here?"

"No, sorry, I don't."

"You work here?"

"No, I..."

"What are you doing here?" asked the other.

"That's none of your business," Loomis answered churlishly.

"It is our business," corrected the first, holding a card out. A police identification card – Special Branch. "We're having trouble with some of our students," the man resumed. "We know there are outside people stirring them up. Can we see your identification please?"

Loomis took out his wallet, picking out his job I.D., his business card, his driver's license, and a photocopy of his residence-work permit, and handed the items to the officer who addressed him. The fellow in turn displayed them to his comrade who wrote down the particulars in a small notepad.

"Mr. Loomees? Is that your name?"

"LoomIS," he clarified. "Isn't that the name written on my papers?"

"Mmm," he droned as he examined the documents.

"I was just visiting someone," Loomis tried to explain. "I'm not an agitator. And if it makes you happy, I'm leaving now anyway to go back to town."

"We'll escort you."

The threesome walked in a hostile silence, taking the lane that led out of the campus. When they reached a deserted bus-stop along Chiromo Road, the man who seemed to be the ranking officer turned and said, "We shall leave you here."

"Kind of you to...uuuh!"

Only a slight dip of the shoulder, that's all Loomis saw. Then he felt a vacuum sucking his insides out and he crumpled to the ground, frantically searching for his breath. He lay groaning. It was the meanest right to the stomach he had ever received.

The man who had delivered the blow crouched over him. "It's over, Mr. Loomees, understand? Finished. Don't come back." He stood erect, and joining his associate, left him lying on the concrete.

Loomis had felt pretty lousy before this unexpected confrontation. Now he felt even lousier.

And to make it worse, she kept staring at him, her glass bead eyes glittering like black diamonds from the reflections of a neon streetlamp, almost mocking him. He rose to his feet and picked up the doll, and headed off to nowhere in particular.

* * *

He opened his eyes and immediately panicked. There was a painful pulsing in his head, his throat burned, and he had no idea where he was; in a bed, with a woman, inside a strange room. No, the room...there was something familiar about it. He recognized the pea-green concrete walls, the faded blue-cotton curtains, and the big bureau in the corner crowned with framed photographs and a Japanese-make cassette player. He was in Teresa's one-room flat in Ngara, right outside of city center. He looked at the woman beside him just to make sure. It was Terry alright. Her slim, sexy figure was still clothed in an iridescent-green belted blouse and a provocatively tight pair of designer jeans.

Good old Terry. Just like old times. In those days of carefree carousing, whenever he got excessively inane with alcohol, if any of the girls were around, one of them, whoever was having a slow night, would take him to her place and keep him out of trouble. He knew many of them: Vicky, Maria, Monica...girls working in the tourist trade; a bit of heaven for five hundred shillings. But to him they were friends. Just friends.

"Terry, Terry?" He shook her. "Teresa?"

"Ummm, nini? What?" she muttered in her sleep.

He spoke to her in Kiswahili. "Terry, get up. Get up and tell me what happened last night."

"Daryl, please, go back to sleep," she said drowsily, without moving. "In a little while I'll make tea." She rolled away from him, over on her side. "Let me rest a little."

"I don't want any tea. I have to get going. Tell me what happened before I leave."

With much effort, she struggled to sit up on the side of the bed and proceeded to rub the sleep out of her eyes with both hands. Then, dropping them, lightly slapped her thighs with her palms. "You were very bad last night."

"How?"

"You were yelling out insults to the Special Branch, asking strangers if they were working for them, daring any Special Branch people to come out and show themselves...going on and on about the Special Branch in a loud voice. That type of talk is dangerous here in Nairobi. I had to get you out of there."

"Out of where? Where were we?"

"The disco at the Ainsworth."

"I don't remember."

"Daryl, it's one thing to get into fights, but to insult the security people, that is extremely bad. You were lucky."

"I'm sorry."

"Daryl, are you in trouble?"

"No, there's no problem...really." He looked at her and felt ashamed. How could he explain? He had acted like a jerk over something which Terry herself could rebuke him about – love. A mother at fifteen, abandoned by the child's father, her parents impoverished peasants, she had fled to the big city to seek employment. Except there was no employment for an uneducated village girl like her, so she became self-employed, renting her body out so that her kid could eat.

That was love. Real love. At least she hadn't thrown the infant down a pit latrine like so many other young, unwed mothers were doing these days.

"Mama!" cried a small voice outside.

"Wait!" Terry called back. She got up and opened the door to let in a little half-caste girl about four years in age, her second child. She slept in the kitchen room next door. Her name was Patricia, and she represented one of the risks of the business. Or one of the blessings. Loomis often couldn't tell which.

"Say hello to Uncle Daryl, Trish," Terry told her, returning to sit on the bed.

The cream-colored girl in the yellow pajamas went shyly over to him and mutely held out her hand.

"Hello, Tricia, how, are, you?" he asked in primary-school English.

"Fai-eeen," she whispered, barely audible.

"She's learning English already," Loomis commented to the girl's mother.

"Yes, and next year we start school, don't we, Trish?" She picked her daughter up and placed her on her lap, hugging her.

"Where's Fortunata?"

"She's with my parents in Nyeri."

Loomis put on his shoes, then stood up and slipped on his cashmere sport coat. Searching through the pockets, he eventually came up with two hundred shillings. "Here, take this, it'll help to pay the rent. I have to go now."

Teresa, putting the child down, took the money and rose to escort him to the door, a journey of about three steps. As he opened it, she tapped him on the shoulder. "Don't forget this," she said, handing him the goatskin doll.

"Was I still hanging on to that thing?"

"You don't remember where I bumped into you?"

"No."

"It was at the admissions door. You were having an argument with the ticket clerk. You were insisting on paying admission for the doll. He thought you were making fun of him and I had to straighten it out. Then inside the disco you kept dancing with it and introducing it by some name I don't even remember."

Loomis's face simpered into a goofy smile. "God, I must have been shitfaced."

"You were the worst I'd ever seen you."

"Give it to Trish. I don't want it." And with that, he turned and exited.

TURKANA DISTRICT, APRIL 1980

His reappearance at the site was awkward. He had trouble looking his men in the face, so great was his embarrassment. A most unpleasant experience was swallowing all his pride and apologizing to Greenbottom, who was still present, and who had decided to remain on site until Loomis proved emotionally fit to carry on.

It was in the office caravan that Loomis carried out his apology.

"Hello, Reg."

His greeting was met by silence.

"It would be an extreme understatement to say that I'm sorry, and that I apologize for my ridiculous, uncalled for, and despicable behavior."

Greenbottom was looking down at something on his desk, more for the purpose of avoiding looking at Loomis than anything else. "I really don't want to discuss it, and, to be frank, I am not interested in nor will I accept any apologies. Nothing you say can revoke my utter disrespect for a man who has shown himself to be so weak, so utterly lacking in self-respect, as to display himself in such a manner, particularly in front of our employees."

"I understand, and I totally concur. However, I think that it is only fair for you to know the circumstances behind my actions."

"I'm not interested, as I said."

"No, it is important that you know that in my alcoholically deranged mind, you were someone else."

"I don't care. The only thing I care about is your ability to carry out the rest of this contract in an efficient and productive manner." He finally looked up. "Is that understood?"

"Clearly."

"Very well. Now, I've been looking at your schedule of works and I've come to the conclusion, that instead of going to Lokitoptop, we proceed next to Kokolok. There is a new murram road that intersects with the road we used coming here. It's not on the maps, but I have already scouted it and driven all the way there. I know that you planned to work there on the way back south, but it would save us some time if we go there directly."

"Yes, if you think so, we shall do that."

Kokolok. Anyway, they would have to go there sooner or later.

"Now, as for the current situation, the rig has been positioned, and we expect to spud in this evening and to grout the surface casing. We start the pilot hole in the morning, and I expect you to be ready for work."

"I'm ready, Reginald."

"Don't call me by my name, not Reginald, and certainly not Reg."

"Right."

Loomis took that as a cue to leave, and he did so with a sigh of relief. *Glad that's over.* Now it was just to sort of explain it to the men.

So in the evening, he gathered them together, where they sat in front of him on assorted camp stools and on convenient places on the ground.

"I can only say, I'm sorry, and that I had some problems, but now it's over."

"A woman!" someone shouted, laughing.

"Yeah, can you believe that!" he said, laughing himself.

Now, everyone was chuckling.

"They are the worst disease," Ben commented.

Another round of harmonized mirth.

"Don't worry, Bwana Loomis," Shigoli assured. "Forget it and let's go back to work. You are a good boss."

"Sawa."

O.T., the welder, made his terse contribution. "Remember. One, Time. That's how to do it," which sent everyone into a minor laughing fit, and it brought Loomis just a little bit closer to his former philosophy regarding women.

Sikhendu got up and went into a little dance, singing some raucous BaLuyha song that made everyone cheer.

McKracken was next. "You are strong, stronger than them, you are the White Hyena!"

This gave rise to a wave of merriment among them, chortling, guffawing, and slapping their knees.

"Okay, no need to say anymore," he told them, grinning. And with that, the meeting was adjourned.

Oh, the brotherhood of men. It was the shot in the arm for the reclamation of his previous self. He began to take a more poignant, philosophical view on what happened to him. Funny, he even thought of the words to an old Charley Pride song, a favorite in Kenya: 'Well, I'd rather love and lose you, than never know your love at all'.

Amonee wasn't really better than any other woman, and it was self-delusion that made him think otherwise. Sure, the initial infatuation was always euphoric, but what happens later? She probably would have gotten fat, started nagging, complaining about his habits; he probably would have had to ask permission whenever he wanted to go out for a beer. No, it was nice while it lasted, but now it was over and it was time to look ahead.

Thinking this way calmed him, despite isolated moments when the memories of things they had done together and the words they had spoken to each other gave him temporary pangs of pain. He forced himself not to look at the photos of the kids and the balloons, although he was reluctant to throw them away. But in time, all this reminiscence would pass, he rationalized.

Quite contrary to how he felt before, work became a relief to him by preventing him from dwelling too long on his personal life. And so he began to plunge all his energies into it.

Borehole number fourteen was a great success. They did not even have to test it by pumping, for the water erupted in huge spouts all on its own – a flowing well under pressure – the water shooting into the air in great gusts, free of its confinement. Everyone, the crew, the casual laborers, and dozens of local Turkana, shouted and danced with glee under the spouting water, intoxicated with the cool wetness that splashed over them; even hard-crusted Greenbottom was enthused to the point of grinning widely.

"Ebu Lakwan!" McKracken shouted.

That elicited a chanting chorus: "Ebu Lakwan, Ebu Lakwan, Ebu Lakwan!"

And all this showed Loomis that life was more than just personal worries, and made him feel stupid about his recent lament over romantic love.

* * *

On the way to borehole number fifteen, located in the area of Kokolok, everyone was in good spirits, even Greenbottom. There was no reason to suspect that their fortunes would take any radical diversion from the course they were on. In fact, access was so good, they didn't even need to build any entrance road; the way was as clear as a jaunt over a football pitch. Because of this, they were able to set up quickly.

Yet, some vague perturbation in his mind haunted him. He was timorous, but was not sure why, other than the map-reading episode that had taken place less than two months ago.

And sure enough, everything started out fine. Until the drilling got underway.

There were devils in the borehole. Although they had drilled a one-hundred-meter hole, the linings were refusing at twenty-two meters, even after reaming the hole to a diameter twice that of the linings. Loomis knew there were technical explanations: the swelling of a hydroscopic clay layer in contact with the drilling fluid, or the release of lateral earth pressure in response to the overburden pressure, blah, blah blah etcetera etcetera...in the final analysis, however, the fact was, there were devils in the borehole.

This was not the first time he had had difficulty in placing the linings to the bottom. But in all his ten odd years in the business, this was certainly the most obstinate case he had ever come across. The ground was just too stubborn. They flushed the hole repeatedly, necessitating many trips with the water bowser. They tried driving the linings in with a half-ton drop hammer. Nothing seemed to work. Loomis prepared himself for a long, drawn-out struggle.

At one point, the idea came up about slaughtering a goat. Everyone agreed that this was the thing to do, most fervently the Turkana casual laborers. And so they did, pouring all the blood inside the hole. But that didn't work either.

* * *

April 21. Just another hot, bright, dusty day. They were breaking for lunch when Loomis was distracted by a loud ruckus going on under a tall edepal tree some few hundred meters from the well site. He hurried along accompanied by Shigoli to see what was happening.

A shouting melee of Turkanas stood around the tree while two or three others were beating it with large sticks and clubs. Loomis couldn't see more than that through the crowd. He weaved his way through the mob with Shigoli following until he found McKracken. From this new position the view was more revealing. There was a man tied to the tree, writhing and screaming, but for what reason Loomis could not yet fathom. Then he realized that what he had first taken to be black-stained patches on the bark were actually angry hordes of black ants, pouring out of the wood in response to the blows by the clubs. The bound man looked familiar. It was Ekwom, the camp laborer

"McKracken, what are they doing to him?"

"They say he has slept with someone's wife, but he is denying it."

"How do they know?"

"That man," McKracken said, pointing to one member of the crowd nearest the tree, "is the husband. Yesterday he woke up and found all of his animals sitting on their haunches, and that is how he knew. He confronted his wife and she admitted it. That boy took her by force."

"His animals told him?"

"Ndio."

"And you believe that?"

"Ndio."

Loomis couldn't take his eyes off the tortured man, despite the discomfort the sight imparted. Here was a sight, similar to the beating of the thief, which brought back painful memories. He wanted to leave immediately but he just had to ask, "Is he going to be eaten alive?"

McKracken laughed, and none too quietly neither. "No. In a short while they will release him, when he admits he did it. He is just too stubborn; he doesn't want to pay the fine. Should be many cows, and the boy is poor. But he will pay it, and he will be very sore for the next few days and then itch for a month. He will remember his mistake. They are purifying him. Nothing more."

Loomis was pushed violently to one side and realized it was Greenbottom fighting his way through the crowd.

"Get out of my way! Get out, get out!" he hollered with contempt. When he made it past the first row of onlookers he turned and faced them shouting, "You primitive beasts! Ignoramuses!" He tried shooing the Turkanas back with his arms. "Get away!" He then approached the tree and upon reaching it, while still yelling disparagingly, began to untie Ekwom, inciting the Turkanas to indignant protest.

McKracken became agitated. "He is making a mistake!" he shouted. "It is bad for him to let the boy go. They are purifying him," he repeated futilely.

Greenbottom continued his ranting in English while untying the ropes, stopping frequently to brush and slap at the ants which were now biting him as well. Several of the Turkana men approached him and screamed their dissidence in his ear. But they seemed afraid to physically stop him. This white man, they thought, was a madman, and they feared to touch him. Ekwom, once freed, dived on the ground rolling himself over in the sandy gravel. Greenbottom picked him up by the arm and led him stumbling away, while the

Turkanas followed behind them, truculently voicing their vehemence.

"This is very bad," McKracken stated. "Turkana believe if he remains impure, very bad luck will follow all that are present."

"And you maybe believe that too?"

"Ndio."

"Well, I can't. I can't believe that my luck could get any worse than it's already been."

The crowd resigning, they dispersed, and with nothing more to be seen, the Hydro-Drill staff that were present returned to their camp.

Over dinner, which he took alone in his tent, Loomis pondered Greenbottom's reaction to the Turkanas. He couldn't really blame him – the sight had appeared pretty gruesome. The key was understanding people, he reflected. Greenbottom was among the group of white Kenyans who were still mourning the death of the world they had come from, a world that Loomis could not know about. From post-Victorian England straight to Imperial Africa. The country was wilder then, certainly a much more hostile and mysterious place for one of European background than the Africa of today. The strange dangers of ferocious predators, lethally poisonous snakes, and horrible diseases added to the tribulations of farming in the rough bush and forests. The indigenous inhabitants, the Africans, were a strange dark-colored people with bizarre customs and seemingly obscene rituals. Their languages were incomprehensible babble and their lifestyles were certain evidence of their savagery. At least, those were the impressions they gave to the white pioneers. So, armed with material superiority, people like Greenbottom, his forebears and his peers, set out to tame the land and civilize its people, and to rid the country of this primitive savagery, never once reflecting upon the savagery of their own race: the tyrannies, the massacres, the World Wars, Hitler, Hiroshima...even now they kept coming, the white people, but now in the cause of development, still blind to the newer, more modern forms of savagery that their own technology had conceived.

* * *

April 22nd. The weather, the persistent wind, the land, the very feel of the day, an exact replica of the day before. Consistent with this, the linings were still obstructed. Loomis stood by the rig, his brain still confounded by the unsolvable mystery below the ground. An interruption by McKracken was particularly annoying.

"Please come. You must see something."

"You don't see that I'm busy?"

"It is important."

"What could be more important than finishing this fucking borehole and getting the hell out of here?"

"More important," McKracken insisted.

"What is it about?"

"You must see."

"Right now?"

"Ndio."

Loomis reluctantly followed him away from the well site and was eventually led down into a small sandy laager, which at some points was fairly steep, and he cursed each time he lost his footing or got caught by thorns, his anger with McKracken increasing. Then he noticed the vultures circling overhead and grew curious. Below, the land leveled out, and was monotonously scattered with wiry brush and short, grey, leafless bushes, one of which McKracken was making straight for. Fixing his eyes on this particular bush, Loomis could now make out a pair of black feet sticking out from behind it. He slowly circled around with McKracken to get a full view of the body. It was lying face down in sand that was splotched with pools of caked and dried blood. A shiny black mound of flies covered the upper parts, and as Loomis drew near, the swarm took off with an amplified buzz. He squatted over the body to view the numerous bloody cuts on the man's back, neck, and head – the work of an abarait. He looked up at McKracken whose sombre face said nothing, then turned to stare at the corpse again for a few more seconds before turning it over. The face was badly slashed but still recognizable. It had belonged to Ekwom.

"Well, it looks like the irate husband got his revenge at last," he remarked noncommittally.

"This is very bad," McKracken said, finally speaking up. He looked worried.

"Nobody has to know anything about this."

"This is very bad," McKracken repeated.

Loomis stood erect. "Look, there's nothing we can do for him now. Reporting it will only bring the police and endless questions. In a few days the hyenas and vultures will finish him off, even the bones, and with any luck we'll be out of here soon and no one will be any the wiser. We'll tell the bishop he ran away."

"You don't understand, this is very bad..."

"McKracken, listen, I agree but..."

"They say that when one Turkana murders another, there will be no rain that year. Many animals will die, and there will be great hunger." Having said that, McKracken turned and walked off, Loomis following him quickly.

"Don't tell anyone," Loomis reiterated, catching up.

* * *

April 23rd. First light. Loomis rose from his bed and stood up stretching himself. Darting his head out of the flaps, he cursed when he saw there was no washing-up water in the basin outside his tent. Then he realized that the person who normally took care of that was now dead. He went to the pack of cigarettes lying on the table, but withdrew from taking one, deciding to wait until he got his coffee. Caffeine and nicotine made up his breakfast these days.

"Bwana Roomis." It was Mutua. "You must come lite away."

"I'm not going anywhere until I've had my coffee. Tell Juma to hurry it up."

Mutua took the liberty of sticking his head in. "Prease, it's Bwana Gleenbottom, he's vely sick."

"I know, sick in the head. I'm also sick, sick of him and this lousy contract."

"Prease, don't make joke. Come and see."

On his way to Greenbottom's tent, Loomis couldn't help gloating sadistically. Only a week and the guy already had a case of the shits. Teach him a lesson. Now that the pompous ass had been initiated into life in the bush maybe he'd run back to Nairobi to his cozy little office.

As soon as he entered, the putrid stench hit him like a brick wall – the stench of faeces, bile, and sickness. Greenbottom was moaning and shivering face down on the bed, his head hanging over the side, and every now and then choking, retching sounds would come out of his throat. He was heaving, but despite the great effort he made to do so, only a small amount of yellowish mucous dripped slowly and viscously out to add to the slimy mess he had already vomited on the floor. With a sudden movement he bent double clutching his abdomen while groaning pitifully. Loomis did not have to be a doctor to know what it was. He was horrified. "*Kipindu-pindu,*" he breathed out, shocked.

"Kipindu-pindu?" Mutua asked in disbelief, frightened, hoping that it was not.

Loomis regained his composure. He grabbed Mutua roughly by the arm. "Keep your mouth shut!" he ordered with a menacing face. "We don't want to start a panic. Go to your tent quickly and bring the first-aid kit."

Mutua departed, trembling and shaking.

Kipindu-pindu. In its grip, you diarrhea until you bleed and puke your stomach inside out, all your life fluids slowly and agonizingly wrung out of you. A severe case needed only twelve hours or so to kill you. Go to bed feeling a bit off, and in the morning, you're dead. And it spread like wildfire. Kipindu-pindu. Cholera.

When Mutua came back with the white, wooden, red-crossed box, Loomis opened it violently and rifled through its contents, searching for Greenbottom's, as well as their, only hope – tetracycline. He found the plastic container he was looking for and opened the cap. The container was empty.

"Mutua, damn you! What happened to all the tetracycline?" he shouted. But Loomis knew what happened to it. The men believed that four or five of the capsules taken before engaging a dubious woman would make them immune to all kinds of venereal disease. Apparently they had been raiding the box before each of their trips to Lodwar.

"Mutua, you incompetent shit! YOU were in charge of the first-aid box!"

Mutua stood frozen, lacking a reply.

Don't panic, Loomis told himself. There was nothing that could bring the capsules back and Greenbottom had already reached the stage where an intravenous was vital. They had to get him to a hospital in any event. "Go and call McKracken to bring the Land Rover here. And don't say anything else other than that."

Greenbottom was sobbing deliriously. Loomis, waiting while Mutua fetched his driver, watched the suffering man with compassion mingled with guilt. He would not wish cholera on anyone. It was a bad way to go.

The Land Rover pulled up, and shortly McKracken was together with Mutua inside the tent.

"McKracken, we have to take Mr. Greenbottom to the hospital. I think it's kipindu-pindu," Loomis calmly explained. "Go out and open the back door of the Land Rover. Mutua, help me to lift him up."

McKracken exited as instructed, but Mutua stood his ground, shaking his head in ardent refusal.

"Mutua, listen to me, it's alright as long as you wash your hands after touching him. I'll take the head-end of the mattress, you take the lower end, okay?"

Mutua still didn't move, but continued to say no with his head.

His fears were not unfounded. Even perspiration carried the deadly bacteria.

McKracken returned.

"Help me get him into the Land Rover, McKracken, Mutua is a coward."

The ex-police officer did not hesitate, taking hold of the head-end while Loomis took the other. Mutua stepped gingerly out of their way as they brought the sick man and his mattress to the vehicle, and placed them in the back.

"Kakuma is the closest place with a hospital," Loomis remarked to his driver, slamming the back door shut. "Let's hurry." He started briskly towards the passenger door but stopped dead in his tracks before he got to it.

There is something particularly frightening about the sound of a gunshot – it possesses a terrible ring of finality. All hopes and plans, loves and hates, joys and problems, all obliterated in a split second, erased as if they had never existed, by a well-placed bullet in the brain. Directed from an unseen distance, a bullet was instant death concentrated into a few centimeters of metal and a sharp crack of sound. It was this quality of the sound that made Loomis freeze when he heard it.

"DODOTH!" McKracken screamed.

He could see them now, dark figures rising up out of the laager he and McKracken had been in the day before. They almost resembled Turkana, with their blankets wrapped around their waists as they ran towards the camp, but the white war paint patterned on their glistening black bodies gave them a ghostly supernatural appearance, much like the skeleton costumes that kids wore on Halloween. Periodically, they broke their strides to aim and fire their weapons. The quick snaps of SLRs and the terse staccato bursts of rapid-fire automatics ripped the air. Loomis, still standing, his body jammed with fear, strained himself against making an involuntary bowel movement, and looked on in bewildering horror.

The crew and casuals had already reacted, clambering into vehicles whose engines the drivers frantically turned over. Some of the trucks had begun to pull out with many of the casuals running behind still trying to board them – a panicked frenzy, filled with a confused cacophony of shouts, gunshots, and roaring engines, enclosed in a halo of dust. Loomis, driven by a reflex of survival, snapped back to himself and the next thing he knew he was sitting in the cab next to McKracken. Mutua was in the back with Greenbottom; evidently his fear of bullets overpowered his fear of cholera.

"Why are they attacking us?" Loomis whined in helpless protest. "I thought they were only after livestock!"

McKracken lurched the Land Rover in first gear and they pulled out behind the Cruiser. "These days also food! And money! Money to buy more guns and ammunition!" he shouted in reply.

Loomis's heart thumped painfully against his ribs and an overabundance of adrenaline made him feel faint. Getting up that morning, life seemed to contain only the humdrum routine of work. Now, less than an hour later, it had become an unreal nightmare of fear and chaos. A dull whop of sound burst from behind him and his earlobe was pinched by something sharp. He turned to find the passenger window shattered away and looked again to the windshield at the small round hole where the bullet had gone through. Mutua screamed but McKracken made no sound as he feverishly negotiated the vehicle over the rough track. Then a muffled explosion and the Land Rover was sliding all over the place. Front tire hit, out of control, they soared up, then hurtled down, down into the laager and straight into a thorn tree.

* * *

Everything was moving: up, down, like a television set on the blink. A tremendous ache chiseled at his head and sinuses. Somewhere on the right side of his body, a live wire was dangling, shorting out with pain. He felt a nausea, the kind that comes with a sudden acceleration, and he lifted himself to vomit. As he did so, his right arm screamed with pain, and he blanked out.

When he came out of it, his head and arm were still throbbing and he was still queasy, but at least everything had stopped spinning. A raw thirst gnawed at his throat and the left side of his face was burning. Moving his eyes only, he realized he was lying outside in a scrubby desert, then caught something moving on the edge of his vision: smoke. With great effort he moved his head and his eyes fell upon the smoldering ruins of a vehicle. He tried, but could not remember anything. Had he been in that vehicle? How did he get out? Shifting his leg, he winced as he discovered that his left ankle also pained him. What had happened to him was a mystery, and he wondered just how long he had been lying there. By the feel of the heat, it must have been at least mid-morning. He slid his good arm along the ground so he could look at his watch. Miraculously it was still working. Nine-forty-five. Why did he feel so hot, so thirsty? The little window with the date inside said it was the twenty-fourth. The twenty-fourth of what?

His consciousness altered between states of blankness and dazed lucidity, and all the while he was aware of the land getting hotter and brighter, feeling the sun broiling him. By noon he was receiving company: sinister-looking vultures, with twisted bills, their ugly bald heads dangling at the ends of drooping, snake-like necks, were landing nearby, keeping a distance of twenty meters or more, looking him over. In one of his more lucid moments, he decided that his last goal in life would be to keep them off him until he was completely dead. He would make them wait. Then the whole thing struck him funny. Don Quixote and the windmills, Daryl Loomis and the vultures. He felt giddy, relieved. So this was death? The Great Secret about to be revealed to him? Not so bad. He was going to enjoy it. After all, he laughed in his head, it only came once in a lifetime. Maybe he was dead already, had died in that car crash, and was having a post-mortem dream, an out-of-body experience, sort of an interlude while waiting for his trip up or down or wherever he was going; maybe he was in the 'bardo state' of the Tibetan Buddhists, about to battle his way through demons and illusions of the netherworld and make it to Nirvana; maybe... His thoughts receded into a grey mist, where they remained for a long time.

He faded into a coastal scene, lying on a beach of blindingly white sand in front of white coral cliffs, shaded by luxuriant vegetation, facing a jade-colored sea. Mombasa, maybe. He was no longer hurt, and Amonee was with him. They were frolicking in the sand, naked, and although they appeared to be alone, there was a great cheering and applause coming from somewhere, or rather, everywhere, and he was indescribably elated. But a vague apprehension made him wary of this vision, and the grey fog came back, a coiling, nebulous haze, but this time alive with quick-moving shadows – jumping up, flying off – silhouettes of vultures. Then the phantoms disappeared and the silver-black miasma began to turn in upon itself in a grand vortex, revolving, revolving, sucking him into a bottomless blackness... *No! Not yet!* he cried in his nightmare. There were things left undone, he protested, unfinished matters... The black void answered with a throaty drumbeat, slow and ponderous, but increasing in volume, getting closer...no not drums... thunder...thunder, peals of thunder so loud they vibrated his body... A great vision opened up before him. A camel's head of monstrous proportions towered over the land, floating in the sky, his beastly face wearing an expression of extreme disdain, stinking of fur...it moved towards him, followed by a long woolly neck, then giant padded hooves coming down to crush him...no, stepping over him...the creature passed and all that was visible was an interminable expanse of pink underbelly, until more hooves and it was gone, but just as quickly a second gargantuan camel stopped before him. They were bringing a message he knew, a message from God. No, the Virgin Mary, a black Virgin Mary, naked to the waist and donning an apron of animal hide...a Turkana Virgin Mary! Another! Two of them, angels, Black Seraphims, with noble breasts jutting proudly from cello-shaped bodies. Goddesses, beautiful, death is

278

beautiful...they embraced him, with both love and adoration, and offered him a creamy white substance in a sacred vessel – the Milk of Life! He could feel the sublimely sensuous wetness in his mouth and he wanted it more than anything in the world and then his throat cracked and splintered and he coughed and choked...a trick! It was the Milk of Death and the angels weren't angels, they were she-devils taking him, taking him to...

...He was sitting in a shady place outside. Little shadows, like cockroaches, were scampering around him. A Turkana woman sat across from him whittling a stick, another woman off to the side having a boxing match with a camel. What was he doing here?

Death took a long time. Was his life so complicated they couldn't decide where to take him? The Turkana girl looked up at him and the black moon of her face ripped at the bottom into a gaping smile with Cheshire-Cat teeth...

...He was astride a great hairy beast with long ears, a shaggy-winged horse perhaps, which he was bound to by ropes to prevent his escape. He was flying but it was bumpy, too bumpy. *Feel sick, too many thermals, ah you just don't like flying, Daryl...flying, falling, guns, fire, where am I going...long journey, final journey...*

...Blackness. It returned and returned, but he always woke up traveling mounted atop the beast...

...He was in a closet-spaced box with windows. He was going to be interrogated. The Face of God appeared in one of the windows. They were right. An elderly white man with a great grey beard! How did Michelangelo know? God turned his head to someone else, one of his angels maybe, and began talking in Turkana language...God was a Turkana! Then, God spoke to him, "WHO ARE YOU?"

Who am I? I don't know. Who are you?

"Are you Ebu Lakwan? Are you the White Hyena?"

"Yes, and I know who you are now, God," Loomis sedately told him. "You're a Turkana, but you're disguised as a white man..."

He must have been too bold; he must have said a bad thing.

Maybe God didn't want anyone to know his secret. Because soon after he badmouthed to God, the whole universe started to shake and tremble, then broke up into pieces, and objects – bushes, trees, and pieces of earth – were being hurled at him, until he fell into the blackness again...

"...Dr. Ekidor..." the looming black face told him, pulling its flesh to form a leering smile, Cheshire Cat again "...Lodwar hospital...not God...not heaven..." the face said it as if answering a question. Had he asked a question?

"Are you a Turkana?" Was he asking another question?

"Yes."

"No you're not," Loomis challenged with a knowing smile, "you're a white man but you're disguised as a Turkana..."

Again he must have said something wrong, for the universe quaked once more, this time with greater motion and louder noise until it was almost unbearable...deafening rumble...jumping flying...throwing him...

He couldn't take it anymore. "IT'S THE END OF THE WORLD!" he screamed.

"Take it easy, easy now," said someone out there.

"FOOLS!" Loomis yelled back.

...Everything was white. It was the end of his journey. Swift white angels with long flapping wings swirled and hovered like moths as he floated past them...

It was noisy: alarming bells and incoherent babbling...noise becoming darkness, darker than black, except for a pinpoint of light in the middle, growing larger, brighter...a star, a sun...drawing him in...being pulled into it...falling into the sun...cast into a fiery furnace...he would burn...it was...he was going to...NO!!!!

"Good morning."

Loomis looked at the pretty black woman in the nurse's uniform. He blinked. He still wasn't sure. "Where am I?" he asked her.

She took his left arm and wrapped a piece of rubber around his bicep. "Nairobi Hospital," she stated, pumping air into the rubber strap.

He noticed the cast on his right arm and the drip connected to his left. There was a tight stiffness gripping his left ankle. "How long have I been here?"

"About a day." She placed the cold metal disc of a stethoscope on his forearm. She offered no further explanation as she listened to his pulse.

"Where was I before that?"

"Lodwar," she answered without looking up, still listening intently.

"What happened to me in Lodwar?"

She ceased her listening, deflated the rubber arm band and removed it, returning it to a grey metal cart. "Get some rest," she told him, "I'll explain everything later. You must sleep now. Aren't you tired after returning from the dead?" she asked rhetorically as she chuckled.

"Was I dead?" he asked in childlike ignorance.

"It's what everyone thought. Sleep now." She opened the door and went out pushing the cart in front of her, leaving him alone in the small, white and quiet room.

He woke up again. The nurse, as if she never left, was now changing the I.V. bottle. "How was your nap?" she asked.

"I don't remember. I guess it must have been good then. Are you going to tell me what I'm doing here?"

"The doctor will be here shortly. He will explain. What is your name?"

"Daryl Loomis...isn't it?"

"Very good. You will be alright." Then she left again.

Fifteen minutes later, another nurse came in rolling a food cart. She smiled while helping him to sit up, propping pillows behind his back.

"You wouldn't happen to know what I'm doing here, would you?"

"You are recovering." Placing the tray on his lap, she too left him, and Loomis wished she hadn't, for he was famished and had trouble eating left-handed. While finishing off what he had spilled, the doctor entered, a handsome Indian who spoke with an Oxford accent. "Good afternoon, Mr. Loomis."

"Good afternoon. Am I ready to be told what happened to me, or is it a secret?"

The doctor fingered the clip board tied to the foot of the bed, lifting it slightly so he could read it. "Severe cerebral concussion, extreme dehydration, shock, and electrolyte depletion, compound fracture of the right humerus, severe sprain and torn ligaments of the left ankle, multiple contusions, not to mention heat-stroke," he recited. "Do you remember anything, Mr. Loomis?"

"Well, it's a bit confused. What day is it today?"

"Tuesday, May the second. Do you remember the accident?"

"We were being attacked."

"Mmmm." The doctor let go of the chart and looked up. "Your vehicle crashed, somehow you got out. It was probably a day or two before some Turkana women found you lying injured, and they brought you to a Catholic mission in Oropoi. An aid worker there drove you to Lodwar. From Lodwar you were flown here by the Flying Doctor Service."

"Did he have a big grey beard?"

"Who?"

"The aid worker."

"I don't know. Did he?"

"I think so...the nurse...she said everyone thought I was dead..."

"There were three bodies found in the Land Rover, all burned beyond recognition. One of them was assumed to be yours. I'll have the nurse bring you some newspapers. You can read it for yourself. How do you feel otherwise?"

"Fine. My arm is itchy."

"You'll get used to that. The cast will be on for some time. We had to reset the bones. The Turkana women who found you patched you up with crude splints. Rather sloppy job, but it probably saved your arm. Tell me, do you have any headaches?"

"No."

"Good. Sleep as much as you can. I'll try to stop in later." He made for the door.

"Doctor?"

"Yes?"

"Could you call the nurse? I think I wet my pants."

There were two stories reported. One was on page two of the Daily Nation of April 27 – AMERICAN, TWO OTHERS, KILLED IN TURKANA DISTRICT. It was the story of a spectacular car crash with no mention of bandits. It figured. Nicodemus Mutua and Reginald Greenbottom, Kenyan employees of Hydro-Drill Ltd., were also, along with Loomis, cited as dead. There was no reference to McKracken. Loomis had taken the Turkana on without submitting his name to Hydro-Drill nor the Diocese of Lodwar, and nobody close to the ex-policeman had been aware of his where-abouts, except perhaps for people like Lokori. Sloppy investigative work failed to uncover the bloodstained patch of ground where he had fallen and the tracks of the small caravan which had picked him up. Not surprising. They had never expected anyone to have gotten out of the vehicle and disappear into the desert. Even he himself did not know how the hell he had gotten out of that Land Rover. So it remained a simple case of mistaken identity, and as far as the world was concerned, Loomis had been killed. That is, until yesterday.

The headlines of yesterday's papers, that of May first, shouted AMERICAN FOUND ALIVE! The story was pretty much the way the doctor had told it. There was an amusing part where the aid worker to whom the Turkana women had brought him gave his small account "...*they told me they had brought a white hyena, so I was expecting some sort of animal, but when I got outside to check, I saw it was a man...*"

After the injured Loomis had been identified, a CID officer, Mr. Rashid Hemed, in conjunction with statements from the survivors of the tragedy (the nature of the tragedy now being disclosed as a bandit attack) had helped to shed light on the fate of Peter Ekal Lokimat Imana, whose body was mistakenly assumed to belong to Daryl Loomis.

When the nurse came in to perform her measurement-taking, he persuaded her to find him a pair of scissors which he used later on to cut out the story. Upon completion of this exercise, he continued skimming through the newspaper and noted another interesting news item:

NETHERLANDS/EEC, MINISTRY, SIGN AGREEMENT
The Netherlands financial representative to the European Economic Community (EEC), together with the Permanent Secretary for the Ministry of Regional Development, signed an agreement yesterday promising Ksh five million for famine relief operations to be carried out under the Turkana Rehabilitation Program (TRP), in the face of what experts fear may be the worst drought in Turkana district in ten years...

A phone call interrupted him. It was from Barnes, assuring Loomis that he would be well taken care of, the fear of a possible lawsuit evident in his sycophantic tone. The project had been officially rescinded, naturally, and Hydro-Drill was pressing the client for damages, in which, if awarded, a large portion of the claim would go to Loomis and the affected staff. Meanwhile Loomis was to rest up for a month on full salary.

NAIROBI, MAY 3-10

Not everyone is fortunate enough to be able to see how their death would affect others, so Loomis, immersed in a rising tide of visitors, regarded himself lucky to receive such a rare opportunity. He was gratefully surprised at the numbers of friends and acquaintances who showed up to demonstrate their concern, putting him in a mood of happy delirium. People who knew him, not only Okova and others from Nairobi, but from all over the country, from Mombasa to Kisumu, Nyeri to Loiktoktok, came to see him and celebrate their relief. Shigoli turned up with a delegation of drillers, reporting that Sikhendu, with a gunshot wound, and Juma, who busted his leg falling off one of the lorries, were the only other casualties. Godfrey from Nyakach and Michael Masitsa from Mbale, were among the others in a steady stream of well-wishers which flowed from morning till evening, while the phone constantly rang. Flowers and cards lined the window sills, and the bottles of booze and beer which were smuggled in were hidden under the bed. Even people he didn't know showed up, including some from the ministry. Loomis had become a minor celebrity.

By evening he was emotionally played out. A nurse entered the room to record his temperature and blood pressure. "I know it's late," she said as she finished her chore, "but are you able to see one more visitor?"

"Sure, why not? Tell him to come in."

"It is a *she*, and you can tell her yourself."

On the threshold of the open doorway, absolutely motionless, hands hanging straight down the sides of her blue caftan, stood Amonee, her face solemn, her eyes riveting his.

He thought that he had gotten over her. That's what he had thought.

The nurse brushed past her on the way out, cuing Amonee to enter, which she did, silently, in small, deliberate steps. Reaching the bed, she sat herself on the edge of it and took his hand in hers. No longer able to bear staring into his eyes, she put her head down and gazed at his hand, which she began to stroke. Her mouth trembled to form a smile. "Hello," she managed in a weak whisper.

"Hello."

"They said you were dead."

"I'm not."

"I'm glad."

"So, how are you?"

"Fine," was all she could manage.

He made a bold move raising his good arm to caress her head, smoothing her soft cottony hair.

"You love me, don't you?"

"Yes."

"Why can't we give it a second chance? We love each other, that's all there is to it. Please, Amonee, let's pick up where we left off."

"No. It's too late."

"Too late, how? I should have died, I don't know how I escaped from the Land Rover...one moment I'm crashing to my death, and the next thing I know I'm here. I'm alive and there's a reason why I'm alive, just like there's a reason why you're here right now with me. The reason is that we were meant to be together.

"No. We're not. We could never be. Not ever again."

"So that means after this visit you intend to disappear from my life again? Is that it?" he asked fretfully. "A mundane visit to the hospital to cheer up a sick friend, that's all, right?"

She didn't answer, only stared at him with a reticent face.

"Okay, I'll be patient. I have a whole other lifetime now to wait. You're only human. Sooner or later you'll give in."

She rose to her feet. "I'm sorry, I shouldn't have come." She walked towards the door and opened it with a swift, determined motion.

"Then why *did* you come?"

She turned her head. "I wanted to be sure."

"Sure of what?"

"That it wasn't for nothing."

"What do you mean, for nothing? Why are you speaking to me in riddles?"

"Goodbye, Daryl."

"You know where you can find me!" he called out as she fled into the corridor. "I'm getting out of here on Friday. I'll be waiting for you!"

He didn't have to wait long. She came to the house on the second day following his discharge from the hospital. He was upstairs lying on his bed, thinking of nothing in particular when he heard the knock on the door, heard the low voices as Okova welcomed her in, heard their footfalls coming up the stairs. He grabbed his crutch and stood up, ready to receive them.

The door opened. "You have a visitor," Okova gravely announced.

A weighty pause followed as the three of them stood wordless: Okova with his hand still on the doorknob, Amonee with her hands in front of her clutching her handbag, and Loomis, leaning lopsidedly on his crutch.

"Ah, well...I'm going into town," Okova stammered hastily. "Probably won't be back until the morning. See you." He shut the door behind him, leaving them to each other.

"I knew you'd come," Loomis said.

She said nothing, but mutely approached him and helped him to the bed, where they fell upon each other kissing, fumbling to remove each other's clothing.

"Wait," she gently commanded. Stilling him, she undressed him tenderly, taking particular care of his cast, then disrobed herself.

* * *

Floating in a post-coital trance, Loomis reflected upon what had just taken place in his room. It was like a dream, only more powerful, for he could still taste it. She had been desperate in her passion, wrapping herself around him so tightly that she raised herself off the bed, the whole weight of her body hanging from his back. Her desperation had excited him and his own lovemaking became frenzied. He hurt both his arm and his leg tumbling on to the floor with her, painfully chafing his knees and elbows in a violent convulsion that seemed beyond his control. He had bellowed and growled, shouting questions at her, aggressively: "You're mine, aren't you! You love me, don't you!" demanding her to answer, making her cry out "Yes! Yes!" until she was screaming it out with tears. And now, that whole scene, playing back in his head, frightened the hell out of him.

He felt her getting up from the bed and turned to see her putting on her clothes with a haste that offended him.

"Where are you going?"

"Home."

He struggled to sit up on the bed. "Why?"

"I have to."

"When are you coming back?"

Her head was down, her eyes fixed on the buttons of her blouse which she was busy fastening. "I'm not. I can't."

"We're not going to go through that again, are we?" he cracked irritably.

She grabbed her handbag and headed towards the door. As she opened it she turned around, and with moist, limpid eyes, she said, "Jon and I are married. We were married ten days ago. Next week I leave for Holland, to live." Then she disappeared from the doorway, vanishing like a spirit, leaving the door ajar. He heard her galloping down the stairs, heard her rapid steps across the sitting room, heard the slamming of the front door. She was gone.

INTERLOGUE

It was the search for the source of the Nile that originally brought Europeans to East Africa, stumbling over each other in a frantic race to be the first to claim the headwaters. That, and the Arab slave trade, which Britain was determined to end, led to a 'scramble for Africa'. The European countries sent missionaries and traders to mollify, pacify, and bring the indigenous people under their own control; to transform the populace through the enlightenment of Western civilization and its values. The clash of cultures and appropriation of land and goods that followed required more than just winning hearts and minds, but often necessitated military force as well. And the result was a new type of entity, a colony, a child nation under the wing of a foreign mother country with radically different traditions and beliefs. And with that came a new type of African, where those who best adapted to the white man's world would become the most successful.

This clash of cultures caused new divisions among the people, and its effects continued for more than a century, right through the time that Loomis and Amonee were grappling with their chaotic romance. It was at that time, also, when the political manifestations of this cultural dissonance became perceptibly clear, during the event that came to be known as the Muthongo Inquiry.

The Kenyan President in the early 1980s was a man who had started his life as a nomadic herdsboy, a life that was not too different from that of other pastoralists such as the Turkana. But with a primary-school education, he became a teacher, and afterwards, because he was one of the very few from the wilderness of the Kerio Valley erudite enough, he was chosen to sit on the nearly all white Legislative Council of the Colony, representing his homeland. This would be the start of his political career, for not long after, and for the same reason – the paucity of eligible candidates from his district – he was elected to parliament.

For others, such as Everret Muthongo, the path to political achievement took a slightly different course. The British colonial government had made his father a chief, and the power and affluence that his position had gained for him was used to groom his son, whom he sent not only to the finest schools in the land, but to higher institutions in South Africa and even Britain. He studied and subsequently practiced law, in both Durban and London. His profession enabled him to hobnob with refined European families, and he wholeheartedly embraced his new cultural milieu. When he finally returned to Kenya in 1959, due to his impressive qualifications, he was appointed as the head of the civil service.

Kenya gained independence in 1963. Jomo Kenyatta became the first president, and he chose the herdsboy, a simple man with low profile and a member of a minority tribe, to be the vice-president. And thus, as irrelevant as it might appear, the backdrop to the destiny of Daryl Loomis and Amonee Emuria was beginning to unfold.

To the civilized world, Kenya was no longer a colony; such a concept was outdated. Kenya was now a 'foreign market'. Immediately before independence, and in the many years to follow, foreign entrepreneurs wooed a good number of the new national leaders with shares and directorships in their economic enterprises both at home and abroad, thus forming a powerful group of 'lobbyists' who would protect and facilitate outside interests in Kenya. The first of such elitist cliques was referred to as 'The Family', and included highly placed ministers and the closest people to Jomo Kenyatta, who had held the political reins in the first decade and a half of Kenya's independence. As the president grew older and more senile, The Family extended its influence over government policy by securing top positions in the Kenyan African National Union, KANU, the ruling (and only) political party in the country.

Of course, there was opposition, mostly along tribal lines, since The Family was almost exclusively Kikuyu, and the opposition was spearheaded by the Luo, the rivals being the two largest ethnic groups in Kenya.

Despite being a Kikuyu, Everret Muthongo was not a part of The Family. They were old, greedy men who had no vision, and would risk the division of the republic in order to maintain their political and financial position. They belonged to the past and their demise was inevitable. Muthongo knew that Western governments and outside foreign interests were growing tired of dealing with them and were looking for new links and relations. In 1967, Muthongo resigned his post as head of the civil service in order to join politics and was elected as M.P. for Gitango constituency.

The real showdown came when the health of the first president degraded so severely that it was certain his time was near. It was then that The Family saw the threat to their power, a threat which came from the Constitution itself, specifically Chapter II, Part I, Section 6, which stipulated that in the event of the president's death, the vice-president shall assume the office of president for a period of ninety days until new elections are held. Three months as the 'Top Man' was certainly enough to consolidate one's power, and once one was entrenched as an incumbent, he would be very difficult to remove.

In 1976 The Family engineered the 'Change-the-Constitution' movement, i.e. change it so that the vice-president could not have access to the presidency. The ensuing rift over the issue effectively split the nation's leaders into two camps: The Family on one hand, and those opposed to The Family – known as the Constitutionalists – on the other. The Constitutionalists were led by Mwai Kibaki, the then Minister for Finance, Charles Njonjo, the M.P. from Githere, and the backbencher Everret Muthongo, the M.P. from Gitango. The vice-president himself kept a low profile.

Muthongo proved to be an important ally. He was a vociferous campaigner in the National Assembly, managing to win over a number of converts from the enemy's camp. But more importantly, Muthongo successfully wrested the control of the civil service from The Family, for he was still favorably remembered there by many faithful adherents. Through Muthongo's efforts, the motion to change the Constitution was eventually defeated in parliament.

If The Family had been bested in the legal domain of the National Assembly, this did not mean that they were ready to give up. They had other means, not so legal, not quite in accordance with democratic procedures, and their machinations led the country into the 'Ngoroko Affair' .

The Ngoroko Affair. An incredible plan. The funding of a private army through public funds and foreign aid. It involved the setting up of the Rift Valley Operations Team, an anti-stock-theft unit whose purpose was supposedly to tackle the vicious cattle rustlers in the remote arid districts of the north, mainly the Turkana, but in reality it was a trained commando unit and hit squad designed to assassinate the enemies of The Family immediately upon the death of the ailing president. Among the targets on the death list, besides the vice-president himself, were Kibaki and Everret Muthongo.

But two things thwarted this plan. Muthongo, once again relying on his contacts in the civil service, got wind of the plot, and through informants planted in The Family's organization, was able to keep abreast of its progress. The Constitutionalists were therefore prepared. The other spanner in the works was that Kenyatta inconveniently died while on holiday in Mombasa instead of waiting to expire at the State House in Nakuru, the planned assassination site.

On August 22, 1978, without a shot fired, the presidency fell smoothly into the hands of the man who was once a herdsboy on the lonely plains of the Kerio Valley.

The fact that Muthongo had risked his life in support of the new president meant new opportunities would open up, now that The Family had fallen out of power. The friendship between Muthongo and the new president was thus welded stronger, and for his loyalty Muthongo was rewarded by being appointed the Minister for Justice, a ministry which carried the most potent portfolio in the entire cabinet. Now, under Muthongo's authority, came the whole of the civil service including the police force and Special Branch as well as all of the elements of regional administration, a bureaucracy of provincial and district commissioners, officers, and local chiefs. In addition he had complete control of the Immigration Department (foreigners who needed resident permits, including friends from South Africa and England, were especially pleased with that). The Minister for Justice was also the immediate superior of the Attorney General; ergo the law courts were now added to become another easily accessible sphere of influence. All this made Muthongo the second most powerful man in Kenya.

These power changes, along with the sudden establishment of a new regime in Kenya, threw the West into confusion. They had been accustomed to dealing with The Family, and now that The Family's power had been shattered, they were unsure of the approach to be taken towards the new leader. Because of his mild demeanor and low profile, not much was known about him, except that he was from a humble background, with only a primary-school education. Would he be astute enough, shrewd enough, and ruthless enough, to stay in power? What was his position on foreign investment, trade restrictions, and the use of Mombasa as a naval base? No one was certain.

Muthongo, on the other hand, looked more attractive to the world's power brokers, being highly educated and having business connections in Europe and South Africa. And he sustained an image that appealed to their sensibilities: his deportment and manner of dress, his ardent identification with anything European, and his relaxed, affable presence in the company of non-Africans. His worsted and pinstriped suits were imported from renowned tailors in London, while his monocle and gold pocket watch became his symbols of Western refinement. His wife was an upperclass Englishwoman; his children attended boarding schools in the U.K. The gourmet fare offered in his household could have been taken from the menus of the finest restaurants in Europe. Gauged by Western standards, Muthongo posed an exemplary example of an enlightened, progressive African.

The political and business communities of the world were, at the moment, caught in a wavering, vacillating stance concerning the new president, and Muthongo set out to exploit their doubts and procure outside support for his secret campaign.

Some funny things began to happen. First, the Attorney General resigned and was replaced by another. After that came the Kimuli Trial. A prominent Nairobi businessman was apprehended while conspiring to illegally purchase sophisticated weapons from the armed forces and plotting to kill the president. His defense, as it came out during the trial, was that he was working under the authority of the Minister of Justice, Everret Muthongo, whom the defendant claimed was his cousin, and the whole idea had been to test the nation's security. Muthongo himself was subpoenaed to testify in court, where he denied all knowledge of Kimuli and his actions. And yet, as ludicrous as Kimuli's defense had appeared, the defendant was acquitted.

Then there was that attempted coup on the communist island state in the Indian Ocean, staged by mercenaries from South Africa. Luckily it flopped. But why did the leader of that little nation accuse the Kenyan government of complicity, of aiding the mercenaries with an airplane, landing rights, and other logistics, and even name Muthongo himself as the main antagonist? Of course Kenya denied those claims, but the president had by then decided that Muthongo now needed to be watched very carefully.

But most disconcerting of all was the aborted coup in Kenya a year later. The air-force mutineers' story, that their intention was to pre-empt and upstage an even more organized coup planned by people high up in the government, was, perhaps, more than the hysterical pleas of men facing the gallows?

Yes, some funny things had been happening since Muthongo became the Minister for Justice. And then it all blew wide open in the middle of 1983.

PART IV

JOURNEY TOWARDS A FALLING SUN

NAIROBI, AUGUST 24, 1983

The sidewalks were crowded that day; a Monday morning, like any other Monday morning, the pavements stirring with a medley of bobbing pedestrians returning to routines they had abandoned on Friday afternoon.

On that day he casually sauntered along, finding himself immersed in a sea of ethnic diversity: African businessmen nattily dressed in three-piece suits and tasteful ties; circumspect Indians in drab-colored buttoned shirts and polyester slacks; Sikhs sporting their extravagant turbans and prominent beards; Somalis with Kushite faces of burnt copper marked by aquiline noses; Arabized-Indianized Swahili, an indigenous race from the coast of East Africa; and even more striking, quite incongruous in this urban setting, Masai warriors robed in their flashy red tunics and carrying their spears. All of them contributing to a potpourri of races and cultures jostling under a gentle August sun, in streets congested with horn-blaring traffic. Nairobi. Green City in the Sun. A venue for international conferences. The Great Metropolis of Black Africa. It had grown larger, and like an insatiable beast, proceeded to swallow up the mortals who had created and served it.

Little Kamau flitted from person to person, performing his well-rehearsed cant of destitution for a small fee of a shilling or two. His ten years of life in the streets, his birthplace, had made him a keen observer of human nature, a social psychologist attired in tattered rags, and he utilized this knowledge when selecting his audience. Women were almost always good for something; so were the wazungu. The boy's eyes now widened with attention at the sighting of a potential benefactor. He set himself in motion, his trajectory charted along a collision course with the light-skinned brown man in the dark grey suit. Where their paths intersected, Kamau adopted a sideways style of walking, advertising his face to the man he was now keeping pace with alongside. Always show them your face.

"*Saidia*? Help me?" he entreated. The whine of his voice and the pleading face were overly affected. "Saidia?"

To the boy's dismay, the man totally ignored him. Kamau had to make him look. He grabbed the bottom of the man's suit jacket and tugged. "Saidia."

The man raised his arm as if to strike him. "Fuck off, you little shit!"

The boy abruptly halted and stood rooted, like driftwood caught on the bank, and the man disappeared into the crowd.

'Fuck off' was the most useful expression he had these days. *Don't bother me. Leave me alone. Fuck off.*

Daryl Loomis brushed with his hand that part of his jacket where the boy had touched, maintaining an eye on the pedestrians in front of him, searching for openings to pass through. Walking in Nairobi these days was like playing musical chairs where the music, the pulsing hum of the city, was never switched off. The sidewalks were bursting with people, many of them spilling on to the street, and it made Loomis wonder: where did they all come from? Where were they going? What were they all doing here at eleven o'clock in the morning? Many of them, he was certain, were simply wandering the streets in a vain search for jobs that didn't exist.

The cigarette that was clenched inexorably in his teeth burned down to its filter and Loomis tore it from his mouth and threw it down, still striding steadily, pushing his mid-morning shadow ahead of him. In a way he was grateful for the amount of urban density that surrounded him; it was easy to hide in. A year had passed since he had last been in Nairobi, and he quailed at the thought of bumping into someone he knew. Feigning his way through casual talk and banal conversation, especially about old times, proved an unbearable exercise. He had nothing to offer in the way of conversation, misery being such a lousy topic. He preferred loneliness over company; loneliness was a good listener, never offering useless advice. The only exception was Okova, but that was different. Okova understood. Okova had been his witness. And he never asked questions.

Picking the last cigarette out of his lapel pocket, he was reminded of their depletion, and detoured over to a newspaper vendor whose wares were displayed on the ground. Bending down to grab a pack of Sportsman, he glanced fleetingly at the headlines of the *Standard* and the *Nation*, both papers broadcasting the same topic: MUTHONGO IS TRAITOR – MPs and MUTHONGO SUSPENDED, INQUIRY TO BE HELD.

He had resumed his weaving through the throng for another block or two before being distracted by a black Renault cruising slowly beside him, its horn blaring insistently. It stopped, and the window slid down. "Need a lift?" inquired the dark, jolly face of Peter Njenga.

It appeared as if the city still wasn't big enough; he had been found.

Loomis approached the car and bent down. "Hello, Peter. I'm just going to Shell House."

"Well, get in, will you."

He opened the door and got in wearing a grim face, bracing himself for an uncomfortable chat.

"Long time," Njenga began. "Two years at least. Or is it three?"

"Three."

"That's right. The last time I saw you was when you were in the hospital. Jesus, the time really goes, doesn't it?"

"Yeah, it goes and goes."

"So what are you up to? I thought you had left for the States."

"I've a...I've been in Uganda, and now I'm in the Southern Sudan, just north of Juba. Towne Oil Services. Got a contract to provide water for the oil rigs."

"Who's doing the oil-drilling? Blocker?"

"Yeah."

"Southern Sudan, eh? How is it there? Heard it's a bit tricky now."

"Ah, things flare up and cool down. You get used to it."

"There's still plenty of work here, Daryl. This place is starting to boom. What are you doing in such a miserable place? Come back to Kenya. They've begun to tender for the Turkwel Gorge investigation, a dam site, right up your alley."

"Believe me, Peter, I've tried. I seem to get only the jobs nobody wants, like Tororo and the hellhole I'm in now."

Njenga stepped on the brakes to stop for a red light. "Oh, c'mon, there's so much work. You haven't tried hard enough."

"I'm telling you, I've been applying. But nothing, nothing ever comes up except 'regretting to inform you'. I'm under a curse. The Kokolok curse. Since the Turkana job. Or don't you know that I've been cursed with rotten luck?"

"What?"

"Never mind. I'm just babbling."

"How's that lady, what's her name? Still seeing her?"

He knew that question had to come up sooner or later. "No, that ended long ago."

"Figures. I was surprised you were with her for so long. I should have known no female could hold down Daryl Loomis."

"Yeah," Loomis mumbled.

"Still, you should think about some stability," Njenga said, pulling out as the light turned green. "You're not getting any younger you know."

"What? And saddle myself down with problems, like you?" he remarked, faking smugness. He waited impatiently for Harambee Avenue, wishing he had lied and told Njenga a closer destination.

"I tell you, it's worth it," Njenga went on. "Especially the kids."

Outside of the parliament buildings a large crowd had gathered, parading, shouting, chanting, and thrusting placards in the air. They were making a noise that rose noticeably above the usual din of street sounds.

"What's happening over there?" Loomis asked, trying to change the subject.

"They're demonstrating against the 'traitor'. Have you heard about it?"

"I saw something in the papers."

The Renault swung around a roundabout. "Yes, they say Muthongo tried to take over the government. Is here alright, Daryl? I want to get on Uhuru highway. I have to go to the industrial area."

"This is fine."

Njenga pulled the car over to the curb. "So how do I get in touch with you?"

"Just contact the Towne Oil office in Shell House," Loomis answered, getting out of the car. "They'll send the message or letter along. See you, Peter." He shut the door.

"See you, Daryl. Good luck."

The session at the Towne Oil offices had been mercifully brief, his presence in Nairobi necessary only to pick up another Land Rover to replace the one that was shot up, and to drive it back to Juba. But even the fifteen minutes had been too long, too long to avert the patronizing of his administrative superiors, with their looks of false concern and solicitous questions: Has it got any worse up there? Are you happy with the security situation? Should we request more armed guards? Don't worry, the Khartoum government will soon mop the whole area up, and after this job we may have something quieter for you.

"What about the gun?"

"Yes, it's all been arranged," Saunders said, a tawny-haired fellow, handsome in a way, but with lackluster features, typical of someone whose main purpose in life was to get ahead and who put career advancement ahead of anything else. "Beretta, nine millimeter." He pulled it out of the drawer of his desk, complete with shoulder harness and five boxes of clips, and also gave Loomis the papers that went with it.

"Thanks."

With no more business to attend to, he left.

All Loomis wanted to do now was to pick up the Rover and go to the house in Buru Buru to sleep off the rest of the day. There would be no one there, thank God, for Okova, now working freelance, had gone to Mombasa to tutor the U.S. consul. Loomis, even though his appearances in Nairobi rarely exceeded once a year, still paid for the house out of sympathy for his struggling friend, and it was a small thing anyway; the house allowance he was given in these risky contracts came in the form of cash and the amount was several times greater than Kipkoech's rent. Besides, it provided a quiet place to hang his hat on the few occasions he was around.

He walked carelessly, blankly, past the black iron gates that closed off the lawns of the Kenyatta Conference Center, whose tower pointed proudly to the sky as a symbol of progress and achievement. Further on he approached the adjacent Law Courts, enduring colonial structures of buff-colored bricks that displayed a regal and imperial officialdom.

He suddenly stopped short. "Ah, shit," he muttered, spotting Geoffrey Wanyonyi passing through its gates and entering the sidewalk. Loomis stood still, waiting for him to get lost in the street crowd, but no such luck; the figure in the powder-blue suit, holding an attaché case, was heading right in his direction. Now, realizing that avoidance was futile, Loomis resumed his shuffling gait.

"Hey, Daryl!" Wanyonyi called out.

"Hello, Geoff," he responded as they got closer.

"I didn't know you were in town."

"Got in yesterday."

"It's too bad Okova is in Mombasa."

"Yes, I know, he left a note on the table."

"It's good to see you. Been a long time. How are things?"

How are things? Loomis had come to hate these little niceties that demanded false answers. "Not bad," he lied.

"How long are you going to be around for?"

"Tomorrow I drive back to Juba. I'll be off early in the morning."

"Drive?"

"Yes, I'm picking up a Land Rover for the site."

"Why don't we meet for a drink at the Norfolk? In the evening."

"I don't know, Geoff. Like I said, I have to leave very early in the morning."

"Daryl, I haven't seen you for over a year. I'm not going to accept that as an excuse. You can spare time for one drink."

"Alright. One drink."

"Good. Around six," said Wanyonyi. "Let me go, I have to prepare for another case at two. So I'll see you then."

"Guess you will."

Loomis took a taxi to the house in Buru Buru, got out, paid the driver, opened the front gate, unlocked the door, closed it, locked it, went upstairs to his bedroom, and took a nap. He was to pick up the Land Rover at three, he reminded himself before he got into bed.

* * *

The Norfolk Hotel stands on Harry Thuku Road. Once a bastion of colonial leisure, it was now a five-star hotel drawing European tourists, who, charmed by the romantic nostalgia evoked in the books of Elizabeth Huxley and Karen Blixen, slept in its rooms with the hopes of being touched by the spirits of the great white pioneers; to mingle with the ghosts of legends such as Grogan and Delamere; sampling the nuance of grand and adventurous bygone days to spice up their holiday safari. Most of them had never heard of the person the street was named after, Harry Thuku, a Kenyan nationalist in the 1920s, nor of the incident that gave fruition to the street's name, unaware that the very lane they strolled upon right in front of the hotel was once, on a sunny March day in 1922, stained with the blood of one hundred and fifty unarmed Africans. They had been protesting Thuku's arrest by the colonial authorities when they were fired upon by gun-wielding police and some of those very same great pioneers who had been drinking in the bar at the time. But Loomis, every time he walked down Harry Thuku Road, never missed the irony.

He walked in and passed the outdoor cafe and entered the Lord

Delamere Bar. Through the buzzing crowd, and behind a table littered with amber-colored beer bottles, he saw Wanyonyi seated with a white man. He joined them with diffidence, more doubtful than ever of the soundness of this rendezvous. He just wasn't in the mood.

"Daryl, this is a friend of mine, Scott Richardson, an American like you."

Loomis sat down hurriedly, effacing any opportunity for handshaking.

"Scott, this is Daryl Loomis."

Richardson was in is early thirties with neatly parted dark hair, a bit overweight, a plumpish oval face with pretty blue eyes. "Hello, Daryl, is it?"

"Yeah, hi," Loomis reciprocated sullenly.

"Scott is a journalist. He's also working on a book about Kenya," Wanyonyi said. "A beer, Daryl?"

"If you're standing, a whiskey double, neat."

"Yo chief!" Wanyonyi called out. A waiter appeared. "Whiskey, *tot mbili, bila choch*ote." Then, to Richardson, "Daryl works as a geologist."

"Oh, I see. Gemstones? Oil?"

"No. Water. And civil works."

"You must be pretty busy. There's always a demand for water." Richardson's fleshy face was pathetically overflowing with cordiality, his large wet mouth stretched into a self-satisfied smile.

"Busy enough."

"Been in East Africa for a while Geoff tells me."

"Long enough."

"We were just discussing the Muthongo thing," Richardson said.

"Keep your voice down a bit, Scott," advised Wanyonyi.

Richardson leaned towards Loomis and asked discreetly, "What are your views about it? You being a foreigner working here for some time, perhaps you could fill me in on the stuff between the lines?"

"Could I? Politics doesn't interest me, Mr. Richardson."

"Well, a lot of expatriates I've talked to are pretty nervous about it."

"Is that so?" Loomis commented sourly. "And you?"

"I get the hunch it's a bad portent. The man is extremely intelligent, the most educated man in the government. He stands for development. Unfortunately, as so often is the case in these countries, he didn't fit in with the jealousy and petty politics of all the other incompetents around, in particular the 'Big Guy'."

"You're going to put that in your book?" Loomis asked wryly.

Richardson laughed frivolously, "Oh no, no, no! No, the book deals with settlers who remained in Kenya, what you might say, a last glimpse at what was. That kind of stuff sells better."

"Oh right, current affairs is for your newspaper. That's the place to expound your opinions, am I right?"

"A good journalist doesn't insert his own bias in a piece."

"Don't give me that bullshit, Richardson."

Wanyonyi intervened. "Ease up, Daryl. We've come for a friendly drink, so let's enjoy, eh?"

"Well, what's *your* opinion on the matter, Geoff?" Loomis asked in a tone that was somewhat mordant.

Wanyonyi dropped his voice discernibly lower. "Myself, I always make it a policy of going with the prevailing wind. If it's time for him to go, then he'll go."

"Geoffrey, my, how you surprise me," Loomis rebuffed with acrid sarcasm. "And you a lawyer tsk, tsk. I thought you would be a little more adamant about it. Isn't justice the premise for your trade? Muthongo was the Minister of Justice, wasn't he? Well, what kind of justice are we talking about?"

Loomis broke off speaking as the waiter placed the drinks. He picked up his whiskey and took a large sip. "I probably don't follow politics as closely as you do, Mr. Richardson," he continued. "But I do remember a controversial trial a couple of years ago. That American sailor that butchered a prostitute with a beer bottle? His sentence was a fine of five hundred shillings, about thirty bucks, the same price she probably charged for the screw. Is that how much that girl's life was worth, and the life of her daughter that she left behind? I remember the sailor's mother flew in for the trial, and after the sentence was pronounced she said something like, 'Thank God I have seen justice carried out!' Is that the justice we're talking about?"

Wanyonyi tried to say something, but Richardson got in first. "It's not like in the States, Loomis. The problem in these places is the extent of corruption, especially low-level corruption, not only the guy at the top, everyone is on the take. The judge was probably bought off."

Loomis finished gulping his drink. "The judge was an expatriate. British. A white man."

"Daryl, want another?" Wanyonyi asked, gesturing towards Loomis's empty glass, figuring the interruption would close their discussion.

"Another whiskey? Sure, why not," replied Loomis. But he shouldn't, he thought, and he knew why not. "You know, I also remember Muthongo justifying his recruitment of expatriate judges on the grounds that there weren't enough competent African judges. Tell me, do you think that white judge was competent?"

"Let's drop the political issues," Wanyonyi said, tired of the topic. "You never know who's listening." He called the waiter over once more.

It was funny that Geoff should say that, because Loomis had been covertly watching an African in a black suit with short hair and glasses sitting at the table behind them, who seemed to be looking at them in a way that seemed just a bit too attentive.

When he heard that Loomis was now working in the Southern Sudan, Richardson turned to Loomis with renewed interest. "Oh really? How's the situation there?"

"Why? Figure there's a story in it?"

Richardson's cordiality was used up. "No, dammit! It was just a friendly question!"

"There's nothing friendly about that part of the world."

Richardson glared at him.

Wanyonyi looked embarrassed. "Scott, uh, there's a rugby match on Saturday afternoon. Are you free?"

The conversation between Wanyonyi and Richardson took a genial turn while Loomis silently watched them, hating them, hating everybody, hating himself.

"Listen, Richardson, why don't you go back to the States," Loomis suddenly said out of nowhere, "and use your journalistic incisiveness to expose the dirty laundry in your own country, and keep in mind what they say about glass houses." He threw back what remained of his whiskey in one swallow. "Thanks for the drink," he said, rising to his feet. He turned and stormed out of the bar.

"Your friend's a fucking asshole."

"Not usually. Of course I haven't seen him for a while. I think it's that job of his, he never used to be like that."

* * *

Loomis sat by himself at a table near the edge of the rooftop bar atop the Six Eighty Hotel, a cigarette burning in between the fingers of his left hand, his right hand idly picking at the moist label of the beer bottle in front of him.

Why did he try at all? He knew he wasn't fit for social occasions, however trite and casual. The reality was that he couldn't stand people; they were all so full of themselves, all bubbly and caught up in their own personal dramas. It's not that he felt superior to them, for what was the gain in that, and after all, he had once been just like them. It was bitterness that he lived with, the bitterness of having to be alone, alone with the oppressive, arcane revelation that everything was bullshit.

A chilling breeze streamed in over the concrete balustrade and he looked out at the buildings across the street. The shade of night was being drawn and the artificial lights of the city turned on. He lit another cigarette, his fifth in an hour.

What was it festering inside him? Why, day in and day out, did he carry himself around like an empty, hollow shell with despair as his only theme in life?

He poured the remaining contents of the bottle into his glass, watched it foam, then called the waiter over for another beer. He regretted the order as soon as the waiter had gone – he really didn't enjoy drinking nowadays. The alcohol would only amplify his self-pity and raise his deeply imbedded anger.

A man in a suit walked over to ask if he could borrow the single empty chair at his table.

"Sure, take it," Loomis told him. "My loneliness doesn't need a chair. It sits in my lap."

The man, whose brown face had been amicable and friendly, frowned as he dragged the chair away, puzzling over whether the foreigner had been rude or not.

Oh, no, I'm starting again, he realized. This next beer would be his last. He should stay away from drink, stay away from social contacts, and confine himself in a self-imposed exile. Because the past three years had made him repulsive to other human beings.

He was distracted from his thoughts when, just out of reflex, he looked at the man hauling the chair back to his table, and noticed another man, at another table, an African in a dark suit with short hair and glasses. Was it the same guy that was at the Norfolk? Or was it just paranoia? The rooftop bar was poorly lit, so any conjecture would be inconclusive. Still, he was haunted by a feeling that people were watching him whenever he came to Nairobi, although he could never comprehend the reason why he felt that way. It probably stemmed from the time when he was accosted by those two Special Branch guys, when he stupidly, like a fucking jerk, had gone to her house.

They started to play music, which came over the speakers set in each corner of the roof.

Fuck, he hated to listen to music these days. Any kind of music.

And what it made it worse, it wasn't some inanely happy love-you pop song, but a rather depressing one with lyrics that seemed to be summing up his situation in life. The last fucking thing he needed to hear: 'Holding Back the Years'. He tried to filter out the words, but they penetrated through the wall in his head anyway. 'Wasting tears, wasting years, without a chance of anything good'...the song was just rubbing it in his face.

It was so easy to blame it all on the affair he had with Amonee; he was continually convincing himself that in all his life before meeting her, he had never been as despondent as he was now. But it wasn't just that; it was only one scar among many that had lately branded him a pariah.

In some subtle way, he communicated to others the suffering he had witnessed, the shadows of civil war and starvation, though not so much with words; the gaze of his eyes and the quality of his voice were enough to mirror the refugee camps, the bloodied corpses in the village just outside of Kapoeta, and the living skeletons that slowly withered away staring out at death.

Or perhaps that was her fault too? Maybe he would have been protected by a convenient coat of callousness had she not opened up his Pandora's Box of feelings? Perhaps he could have just shrugged it off?

Then there were those fruitless, absurd jobs, like that bridge they kept repairing only to have it repeatedly blown up by the rebels. Why did he take such jobs? At first he had been driven by the desperation of unemployment, but now, in a fleeting state of alcoholic insight, he realized it was a morose yearning, a death wish.

The beer came and he drank some, but left most of it, knowing he was tanked-up enough. After paying his bill he departed downstairs to the light-brown Land Rover he had parked on Kaunda Street.

* * *

The drive east out of town was unpleasant. There was a small traffic jam on Jogoo Road and he banged the horn so hard and so often he bruised his fist. Again, he found himself thinking, what were they all doing here?

What was normally a fifteen-minute drive took him nearly forty minutes. As the traffic cleared, his thoughts turned to the Land Rover. He should take off the Kenyan number plates and put on the Sudanese ones under the seat, and he should do it before setting out the next day. Ideally he should do it that evening so he wouldn't forget, but the booze had made him sluggish and miserable and sleep was deemed a priority.

After parking the car in front of his house, he went into the glove compartment, took out the gun, holster, and ammunition, and stuffed all of it in his jacket pocket. He locked up the Land Rover and fumbled for his house keys.

Inserting the keys, he cursed under his breath; today he was worse than usual; he had left the door open. Or did he? No, he didn't. Definitely did not. He distinctly remembered locking it.

Drunk as he was, he was convinced someone was in the house. He reached into his coat pocket, pulled out the gun and removed it from its holster. He took out a box of clips, and walked away from the house so he wouldn't be heard slipping the clip into the gun. He returned to the door with gun drawn, filled with fear. Turning the knob and pushing the door slowly, the slight squeak of the hinges made him cringe, and so he only opened it enough for him to squeeze through. He didn't bother to close it.

There was a shadow in the darkness, a vague outline highlighted by the weak light coming through the front windows. He had an urge to shoot first and ask questions later, but instead he called out, "Don't move, I see you, I have a gun and it's aimed at your chest."

"Daryl?"

He took a half-step back, struck by both sudden shock and sublime joy, strangely mixed. Her face, dimly lit by the glow of a neon streetlamp filtering through thin curtains, hung like a disembodied, phosphorescent visage in the surrounding blackness as she moved toward him, a ghostly hallucination. For a moment he wavered, seized by a paroxysm of confused feelings, until finally the amalgam of fear and joy emptied out of him, and he could taste a black and rancid anger climbing up his throat. "How the hell did you get in here?"

"I'm sorry, Daryl, forgive me, I asked Mr. Kipkoech to let me in."

He lowered the gun. "And so he did, did he? Well, he's going to get one bloody nasty letter of complaint about that, I can assure you."

"Oh, Daryl, I'm..."

"You must excuse me for being so discourteous," he said with nettling sarcasm, "it's just that I had such a lousy day, today and every day..."

"Daryl, I know..."

"...I should greet you properly and say how nice of you to drop in...how's married life? ... How's hubby?" he spat out maliciously.

"Daryl, please..."

He shut the door, finally, and then, without switching on the sitting-room lights, strode towards the kitchen as if fleeing her, intuiting just how emotionally dangerous her presence was to him.

"I beg you to listen," she implored, following him through the shadows of the house. "Please don't act this way..."

Inside the kitchen, he turned on the light, put the gun on the counter, and proceeded to violently bang open all the cupboards. "Would you like some tea? I hope you won't think me rude if I tell you to help yourself, but I'm much too tired to entertain this evening..." He slammed the items hard on the kitchen counter. "...This is the tea...here's the sugar...I think you do remember where the kettle is..."

His intensity startled her. She stood silently in the kitchen doorway, waiting for his harshness to die down. She was beginning to get scared; she didn't know who this man was.

"As for me, I feel like something a bit stronger," he continued, bringing down a whiskey bottle from one of the cupboard shelves. He opened it and took a long pull.

"Please, Daryl, stop it..."

"So why did you come here?"

"If you calm down and listen, I can explain..."

"Do you know how the very sight of you torments me? DO YOU!" he shouted, not listening. "But of course you do, you couldn't be that stupid." He took another gulp.

"Daryl, please, give me a chance to ..."

"What's the matter, hubby not giving you enough?" He took another swallow of whiskey, only vaguely hearing her anxious chattering.

"They're looking for me...they came to Bungoma, I didn't know anywhere else I could go...I..."

"You miss it, don't you?"

"What?"

"I was real good, wasn't I?"

"Daryl, you're not listening..."

"Just like the old Swahili saying, he who has tasted honey will return to the honey pot..."

It was becoming too much for Amonee. She started to break out in moans of frustration, defeated, broken. "Oh, why won't you listen to me?!"

"Well, I think I can oblige you, for old times' sake." He brought the bottle to his mouth one more time, then putting it down, came towards her.

She was weeping now. "I don't care about myself, it's the child...no, Daryl, please, what are you doing, stop!" she pleaded as he grabbed her roughly around her waist. "Don't..." He was hurting her; he shoved her hard against the refrigerator; now she was genuinely frightened.

It's going to happen again, she thought. *It's happening again.*

He tried to kiss her forcefully. "No...don't..." She turned her face, her body heaving with her sobs, and attempted to push him away, but her struggle only aroused his fury and he struck her hard across the face, so hard that she fell against the counter and collapsed to her knees. She let out a loud moan, "No, Daryl, dear God, please..."

He dragged her up onto her feet.

She was screaming hysterically now. "Please! You've got to help me save my son!"

Still deaf to her utterings, he grabbed her by the hair and pulled her head back, snarling like a wild animal, his lips curled back, "You took my soul away, you bitch, and now I want it back!" He clawed at her dress, ripping it down over her shoulder and she screamed again. Then, between her squeals of fright, he thought he could hear another sound, like a weak echo, a tinny reverberation, another voice crying, a small voice...

"Waaaa!"

Into the light of the kitchen walked a small, honey-colored boy, roughly two years old, bawling hysterically, and covering his eyes with the backs of his hands. "Mama!" he wailed scampering towards her.

Loomis released his hold on her and backed up in shock. The kid must have been napping in the dark sitting room all this time. His jaw dropped open while his eyes strained outwards in disbelief at the little figure. Amonee knelt down on the floor and took the weeping child in her arms as Loomis continued to retreat, backing into the counter and knocking the whiskey bottle over, which streamed out its contents. He turned and picked it up, righting it with shaking hands, then addressed her with a face full of revulsion. "You...brought your...fucking kid here!"

"Stop shouting!"

"I'M NOT SHOUTING," he said, shouting.

Then everything went quiet.

The array of intense emotions in only a matter of minutes made him nauseous. Feeling weak and dizzy, his back slid against the counter as he sank down on his haunches to the floor. "Oh my God..."

Amonee, on her knees, cradled the boy, rocking him gently; she herself was no longer crying, but consoling him in a cooing, maternal voice, "It's alright, my sweet,...look, Mommie's not crying anymore..."

"Oh my God, I'm sorry." Loomis buried his face in his hands for a brief moment. Then he brought his head out of them to ask, "What the...what's going on? Why are you here?"

Stifling her grief, she continued to engage herself in comforting her son who continued to drone with fright and confusion. "It's okay, baby," she told him, stroking his hair.

Loomis just sat on the floor, trying to compose himself. "What...you said what...what...who...who's..." he stammered, searching for a reason behind the morbid encounter. "What's happening? Who's looking for you?"

"The...Special Branch," she managed to cough out.

"Why?"

"Jon...he has something to do with the traitor."

"Muthongo?"

"Yes."

"What something?"

She sniffled. "I'm not sure what...it's complicated. Business. Money." She sniffled again.

"And where the hell is he now, your husband?"

"In Holland."

"You're in Kenya by yourself? With just the child, I mean?"

"Yes," she answered, gazing at her son. "He didn't want me to come. He forbade me. He warned me it was a bad time. I left without his knowledge." She looked up at Loomis and said, defensively, "But I had to come, I had to come, my father is dying." She glanced down at her child again. "I wanted him to see his grandson. And I wanted my son to know that part of his heritage."

"I'm sorry."

"No! Don't keep saying that!"

The small boy was now quiet, feeling safe in the warmth of his mother's bosom.

"Let's go back to sleep now," she said, soothing him, "...sleep in my arms, my sweet." She faced Loomis again and, in a controlled, authoritative voice, said, "I'm not concerned about myself. I know I don't deserve any help or sympathy from you. I understand that you should hate me. But you should know...and it's time for you to know...I also hate myself...have hated myself every day for the past three years."

"What, you too? So then why did you do it? Why did you leave me?"

"You still don't understand."

"Oh, I think I understand. This guy, Jon, whatever his fucking name, is a boring dickhead, and I gave you a few laughs and showed you a good time, but there was no future with me. So although it was fun while it lasted, you made up your mind to choose the stability and security a rich man can offer."

She shook her head. "No."

"No?"

"If you look in your heart, you know that's not true."

"So, what is it then, he went into a jealous rage and he threatened you?"

"Yes."

"With your life?"

"No."

"Well then..."

"With yours." She looked at him, and was close to breaking out in sobs again, so she took deep breaths to control herself. "When I told him...he said...he said...I should take care of it, and if I couldn't... then...then he would."

"Take care of it? Take care of me? I can take care of myself, and I should have taken care of him when I found him at your house."

She didn't quite comprehend what he had said about her house, but his meaning, that he could just confront Jon like a macho boyfriend claiming his girl, was ridiculously simplistic. She attempted to tell him as much. "Do you think that he would just show up, by himself, slap you in the face with his pretty white glove, and challenge you to a duel? Is that the way you think it works? Do you remember what happened to Elijah Otuko last year?"

"The Assistant Minister of Health? The guy that was killed by thugs?"

"He was another problem that had to be taken care of."

Loomis went quiet. He heard the boy snoring, or some similar baby sleeping noise, and was at least grateful for that. But he still didn't understand what was going on. "So what does all this have to do with you?"

"I just told you something that isn't supposed to be known. I know other things as well. That's why the government wants to find me."

"Don't you think it's best if you turn yourself in to the authorities?"

"Yes, but not with my child. I don't want him to be involved. They might use him as bait to get Jon to come to Kenya. I'm not going to play that game. That's why I've come here. I want you to take him, keep him safe."

"Safe? Do you know where I work? Huh? Southern Sudan. I have to go back tomorrow. Over there, it's not just the government against the rebels, everyone is fighting each other; it's a fucking blood bath. So, what you're suggesting is out of the question."

"Oh... But I thought you worked here in Kenya."

"Not for three years. No jobs for Daryl Loomis these days."

"I see," she murmured contemplatively. "He was making sure."

"What?"

"The Department of Immigration is under Muthongo's office."

"Are you saying that prick of a husband got me blacklisted?"

That question was answered by silence, as the both of them, sitting on the floor, took time out to think.

"But you have many friends," she said. "Couldn't they take him for a while?"

"I don't have friends anymore. Except Okova, but I don't think he would be very good at parenting." He paused. "So what do you want to do?"

"I don't know now," she moaned, feeling defeated. "You'll have to do the thinking for the both of us."

A wearied stillness ensued. Two desperate people, sitting on the kitchen floor.

"He is my sole reason for living," she declared, looking endearingly at her child.

Loomis studied the boy, a half-caste with a homogeneous, butterscotch complexion, black lustrous, curly hair, and large almond eyes, his mother's. There was something familiar in the pout of his mouth.

"What's his name?" Loomis decided to ask.

She smiled wistfully. "I wanted to name him after his father, in the hopes he would grow up to be just like him, but I couldn't..."

That statement obliterated the sympathy he was starting to feel and replaced it with rage. How could she say something like that? How could she be so insensitive to his feelings? Just because she was in trouble was no excuse. Was she cruel or stupid or what?

"I didn't ask for a fucking song and dance about his daddy, I just asked the kid's name!"

"Jon."

"Jon. Figures, what else...wait a minute...you just said...you're not telling me..."

But she was telling him, telling him now with her eyes, her intense gaze pinning him against the bottom cupboards, blocking any escape from the outrageous, irrevocable truth.

She spoke again. "That night, the last time I saw you, after you got out of the hospital, when I came here..."

At first her words fell away into a distance to become hollow, meaningless sounds, but after a few seconds, like the time lag that precedes a sonic boom, the impact of what she was saying shook him with full force. Suddenly his whole world crashed down upon him. He slapped both his hands to his face to cover it once again. "Oh,

Jesus, Jesus!"

"I didn't plan it, it just happened."

"...Jesus, Jesus..." He removed his hands from his face. "Wait, how do you know? Are you sure?"

"I'm sure."

"How...but?"

"Do you need to know the details, the feigned headaches, the abstinence, my menstrual cycle?"

"No, I guess I don't." He went quiet, before asking, "Does he know?"

"No, he never questioned the birth, even though he was a bit perplexed at the timing. Maybe it's denial."

"This is, I mean, really fucked up."

Then suddenly, he was filled with a great happiness that the kid was his, that she had borne him a child. He looked back at Amonee. Her chest was heaving deeply and rapidly, her mouth taking in large sucks of air, and she was wheezing and gasping as if asthmatic. Then Loomis realized she was crying, crying voicelessly. He sat beside her, and timidly, hesitantly, put his hand on her shoulder. She didn't mind, she was no longer afraid of him.

After a few minutes, she composed herself. "That's why I came here. If anything should happen to me, I'll at least know that he is with his father, and that you would keep him safe."

"What do you mean, 'if anything should happen'? You've done nothing wrong, just report to them and tell them what you know."

"That would be a very big problem for many people, including Jon, a problem that would have to be taken care of."

"You would be safe in the hands of the government."

"Would I? They're still in the process of finding who in the government is allied with these people." She paused. "John Sabunda, a key witness for the State, found dead while in detention. No official cause of death. Right now, it's difficult to know who is on whose side."

Alarm bells rang off in his head. They could have been on their way right at that moment, they knew, didn't they? They knew that he had been connected to her in the past – those two guys on the university campus...they had been keeping tabs on him...people following him...the guy at the Norfolk...at the Six-Eighty...

"Amonee! Amonee, we can't stay here!" He got to his feet, grabbing her arm and helping her up with the boy still in her arms. Then he swiped the gun off the counter and put it in his pocket.

"What do we do?"

"We have to get out of the house. The rest we'll discuss in the car. Are your things here, bags, passports..."

"Yes."

"Okay, let's take them and go."

* * *

They had left the house, Loomis driving aimlessly, randomly, just to get away, to get lost within the urban night.

"We have to leave Nairobi tonight," he announced inside the Land Rover. "All three of us."

"Where are we going?"

"Juba, via Lodwar. Then on to Khartoum."

"Me as well? No, Daryl, just take our son, I'll stay here, report to the police, and take my chances."

"Goddammit, do you trust me?"

"Yes."

"Then do as I say. You said I should do the thinking for the both of us. Well, I have. I'm not going to leave you here. We leave as a family. End of story."

"Alright," she agreed with a faint smile. She liked that part about family.

"What are you smiling at?" he asked.

"I'm happy. We're together again. And my son is with his father."

Loomis grinned back, tenderly, as he turned left onto an unobtrusive backstreet. "I'm happy too. It's the only thing I ever wanted."

They were quiet for a while, bathed in a warm glow of attachment.

"I should've known it was mine," he said. "Handsome little devil."

They both chorused out together, predictably, "Just like his daddy!" causing the two of them to laugh. Then Amonee became reticent once more.

Her face turned fey. "I'm sorry for what I did. Do you forgive me?"

"Of course I do. Do you forgive me?"

"For what?"

"I almost raped you."

"You wouldn't have done it. I was scared, but I know you would have stopped, ashamed at yourself. Even if our child didn't wake up. It was only anger."

"Yeah, you're probably right," he confessed with a simpering smile. He knew she was right. He hadn't even been close to an erection. "Well, I'm sorry anyway. And I'm sorry I ripped your dress."

She put her arm on his shoulder and gently stroked him. "You'll have to buy me a new one first chance you get."

"No problem."

He shut up for a while as he turned right, now trying to get his bearings. He realized that he was entering Eastleigh.

"What passport are you holding?" he asked abruptly.

"Kenyan. I'm still a Kenyan. I'm only a resident of Holland, but Jon, I mean our son, is a Dutch citizen."

"Good, perhaps the Dutch Embassy in Khartoum will be able to help you get a flight out. You can take KLM. You buy a ticket for Amsterdam, but the plane makes a stop in London. You get off there. Do you know anyone in London?"

"I have a cousin studying there, at the London School of Economics. I could look him up."

"Anyway, I'll give you money. Maybe it's better you don't contact anyone. I'll finish this contract and join you. I have two months to finish that contract and we will need the money."

"We drive across the border? Into the Sudan?"

"I don't see any other way. I don't think the authorities would expect you to slip out through the Sudan. Remember the 'Ngoroko' thing? When they formed a hit squad to kill the president? That guy, the Rift Valley Provincial Police Commissioner, the man who had charge of the Ngoroko unit? He fled the country by road, taking a route that went through Turkana District and into the Sudan. Later, from Khartoum, he flew to Geneva where he was granted political asylum. So we do likewise, because I always go that way, and they know me at the border. "

"But it's so far. Lodwar alone will take several days."

"No. Twelve hours, tops, and we should be there. The road is tarmacked now, except for the last thirty kilometers or so. It's called the Kenya-Sudan highway these days."

"I can't enter the Sudan, Daryl, I don't have a visa." She had not expected that she herself would embark on such a journey, and she was searching for reasons why she shouldn't.

"I'll hide the both of you in the back, throw some gunny sacks over you. They won't search the car. They know me both at Lokichoggio and Kapoeta, I'm always shuttling back and forth across the border."

Even though the intense melodrama they had just gone through had jolted him back to sobriety, he knew that an all-night drive, even without the alcohol inside him, would be a serious challenge to his nervous system and quite risky. This difficulty thus engendered a trip to town, to the River Road area, where Loomis bought two bundles of miraa, choosing the short-stemmed, extremely potent variety known locally as Giza, the Swahili word for darkness.

Now, at eleven p.m. they were indeed traveling through darkness, along the Naivasha-Nakuru road, having passed the last of the neon streetlamps miles back. Not much had been said since they had made their hasty departure from the city, and the boy had fallen into a deep, slack-mouthed slumber.

Amonee stared straight ahead, wordless, a hauntingly baleful expression on her face. The sound of the Land Rover's engine seemed to be the only sound in the world. "After three years of not seeing each other, we had our first argument."

"Get some sleep, you're going to need it," he told her. "First, open that bundle of miraa for me. I have to keep awake."

THE JOURNEY, AUGUST 25 – AUGUST 28

Passing Nakuru, passing Eldoret, passing Kitale, into the Cherenganyis and out again at Marich Pass, the Land Rover hurtled through the night following the moving bubble of light formed by the glare of its headlamps. Illumined by this light, the trees and bushes appeared as eerie silver spectres. The eyes of nightjars, caught in the bright beams, sparkled like flakes of gold as the birds stood stock still in the middle of the road until, at the last moment, they would fly off in a tardy, slow-motion panic. From time to time, other strange, nocturnal creatures, small, grey, and furry, were spotlighted when they scooted across the path of the oncoming vehicle, typical of a night drive through the bush.

Loomis, while driving, busied himself by chewing his miraa. From time to time, while keeping his left hand on the steering wheel, he would clutch one of the twig-like plants with his right, peeling the green fleshy skin off the stem with his teeth and collecting it into the wad already formed on the inside of his cheek, chucking the remains of the stem outside the window. Otherwise, he sat rigidly behind the wheel driving as fast as he safely could. Amonee and the child were both asleep, and in his solitude his thoughts raced on along with the Land Rover.

Norepinephrine, the intoxicant in the plant, was an upbeat drug, so his mood was positive. They were going to get through this; it was an adventure, an experience of a lifetime. He was back with Amonee. She had a borne him a child. He had a kid, her kid, what more wonderful news could he get? Life was great. There wouldn't be any problems. And they would live happily ever after.

He looked at the both of them, but more so the child, still snoozing. "Hey, kid, I'm your daddy," he said. He felt giddy. "I'm your daddy," he repeated to himself.

At around three o'clock in the morning the child woke up crying, awakening Amonee who set about pacifying him with hushed, motherly assurances. "Ah now, my sweet..."

"Mommee, 'ome Mommee."

"Yes, we're going home, my sweet. See, we're going bye bye car."

"Ba ba coor," repeated the two-year-old.

"Where are we?" she asked Loomis.

"We're nearing Kainuk. There's a routine police check up ahead, so don't panic."

Sure enough, five minutes later, the iron spikes of a roadblock were revealed in the beacon of the headlights. He downshifted, approaching the barrier slowly as an armed policeman came out to meet them. The Land Rover came to a halt and Loomis extinguished the lights as was the rule.

"Wapi? Where?" the askari shouted out in question.

"Lodwar."

"Saa hii? At this time?"

"This car overheats; I would never make it in the daytime."

The policeman, rifle slung over his shoulder, walked closer to the Land Rover and peeked inside the cab. "Haya," he said as he waved them on.

Soon after they drove off, Loomis began talking to the boy. "Hey, kid!"

The boy looked in the direction of the voice in the dark, a bit stupefied, putting his fingers in his open mouth. He then turned to his mother, protesting in whiney complaints, even going so far as hitting her shoulder.

"He's hungry," she said, taking out her right breast, which he immediately pounced upon to suck.

"No bottle for him, eh, he gets to have the real thing?"

"He's almost weaned. It's just that he's stressed. For us Africans, we're not at ease using a bottle."

"Is that a problem in Holland?" he asked, referring to the breast-feeding. "European women don't normally nurse a child of that age."

"No, the people there are very tolerant. And they are exposed to a lot of cultures. Indians, Africans, people from Guyana and the East Indies..."

Somehow, her praise of her new home affronted him. Despite himself, he risked putting salt in his wounds by asking, "So you like life there?"

"I would say that it is probably one of the best countries to be in if I had to live abroad. Racism is very rare. And I have everything I want. Except you."

The conversation was heading in a direction that he didn't want it to go. Too serious. It would ruin his high. But now it was too late.

"When you said I took your soul away, I guess I did," she acknowledged. "In a way I didn't anticipate. A part of it, anyway."

"You mean the child? Don't feel guilty, I'm thrilled about it. Now we're together, so let's just be happy." Then, since they were already in a serious mode, he just had to ask, "Why did you throw away the doll? That hurt me."

This question disturbed her. "How do you know about that?"

"A few days after I received your letter, I was in Nairobi and decided to go to your house."

"And Jon was there?"

"Yes, didn't Katy tell you?"

"No, she didn't mention it at all."

"I just hung around outside for a few minutes. Then I saw it in the garbage." He paused. "So, why did you do that? You really wanted to forget me that bad?"

"I didn't throw the doll out. I kept it in the bottom drawer of my dresser, together with your letters. He found them. He was very angry. He burned the letters and put the doll in the trashcan."

They both became quiet, as the toddler continued sucking.

"I feel like we're in a Greek play," she said out of the blue.

"I hope it's a comedy."

"No, they're usually tragic, with a lot of irony."

"Oh, like the guy who slept with his mother?" He was trying his best to lighten things up again.

She gave out a short chuckle. "Yes. Full of pathos."

"Pathos? What's that?"

It amused her that he didn't know the word, as if his unfamiliarity with it expressed his humble, down-to-earth personality. "It means it makes you feel sad."

"I'd rather be in a Charlie Chaplin movie."

This time they laughed together, and the baby stopped feeding to look up, trying to find out what was so funny.

For four more hours Loomis continued driving and chewing, and making stupid jokes under the influence of the drug, trying to exude an atmosphere of frivolity. He even made farting noises with his mouth to amuse the kid.

Within a short time the darkness slowly thinned as the sky diffused a pale light, raising the curtain on a stage of golden sandy desert where isolated acacias stood like battered umbrellas. In no time at all it became blindingly bright. They had reached the central basin of Turkanaland: hot, scorched, and dissected by thousands of lightly forested laagers. The road engineers had designed concrete drifts to get across these numerous dry river beds, and the leap up and dip down when driving over them made the little boy squeal with delight.

"Wheeee!" said Loomis, joining in the fun.

"Daryl, maybe you should slow down."

"No, don't worry. He likes it."

They headed steadily towards a cluster of rounded brown hills where Loomis pulled over.

"Excuse me for a moment," he said as got out.

He didn't want to have a bulging cheek stuffed with miraa when entering Lodwar, so he stuck his fingers in his mouth and plucked out the wad, and then spat out the rest.

At ten o'clock in the hot morning, they crossed the bridge which spanned the dry chasm of the Turkwel River, and entered Lodwar.

Lodwar was getting bigger. Just a glance at the number of people shuffling in its sandy streets was enough to tell. Loomis pulled up alongside one of the bigger dukas on the main street that led north out of town.

"I'll just be a minute," he said as he got out, his smile expressing the drug-induced exuberance he felt.

A few minutes only had passed before the child began to make a fuss.

"Pee pee, Mommee, pee pee."

Amonee now regretted that she had toilet-trained the boy so well that nothing could induce him to wet his pants. His protestations became desperate.

"Alright, wait...wait." She opened the car door and climbed out first before grabbing hold of him. Setting him down on the ground, she undid his pants.

"*Safari ndefu inasumbua watoto.* A long journey is hard on children."

She looked up into the hawk-nosed face of a Somali in a suit and tie. "Yes...yes, it is," she agreed, diffidently.

"Where to?"

Little Jon was still peeing as Amonee searched for an answer.

The Somali graciously offered one. "Kakuma?"

"Yes." She looked away from him as she pulled up her child's trousers and bundled the boy back to the car. She got in and shut the door, and looking in the rearview mirror, noticed that the man did not move off.

The driver's door opened and Loomis struggled in holding a carton containing heat-treated milk, biscuits, and tinned food. "I think this should last us until we get to Juba." He placed the box in the back, then plopped forward in the driver's seat. "We still got a long way to go."

He turned over the engine and, with the clutch let out, the Land Rover jumped to a start and sped off.

Standing in the scanty shade of a young acacia, stroking his pointy chin and staring at the vehicle as it disappeared behind its wake of dust, was Rashid Hemed of the Criminal Investigation

Department. He turned and broke into a brisk walk as if he had just remembered something he forgot to do.

* * *

The road dwindled into a degenerating track, and the ride became bone-jarring. The Land Rover jumped, swerved, and rocked to the whims of Loomis's driving, and Amonee was grateful for the few good patches that had been recently graded. The heat inside the metal-bodied cab approached that of an oven, while the hot blasts from the half-open windows offered no solace. The windows were only half-opened because the dust stirred up by the moving tires had a tendency to smother.

Several hours went by and both the Baboon Hills and Pelekec Mountain came into sight. Shortly afterwards they reached Kakuma, which was little more than a ramshackle collection of dukas clustered together in the barren flat space between the mountains and sustained only by the lorry traffic going into and out of the Sudan. They drove through the settlement, continuing on to the dangerously deep laager of the Tarac River where, down its rocky banks, Loomis negotiated the Land Rover with patient concentration. On coming up out of the dry river bed, they came face to face with a lorry waiting to cross in the opposite direction. The driver was a kinky-haired Nubian that Loomis had seen on a few occasions in Juba.

"Ahmed!" Loomis called.

"Oh-ho, Loomis. How is you?"

"I'm fine. How is the road today?"

"Quiet. No trouble today," the driver shouted back. "Just hot. And dusty. You going back?"

"Yes."

"Something strange in Lokichoggio," Ahmed continued. "They awake today and check vehicles who goes out. Not coming in. Me, I just pass and see long queue on the other side."

"I see. Was Mwangi there?"

"Eh, right outside with his askaris. Searching vehicles. Only going out but. You carry anything?"

"No, just the usual." Loomis was relieved that Ahmed paid no attention to his passengers, probably assuming Amonee was from the area and had solicited a lift.

"Ah, they know you anyway. You have no problem. Good journey."

"Haya, Ahmed, you too."

With that the lorry proceeded down.

"What does all that mean, Daryl?" Amonee asked.

"I don't know. But we can't take the chance of going through Lokichoggio now."

The plan, sounding so simple when proposed, was now fucked up. This unexpected turn of events unnerved him.

"What do we do?"

"I don't know. I have to think." Seemingly composed, Loomis engaged the gears while hiding his growing panic. He had to come up with an idea quickly but until then, keep pushing on ahead, for if the worst that he feared was true, there were police Land Rovers not far behind them. "Could someone have recognized you in Lodwar?" he pondered aloud. "I can't see how. Did you get out of the car?"

"He had to pee," she confessed.

"Yeah but...who could have possibly recognized you...ah, well, we're not even sure yet if that's what it is. But Lokichoggio is out in any case."

After that there was a strained silence between them, intruded upon only by the rattling of the vehicle. Loomis continued to feed the last of the miraa sticks into his mouth, forming a new clump in his mouth and driving more slowly now, trying to assess their situation. Obviously, the apparent alternative was to cross the border through the bush. But was there any decent track to make that idea feasible? Even if there was, it would take a great deal of wandering and circling to find it, and then there was the risk of being caught by the police patrols around the border. And there was the added danger of bandits.

It was clear that they needed to enlist the aid of someone who knew the land. Would the Turkanas help?

He'd have to find some first: since the Tarac River they had seen no signs of any human habitation.

A short time later, they were driving alongside the Songot mountain range, an elongated, somewhat greenish tableland of undulating hills, draped with patches of cloud shadows, rumpled and rucked with folds and crevasses like a giant wool blanket carelessly dropped on the Rift Valley floor.

There was something he vaguely remembered about Songot. Sifting through his memory he came up with the image of Lokori, the amiable herdsman he met during the Turkana contract, and he recalled those words that seemed so trite at the time "...and I have many many cattle on top of Songot Mountain...they are with my brother's herd."

Could he find someone he used to know up there? Songot was an extensive upland: twenty-five miles long and five miles wide. The chances of finding anyone, let alone a casual acquaintance of three years before, were very slim. But it was a chance they would have to take. They could not go much further on this track.

Loomis pulled the Land Rover off the road and drove through the bush, away from the mountain.

"Daryl, what are we doing?"

"You see those hills?" he asked her, jerking his head back over his shoulder. "We're going to climb up on top of them. We have to look for some friends."

He drove until he found a suitable place to leave the vehicle – behind a series of large termite-hills that merged together to form a mound the size of a small mausoleum.

"Take some of your things." He reached over to the glove compartment, took out the gun, holster and ammunition, while Amonee looked on with some dismay as he put the holster on.

"It's only for emergency use. I hope I don't have to use it." He got out, grabbing the panga he kept hidden under his seat, and then spat out his miraa.

She opened the door and stepped out of the car with the child, and was immediately met with a slapping wind, reminding her that she was in the desert again.

Loomis was already at the rear of the vehicle, opening the back door, unfastening her two suitcases, one big, one small, sifting through her stuff, throwing some on a pile which began to form between the two bags.

First, the passports, which he placed inside a spare plastic bag; then hats, scarfs, and toiletries that included all types of creams...

"Tampons?" she asked, with a confused face.

"Well?"

She threw them on the pile herself. Then she let the baby down so she could absorb herself in the collection of things, the boy at once inspecting the ground for interesting things to pick up.

"My evening gown?"

"I'll use it to make a sack I can carry on my back. I hope it's not one of your favorites."

"Well, if we make it through this, I can always buy another one, and if we don't, I won't need it anyway."

She took her head-kerchief and tied it around her head.

"Is that enough protection? Sure you don't want a hat?"

"I'm an African, it's enough."

He handed her a pair of white cotton slacks. "Here, put this on under your dress so that you don't get cut up on the rocks and thorns. She did as he instructed.

"Hey, keep an eye on the kid, he might pick up a scorpion."

She grabbed the boy and bundled him up, the child screaming and flailing his hands in protest. She wrapped the shawl around her to bind him to her.

Loomis inspected the pile and noticed a child-size peaked cap, with the New York Yankees emblem stitched on the front. He picked it up. "Huh," he chuckled.

"What?"

"New York Yankees; a baseball team from my home town. I bet this logo is all over the world by now."

He fitted it on the little boy's head, the child not seeming to mind. Loomis gave out a weak smile. "There you go, kid; wear it with pride."

She looked at him, perhaps a bit more intently than expected and said, "I love you."

He leaned his chin against the top of her head, then kissed her forehead. "Don't worry, we'll get through this."

He finished feeding the pile of things on top of the evening gown, including the milk and biscuits he bought in Lodwar, electing not to take the tinned stuff because of its weight. Then he planted his floppy brimmed bush hat on his head and brought the sack over to the shade of a large bush. "Rest here," he told her, "I won't be long." He left her to set about cutting down small trees and bushes and throwing the cuttings on top of the Land Rover. It was fortuitous that the color of the vehicle approximated very closely the color of the ant-hills, or perhaps not; perhaps, Loomis smirked to himself, his bosses had chosen the sandy color to make the Land Rover more difficult to shoot at.

His labors were completed in just over half an hour. After that he tied the evening-gown sack under his armpits.

"Start walking towards the road," he instructed her.

Carrying the child in a shawl on her back, she turned and headed off without waiting for him. Loomis followed behind, walking backwards, trying as best he could to erase tire tracks and footprints with a makeshift broom of bush branches. He continued to do this even after they had crossed the road and were approaching the foot of the mountain. Several hundred meters later he dropped the broom and joined her.

"I hope it isn't too obvious," he reflected aloud, trying to judge whether his sweeping left any discernible trail.

"Is there someone following us?"

"Maybe. We can't be too careful."

"And will we find people on top of that mountain?"

"There are Turkana up there. That's where many of them graze their cattle. I admit it's a shot in the dark, but I don't have any other ideas."

Without further discussion, they trudged towards the hills through the sweltering heat of early afternoon, Loomis carrying a five-liter plastic container of water in his hand and a few packets of milk and biscuits stuffed in his pockets and in the evening-gown 'knapsack'.

The land began to rise, first gently, then abruptly. They climbed slowly, picking their way through bushes, avoiding the barbed thorns, bending under the branches of dwarfed trees, stepping over shelves of exposed rock, attempting to choose routes which favored the least effort. The exertion made the couple breathe heavily, precluding conversation, while perspiration soaked their clothes and dripped from their arms and faces. The little boy stared about him, wide-eyed and curious, content enough to be perched upon his mother's back.

Higher up, they found themselves amidst a profusion of sansierva and cactus, and the rocks around them were spotted white with the excrement of hyrax and baboons. As the slope became steeper, they had to bend their bodies forward, leaning into the gradient to keep their balance, straining the muscles in their calves and thighs.

"I can't believe they bring cattle up here," Amonee finally blurted, out of breath.

"They do, but they must use another way. I don't see any signs of cattle crossing here. I doubt that their route is all that much easier though."

"Can we rest, please?"

"For a few minutes only."

They set themselves down on the most comfortable spots they

could find and nourished themselves with the milk and biscuits Loomis produced from his pockets.

"He's pretty cool, that kid, considering what we're doing."

"Yes, he normally doesn't make a fuss. Happy go lucky, just like his daddy used to be." She caressed the boy's head, and then said, "I'm sorry."

"For what?"

"For everything."

"Forget the past. This is where we are now. We're fighting for the chance to be together, isn't that right?"

"Yes, you're right."

A contemplative pause.

"Maybe I better carry the kid."

Amonee undid the shawl, swung the baby around, and set him lightly on the ground in front of her. He immediately engaged himself in trying to climb into her lap.

"Come here, Jon," Loomis entreated.

"Call him 'my sweet'."

"Come here, my sweet."

The boy turned his face toward him, and with his fingers in his mouth, stared at Loomis with no intention of wandering from his mother. Loomis rose and sat down beside him, making the funniest, most laugh-provoking faces he could muster. At first, he would puff up his cheeks and blow out one side of his mouth quivering one cheek like Huntz Hall used to do in the Bowery Boys flicks, making blubbering noises as he did so. The boy went into hysterical giggles. He did this repeatedly, eliciting the same response each time, the kid never tiring of the trick. After that Loomis stuck his finger in his mouth and pulled it out to make a popping sound, and of course the kid tried to emulate him. The boy, smiling and at ease, finally permitted himself to be touched, and Loomis eventually persuaded his son to sit on his lap. Touching the child unleashed his feelings, and he found himself hugging the boy, close to tears.

"Are you okay, Daryl..."

"Yeah, I'm fine."

They all became still, listening to the wind singing through the bushes and the lonely chirp of a solitary bird nearby. A minute or two passed while the boy fingered Loomis's face and played with the buttons on his shirt.

"Let's try it," Loomis proposed. He grabbed the shawl while Amonee positioned the child. The boy offered no resistance to being secured onto the strange man's back.

"Shall I walk in front now?" she asked.

"No, stay behind me."

They continued upwards. The sun by now had hidden itself behind one of the higher crests, resulting in a partial shade on the mountain's eastern face, thus providing some relief from the heat. But the euphoria of the miraa had leveled off some time ago and Loomis was beginning to crash. His nervous system rebelled, causing his cranial muscles to contract and twitch while his jaw became locked, giving him an ache in his head and a pain in his neck. The withdrawal of the drug also heightened his anxiety and filled him with doubts. What the hell was he doing up here with his woman and his child? He was making the wrong decision. They should go back and turn themselves in; he would make sure she was kept safe. He had been doing the thinking for the both of them, but he had screwed up royally with his ideas. This was definitely a mistake, a voice somewhere in his head was telling him.

Don't think, he reprimanded himself. This was a time for action, not reflection. *Just keep going up; nowhere to go but up.*

Three quarters of the way towards the first apparent crest they were faced with a wall of earth that offered no chance of any reasonable footing. They instead opted to follow a broad ledge of soil and talus that seemed to contour the slope. For a while they were no longer climbing and they hoped that the contour they were traversing would eventually lead upwards. They rounded a sharp corner and the sudden sight that confronted them took their breath away – a spectacular hanging canyon cleaved in the side of the mountain, suspended as it were by a terminus which ended abruptly in a sheer cliff falling a thousand feet to the stony plains below. The canyon itself was enfaced by precipitous, smooth-faced walls of granite, stained red and black with iron and manganese, giving the impression of gigantic Neolithic murals. On the water-cut floor of this grand chasm sat abandoned immense rocks, elephantine and rounded, the size of small houses.

"Jesus!" exclaimed Loomis.

They stood in awe for a few seconds.

"Well, we're not far from the bottom of it. Going down shouldn't be much of a problem. But to get over to the other side is going to be a bitch. Nothing but sheer cliff face all the way to the end. It's either that or going all the way back and trying a northern approach."

Amonee had no response to that.

Loomis twitched his ears and looked up. He heard something: a whine that weakly drifted in and out with the breezes. Then the sound of air being cut. "Get down!" he warned with a muffled yell.

His eyes searched the sky but he couldn't see it. The sound, however, was unmistakable. Then he spotted it. A helicopter, small, military in shape, probably a Hughes 500. A police helicopter.

They crouched down, staring at each other in suspenseful silence, afraid to talk, afraid even to breathe, as if in their terror they expected those in the chopper to be able to hear them. Loomis followed the helicopter with his eyes, the aircraft through the distance appearing as a giant flying insect skimming across the sky.

"They're looking for us, aren't they?" she whispered, controlling her fright.

"Hmmm, it looks like it. Or could be they're after the Ngoroko – livestock raiders," he added, not believing it.

For a few minutes the pulsing drone seemed to get louder, and the silhouette to grow larger, come closer, before it slowly disappeared to the north.

"Good! They didn't see the Land Rover! Let's move, they might come back."

Loomis had been right about the way down; it wasn't much of a problem. Except at the end near the canyon floor where they had to find their way around car-sized boulders. By this time the canyon had begun to subside into shadow as the sun continued to sink lower. The boy was certainly unruffled about it all, playing with the thatch of hair that stuck out of Loomis's hat at the back of his head.

"Can we take another rest?" Amonee pleaded when they reached the bottom of the gorge.

"Alright, but not too long. I don't want to have to climb up there in the dark."

But there was something else worrying him, although he did not voice it to her. This place, without a doubt, was leopard country, and it was prudent to make haste, for while a leopard may think twice before attacking a full-grown human, swiping the little boy off Loomis's back and making a clean getaway would be a facile feat for such a nimble predator.

Loomis took the boy off his back and left him to sit with Amonee while he himself went off to scout out a route up. When he came back, his signs of exhaustion were clearly visible. On his face he wore a grimace of pain and he seemed to be hyperventilating.

"Daryl, are you alright?"

"It's the miraa. Together with this exertion, it's raising my blood pressure. My heart is racing like a speedboat."

"Take a rest, please, sit down and rest."

He did so, upon a medium-sized rock. They drank almost all of the water that was left, and munched on more biscuits.

She stopped caressing the boy to shoo the incessant flies about her face. "So many flies!"

"Maybe we're getting close. Where there's livestock, there's flies."

They sat for a moment or two longer.

"Okay, let's go on," he said, undaunted. "I've found an easy way up."

What he meant to say was 'relatively' easy. The trail he picked out required them to step and hop from one ledge to another, all on a cliff angle of seventy degrees. The way was sometimes barred by bushes and short trees which obstinately grew out of broken crags, and the only way past them was to wiggle through, causing great difficulty in the handling of the boy. The air was alive with the birds they disturbed – swifts, larks, crag martins – birds of high rocky places, while above them a bateleur eagle circled lazily. In his present state the power of flight seemed especially appealing to Loomis, who now started to worry about how much farther he could go on. The route did not get easier. Towards the top of the cliff the rock surfaces became rounded and smooth and they climbed using their hands and arms as much as their legs to support themselves. With the water finished, the empty container became a hindrance, and Loomis decided to throw it away. Every so often along their ascent came a heartrending moment when one or the other of them would slip, and they would throw themselves belly down to avoid falling, after which followed the hollow, ominous clattering of the pebbles and debris cast loose by their scrambling. Neither of them dared to look down. Loomis found the responsibility of carrying the boy more and more wearing on his nerves, but luckily the boy had fallen into a deep slumber about an hour ago.

They stopped to rest on a precipice very close to the top. The last fiery rays of sunlight effused over the western peaks of the range, trimming the gorge with an orange luster and imparting the scene with an air of enchantment. But Loomis was too tired to appreciate the beauty of it. He looked up at what remained of their ascent. Only about five meters, but it was nearly vertical. He suddenly realized the value of having been a rock hound – his work had put him in positions like this before. In fact he had seen worse. This little patch he felt sure they could handle without ropes. "Stay just behind me, we'll go very slowly. Watch carefully where I put each hand and foot."

He worked his way up at a snail's pace, sometimes taking a few minutes before deciding on a hold, and always looking back to check how well Amonee was reproducing his movements.

"How you doing, alright?"

Her black face was gilded with a silver sheen of sweat. "I'm okay. A bit nervous. If I was alone, I would be terrified."

"Well, just hang on. There isn't much more left to go."

"I'll be alright. I trust you. Trusting you gives me confidence."

"Now, you see where my heel is? Grab hold there and pull yourself up...good, now put your left foot on that ledge where mine was."

In this manner they slowly inched their way up, as Loomis's head continued to reverberate with nausea-inducing throbs, making him feel precariously faint. But approaching the end of the climb gave him new strength and impetus. Ten minutes more and his hands reached the final lip. He pulled himself up, ready to crawl over, when he looked up and, to his shock, stared straight into the dark muzzle of an automatic rifle. A split-second later he heard a click and then he closed his eyes.

He remained clutching the rim of earth above, lowering his head and waiting in utter capitulation for seconds that seemed forever, before he heard the man shout "Ebu Lakwan!"

He returned his head up and saw the rifle barrel rise to point at the sky, and studied the figure looming over him: a tall man with tar-black complexion, covered in a gray blanket he wore as a tunic, with thick lips that stretched into a wide smile lacking the front lower teeth, a prominent nose that somehow looked familiar. As the man bent his head to peer at him, Loomis could see his large rheumy eyes framed with long lashes. He had an intricately patterned blue mud skullcap at the back of his head, and a strap of brightly colored beads that went around his forehead. Loomis was sure he had never met this fellow before.

"Daryl, who is it?" Amonee shouted from below.

"Ebu Lakwan! White Hyena!" the stranger shouted again, grabbing hold of Loomis's wrist and pulling him up. Then he fired a shot into the sky.

"Daryl, what's going on, who's shooting?" she asked, panicking.

"It's okay," he shouted down. "This guy knows me."

Then he went into the Turkana handshake, the one that doesn't seem to stop, clasping palm to palm, shifting to grasp each other's thumbs, then interlocking fingers, back to clasping palms, over and over again in a repetitive pattern, all the while shouting questions at each other.

"Naa?"

"Payaa!"

"Naa?"

"Payaa!"

"Mata?"

"Mata?"

"Mata abero? "

"Mata ibaren? "

"Mata nawi?"

"Mata ide?"

The boy, having been woken by this commotion, began to giggle. The man with the big smile was funny, and the yellow beads and the blue stuff on his head were pretty.

"Daryl, help me up, I'm getting tired."

"My wife," Loomis told him.

The Turkana took a couple of steps down, and balancing himself precariously, brought Amonee up in one swift motion.

"I see you've found your friends," she said panting, trying to catch her breath, yet very much relieved.

"Ebu Lakwan!" the man shouted to his left, and then again to his right. It was then that Loomis saw two other men loping towards them from each side. When they joined up, Loomis had to undergo the Naa-Payaa routine two more times, and they then broke into a babble which Loomis couldn't quite catch.

"What are they saying?" he asked Amonee.

"They say that after you left, there was no rain. Some sort of punishment. But last year it started raining again, and so they knew you would return. Something like that."

"I'm surprised they remember me."

"Well, I guess there aren't too many white hyenas around."

The trio of men began to walk off, their guests following them without any idea where they were going.

The man who they first encountered suddenly turned to Loomis.

"You know me?"

"No. You know me?"

"Yes, I know you. I am Emanikor. I am brother to Lokori. He tell me about you." Then he went into some spiel that Loomis did not understand, except for yet another mention of Ebu Lakwan.

"Can you help me out here?" he again beseeched Amonee.

"He says that you are the one who is neither white nor black, neither European nor African, an outsider, but who has the spirit of a Turkana, the White Hyena."

The land they found themselves in was cooler and greener than the desert below, with ubiquitous acacia, an abundance of edipal trees, candelabra euphorbias, and patches of lush verdant grass.

"Ebu Lakwan, you have a gun," Emanikor noted, pointing to the shoulder holster.

Loomis took the small Beretta out, and the three men laughed in chorus. Looking at the AK-47s and the Chinese burp guns they carried, he felt embarrassed, akin to being ridiculed for his penis size.

First the odor, and then the sight of herds of cattle amidst the vegetation: large, white, long-horned Zebu, with the characteristic humps just past their heads, their cowbells tinkling like wind chimes as they shuffled along with bent heads browsing the grass.

"Cow, Mommee, cow!" the little boy said.

She grabbed Loomis's arm. "Let me take him now." She undid the shawl and transferred the boy to her own back.

"Cow, Mommee!"

"Yes, cow, my sweet!"

"Do you ever call him by his real name?"

"I try to avoid that, it makes me feel uncomfortable. I thought that maybe with time, when he gets older..."

"Ebu Lakwan!" Emanikor announced to the village.

Dome-shaped huts of sticks and grass came into view, and the people milling around hastily scattered about, going into their huts and coming out again wearing their dancing bells, and then began to approach them.

As they got nearer, they did something that touched both Loomis and Amonee quite deeply.

They went into a welcoming dance.

The women started with a chant, followed by a female refrain. Then the men joined in. A beautiful choir, Amonee thought.

"Ngen-yeni, bi bai yen, hai yaa a yaa ya...aburinyenya..." Each refrain was followed by a woman giving out a whooping ululation.

The singers formed a circle around them, repeating their chorus, clapping their hands and stomping their feet to jangle their bells to form the beat. They put their right foot out, drew it back, put their left foot out, took it back, jerking their heads in the same direction as their feet. Several of the elders came out from nowhere, took the couple and child from the middle of the circle, and led them into a large hut, with many of the dancers following. They stooped and entered, and soon after others came in, filling the space available, their dancing finished.

No sooner had they sat down, they were faced with a barrage of questions. Where did they come from? Why did it take so long for the White Hyena to return? Your boy looks strong and healthy, what is his name?

The couple just shook their heads and nodded, too overwhelmed to respond. It wasn't until Emanikor arrived and sat down beside them did they have a chance to explain their situation, which Loomis chose to do, with the help of Amonee.

And the situation was this: Amonee, Black Diamond, knew a man that was bad. The police want to catch this man, but they also want to catch Black Diamond, even though she did nothing wrong. They don't trust the police, so they want to get away from them.

"Daryl, are you sure that's the right thing to say?"

"Believe me, the Turkana warriors often say that the police are like their wives. They would just love a chance to outfox them."

Everyone was smiling, and one of the young men shouted, "The police are our wives!" A chorus of hearty guffaws naturally followed.

"Well, no problem there," he said to her.

This disregard, even abhorrence, of any outside authority was a trademark that the people of the region had held for more than a century, and the British themselves had paid a high price in their attempts to subjugate the Turkana tribe. And for every post-colonial government since then, the 'war on cattle raiding' was just as futile as America's 'war on drugs'.

He addressed his audience again. "Is there another way besides the main road?"

"Yes, many ways!"

"We need to get to Juba," Loomis informed them. "Can someone help us?"

More jabbering among them, until Emanikor announced that a meeting with all the people should be held to discuss the problem.

In the meantime, food was brought, wooden bowls full of fermented milk mixed with a bit of blood. The crowd departed after that, leaving them alone in the hut.

Amonee was worried, needlessly as it turned out, that her son wouldn't eat the milk and blood porridge. But he liked it, and it was fun to eat too, because you got to put your hands in it and play with it before putting it in your mouth. His whole face soon became smeared in a pasty mess.

"Maybe we should put this stuff on the kid's menu," Loomis commented.

Amonee responded by scooping a handful of the thick gruel and feeding Loomis by hand, sticking her fingers in his mouth and wiping the excess milk off his lips with a gentle wipe of her wrist.

He did the same for her, except that he kissed the coating off her lips and chin, much to her giggling.

It was not long after that the meeting was held, and the couple was summoned outside to the middle of the encampment. It was night by now, and the quiet murmurings of the people who had already assembled were complemented by the chirping of the crickets. The twosome sat down in the front row of the gathering and soon the boy was clambering over Amonee, making one-syllable sounds to amuse himself, "Ah doo, ah mee. dah, dah, ah boo goo..."

Then the meeting started with an intro by an elder, who apparently explained the 'situation'.

What followed was a discussion of the main issues.

Loomis brought up the first issue. Could they show them another way to cross the border without going on the main road?

Yes, there were many ways, was the answer.

Could a vehicle pass on these alternate routes? That question provoked a short debate, with the end result being 'no'. No, could only walk.

Second issue. They needed to go to Juba. They could not walk the several hundred kilometers distance to get there.

But didn't White Hyena and Black Diamond come there by vehicle?

Yes.

Were the police trying to catch the White Hyena?

No, only Black Diamond.

Then the answer was clear. Black Diamond could walk, while the White Hyena took his vehicle. No need for her to walk to Juba. They could reunite once they had both crossed the border near Kapoeta.

Third issue. They would have to go through the land of the enemies. Would the Turkana be willing to take the risk of escorting Black Diamond?

There were 'pros' and 'cons' on this matter that stirred a rousing deliberation which lasted for a quarter of an hour. But the 'pros' eventually won out based on two key points. Were not the Turkana the most formidable, the most militarily superior tribe of all the Ateker people, as hundreds of years of history had shown? Of course, yes, was the answer; that is why the Turkana had held an area that was at least five times larger than any of their enemies. The second point was even more persuasive. Could the task be interpreted as a sign from Akuj, a test to show that they were worthy of the rain he gave them? If so, then there was a much greater risk if they did nothing – a drought could follow. In order to answer this question, they required the services of an emuron.

The emuron called on to perform the divination was the kind that tossed sandals and read the configuration they formed when they landed on the ground. He had been sitting in the front row of the gathering before he stood up and then took a new seat on the ground in front of the crowd, who now jostled for space as everyone moved forward to get a good view. Loomis and Amonee were urged to go and sit beside him, which they did after she secured the baby on her back. The emuron extended his arms for them to hold his hands, Loomis the left one, Amonee the right, which he held tightly before releasing them. He then removed his sandals and flipped them up in the air. After they fell, he studied their positions and made the first of his proclamations.

"What's he saying," Loomis whispered to Amonee.

"Shhh, wait. He says that the journey to the enemy's land will take place...the day after tomorrow, and will be...let me see," she paused, "ah yes mostly...successful, but there will be some problems along the way for both of us."

He threw the sandals up a second time, and again interpreted the subsequent arrangement.

"Now he says that the ones who will escort me will...uh, pose, I think that's the right word...pose, or act as traders. They will carry the maize and beans from the store. If they do that, the enemy will not attack us. And he doesn't see bandits, but he is not sure, so we must be careful."

Maize and beans, which the Turkana obtained either through relief organizations, or by trading with the southerly Pokot tribe, were very valuable commodities in the famine-stricken Southern

Sudan.

Again, the emuron tossed his sandals. Again Amonee translated his divinations.

"Only six shall accompany me, one married male, two unmarried males, one married female, two unmarried females. I must dress as a Turkana woman, so no one suspects. We will go with two camels for milk, and four donkeys. He says that Emanikor, as the married male, will lead us."

He repeated his throwing a fourth time.

"The White Hyena's vehicle is south of Agrilok," she conveyed to Loomis.

"Is Agrilok the hanging canyon?"

"I think so. Wait...now he says that the group will meet White Hyena at the mountain that looks like a camel."

The emuron flipped again, this time shaking his head slightly, looking a bit puzzled.

"Uh, oh," Loomis voiced, "that doesn't look good."

"Shhh...he says the journey doesn't end there...it continues...another journey...a journey towards a falling sun...but he can't see anything beyond that."

After that last declaration, it seemed the emuron was finished with the sandal tossing, and a general discussion took place, mainly concerning the arrangements that he had advised. One thing more they had to do, according to the emuron, was to slaughter a bull as a sacrifice to Akuj, to make sure he was paying attention to their endeavors, since the Turkana knew that Akuj, God, was indifferent, heedless, and sometimes downright callous.

Once the talk died down, people began to leave for their respective huts. Amonee and the baby were taken to a hut where she would sleep with the women, while Loomis followed a group of young men to the etien, the male sleeping quarters.

* * *

Loomis opened his eyes to a pastel blue sky, having been woken up by the myriad flies on his face, and the smells of cattle and the sounds of cowbells. He rose to wander amidst the coppices of trees and around the scattering of huts to find Amonee sitting outside one of them. She rose to receive him. The toddler, dressed now only in his underpants, was making a circumspect acquaintance with three other similar-aged Turkana children and an older pubescent girl.

"Hi, how did you sleep?" he greeted her.

"Not bad, a bit chilly, but I was so exhausted I just fell right out, and he only woke me up once."

"Have you had breakfast?"

"Yes, we've already had our milk."

"Seems he's starting to make friends," Loomis commented, watching the children, now touching the honey-colored skin on his son's arms and belly.

"Do you think his skin color will give us away?" Amonee asked with some concern.

"Well, I've seen light-skinned Turkana before, particularly children, but, he is a bit lighter than that. Still, I don't think anyone is going to pay too much attention to him."

"In a little while I will go with the women for my make-over. They have to shave his head too," she said, referring to their son. "I don't think he'll be very cooperative, I might have to do it myself."

"Good luck with that."

He saw women passing by, walking gingerly with wooden bowls full of fresh blood.

"I guess they must have slaughtered the bull already."

Emanikor approached with one of the elders and grabbed his arm. "Ejok, White Hyena. Come with us to help arrange things."

"See you later," he told her.

The day went by with Loomis involved in the manly things, while Amonee spent her time with the women. He had to inspect the loading of the maize and beans, approve of the two young warriors that were preliminarily chosen, and to help select which camels and donkeys that were to go. Basically, as he knew next to nothing concerning these matters, he just agreed to whatever were their predetermined choices. When finished with these duties, on his way back to his etien, he noticed two women constructing a new hut, planting curved sticks in the ground and thatching branches with fresh green leaves onto the top.

"A new hut for you and Black Diamond," Emanikor informed him.

It wasn't until mid-afternoon that they were able to meet again.

He found her standing outside the same hut where they had met in the morning. She had that same radiant smile that by now he knew so well, but everything else was different.

Her head was bald except for a row of stringy braids that ran down the middle. She had two pairs of metal rings in each ear. From just below her chin there was a beaded collar, and below that a stack of stringed beads that went down to the top of her shoulders. She wore a goatskin cape that covered her chest, and a cow-skin apron that fell to her ankles. Encircling her wrists were metal rings, and around her biceps were multicolored bracelets, glowing alluringly against her black sinewy skin. Their son, whom she was clutching in her arms, was naked, his little dinky penis exposed, and he too was shaven-headed save for a little tuft of hair at the back.

"Take off the cape," he ordered her gently.

She put the child down and delicately removed the leather bib. He looked at her: her breasts, rounded ebony gourds with erect nipples, the slender curve of her waist expanding into svelte hips that teasingly disappeared into her leather sarong.

"God, you're beautiful."

He stepped towards her and took her in his arms, then gave her a light kiss. "But you smell like a goat."

She lowered her arm to smack his backside. "It's the animal fat they smeared on my skin!"

"But I like it!" he told her, laughing.

She hugged him. "You're a goofy person."

He pulled his head back to look at her in mock amazement. "Really? I thought I was witty."

"Only with you!" she burst out with a laugh.

"Huh?"

"Only with you could I be here right now, looking like this," she said, still laughing.

He hugged her tighter. It seemed their romance was being rekindled by the extremity of their predicament. Or the absurdity of it. Loomis wasn't sure. But, whatever it was, he didn't care.

* * *

There followed a feast. There was enough meat for everyone, despite the fact that they were over a hundred strong. Some of the blood was offered as well, given only to special persons, for the rest should be stored. Of course, Amonee and Loomis were among these special people and they therefore had to take perfunctory sips, regardless.

And then came the night dancing.

The leaping, the jumping, the beat, the rhythm, the chanting, the jingling bells, and the fused singing, sent waves of therapeutic excitement over Amonee, allowing her to briefly abandon her anxiety over the next day's safari. A release of all her tensions. A frenzied purge of all her doubts and qualms as she bounced her body up and down with her female partners, their bells clangoring brazenly through the night air. She was on a high; deliberately receptive to the energy, so that she could counterbalance her fear of what lay ahead. A high she knew would end soon after.

Later, alone in their private hut, they lay together, the boy crawling on top of them.

"I'm scared," she said.

"Don't worry. You're in good hands. These people will defend you with their lives."

"I know. But I don't feel comfortable being separated."

The boy soon fell asleep between them, snoring.

"I have to walk all the way," she bemoaned.

"Yes, the Turkana don't ride their animals. You would look ridiculous and out of place on top of one of them."

"They gave me a pair of sneakers."

"That's nice. Turkana women usually walk barefoot."

Although the men wore sandals, Turkana women did not, as if sandals were distinctively male apparel. On the other hand, a Turkana man wouldn't be caught dead in sneakers.

"I love you," she confessed.

"I know that already."

"You don't want to say it back?"

"Do I have to?"

"No."

"You're not going to make me?"

"No!" she answered laughing.

They hugged each other. Then she put their sleeping boy on the outer part of the cow-skin mat, cuing Loomis to draw near her.

He held her, and they joined their bodies, and stayed that way until they merged together, melting into one another.

THE JOURNEY,
AUGUST 29 – SEPTEMBER 1

It was still dark, but dawn was approaching fast, heralded by a madrigal of birdcalls. Whiffs of woodsmoke from early-morning breakfast fires were carried by the breeze. The animals for the journey were being prepared, the camels being the most noisily recalcitrant. The little troupe was just about ready to get underway. It was to be journey of four days. To get down off the mountain, they were to take a northwesterly route, a wide, well-worn trail the Turkana used to drive their cattle. Loomis proposed to escort them at least halfway down, as he had nothing to do but wait in the hilltop encampment for another two days in order to bide the lead time that the travelers required for their rendezvous. It was safer to wait here, rather than for him to delay in Lokichoggio, where the possibility of unwelcome questions could put their mission in jeopardy.

As it turned out he walked down the entire length of the mountainside, so reluctant was he to leave her. On the way, he joked to her with the intention of keeping her in buoyed spirits, praising her new sneakers, making ribald comments about the way her hips rocked and swayed her leather apron, as well as clowning around with the boy. The child, shawled onto Amonee's back, was his usual unflappable self, looking around at his environment in analytical curiosity. The Turkana men were involved in their own discussions, the females merely listening to, and laughing from time to time, at the apparently funny stories the men were narrating.

Emanikor, the leader, wore his blanket, while the young bare-chested men had red checkered cotton sarongs wrapped around their waists. The older Turkana woman, like Amonee, was covered in leather hides, while the maidens, barely fifteen years old, were half-naked and their aprons were cut in the arrac style, with only a short flap provocatively covering their loins. One of the girls was covered with red ochre: head, face, chest and back.

"Why is she painted up like that?" Amonee asked Loomis, expecting he might know the answer.

"Yeah, odd isn't it, prettying herself up to go on a serious expedition. I would imagine that perhaps the emuron suggested it, though I can't figure out why."

As they neared the bottom, and the time for separation grew closer, the angst of both of them intensified.

Eventually, they reached the desert floor. He double-checked that her passports were packed, that the kid's hat was on tight enough so it wouldn't be blown off by the wind, and other little details, all designed to marginally defer their parting.

"Well here we are," he said. "God, I wish I could go with you."

"Don't worry, please, I'll be okay."

"I love you," he said. "More than anyone in my life. More than my own life." He grinned. "See, you didn't even have to make me say that."

She gave him a faint smile, one with closed lips, something she rarely did. She stroked his cheek, and he stroked hers in turn.

"Please," she implored, "you be careful too. I have people to help me, but you'll be alone. So of course, I'll also worry about you."

Emanikor halted to give them time to say goodbye, while the others filed past.

She kissed him on the cheek, and then turned to walk away. Emanikor followed behind her.

He watched them walk into the desert, until their silhouettes were blurred by the heat waves emanating from the ground.

Loomis almost never thought about God. At best, he adopted the same attitude that the Turkana did. If such a thing as a God existed, it was an uncaring, unfeeling, and negligent being. Yet despite his beliefs, he found himself saying, "Please, God, protect her. Help her make it through."

Then he turned to walk back up the slope, along with the young Turkana boy assigned as his guide.

* * *

She marched with them over moderately rough ground that became more level as they went ahead, feeling comfortable with her sneakers despite them being a bit undersized, and content with her compliant son on her back. Buffeted by an agreeably convivial wind, she contemplated the beauty of the desert. The sprinkling of acacia trees and the intermittent baobabs were like decorations adorned over the vastness. It was refreshing. Maybe she would even enjoy the trek.

And for most of the morning she actually did. Although, towards noon, it became unpleasantly hot and her feet began to sweat inside her ill-fitting sneakers.

They walked and walked and walked, a little caravan of seven people and a baby, two camels and four donkeys. The donkeys, loaded with sacks of maize and beans, and the numerous diverse gourds and wooden vessels of every shape and size, were generally quiet, but the camels grunted frequently, a sound she didn't like. They were rather large animals, and so she didn't trust them, notwithstanding the ostensible control of the beasts that her Turkana comrades displayed.

In the afternoon, they stopped under the shade of one of the larger Doum Palm trees. "We rest here," Emanikor announced.

They drank fresh camel milk for lunch. The men lay down with their heads resting on their ekicholongs, the women sat and played with the boy, who by now showed no apprehension toward the strange-looking women, especially since his mommee now looked just like them.

Amonee took a nap while the wind washed over her.

* * *

Once back in the village, Loomis became restless, having nothing important to do. In his idleness, he could not restrain his mind from wondering where she was at that moment and how she was faring.

The Turkana men, sensing his anxiety, brought over a plastic container of palm wine. They drank, chatted, and generally tried to cheer him up. One important discussion they had concerned the place he was to meet Emanikor's group. It was a frustrating dialogue, as his ability to speak Turkana was as bad as their proficiency of Kiswahili. A topic that should have been covered in minutes took up a whole hour. But at least he had an idea. The mountain was ten miles north of Kapoeta, and clearly visible, as it only took an hour by foot to reach it from the road.

For much of the rest of the day, he remained lying down under a tree, ruminating over Amonee and their son.

* * *

She reckoned it was nearing six o'clock when they finally gave her and her son some water to drink. They also gave them something to eat. 'Akibok', the older matron called it. It looked like the usual milk and blood, but it stank to high heaven, which made it difficult to imbibe; it tasted awful as well. The child would not eat it, and Amonee got angry when the married woman, whose name was Aite, had tried to force feed him and made him cry. Amonee grabbed her son. "He doesn't like it."

"He must eat," Aite demanded, then walked away, somewhat irritated.

Shortly after, they were on their way once more. The sky was searing with the orange light of a fiery sun going down beneath the horizon, and it was then that she became a bit frightened for the first time, frightened at being lost in a severe wilderness, and realizing that her life and that of her son's depended on the strangers who were guiding them. They advanced through dusk and into the night. Hours went by and she was truly exhausted. What made it worse was that her little boy was also becoming tired of the trek, as he began to cry for some indiscernible reason. Assuming it was the discomfort of being in the same position for a long time, she removed him from her back and carried him in her arms, which seemed to pacify him for a while, but at the same time, made walking more arduous for her. Still, they did not stop until hours later, in a place that seemed to be picked at random.

Her legs and feet were aching as she lay down upon the cow-skin mat, but fortunately, her son had fallen asleep about an hour before and so that was one less problem she had to attend to. Again she was offered a bowlful of the akibok, which she took and even tried to eat as much as she could, but did not bother to wake the child.

She stretched out on her back to look at the stars. It seemed as if they were humming to her, and then she remembered that night three years ago, gazing at them together with Daryl. He must be looking at those same exact stars at this moment, she guessed.

"Good night, Daryl," she murmured to herself before she went off into a slumber.

* * *

In the evening, Loomis had once again sat down with the men, and once again had felt defeated at his lack of comprehension of what they were saying. He had been involved only in the beginning of their conversation, and thereafter only intermittently, whenever the Turkana remembered his presence. Otherwise they mostly talked amongst themselves, leaving him the opportunity to think of Amonee and the kid. He ate his food, the stuff he didn't like, the akibok they made with camel piss.

Lying on the ground under the open sky, he focused on the stars. He smiled. *They're singing,* he thought to himself. "Sing for Amonee," he said out loud.

The second day was even more boring, and he spent most of it sleeping it away. Which, in a sense, was what he needed. But at night he found himself tossing and turning, and fretting. He eventually had to convince himself that worrying about them would not help them, regardless of whatever situation they were in. Yet, he couldn't wait for the morning; the time of his departure, which would give him a sense of purpose, a progression toward the time when they could be together again.

And then it came, with all those beautiful bird songs, the bellowing of the cattle, and the early-day chatter of the people around.

After breakfast, this time a maize porridge, he was given the same adolescent boy as a guide to take him to the Land Rover.

It took three hours to get off the mountain. He was carrying the evening-gown sack full of her things, which gave him a perception of continuity. *She'll need these things later,* he told himself.

The trail went basically southwest and came out just north of the great canyon that he and Amonee had traversed. After that they had to go south to try and find where Loomis had parked the vehicle. It was another two hours before they found it. After the both of them had removed the cover of branches, Loomis thought of something he had previously not considered: he would have to get rid of everything that suggested her presence, not only the suitcases, but the evening gown full of things that he had stupidly brought down. He opened the rear door and contemplated the best way to ditch her belongings. He looked at the teenage boy. He figured he was tough enough to carry the things back up the mountain. Not only would that be less obvious than just dumping them here in the desert, but the articles might find some use up there. He snickered to himself as he envisioned one of the Turkana women attired in the evening gown.

Then he remembered the vehicle plates. He would change them now, which he set about doing while the lad waited. He took the Kenyan plates and decided to stick them in the larger suitcase. This was a big decision, as he was required to hand them in at the border, but he figured it was better to take a risk and try to bullshit his way out of it, rather than the bigger danger of discovery in the event that indeed the authorities had identified his vehicle in Lodwar. He wondered amusingly at what implements the Turkana blacksmiths would make out of them.

He motioned to the youth that he should bring the stuff back with him, saying 'zawadi', the Kiswahili word for 'gift', as he did not know the proper Turkana word, and using some rope, tied the suitcases to the boy's back before bidding him farewell. By now it was nearing noon.

His plan was to start driving, but slowly, and sleep in the Land Rover a few hours' distance from Lokichoggio. Of course he had to get the car to start first. Leaving the vehicle for two days exposed to the elements, namely heat and especially dust, turning over the engine was an optimistic assumption. It was about seventy-thirty, he reckoned. *Maybe it will, and maybe it won't.*

He switched the ignition on and the engine came to life with a sonorous whirr.

"Atta baby."

* * *

In the darkness just before sunrise, Amonee awoke with a painful cramping of her bowels. She rose hurriedly and took a few steps and managed to quickly lift the back of her leather apron before she violently and noisily discharged a liquidy mess. Then she was struck with the conundrum of cleaning herself; she didn't know what to do, and was too ashamed to ask advice from Aite or the girls, and was equally loathe to use the shawl she used to carry the baby. She remained squatting, deciding to do nothing about it, feeling so debased that she broke down crying.

Again they were off before the break of dawn. Her legs felt like plywood boards, and now her anus itched and burned with every stride. To add to that, the baby was crying again and she tried in vain to placate him. Resigning herself to her situation, she secured him onto her back anyway, despite his protestations, and continued her march with the rest, hoping her day would improve.

Four more hours of walking, walking, walking. The wind brought with it the acrid odour of dust, carried over miles and miles of rocky ground strewn with cobbles and scrubby with bushes. By now her feet began to burn with blisters, and she was tempted to take the sneakers off. Her son had been crying all the way, and when they had finally stopped to rest, she removed him from her back to inspect him. He had a rash, complete with numerous pimples, and it seemed to be over most of his body. He had also been suffering with diarrhea, and it was all over the middle of the shawl.

Aite came over, and after inspecting the child, fetched a gourd of goat fat from one of the donkeys and applied it to the child's skin with Amonee's acceptance. But Aite would not give her any water to clean the shawl. In fact, they themselves drank very little of it, and a constant thirst was another discomfort she had to endure.

After that they continued with the same monotonous, and for Amonee, painful, steps forward, one foot ahead of another, left, right...pressing on into places that looked exactly like the places they had left behind them, a repeating pattern that made her feel she was going nowhere. The child still persisted in his bawling, making her cringe with a vicarious distress, and the putrid smell of dried excrement on the shawl made her plight even worse.

It was around noon, she estimated, that they saw a vehicle in the distance, moving at right angles to their direction, its appearance made more obvious by the plume of dust stirring up behind it. It stopped, apparently for the purpose of scrutinizing the little caravan.

"Wait here," Emanikor ordered.

Amonee felt nervous as he strode towards the Land Rover, seemingly a police vehicle. Upon reaching it, Emanikor leaned his arm on the half-closed window as the policeman addressed him.

"Habrari, how is it?"

"Fine," Emanikor responded in badly pronounced Kiswahili.

"Where you going?"

"Not far."

"What are you carrying?"

"Maize and beans." Emanikor spat a missile of saliva out of the gap in his lower front teeth. "Any problem?"

"No, no problem." And with that, the border patrol drove off to the east, continuing on in their original direction.

When Emanikor came back he informed her, "We are very near the border. No problem."

They walked for another hour before they took their afternoon respite.

Food was dished out; again, the akibok. Not long after that, a commotion broke out. It was between the two bachelors: first words, then a physical confrontation, like two boxers in a hold, but trying to trip each other up as well. The fight was made even more graphic by the blows they dealt each other with the abaraits around their wrists, slashing each other's backs and arms, the blood a bright gleaming red against their black skins. Emanikor and Aite intervened, striking at the both of them with their walking sticks, and screaming Turkana expletives until the two youths were separated.

Amonee, to say the least, was unnerved.

Apparently, it had been an argument over the one or the other of the two young maidens. Probably the one made up with the red ochre.

"Don't worry," Emanikor assured her as he approached to calm her. "They have hot blood, that's why they were chosen. They will kill anyone who tries to harm you."

During the night, she felt so awful that she could not ponder too much about Daryl's own situation, except for believing that his own wits and courage would keep him safe, despite the fact that he would be alone in a stark, perilous night. She herself could not find sleep, distracted as she was by her numerous discomforts, but apprecia- tively, her son was able to doze off in between his bouts of bawling. Whenever the self-pity over her predicament overwhelmed her, she would remember that they were halfway. Halfway…halfway…and this enabled her to fall into a series of fitful naps.

She welcomed the morning, regardless of the agony of getting on her feet and resuming the endless walking, only because the passing of every moment meant that the end of her journey was drawing that much closer. Still, she could not fight off the oppressive notion that she and her comrades were only tiny insignificant figures, wandering hopelessly in a desolation that stretched to forever.

As the morning progressed, the land seemed to get bleaker, and strong winds from the west began to buffet them with bullying gusts, explaining the origin of the alien-looking pillars of stone, burnished by wind and sand, that marked their way. Since dawn they had been on the move, except for the occasion when they had stopped to milk the camels and drink fresh milk warm with their body heat. The beasts they walked with had begun to pall for Amonee, especially the supercilious-faced camels who farted, slobbered, and made frightful, sonorous bellows which further upset her son.

In the heat of the day, when the sun bleached the land white, they took shade underneath a single edepal tree. There they drank more akibok, and Amonee persevered through another diarrhea attack. Sleep proved impossible for her. Flies landed and crawled over her face, arms, and ankles, wickedly tickling her till she thought she would go mad. Cicadas hidden in the bushes screamed out the heat in an incessant ear-piercing shriek that pressed upon her ears. Frequent gusts of wind blew sand in her face. On top of that the child, because of his heat rash, had become implacable as he howled out his suffering.

Later on the child quieted down into a slumber, but Amonee was still awake. She looked up when she saw Akiru, the girl in the red ochre body paint, run over to a urinating camel, and was shocked to see her intercepting the yellow stream with a cup. Morbidly intrigued, Amonee rose and followed the woman over to the donkeys where she saw her pour the cup's contents into one of the vessels of milk.

Hearing Amonee stirring behind her, Akiru turned around. "Akibok," she said smiling.

Amonee ran off to vomit. Convinced it was the cause of her stomach troubles, she swore to drink it no more.

The afternoon had not yet ended when they embarked on the next leg of their journey. The winds picked up in intensity and dust devils soon sprouted around them, with some of the miniature tornadoes whirring and wobbling across their path; the ones the marchers could not manage to evade slapped at them with revolving fists of dust. To the west, the sun got lost behind a malevolent curtain of charcoal-grey clouds, and the dull radiance of the steel-grey firmament threw an eerie, metallic storm-light over everything. Emanikor hurried them along, at times pointing dramatically to the west and shouting frantically, emphasizing the need to make haste. They took shelter behind one of the eroded rock pillars as the wind increased its fury, roaring its rage, blowing in wild fits, and letting loose with serried waves of flying sand until the whole concern of camels, donkeys, and humans was engulfed in an angry tumult of dun-colored, dust-laden air. The wind flogged at them with lashes of stinging particles, making it difficult for the men to restrain the animals, the donkeys braying and the camels raving in fright. Amonee screamed for her baby. Aite brought the crying boy over, bundled in a blanket. Then all of the women dived on the ground, covering themselves with cow-skin capes.

In the face of this rising gale of sand, Ereng and Kem, the two young warriors, had the laborious and dangerous duty of tying up the left forelegs of the camels to prevent them from running away in their confusion. The Turkanas used no ropes or reins on their animals, and getting a camel to stay still while Ereng grappled with its leg required formidable efforts, with Kem at times hanging on to the beast's neck. When the men finished bringing the animals down, they too collapsed upon the ground, pulling their blankets over them, submitting flinchingly to the whipping the elements had deemed to give them.

* * *

He stood by the Land Rover, scratching his head, feeling the day's temperature rising to its zenith, and chided himself for being so stupid. How could he go anywhere without water? None of the Turkanas had reminded him, for they and their stock, if need be, could go for days without it. Although his thirst had not yet become severe (he still had some packaged milk), the Land Rover's had, and a couple of hours driving had been enough to alarm the bloody red light. He opened the hood and checked the water in the radiator. It was less than half-full. It was obvious the car would not make it in the heat of the day.

He opened the door and got in. For now he had to be content with resting here until the night and with luck reach Lokichoggio in the very early hours of the next morning. But he was not content. He was anxious. It was a three-hour slog to Lokichoggio, and the camel-looking mountain, ten miles north of Kapoeta, was another two on a shitty road. He didn't want to cut it too close with the scheduled rendezvous time, for he felt it was important that he get there first.

He lay back in the hot cab, and after stabbing at a tin of corned beef with his Swiss Army knife, consumed its contents, drank some milk, and took a nap. When he woke up, his first thought was that he was still dreaming – a dream that he had found himself on Mars was real enough to frighten him. The world outside the Land Rover was a hazy ochre red, the hills, the ground, even the sky – just like the photos from the Viking probe. He convinced himself that he was not dreaming, that this was Turkanaland, not Mars.

Then he heard the sound of a lorry, and saw a billow of dust to the south steadily approaching him. It slowed down as it came closer. He thought it looked familiar.

The large vehicle, overflowing with goods that threatened to spill over with every lurch, finally stopped alongside. Riding on top of the mound of merchandise were two Turkana tribesmen with Kalashnikovs that apparently were hired as armed guards.

"Hey, is that Loomis?" a swarthy man shouted from the window of the cab.

It was Sanjay, the biggest merchant in Lokichoggio, and perhaps, in all of Turkana District.

"Yeah. Got any water? My radiator is low."

"How you travel no water? You should know better. How long you live in this place?"

"Yeah, well, I got really drunk in Lodwar and I just forgot."

Sanjay turned to his driver. "*Maji*," he told him, 'maji' meaning water, then hopped down. The driver reached under his seat to retrieve a plastic container full of water and also disembarked.

"Big dust storm in the northwest," Sanjay observed, looking skyward. "I hope it not come this way."

"Yeah, hope not," Loomis replied as the driver filled the Land Rover's radiator. A new upsurge of apprehension over the welfare of Amonee and their child started to grip him.

"Okay, we must continue. Need to reach before dark. Too dangerous at night. You go ahead first so you not eat our dust."

"Thanks." The radiator business finished, Loomis entered the Land Rover and pulled away.

* * *

In the evening, an hour after the storm had abated, they set out once more, and Amonee, plodding wearily along, was amazed at how clear and cool the air had become. Everything, vegetation and earth, possessed a subtle sheen, as if the desert had had a good scrubbing. She was envious; she herself felt gritty; the sand particles adhering to the oil on her skin were a constant source of irritation. Her nostrils were swollen shut from the dust, forcing her to breathe through her mouth, the hot air scorching her already parched throat. The ground bounced back the heat that the sun had thrown at it all day, the landscape like the surface of some rocky, barren planet.

Keeping to the pattern of the previous two days, they walked through dusk and into the night, but this time they did not stop to sleep. Amonee's suffering grew. Her feet were plagued by her persistently stinging, burning blisters; the ones that had already broken open were searing from the tobacco that an obdurate Aite had resolutely applied. Her ankles were sore and her knees ached. The muscles in her calves, thighs, and even in her buttocks were stabbed with painful cramps. With every agonizing step she came to believe more and more that the onerous journey was her penance; an atonement for her sins. She was the one responsible for this mess; she had caused pain and heartache to all who came into contact with her, even her own son was now beginning to suffer the conse-quences of her actions. It was all her fault. "Oh God, I'm sorry for what I did," she mumbled aloud. "I'm sorry for what I did."

At dawn they took a short break where Amonee reluctantly accepted some fresh milk and wild honey. Aite had to help her up when they were ready to resume the trek.

During the latter part of the morning, the sky was invaded by bulky, protean clouds; weightless giants scudding stolidly by on a great journey of their own. By that time the terrain had changed dramatically. The troupe were now traveling through a savanna of golden grass, punctuated by huge, gruesome, troll-like baobabs, their enormous trunks thick enough to drive a car through, their maligned, leafless branches arched like arthritic tentacles. Countless termite mounds sat like headstones in an ancient graveyard. The view repulsed her, and at this point in the journey even the most innocuous scenery appeared to her baleful and ominous.

She found that her former affection for the Turkanas had descended into an annoyance bordering on hate. At times they would order her about as if she were a child. They withheld water from her until they themselves decided on the proper occasion to give her some; she resented this control over her and also grew extremely jealous of the attentions the other women were giving her son. Worst of all was the poison they were feeding her: their wretched milk that cramped her belly and made her bowels painfully uncontrollable.

The Turkanas would not answer her questions relating to such matters as to where they were, how long to the next resting place, and how much of the journey remained before the rendezvous point. Her ignorance concerning her situation nurtured a growing sense of impotence which tortured her by making time, distance, and position meaningless concepts obliterated in the all-important, ceaseless, continuum of walking.

"Oh God, I'm sorry for what I did," she murmured to herself.

* * *

In the growing morning light, both Songot and Mogila stood clear and clean. Loomis directed the Land Rover along the road that coursed the narrow gap which separated the two mountain ranges. Lokichoggio, which sat smack in the middle of this little tectonic valley, was less than half an hour away, and he began to rehearse what he would say in response to a variety of possible scenarios. It had been six days since they had interrupted their journey from Lodwar, and this hiatus, along with the new plate numbers, he hoped would be enough to throw off any suspicion.

He passed the road which branched off to the Red Cross hospital at the foot of Mogila, then entered the dusty, sleepy settlement that served as the border post. Clustered around the "town" were the camps of the Turkana Rehabilitation Project, a project which never left after the drought of 1980, but remained with the commitment of bringing total development to Turkana District, whatever "development" was supposed to be. The camps, fenced in with thornbrush, were crammed with Turkana families and their smaller livestock, reluctant to move out of the "town" because of the free food provided and for fear of the enemies who might be encountered out in the desert.

Two rows of shabby, mud-walled shops flanking a dirt road, a school, and a couple of churches formed the spine of Lokichoggio, while at its head, at the northern end of the settlement, stood the buildings serving the police, the GSU (the Government Special Unit, dedicated to battling the Ngoroko or cattle thieves), and the few customs and immigration officials who monitored the inter-border traffic. Stopping at the large timber shack which housed these officials, Loomis found no one there. It was still too early. He thought of driving off, but without a stamp of departure, he might have problems in Kapoeta on the Sudanese side. Besides, he had nothing to hide: he had no contraband, and there was no evidence that he had committed any wrongdoing. There was no need to arouse any undue attention to himself; this was a normal trip back to site.

He beeped the horn for several minutes before they showed up: an immigration official who knew Loomis, and walking beside him, a policeman in green khakis.

"Hello, Mr. Chunga," Loomis called genially. "Sorry to wake you up, but I had a sudden and compelling urge to see your face. I'm on my way back and I'm late."

"Yes, yes, Mr. Loomis. Habari yako, bwana? Don't always be in such a rush. We have got beer in the canteen today, first time in six months. When was the last time you offered me a bottle?" Chunga was a short brown Kamba with a noticeable pot belly, posted in a hardship area where the greatest calamity he had faced was being bored to death. "Besides," he went on to say, "there's someone who would like to see you."

"Excuse me, bwana," the policeman interrupted, "the OCS wants to see you."

Loomis stiffened imperceptibly, then put on a contrived air of nonchalance. "Tell Captain Mwangi I'm traveling empty. The whiskey comes from Khartoum these days. I'll bring him his crate when I come back in."

"You just come," insisted the policeman.

Loomis got out of the vehicle to follow the askari, whereupon they entered the wooden building which was the police station. They passed the duty officer's desk at the front, then turned down a wooden corridor, walking on a timber floor where footsteps made a racket of loud thumps. At the end of this corridor were several offices, one with the door ajar. On this door was written 'OFFICER IN CHARGE OF POLICE STATION, CAPTAIN J. MWANGI'.

Mwangi was a burly man the color of burnt sienna. A squat nose in the center of his face separated his beady eyes, and he had long thick lips which reminded Loomis of a crocodile's, particularly when he grinned. He too possessed a sizeable paunch, a common affliction in Lokichoggio. His head, craned over his large desk, did not adjust itself as Loomis entered; only his eyes took notice, swivelling upwards in their sockets. "Ah, Bwana Loomis. You have really delayed in Nairobi. Too much of the good life there. I know how those city girls go crazy over you light-skinned foreigners." Mwangi offered his hand but did not get up.

"Habari, Bwana Mwangi."

"Mzuri, mzuri sana."

"Listen, I didn't get a chance to pick up anything in Nairobi. Nowadays I have access to duty free at the Finnish Embassy in Khartoum. Next month I'll be through here again and I'll get you another crate."

"Huh? Oh, oh, the whiskey. That's not the reason I've called you. Sit down."

Loomis did so, with a feeling of impending doom.

"When did you leave Nairobi, Bwana Loomis?"

The answer to this question had been one of the responses already prepared in his mind. "The day before yesterday. Around one in the afternoon. I slept in Eldoret."

"In Eldoret, eh? And when did you arrive in Lodwar?"

"Is this an informal chat, Mwangi? Or am I being questioned about something?"

"It is I who asks the questions. Now, when did you arrive in Lodwar?"

"Yesterday. At 2 p.m."

"Why, tell me, are you here so early in the morning? I had barely enough time to throw on my shirt and run in here when I heard your vehicle. I've not even taken tea yet."

"Is that against the law, to come to Lokichoggio before seven? I left in the middle of the night. About three-thirty. I figured that way I could make it to Juba by the evening."

"That is a tough day of driving."

"I think I can handle it."

"Are you in a rush? Don't you want to greet your friends here in Lokichoggio?" There was an insidious tone of intimidation in his voice. "Don't you want to greet me? Huh?"

"I'm in a bit of a..."

"Where are the keys to your car?"

"Mwangi, what is this?"

"The keys."

Loomis fished in his pocket and handed them over. Mwangi, keeping his arm in mid-air, dangled the keys while calling out to one of his askaris. "Corporal Muliro!"

A policeman came in, clapped his heels sharply together, and saluted. "Yes sir!"

"*Chukua hiyo Land Rover ilipo nje, na weka ndani.* Take that Land Rover outside and bring it in."

The corporal took the keys, clapped his heels together, and saluted before exiting.

"It is very disturbing to me that you have broken your usual pattern," Mwangi went on. "You always sleep here before entering Sudan."

"Well, this time things didn't allow that."

"Must be something important in Juba. Driving all night. Continuing on. Not even a decent duka between here and Juba where you could reasonably refresh yourself." Mwangi was taking his time, taunting him, like a cat with a captured mouse.

"The job is behind schedule and I'm getting a lot of noise about it. The oil team is coming in a few weeks and they expect to be drilling right away. They need water. Lots of water." Loomis heard the sound of the Land Rover being parked in the police parking lot.

It looked as though he would be staying for a while.

"You were seen in Lodwar on August twenty-fifth, six days ago," challenged Mwangi. "That does not fit well with your story."

"It doesn't fit well because it's not true. I was in Nairobi on the twenty-fifth."

"But you were identified in Lodwar on that day."

"By who? How? Can whoever claims they saw me confirm that? Did they ask for the person's passport? It wasn't me."

"You were physically identified on sight by a police officer."

"Oh, c'mon, Mwangi." Now that it was all out in the open, Loomis felt better, ready to match wits with whatever interrogation followed. "Probably someone who looked like me."

Corporal Muliro returned, clapped his heels together, and saluted, then returned the keys to his superior.

"Corporal, tell Sergeant Tivuli to come in here."

"Yes, sir." The policeman clapped his heels together, saluted, and exited.

"And driving a light-brown Land Rover just like yours?" the OCS continued.

"I suppose my vehicle was identified as well?" sneered Loomis with a hint of impudence. Showing annoyance at this point was a good ploy he figured.

Sgt. Tivuli came in, clapped his heels together, and saluted.

"Sgt.Tivuli, is the radio working yet?"

"*Bado.* Not yet. Sir."

"How long will it take?"

"*Si jui.* I don't know. We are still looking for the problem, sir."

"The problem is the entire radio. Every month it must break down at least once. I'm going to have to send the Quartermaster to Nakuru again... now, bring me that radio message from Lodwar, dated the twenty-fifth."

Sgt. Tivuli clapped his heels together, saluted, and exited.

Mwangi gave Loomis a hard stare. "It has been reported to me that you were seen in Lodwar in the company of a woman who is wanted by the authorities, and presumed to be traveling towards the Sudanese border. Perhaps an attempt to smuggle her out of the country. That's what it seems."

Loomis released a hollow laugh. "Sounds like something out of a Wilbur Smith novel. I think you guys are reading too many paperbacks."

"Her name was Pamela Emuria, before she became married. Know her?"

"Well, I can't say that I do, but then again, I can't say that I don't. The name doesn't ring a bell. But you know me, I'm terrible with the ladies, especially those city girls."

"If you really are in such a rush, why then would you pull over and sleep in the vehicle, forty kilometers south of here, exposing yourself to the danger of bandits. In fact, that was yesterday. You were spotted by Sanjay, the trader, who had a conversation with you. That also does not fit in with your story."

Sgt. Tivuli entered the office, clapped his heels together, and saluted, all before handing to Mwangi a sheet of paper.

Mwangi's crocodile lips parted in a triumphant smirk as he glanced at the sheet. "Is your vehicle registration number KUV 147?"

"No."

Mwangi's face collapsed. "No?"

"No," Loomis said again, slowly shaking his head from left to right for emphasis. "It's registered in the Sudan. You should have bothered to look at it before treating me like a 'jambazi'. Didn't you care to look at the plates before you confiscated my vehicle?" Loomis then told him the number of the new plates.

"Let us have a look," Mwangi proposed. They walked outside in the bright sunshine with Sgt. Tivuli following dutifully. When they reached the Land Rover, Mwangi saw it was exactly the way Loomis had claimed it to be, though his face was still skeptical.

"According to the procedure, the vehicle has to have Kenyan plates when issued, and you're supposed to surrender those plates at the border. So I ask you, Bwana Loomis, first as a friend, then as a police officer, where are the Kenyan plates?

"I lost them."

"You expect me to believe that?" He continued staring at the number plates. "Sergeant!"

The sergeant clapped his heels together and saluted. "Yes sir!"

"Search the vehicle."

Sgt. Tivuli clapped his heels together, saluted, and proceeded to do just that. Rummaging through the car he found nothing, except a small manila envelope with a bundle of American dollars inside, and, of course, the Beretta.

"You're carrying a gun this time."

"I have papers for that."

"Let's go back to my office," Mwangi said, carrying the items.

* * *

Amonee was weary beyond belief, severely footsore, sick, and nearly vanquished. Whenever she apologized to God, she now also thanked him, thanked him that her son was at least holding up and his condition was not worsening. The Turkana women had continually daubed the rashes on his body with animal fat and he began to quiet down, complaining no longer. He too had loose bowels, but as a young child his stomach was taking the vast quantities of milk much better than hers. She had never had so much milk in her life. Now she restricted herself to drinking only the fresh milk that the camels provided in the mornings and evenings, adamantly refusing to imbibe the akibok type, much to Aite's chagrin. The *nakuli*, the preserved meat, had finished long ago and there was no more wild honey; the water was down to the last dregs. The safari had become intensely insufferable for Amonee, and she forlornly accepted that the worst was still to come. "I'm sorry for what I did," she kept repeating in a soporific murmur.

She was walking in a daze, trying to block out a horde of painful stimuli, when Emanikor's voice jolted her to attention.

"Walk slowly to those rocks and stay behind them."

All of them crouched down behind a tor of boulders, all but Emanikor who stood where he was, taking the gun cautiously off his shoulders to grip it in both hands. Amonee, her fear and curiosity having been aroused in spite of her fatigued condition, wanted to ask what was going on, but she knew she would not be answered. She kept still with bated breath, peeking out from behind the boulders. The camels and donkeys were in plain sight, lethargically searching for browse not far from where Emanikor was standing. After several minutes she could make out dark figures in the dusty distance, figures seemingly headed in their direction.

She trembled with fright, her previous ills shrinking into insignificance against all the atrocities she imagined could befall her at the hands of these savage strangers. Would she be raped? Riddled with bullets? What would they do to the child? "Oh God, help us," she uttered under her breath.

After what seemed like hours, the stragglers, now clearly discernible, came within shouting distance of Amonee's contingent. There were two of them, and despite the guns they were carrying, they looked more comical than menacing, as they dragged what appeared to be a sled of lashed branches behind them. In fact, in her exhausted state of mind, it was a scene right from the theatre of the absurd; the two bumbling eccentrics in Beckett's *Waiting for Godot*, aimlessly pulling a burden around in the middle of an existential-istic nowhere. The impression grew even stronger when she realized there was a prone body on the sled. She wondered if she was dreaming this.

One of the men was dressed in grimy army fatigues and wore a square-peaked military cap. The other one, as well as the body on the makeshift stretcher, was traditionally robed with a white cotton shuka. They stopped about fifty meters from Emanikor and called out in a language Amonee could not understand.

Emanikor answered back in Kiturkana, and his words she did

371

hear. "No, we are from Songot."

A conversation ensued with each man using his own language. Amonee heard Emanikor say something like "we are those people". After a short parley the strangers approached closer, still dragging their incapacitated comrade.

Aite and Akiru came out from behind the rocks and Amonee followed suit. Emanikor was crouching down, examining the man on the stretcher whose right shoulder was bound in bloodied cotton strips. The women brought over vessels of akibok, Aite tending to the wounded man, helping him to drink. Following a short exchange, the strangers bade farewell and departed on their way.

"Those men are the soldiers of the SPLA," Emanikor explained to Amonee. "They are taking their brother to the Red Cross hospital in Lokichoggio. He has been shot. They have been walking since yesterday evening." Then, changing his tone, he said, "Let's go!"

* * *

Mwangi, sitting behind his desk, removed the money from the envelope.

"There's five thousand in there," Loomis said, deciding not to sit down. "Or maybe four thousand. I could have miscounted."

Mwangi took the cue, and took ten one hundred dollar notes from the stack. "You really are in a hurry, aren't you?" he said glibly.

"How about my gun? Can I have it back?"

Mwangi returned the rest of the money back into the envelope, and shoved that, as well as the holstered gun, the boxes of clips, and the gun's papers towards the front of his desk for Loomis to take.

"Sergeant Tivuli!"

The Sergeant entered, clapped his heels and saluted.

"Tell them to hurry it up with that radio."

Just as Sergeant Tivuli was about to clap his heels and salute yet again, Loomis placed a hand on the officer's shoulder. "Wait a minute." Then turning to the OCS, "Bwana Mwangi, do you have a plastic container that I could borrow? I'm short of water."

* * *

The radio still wasn't fixed. Mwangi wanted confirmation from Lodwar before allowing Loomis to proceed on his way. For the first hour, Loomis sat around trying to look as calm and cool and unconcerned as he could. But after a while, with his mind dwelling on the appointed meeting with Amonee and her party, he grew increasingly agitated. The strain of waiting was made more taxing by the fact that he was waiting for something not to happen: if they made contact with Lodwar, he was finished. And what would happen to Amonee and the child after walking for four days in the desert only to find no vehicle to deliver them safely away?

He was experiencing the same tension he used to experience when standing in a long queue for a phone booth, waiting to make an urgent call. He looked at his watch. Close to noon. He would have to make an attempt at forcing Mwangi's hand. He rose from the wooden chair in the office where he had been deposited, and crossed over to Mwangi's office.

"Yes?" inquired Mwangi without looking up from the papers on his desk.

"Radio fixed yet?"

"Bado. Not yet."

"What's the problem with it?"

"Generator." Mwangi looked up. "What is your problem, Loomis?"

"*Riziki*. You know, daily bread. Like where am I going to get it after I get fired from this job? Look, I got delayed in Nairobi, and..." Loomis did something he hadn't done for a long time – he went into one of his routines: "...it wasn't my fault bwana...a girl like that doesn't come along every day...Swahili girl from the coast...you know, half-Arab...very light, the color of sand...beautiful hips, you know, the type you can really grab a hold of..."

Mwangi's wide mouth expanded into a smile, bubbles of saliva at the corners.

"...and those girls from the coast really know how to do it, I'm telling you," Loomis went on, "moving this way and that..." He gyrated his pelvis for effect.

Mwangi guffawed.

"So you can understand how difficult it was to leave her arms to go back to that shit-hole where I work. I tell you, I was enjoying her, bwana, the food, the drinks, we went to the Carnivore, Florida 2000...nothing was too good for this girl...maybe she was a genie, I don't know, but she certainly had me under her spell...now I'm late. I should have been back four days ago, and I mean on the site, another three-hour drive from Juba...so maybe I can reach tomorrow, if you let me go...look, you can see that I don't have anybody with me, my vehicle registration is not the one they told you...I just don't understand why you're so suspicious...look, you know me, I'm not a stranger, I'll be coming back again and again, what do I have to gain by trying to deceive you? The only thing you got me on is failing to surrender the Kenyan plates. C'mon, bwana, let me go. You detained me, you checked me out, found nothing wrong...you've done your job, right? If you let me go, I promise you two crates when I come through again. If you don't, well, there's a good chance you won't see me anymore. I'll be out of a job and you'll be out of a regular supply of whiskey."

"You haven't been bringing me any lately," Mwangi stuck in. "I think you have forgotten about me."

"You've just reminded me, haven't you?"

Mwangi made a sly grin. "Let me think about it." Then he added, "You really are a character. And your story, while entertaining, is hardly convincing. But let me think about it."

An hour later, Mwangi came up to Loomis with the car keys. He raised his left hand and made a 'V' sign. "Two," he said.

"Okay, two crates."

"No, two thousand. One is not enough for the risk I take for you."

* * *

Another day. Another day of walking. Heat and wind, dust, sweat, and grime. The agony of wracked limbs. And now, with the water gone, the torment of gnawing thirst. Her throat was so dry it hurt, she could no longer swallow. It would be some hours before she would get fresh milk. But she still refused the akibok.

Early afternoon. The white light of a blazing sun ignited earth and stone, scorching it colorless. The heat came down in hard slaps, only to be flung back up by the scalding ground and quiver in the air above it. A heat haze developed, cutting off the bottoms of hills and trees, releasing them to float in the air. Amonee was dizzy and nauseous. It felt better to look down, look down at her feet, how miraculously they lifted up and came down again, stirring up the dust into puffs of smoke which drifted around her ankles. She became mesmerized, and through some defense in her mind, her prodigious lassitude numbed her until she didn't care anymore about anything. She walked as a somnambulist, half asleep, hypnotized, her legs moving in semi-conscious rhythm. Her mind was so tired no thoughts could form themselves.

It was a dreamlike state where time lost its continuity. She could not remember how one moment led to another; when something occurred, or if words were uttered, the reality of the event dissipated immediately, leaving no trace in her memory. This was why she could not answer Aite's questions – she could not remember what Aite asked her, or indeed whether Aite had actually asked her anything at all.

Night had fallen. Aite watched with concern as Amonee began to stumble. At one point the poor girl fell down. It was clear she could walk no further.

Amonee, by now delirious, lay on the ground, staring up at the stars. They were not singing, not humming, but seemed to be accusing her, castigating her, denouncing her, shouting out condemnation.

"I'm sorry for what I did," she told them.

The procession stopped in the darkness as the two Turkana girls unloaded a donkey of its burden of luggage and struggled to get Amonee mounted in its stead. It was good that they were close to their destination. They hoped that Ebu Lakwan would be there to meet them.

* * *

Several hours earlier, Loomis had had his own problems.

Puncture.

"Shit!...figures." He stopped the Land Rover, not bothering to pull over, then got out and went into the back to get one of the spare tires; that left only one and now came the doubt whether it would be sufficient for the remaining miles to Juba. It was all up to providence, he concluded, jacking up the vehicle. Providence had gotten him this far, had gotten him past Lokichoggio, past Kapoeta; he tried to convince himself it would get him the rest of the way to the journey's end.

Changing the tire took him ten minutes, and he was on the way again, screwing up his eyes in his search for a hill shaped like a camel. A hill that looked like a camel? It wasn't until this moment that he had given it any thought, and he realized that such a description had to be interpreted in the loosest manner possible. In what way could a mass of rock and earth resemble such a creature? It needed imagination, and that was the problem. A new worry entered his mind: how different was the imagination of a nomadic herdsman from that of a kid raised in the big city? Recognizing Camel Mountain was to be the next hurdle on this unorthodox flight to safety.

Whenever he spotted a hill, he would stop and stare at it, trying to imagine how it might appear as the animal in question. He saw ones that reminded him of hippos, one that could have been a headless zebra, and another that could have been creatively called a lion. But no camels. In no time at all he became overwrought with the fear of missing it.

"Dammit! How am I supposed to know which one it is!" he cried aloud, his panic rising. He drove on, muttering to himself, calling the Turkanas crazy bastards, calling himself a crazy bastard, knowing that the speedometer already showed twelve miles since Kapoeta. He was debating whether he should turn back to check if he had missed it, when the sight ahead of him made him brake so sharply his chest slammed into the steering wheel as the Land Rover skidded to a dusty halt. His face slack with disbelief, he went into a laughing fit.

"Ha... Holy mother...ha ha ha...look at that...un-fucking-believable...ha!" he coughed out, then proceeded to choke from the violence of his guffaws. Just up ahead, not more than three or four kilometers off the side of the road, was a hump of a hill, but even more amazing was the inclined pinnacle of stone which seemed to sprout from one end of it. Balanced precariously on the point of the pinnacle was a rounded, oblong block of a boulder. The whole thing had the appearance of a dinosaur, or perhaps, if one did not know of dinosaurs, a camel.

He continued, keeping to the road until he was even with the mountain, then pulled off and drove straight for it. Parking the vehicle about 500 meters from the hill, he alighted, somehow feeling it was safer to walk the rest of the way. He strode quickly through the elephant grass, euphoric with the idea of finding them already there. They should have arrived, he told himself, for he, certainly, was at least a half day late. But upon reaching the base of the strange landform he knew he was alone. His euphoria died and in its place was an intense disquietude. This would be the most difficult part – waiting. He should have known it wasn't going to be like in the movies, falling dramatically into her arms as soon as he arrived.

He circumnavigated the bottom of the hill until he was sure there was no one else around, before plopping himself down in the shade of a rather large termite mound. He waited. The sun moved across the sky, and still he waited.

"Oh, where ARE they?!" he whined to the impassive hulk of stone and scree above him. "WHERE ARE THEY?!" he screamed at the silent savanna. Nothing, not even the wind answered him. The only sound he could hear was that of his own frail breathing.

He waited through dusk as the bushes, the rocks, the termite mounds, became clearly defined in the lucid glow of a dying day, taking on an imposing prominence before melting into grayness. A few birds sang their evening song and the crickets began to chirrup. He didn't remember falling asleep.

An abrupt surge of fright brought him back to consciousness. It was nighttime, and in front of him the shadow of a man was outlined against the stars.

"Ebu Lakwan, we have come."

Loomis jumped to his feet, and in the starlight he could make out the other Turkanas and the animals. The two women were removing something like a sack from one of the donkeys. It was more than a sack, it was a body. *It must be her*, he figured. He ran to her as they placed her on the ground. "Amonee! Oh, Amonee, thank God!"

She opened her eyes slowly and stared up at him with a distant look. Even in the dim glow of night, he could see her face looked terrible – puffed and sickly, and her lips swollen and cracked. Her breathing was labored, and when she finally spoke, her hoarse voice was barely audible. "Is this a dream?"

"No! We've made it! We're in the Sudan!"

"Daryl?"

"Yes." He hugged her limp body tightly.

With great effort she craned her neck forward and strained to put her mouth close to his ear. She whispered, "I'm...I'm sorry for what I did."

His body heaved from the emotion bubbling up inside him, his eyes became moist, and his face contracted. "Oh baby!"

Then he did something that he had never done in front of her before.

He wept.

NAIROBI, SEPTEMBER 30, 1983

The American Ambassador
United States Embassy
Co-operative House
Nairobi
September 27, 1983
Dear Sir:

My name is Daryl Loomis. I am a United States citizen, holder of U. S. passport F121046, and I am an engineering and groundwater geologist by profession. I have lived and worked in East Africa for the past ten years, having resided in Kenya, Uganda, Tanzania and the Sudan. I am currently employed by Towne Oil Inc., a U.S. firm, and stationed in the Southern Sudan where I have been involved in drilling water wells for Blocker Drilling, another U.S. firm, who require the water for their own oil-drilling operations. I have been working on a site near Chaka, about twenty-five miles west of Juba in a concession granted to Texaco (which I remind you is another U.S. firm), since early March of this year.

Having been promised that this letter would find its way into your hands, I hereby undertake to give an account of what has happened to me between the days of September 14 and September 27, the date of this letter.

On the morning of September 14, I was in the Towne Oil sub-office in Juba, a small space used for minor administrative purposes, located in a run-down three-story building on Hezbollah Road in the old section of Juba, where I was busy finishing up some of my reports. At approximately 1900 hours on that same day, four Sudanese policemen, two plainclothes, two uniformed, attached to the Juba North police station, entered the office where they approached me and requested I identify myself. I willingly produced my passport, which they examined. Then, abruptly, they handcuffed me, and without any explanations, forcibly brought me to a police Land Rover waiting outside. No charges for any offense were mentioned to me. I was told nothing, and my questions were met with harsh orders to be quiet. We drove seven hours non-stop on the southeastern road which leads to the Kenyan border. In the middle of the bush, in a place I assumed to be the geographical border, we were met by a Kenyan registered police vehicle and I was handed over to a Captain Josephat Mwangi, the officer in charge of Lokichoggio police station, and three other Kenyan policemen. Upon taking custody of me, Captain Mwangi said nothing to me concerning my abduction except for the words "You didn't bring the whiskey."

Without further conversation, I was driven to Lokichoggio. I was locked up in the cells of the police station where I spent the night without food or water and slept on a cold concrete floor. At 0700 hours the following morning I was brought, handcuffed once more, to a waiting Kenya Police plane which took me to Nairobi, Wilson Airport, police wing. I was still not told why I was illegally and brutally removed from my country of residence. At Wilson Airport I was ushered into another police Land Rover and brought to Kamiti Maximum Security Prison.

Upon arrival at the prison I was taken to the S.S.P.'s office where I was interrogated by several officers of the Special Branch concerning a woman I used to know some three years ago. Still no charges were filed. Then I was put in cell 14 in the Isolation Block, where I remain a prisoner to this day. I therefore urge you to make a formal complaint to the Kenya Government for what amounts to the kidnapping of a United States citizen, and demand my immediate release.

Yours obediently,

Daryl Loomis

That was the letter he wrote three days ago. Lying on his sisal-stuffed mattress on the iron-framed bed, the only piece of furniture in the cell, he stared at the naked light bulb that burned unceasingly twenty-four hours a day, trying to figure out how he got here. A windowless, concrete room, roughly six feet by twelve, hemmed in by filthy grey walls. Cell 14 in the Isolation Block, the Isolation Block a passageway with eight cells on each side; the block that was sandwiched between death row and the block for the criminally insane; a place designed to suffocate its victims with an overwhelming atmosphere of hopelessness. In this cell he was kept for twenty-two of the twenty-four hours which constitute a day, and even for the two hours he was allowed in the courtyard he was alone, kept separate from the other prisoners. At least two other inmates were incarcerated in the Isolation Block – he could hear them – but after his initial attempts to talk to them had ended in vain, he concluded that they had been forbidden to speak to him. Even the warders, the two at night and the two in the day, were silent, communicating only in gestures.

Isolation in a confined space. Sensory deprivation. Social alienation. Whatever it was, they were trying to make him crack. They couldn't have sent that letter to the Ambassador; surely someone would have been here by now to see him; and so they probably didn't pass on his message to Geoff either. And so he remained: alone, and with a future that only promised to be the same as the present – to be caged in silent imprisonment. He was determined to prevent them from making him go bonkers, and so far he felt he was doing pretty well. Every morning and evening he spent an hour doing his exercises: push-ups, sit-ups, leg-lifts, etc. A good deal of the time, he occupied his mind by reminiscing about old movies and television shows, giving himself trivia quizzes, calculating in his head the dewatering of a theoretical excavation, anything to distract his thoughts from the present situation. But there were moments when the terror of it welled up without warning, instances when he could hear time itself passing, as if his auditory acumen were raised to a nerve-wracking level; when silence itself had become deafening.

Love was his strongest weapon against all this insanity. He imagined Amonee in the position he was in now, a position she would have surely been in without his intervention, and the thought that she could have suffered like this was unbearable, making the present reality a meaningful and edifying experience. He was suffering for a cause. He felt like a martyr. He was proud of himself.

But he had been so close to all that he'd ever wanted: to be with Amonee for the rest of his life. He had thought they were home free. He had taken her to a local hospital, where they had put her on a drip to counter her extreme dehydration, given her antibiotics and medicine for dysentery. He spent a night with her in one of the better hotels in Juba, to clean her up and outfit her with new clothes. He had taken her to the Dutch consulate in Juba, and found the consular officials extremely willing to aid in getting her safely to Khartoum and then quickly out of the country on a KLM flight to Amsterdam. They had even arranged the entry stamp into the Republic of the Sudan in order for her to leave without question. They had done all this so rapidly and efficiently, almost as if they had been expecting her. It was then that he realized just how powerful a figure her husband was, and so he did not object when she said she needed a month alone to clear up things, to tell Jon the score, how the child was not his, how she was leaving him for Loomis. They were to meet in London on October 1 – tomorrow.

It didn't look as if he was going to be able to keep that appointment.

He rose from the bed and stepped over to the door, and looked out of the peep slot. "Askari. Askari."

He heard the heavy, menacing sound of the footsteps of the guard approaching – then found himself staring into a pair of cold black eyes.

"Long call," Loomis told him.

The warder fussed with his keys, their metallic jangling loud and brash in the dim, quiet passageway. He opened the cell and led his prisoner to the door-less toilet at the end of the cell block. Then he stood with folded arms, watching as Loomis pulled down his white prison-issue shorts and squatted down to shit in a bucket. Having someone watching him make a bowel movement made him instantaneously constipated. It could be worse, Loomis knew; he could have been the guy who cleans the bucket. As he mused over that thought, the askari did something which shocked him. He spoke.

"You foreigners look the same as we do when we defecate."

"You never knew that before? Did you think we had another opening?" Loomis cracked, trying hard not to feel humiliated. In any case it was a relief to hear a human voice for the first time in three days.

"Don't be impudent, K983."

That was the end of the dialogue. Loomis finished his business and was brought back to his cell to await the last stimulating event of the day – supper. At six o'clock the cell door opened and a tray with stone-cold ugali and undercooked beans was placed on the floor. Loomis looked at the tray for some minutes before fetching it. The food they had been giving him made him suffer stomach pains, but in the end he decided that the little sustenance it offered was necessary to keep up his strength. He ate, then lay on his bed, bracing himself for another sleepless night under the glaring light bulb.

The next morning, the fourth morning of his captivity, there was a bit of excitement. There was a visitor to see him. Loomis was first handcuffed, then brought upstairs to a room that looked like the one he had been interrogated in on the day that he first arrived. Inside, sitting at a small table, was a mid-thirtyish white man in a suit with brown hair and glasses. He had a sort of plastic smile that seemed frozen on his face, and he looked to be an Embassy type; maybe there was good news.

"Hello, Mr. Loomis. Sit down," the man said, gesturing to the other chair at the opposite side of the table. Loomis complied while the man reached over and offered his hand. "Carlson, United States Embassy. Liaison section."

Loomis tried his best to give a decent handshake, despite the fact that his hands were bound together.

"Did you get my letter?"

"Yes, yes, we did. Not only that, but we have been in constant communication with the authorities concerned in this matter."

Carlson spoke with that easy, rising and falling inflection typical of a bureaucrat.

"So what are you going to do about my situation?"

"Do, Mr. Loomis? I'm afraid at this moment, there is nothing much that we can do."

"What do you mean? I've been kidnapped and illegally incarcerated!"

"Oh come now, Mr Loomis, if I were you I would be a bit more level-headed and leave out the theatrics. I admit your seizure was a touch unorthodox, but in some cases it is a procedure which, if all parties are in agreement, can be summarily utilized. You were extradited, somewhat hastily perhaps, but through legal organs of state. I hear there was even some assistance from Interpol. There must have been something you did which was quite irregular to foment such a commotion."

"They have no proof of anything, and so far no one has told me what the charges are. They just keep asking me for the whereabouts of a woman I knew a long time ago."

Carlson's face became suddenly stern. "Listen, Loomis, this is an international situation we have here. This is not the States. There's no Bill of Rights. And the Kenyan authorities are not fools as you may think. Nor are we, Mr. Loomis. In your letter you omitted – intentionally it appears – certain facts and details relevant to your position. Up to now you have appeared unwilling to cooperate. If we're to play ball with these fellows, you have to tell us what you've been up to."

"I've been up to nothing."

"Did you not smuggle a Kenyan national out of this country, a woman who was being sought by Kenyan Security Intelligence? Now, if you intervene in the political affairs of a foreign country, do you really expect the American people and the United States government to be held responsible?"

"On what are they basing these accusations?"

"After being briefed on most of the details, it appears they do have a case against you. The only thing I can do at this point is to give you some advice: get yourself a lawyer, go through the legal system here, and come clean with anything you know. If you explain truthfully your involvement in this affair, maybe, I say maybe, we can ease your plight a bit. But you have to realize how tense the political situation is at the moment. Meanwhile, we'll be monitoring your status."

"My status?"

"Good day, Mr. Loomis." Carlson got up and grabbed the attaché case which had been concealed under the table. He didn't shake hands goodbye.

Loomis, back in his cell, sat on the bed and repeatedly told himself not to panic. If the Embassy had been contacted, then maybe Geoff had been as well. Geoff was not only a lawyer, he was a friend who was sure to take more interest in his fate than an Embassy official who was a total stranger. Besides, Geoff was a Kenyan, and with his experience, should know his way around, should know the ropes, the right people to see. He would get him out of this; have the whole case thrown out for lack of proof.

It was lunchtime: lunchtime for the other prisoners; but for Loomis, it was time to stretch out in the exercise yard, his differing schedule having to do with his enforced segregation from the other inmates. He walked repeatedly around the perimeter of the yard, enjoying the cool refreshing air of outdoors, an askari constantly at his side. Besides the exercises he did in the cell, this was the only form of physical activity he had access to, and he devoted the whole of his two allotted hours to this walking round and round. He had wanted to jog, but they refused to grant him that indulgence. Bodily motion and the simple act of being outside were the only pleasures that were given to him at Kamiti. This was why he could hardly control his ire when he was called in after only half an hour.

Loomis gritted his teeth as he was handcuffed again, but remained outwardly placid, figuring that this attempt at frustrating him was a new tactic they were trying out. They did not bring him back to the cells, however; they brought him to that little room where he had met the Embassy official in the morning. He sat down in the same chair, and, along with the warder guarding him, waited for something to happen. The door opened and Geoff Wanyonyi walked in, accompanied by another warder.

Loomis stood up, elated. "Oh, Geoff, am I glad to see you!"

"Hello, Daryl," Wanyonyi said as he brusquely sat down. "Listen, we don't have much time. Sit down."

As Loomis did so the two warders, much to his surprise, walked out of the room and shut the door behind them.

"Geoff, I can't believe what's..."

"Were you interrogated?" Wanyonyi asked abruptly.

"When I first came here, I was questioned by a couple of Special Branch guys, a superintendent, uh...forgot his name..."

"What did you say to them?"

"I told them I wouldn't say anything until I saw my advocate."

"Did they torture you?"

"What do you mean? This place is torture. Locked up alone, food that makes you sick..."

"They didn't physically beat you?"

"No. Look, Geoff, this is totally illegal..."

"The definition of legality changes from place to place. Welcome to the Third World."

"But I haven't even been informed of any charges. That's not the law of this land."

"Yes it is. You are being held under the Public Security Act, a law white people enacted during the colonial days. It comes straight from the Emergency Powers Act of Britain. They can hold you for as long as they want."

"I'm in detention?"

"Yes, the first foreigner to be held under the Act. Maybe that's why your case is a bit different. In three days' time there is going to be a special session to deal with your issue and to make formal charges. The prosecution is already building up its case. I hope you realize that this is not a simple matter. You're in very deep. To be honest, I don't know how much I can help you."

Loomis looked gloomily away, at a loss for words.

"These people are very interested in why you took so much trouble over Mrs. Van de Velde."

"Who?"

"Pamela Van de Velde, née Emuria. I told you a long time ago she was trouble."

"So you want me to tell you how wise you are?" Loomis snapped petulantly. "It has nothing to do with her, it's her crook of a husband that's been fucking around."

"Do you know who Jon Van de Velde is?"

"Some rich Dutchman?"

"Dutchman? Maybe. He has a Netherlands passport. But he was born in South Africa. He has family and friends in both places."

"A Boer?"

"Looks like it. But that alone is just biographical trivia. Jon Van de Velde happens to be Chairman of the Board and largest share-holder of Duhone Chemicals; in other words he owns one of the biggest pharmaceutical companies in the world."

"So? He's rich, I guessed that already."

"About two years ago, Duhone Chemicals attempted to break into the Kenyan market. First imports, then they sought permission to build a factory. But last year they were kicked out by the Ministry of Health, and their products have been banned."

"Why?"

"They started flogging off expired drugs and other chemicals which are already banned in Europe. Stuff with dangerous side effects. They wanted to use this place as their dumping ground. It was a big scandal. Don't you read newspapers?"

"Only when I'm in them."

"It appears," Wanyonyi went on, ignoring that feckless remark, "that Mr. Van de Velde had known Everret Muthongo from Muthongo's days in South Africa, and in light of current events, one can safely conclude that some kind of deal was recently made between them, something of the nature of 'I help you in your bid for power, and when you're in, you let me bring in my company.' The security people have already uncovered a number of equivocal transactions involving them both. Transactions which suggest treason. Van de Velde probably figured he could wipe up with Muthongo as president. Do you know how much money is in drugs?"

"Of course I know. I'm from New York."

"Van de Velde is only the tip of the iceberg. It may be he's the chief delegate or spokesman for a group of powerful businessmen who would like a piece of the Kenyan pie. He was also on the board of directors of the Nugan Hand Bank."

"So, he's a banker too."

"You really don't read the newspapers, do you? The Nugan Hand Bank wasn't an ordinary bank. It was set up by the CIA and the Mafia to launder money. The clients were high-powered criminals, terrorists, drug traffickers, arms dealers. It collapsed amidst scandal in 1980, and that's when all their dirty little secrets came out."

"What does all this have to do with a poor slob like me?"

"Daryl, I know you have nothing to do with these people, but the government thinks you do, and rightly so. You did smuggle her out, did you not?"

"No. I only arranged it."

"It comes down to the same thing: that you were instrumental in her escape."

"Do they know that for sure?"

"Look. You were both seen in Lodwar on August twenty-fifth..."

"By who?" Loomis demanded to know, still wondering who had started all this trouble.

"A CID officer by the name of Rashid Hemed. Does he know you?"

"Oh shit. Yeah, I remember him."

"Has he ever seen Pamela before?"

"He met her when she came up to visit me during the Turkana contract three years ago."

"Hmmm." Wanyonyi paused, tucking in his lower lip and staring down at the table, ostensibly deep in thought. "If it was only that then..."

"What else have they got?"

"The plates. Why did the Land Rover have two registrations in two different countries?"

"It's a common practice. Well, not that common. But a lot of companies do it. It avoids a lot of red tape and import-export bullshit. But there is a condition that you have to hand the Kenyan plates in, and have it logged against the Sudanese plates. And then there's someone I know in the office in Juba who changes the engine and chassis numbers."

"It's not legal," Wanyonyi said.

"Yeah, well, this is Africa," was all Loomis could think of in defense.

"So what happened to the Kenyan plates?"

"I got rid of them."

"Don't you know that Interpol was called in? These quick and dubious registrations interest them very much. How do you think stolen cars move across borders? If I told you the number of stolen vehicles passing back and forth through Kenya and Uganda alone, you'd be amazed."

"But the vehicle belongs to the company, to Towne Oil."

"Are you naive? They deny anything to do with the double registration, and disavow all your actions. The implication of that statement, or at least the way the prosecution is going to put it, is that you planned the plates thing from the start with the sole intention of smuggling Mrs. Van de Velde out of the country. They also know that you worked in Turkana district before, in fact one time you became very famous because of it, yes?"

Wanyonyi was referring to Loomis's 'death' and 'resurrection' of April 1980.

He continued. "The Sudanese government has now confirmed that you were seen entering the Netherlands consulate in the company of a black female dressed in the fashion of one of the local nomadic tribes. And to seal the whole thing, one of the Turkana MPs just came forward with a statement to the Attorney General's office that there was a story going round about how a group of Turkanas helped a woman across the border, a Teso girl who was dressed as a Turkana."

Loomis clasped his hands together and gazed absently at them. The bush telegraph on this occasion had worked against him, incriminated him, putting him in a corner he would find very hard to get out of. "Geoff," he said without looking up, "do they also know she was traveling with a child?"

"Yes, her son. Van de Velde's son."

"No. My son."

Wanyonyi's face contorted into a grimace. "Are you serious?"

"Yes."

"How is that?"

"We slept together one night. After she was married."

"Are you sure it's yours?"

"I'm sure. She was concerned about our son. That's why she came to me."

"You don't think she lied about the child to gain your help?"

"No," Loomis answered emphatically.

Both became silent. Wanyonyi took off his spectacles, letting them hang from the chain around his neck, and leaned back in his chair with his hands holding onto the lapels of his jacket. It was some minutes before he spoke again. "I think the best thing to do is to admit it. Admit everything, explain the mitigating circumstances, exploit the love angle, your child, and hope for clemency. Then we can ask the American Embassy in to try and work something out."

A knock came on the door and it opened. A senior warder stepped in. "*Saa zenu zimekwisha*. Your time is up."

Wanyonyi got to his feet. "I'll try to see you tomorrow, Daryl. I'm not promising. There's a lot of red tape involved in these visits."

Loomis stood up. "Sure. Thanks, Geoff."

"Meanwhile, I'll try to dig something up. The love plea may not be enough. Let us hope for the best," he said, shaking Loomis's handcuffed hands.

Still alone and ostracized, still locked in his cell, Loomis found the empty hours intolerable. But now he had an idea at least of his position, and this gave him new things to mull over in his mind. The ball seemed to be rolling; in which direction he wasn't certain. He did his exercises, ate his food, walked in the courtyard, and laid in his bed, all with renewed psychic vigor, planning his defense; the earnest, honest pleas he would make and his renunciation of Van de Velde and Muthongo. He worked himself up until he envisioned a paternally understanding Kenyan government pardoning him, forgiving him and Amonee, and recognizing that they were only the victims of tragic circumstances. Perhaps with a bit of good luck, he could get out of this mess.

Wanyonyi did not come back the next day, and his failure to show up caused Loomis to sweat out the night in a festering panic. But he did come the day after that. He briefed Loomis on the session to take place the following morning, a Sunday morning when the rest of the High Court would be closed and empty. It was a secret inquiry to be held in camera. After relating this news, Wanyonyi made Loomis go over everything that had had happened to him from the night he left his house in Buru Buru to the time he was brought to Kamiti. When Loomis asked his lawyer if he had found something, the latter tersely replied that he was going to see someone that night. He also suggested trying to contact Amonee in Europe; maybe a statement from her could help his case. Loomis objected vehemently, insisting that under no circumstances was she to be brought into this. He still worried about her, his own plight notwithstanding. Wanyonyi closed their talk by calling Loomis an idiot.

* * *

October 3rd. He was made to bathe at six o'clock in the morning, washing in a door-less shower, while being watched over by a warder. At seven they came: plainclothes policemen bearing the clothes he had been wearing at the time of his abduction (in his mind he still couldn't help associating his extradition with a kidnapping). He stripped off his prison T-shirt and shorts and, after dressing, presented his wrists for handcuffing. The four policemen, two of them holding him by the arms just below his armpits, the other two closing the ranks front and rear, hurried him out of the prison and into a navy-blue police station-wagon known as a '999'. Loomis was momentarily exhilarated by the racy ride outdoors, and the twenty minutes it took the speedy Peugeot to arrive at the High Court Buildings seemed altogether too short. They parked in the side parking lot and then bundled him up the staircase at the rear of the main building. There was no one about as the five men climbed the stairs, the echoes of their footfalls emphasizing the emptiness of the place. The dispirited vacancy of the building, its lack of any living soul other than himself and his guards, had an adverse psychological effect on Loomis. He began to tremble in fear.

They climbed up until they reached the roof, where rows of wooden courtrooms had been erected to augment the ones inside the building. After going down one row and across another, they came upon the one where his case would be heard and they entered inside. Loomis was disappointed; it was nothing more than a simple room. He had imagined somber paneled walls, huge galleries, and an ornate judge bench embellished with impressive seals and symbols of justice where the judge sat up high, looking down in supreme discernment. Instead, his fate was going to be decided within four water-stained walls with peeling paint, the gallery consisting of unoccupied rows of shoddy wooden benches. The judge's place was a simple, plain, but very large desk with a welled surface so you couldn't see the papers on it. The witness stand was a three-sided wooden affair with no seat. In front of the judge's desk was a long table complemented by a long, backed bench that reminded Loomis of a church pew. Wanyonyi, sitting in it and looking ridiculous in a white, George Washington-style wig, turned around as Loomis and his party entered. There was no one else in the courtroom.

A few steps into the room, one of the policemen removed the prisoner's handcuffs and told him to sit by Wanyonyi.

"This is not how I thought it would be," Loomis whispered to his advocate upon sitting down.

Wanyonyi faced him and said in a low voice, "You don't realize how secretive this whole thing is. For one, nobody wants any publicity at this stage. You're an embarrassment to U.S.-Kenya relations. For another, there's a good chance they may use you for the Muthongo inquiry, and until then they'll do all they can to keep you isolated."

"I know I shouldn't say this, but you look silly in that wig."

"Don't let the courtroom fool you. This is a serious hearing. These wigs may seem pompous, but it's to remind you how grave this function is."

"It's doing just the opposite. I have to try to keep from laughing." It was true. And on account of his risibility, he was already in a better mood than when he had come in.

"It's British tradition. It comes with their law."

The prosecutor came in, a grey-templed, affluent-looking Indian also capped with a little fluffy wig. In one hand he held an attaché case, in the other he carried a black box file. Although Loomis admittedly was not an avid newspaper reader, he did recognize the gentleman to be the Chief State Prosecutor. The only other person they could have brought in more high-powered than that would have been the Attorney General himself. The state counsel took his place at the other end of the backed bench and cast a quick glance in their direction. "Hello, Geoffrey," he said.

"Hello, Dhiru. Nice to see you again."

"Mmmm," was his sole response as he turned his attention to his box file, opening it and shuffling through its pages.

The court clerk came in and sat in a chair opposite the defense, with his back to the judge's desk. He wasn't wearing any wig.

Wanyonyi put his mouth to Loomis's ear and whispered, "The first witness the prosecution will call is that CID man from Lodwar."

"How many witnesses are there?"

"For the prosecution? Should be seven, including Mwangi and that Turkana MP."

"How many do we have?"

"One for sure, maybe two."

"Who's the sure one, Okova?"

"Yes."

"Is he coming?"

"Not today. I'll save him to the last moment. In the meantime I'll concentrate on picking apart the prosecution's witnesses. The less credibility they have, and the more they appear to be in the dark, the better it is for us. Then when we tell our side of the story we'll appear more genuine, not simply confessing because we're in a corner. It won't be easy. We can't deny your actions, only the motives for them which the prosecution will try to put forward. Intent is what I want to focus on."

Another door, at the rear of the room, and one which Loomis hadn't noticed before, opened, letting in the judges, three of them, in black gowns and, of course, with little white wigs atop their black heads, prompting everyone in the courtroom to rise sharply to their feet. One of the judges, in Loomis's eyes, bore a likeness to Aunt Jemima, the Negro nanny on the pancake mix boxes, a similarity rendered by the hairpiece. He sat in the middle while the other two sat on each side of him. The two on the side were the assessors, Loomis was later told.

With the judge and his assessors seated, everyone else sat down.

"Will counsel approach the bench?"

Wanyonyi and the Asian prosecutor got up and stood before the judges' desk. Words were passed which Loomis couldn't hear. Then the two men returned to their places.

"This court has a dual function," the Aunt Jemima judge said. "One is assessing the criteria for which the accused can be held indefinitely under the Public Security Act, pending further investigations into any actions that may have been committed which threaten the security of the Republic of Kenya. The other is to determine whether or not the accused can be charged under Chapter sixty-three of the Penal Code in the Laws of Kenya, section 117 – Conspiracy to defeat justice by the removal of a material witness required in a court proceeding."

"What?" Loomis quietly asked his advocate.

"The Muthongo Inquiry," Wanyonyi whispered back. "That's what they wanted her for."

"Counsel, are we ready?"

The Indian prosecutor stood up. "Ready, My Lords."

Wanyonyi stood up. "My Lords, due to the extreme haste with which this court has been convened, I have not really had enough time to adequately prepare my client's case, and therefore I move for an adjournment of one week."

"I do sympathize with your position, Mr. Wanyonyi, but you in turn must realize that State Security is the issue here and the quicker we can ascertain the involvement of the accused, the better it would be for the whole nation. On the matter of adjournment, I may be able to give a ruling on that tomorrow morning after I hear today's proceedings. Now, Counsel Wanyonyi, has your client received a statement specifying the grounds upon which he has been detained?"

"Yes, My Lord, but we received it only yesterday and..."

"Is he aware of why he is here?"

"Yes, My Lord."

"Then we may proceed. State's Counsel, you can begin."

"Yes, My Lord," Counsel Dhiru assented. "I would like to call my first witness please, Senior Inspector Rashid Hemed."

The door that Loomis had entered through opened once more

and in walked Rashid, still wearing the same suit Loomis used to see him in three years ago. He stepped into the witness stand while the bailiff, a hefty uniformed policeman with the rank of corporal, approached him asking what religion he subscribed to.

"Mwislamu."

The bailiff proffered a copy of the Quran to Hemed. The oath was not much different than that ascribed to a Christian. With his hand on the book, he swore to tell the truth, the whole truth, and nothing but the truth so help him Allah and under the guidance of his prophet Mohammed.

Counsel Dhiru got out from behind the table. "State your name."

"Rashid Ishmael Ramadhani Hemed."

"What is your occupation?"

"Police Officer, Criminal Investigation Department, investigations section, attached to Lodwar police station."

"Have you ever seen the accused before this moment?"

"Yes."

"Can you state when and where please?"

"End of 1979, beginning of 1980, in Lodwar town."

"In other words, on various occasions during that time, is that not correct?"

"Ndio, that's correct."

"Were you acquainted with him at the time?"

"Casually."

"Can you be more specific?"

"We knew each other's names and we exchanged greetings."

"What was the name you knew him as?"

"Mr. Loomis. Daryl Loomis."

"How many times overall would you say you encountered Mr. Loomis in Lodwar?"

"Many times. At least seven. He worked on a water project in the bush but I always met him when he came into town."

"You can easily recognize him, correct?"

"Ndio."

"Is he in this courtroom?"

"Ndio."

"Can you point him out?"

Hemed raised his arm to point at Loomis. "That man."

"Do you recall the last time you saw Mr. Loomis?"

"Ndio. Five weeks ago. The morning of August twenty-fifth."

"And where was that?"

"In Lodwar town."

"I see." The prosecutor turned toward the long table and picked up a 5" x 8" photograph. He returned to the witness stand and handed it to Rashid.

"Do you know the person in the photo?"

"Ndio."

"In other words you recognize her by face?"

"Ndio."

"Do you know her name?"

"Ndio. Pamela Van de Velde."

"May I have a look at that photo?" the judge requested.

"My Lord, there should be another copy in your file."

"Oh yes, so there is," the judge concurred, receiving it from the assessor on his left.

"Do you remember the first time you saw Mrs. Van de Velde?" the prosecutor continued.

"Ndio. It was January 1980. Before she was married. She was called Emuria then."

"And where did you see her?"

"In Lodwar."

"Do you know what she was doing there?"

"She was visiting the accused, Mr. Loomis."

"How do you know that?"

"I saw them together with another white man and I greeted Mr. Loomis. He told me she was his friend from Nairobi."

"Did you ever see this woman again?"

"Ndio. But the second time I did not see her in person. It was in a photo, in the *Standard*, a picture from her wedding at St. Andrew's church. The caption had her name and that of Jon Van de Velde, and of Everret Muthongo. Muthongo was posing with them. I thought it very odd that only three months after seeing her together with Mr. Loomis she was being married to another man."

Geoff flinched. He knew what the prosecution was getting at. They had anticipated his game plan.

"Why did you feel it was odd?"

"I don't know. Maybe the two men knew each other, and Mr. Loomis was indeed a friend of both of them."

"Objection, My Lord," Wanyonyi interrupted, only half rising to his feet, "the witness is speculating."

"I'm in agreement," the judge said. "Witness, confine your testimony to the facts."

"Ndio, My Lord."

"When was the last time you saw Mrs. Van de Velde?"

"Five weeks ago, the morning of August twenty-fifth, together with Mr. Loomis."

"Can you tell us more about that occasion?"

"They were traveling in the same Land Rover, KUV 147. It was parked in front of a duka. Loomis went into the duka and Mrs. Van de Velde came out with a small boy, her son, and took him to urinate. I greeted her and asked her where she was going to. She didn't seem to know. When I asked her if Kakuma was her destination she said yes. Then Loomis came back and they drove off. I thought it very funny that she might have left her husband to go back again to Mr. Loomis, and again I wondered if the two men were perhaps friends, and that the lady perhaps was also nothing more than that to Mr. Loomis. And then I remembered Muthongo in the wedding photo and I went and advised my superior. We contacted our Special Branch department and we were informed that indeed this woman was wanted by Security. There and then communication was made with Lokichoggio via radio call in the event that Mrs. Van de Velde should attempt to cross over the border."

"No more questions, thank you," the Indian attorney said, returning to his place.

Wanyonyi stood up but remained behind the table. "Senior Inspector, the first time you saw Mrs. Van de Velde, before she was married, she was in the company of Mr. Loomis, is that right?"

"That is what I said, yes."

"Why do you think Pamela Van de Velde née Emuria would travel all the way up to Turkana district to visit Mr. Loomis?"

"Sijui, I don't know."

"I object!" the prosecutor exclaimed, jumping to his feet. "He is asking the witness for an opinion he is not in a position to give."

"My Lords," Wanyonyi said, "because the nature of this inquiry is different from most ordinary criminal proceedings, it is imperative that the intent, or supposed intent of any alleged actions, must *a priori* be established. We must also give Inspector Hemed credit for being an observant policeman and allow him to interpret the behavior of the accused and Mrs. Van de Velde in order to ascertain the relationship between them. I therefore argue that my question is relevant and requires an answer."

Boy, what a mouthful, Loomis thought to himself. He now also appreciated the impressiveness of Geoff's deep throaty voice and imposing elocution.

"Yes, but while I'm in agreement with that," the judge said, "I'll have to ask you to rephrase your question."

"Yes, My Lords." He again faced Rashid. "Senior Inspector, when Mr. Loomis introduced this woman as his visitor..."

"He said friend, a friend from Nairobi."

"Yes, friend; even better." Geoff had made the slip on purpose, letting Rashid himself stress the personal nature of the visit. "What did you take that to mean?"

"My Lords, I object!"

"I'll allow that," the judge curtly told the prosecutor. "Witness, answer the question."

"His...girlfriend...his woman."

"Did Mr. Loomis, in his manner toward the lady, indicate that this was so?"

"He seemed very happy that day. Most other times he was in a bad mood, complaining about his job, about one problem or another, calling his bosses idiots...but that time he was cheerful. I almost felt sorry for the woman."

"What was that?" Wanyonyi asked out of reflex. He was known to be good at this: getting the prosecution's witnesses to volunteer more than was asked for.

"I mean, a beautiful woman, coming to him from Nairobi, and him being without a woman for so long, in the bush...like a gazelle walking into the den of a hungry lion; he would show her no mercy..."

The bailiff and the court clerk chuckled audibly while the prosecutor frowned, and the judge got peeved.

"Witness, I warn you to exclude such figurative language in this courtroom."

"I'm sorry, My Lords."

"Now, Inspector Hemed, when you saw them together again on August twenty-fifth of this year..." Geoff, in the strategy of presenting a truthful case, was conceding that Loomis was indeed in Lodwar on the day in question "...you assumed that they were still romantically linked, did you not?"

"Objection! Counsel is leading the witness."

"Counsel Wanyonyi," the judge warned, "I don't want to have to keep advising you on your questions put to the witness."

"My Lords, this question is based upon the witness's previous testimony, his own words..."

"Then I suggest you refer to those words."

"Yes, My Lords." Facing Rashid, he asked, "Mr. Hemed, you said that when you spotted these two people together on August twenty-fifth, you had thought it funny that she had left her husband to go back to Mr. Loomis."

"Ndio, yes but..."

"So again she appeared to you as a mistress visiting her lover."

"Objection! Counsel is answering the question for the witness."

"I'll answer it, My Lords," Rashid volunteered, his manner and timbre that of an injured party. He politely went on. "Yes, that was my first thought, but it also occurred to me that he could be under instructions to aid the woman, especially since there was a child..."

Geoff wouldn't let him finish. "Ah, this child you saw, you had told the courtroom earlier that he was her son. Was there anything that made you certain of that?"

"Well, I just assumed..."

"Did you get a good look at the child?"

"Objection, Counsel is badgering the witness, not giving him enough time to reply."

"Counsel Wanyonyi..."

Geoff quickly defended himself. "My Lords, the witness is being evasive when a simple yes or no answer is required."

"I don't see that he is," disagreed the judge. "Please conduct your cross-examination more appropriately, or I'll terminate it."

"Yes, My Lord." Geoff turned to the witness once more. "Did you get a good look at the child?'

"No, not really. I was concentrating on looking at the woman."

Dhiru stood up. "My Lords, I fail to understand this line of questioning."

"No, I'll allow it. Proceed," the judge said promptly.

"So you cannot say with any certainty whose child it was?"

"No, but it was a half-caste."

"Perhaps the child belonged to Mr. Loomis?"

"Objection!"

"Maybe," Rashid answered in weary resignation.

Loomis now expected Geoff to unload the bombshell about the boy, but he didn't, explaining to Loomis afterwards that he was merely drawing initial attention to the child, and saving the dramatic disclosure of paternity for Loomis's own testimony, and until Okova's corroboration of that night she came to visit him.

Instead, he now changed his line of questioning to focus on matters that seemed unimportant; some in fact, were rather trite, and both judge and prosecutor grew annoyed and bullied him to no end. Geoff shielded himself by citing chapters in the Laws of Kenya, the Evidence Act and other mumbo-jumbo until it dawned on Loomis that his advocate was stalling, buying time. The judge also realized this and gave Wanyonyi a stern reprimand. Geoff had to release the witness.

The second witness was a Sudanese from Interpol who, in response to the prompting of the prosecutor, explained the discovery that the Land Rover with the Kenyan plates was indeed the same as the one with the Sudanese registration. When State Counsel was finished, Wanyonyi announced he had no questions to ask the witness. After that followed a short recess.

Loomis and Wanyonyi were left alone in the little courtroom, except for the two policemen at the rear door.

"I think I've found something," Wanyonyi declared to his client. "But I still need a little time. I might be able to get another witness besides Okova, someone who could reveal a matter important to your defense."

"Who?"

"I didn't tell you yesterday, but a friend of mine, another member of the Railway Club, has a relation high up in Immigration. Last night I went to see him."

"So?"

"Just acting on a hunch, I went to Immigration. That's why I couldn't make it to see you. I managed to persuade some people there to let me have a peek at your file. There is a memorandum in it dated April 1980 which states that under no circumstances were you to be issued a resident work permit on the grounds that you posed a possible threat to internal security."

"Oh that's great! That's the nail in my coffin."

"Shut up and listen. That person I went to see last night tells me that such terminology is the standard way of chasing away certain foreigners without having to have a proper reason. If you were really a threat to security you would be classed as 'persona non grata'. In other words, such an order is a form of harassment. On top of that, this fellow confirms that those instructions came straight from the Minister's office, signed by the Minister for Justice himself, or should I say, the ex-Minister?"

"Muthongo?"

"That's right. They weren't stupid and they weren't blind. They knew you were playing around with their lady."

"Amonee thought pretty much the same. When I told her I couldn't get work in Kenya, she said he was making sure. She told Van de Velde about me. She tried to break away from him. He even threatened to take care of me, you know, have me murdered."

Loomis recalled once more those two Special Branch men who had confronted him near her house. The Special Branch at that time was also under the jurisdiction of the now infamous Mr. Muthongo.

"Anyway, it shows that quite contrary to the contention that you are Muthongo's confederate, you were actually somehow a thorn in his side. Otherwise why else would he try to make life miserable for you? I think with that, if I can get the Immigration official to testify, together with Okova's knowledge of you and the woman, and if..." Wanyonyi wavered, leaving his sentence in the air.

"If what?"

"If I can get you on the stand to tell the whole story, especially about the kid, since that can only come from your mouth, then we'll have given it our best shot. You don't have to testify you know. You'll be facing Dhiru and he can be tough. But I strongly advise you to follow my plan."

Loomis mulled over this as Wanyonyi pored over his papers. The next witness to be called after recess was Mwangi, and Wanyonyi went over again with Loomis the scene at the Lokichoggio police station and the discourse he had with the OCS.

The rest of the day was taken up with Mwangi's testimony, the emphasis being on Loomis's lie about not being in Lodwar on the twenty-fifth and the intentional deception regarding the registration plates, elucidating that Loomis was taking advantage of a radio breakdown between Lodwar and Lokichoggio. Mwangi added a little color to the account by including how he had been threatened with demotion for having let Loomis go. He then explained how he personally went to Juba to discuss with his Sudanese counterparts the matter of extradition and the request to be made to their respective legal authorities. When it was Wanyonyi's turn to cross examine the OCS, the advocate pried out of him certain irregularities of procedure used in obtaining Loomis, and also brought up, for good measure, the matter of the whiskey, while both the prosecutor and the judge verbally ganged up on him, thwarting most of the questions. It killed some time anyway.

By five o'clock in the evening, the first day of the inquiry had come to an end. The judge reminded everyone of the secrecy of the proceedings and apologized for the venue of the next day's court, which would be held in the office of the Senior Superintendent of Prison at Kamiti at eight o'clock, a move which would eliminate undue exposure to the case. Loomis was brusquely delivered back to his cell at the prison.

* * *

October 4th. Again at six o'clock in the morning Loomis was ushered into the shower and again at seven o'clock he was given his clothes. They did not handcuff him this time, but instead, exited, leaving him alone in his cell even after he was dressed. They did not return. Eight o'clock came and went. Loomis wondered what was up. Was someone important, one of the judges perhaps, late? Could a function as official as this run on African time as well? Did Geoff succeed with getting an adjournment? At nine-fifteen Loomis couldn't stand the mystery any longer and he called for the guard.

Their eyes faced each other through the peep slot.

"What's going on?" Loomis asked. "They're late."

The guard made no sound, but brought his hand up into view and, motioning with his finger, wordlessly told Loomis to retreat back into the tiny recess of his cell.

He paced back and forth in the confined space, going over what might be possible explanations. Could it be that Geoff had approached the prosecution with the facts about his Immigration record? Would such a twist in the investigations render necessary a major re-evaluation of the case? All morning he waited in suspense.

It wasn't until twelve noon that the somber silence of the Isolation Block was disrupted by a group of footsteps with low voices. The cell door opened. Two grave-looking Africans in grey suits, one of them a short guy carrying a black attaché case, entered. The taller of the two wore thick, black-framed spectacles, and he was now facing Loomis. He said in a subdued, yet certain authority, "Sit down."

Loomis sat down on his bed like a schoolboy ordered to by his tutor.

The shorter man placed his attaché case on the bed, beside Loomis, opened it, took out a manila folder, and handed it to his associate. The tall guy removed a sheet of paper from the folder and gave it to Loomis. "Is that her handwriting?" he asked.

Loomis looked at the piece of paper. It was a letter:

TO THE EXALTED PRESIDENT OF THE REPUBLIC OF KENYA
Your Excellency:
Forgive me for writing directly to you, but I could trust no one else with my plea. I am ashamed to admit that I evaded the authorities and fled Kenya illegally, but I truthfully plead that I never intended any harm against you nor against the Kenyan nation. I was worried over the welfare of my two-year-old son, and I acted out of a blind maternal instinct. Knowing that you are a devout Christian who loves children, perhaps you can understand how I felt.

I am also responsible for involving Mr. Daryl Loomis. It was I who forced him to help me. I went to him and informed him that he was the father of my child. It is true, he is the father, for Mr. Loomis and I were lovers, and it is only because of threats made by Jon Van de Velde that we are apart. It was under such threats, directed against Mr. Loomis, that I married Mr. Van de Velde.

I swear by our Almighty God that I have nothing to do with my husband's dubious activities. I know that I can prove that by coming back and giving myself up and to tell the Special Branch whatever they want to know. I am willing to do this, although my child will remain in London with trusted friends.

Please do not feel that I want to give conditions for my return, but I must beg you from the bottom of my heart that you forgive Mr.Loomis and release him. He did what he did for one reason only, the love he has for me and our child. It is for that reason that he is now languishing in prison, suffering only because of what he felt was his duty to protect us. With your unbounded wisdom and courage I know you alone of all people can make that decision, as my own courage and wisdom will bring me back to my motherland.

Yours obediently

Pamela Amonee Emuria

(former Mrs. Van de Velde).

"Yes," said Loomis with a vacuous face. "How did you get this?"

"Diplomatic pouch from the High Commissioner in London. It arrived late last night."

"Was this my advocate's idea?"

"No, she was the one to approach the Kenya Mission. She got word of your detention through friends, other Kenyans living abroad, and then through the press."

"What do you want from me?"

"There is a Kenya Airways plane that leaves at five o'clock every evening, Rome-Frankfurt-London. You take this flight. Mrs. Van de Velde will be contacted. The president himself has decided that you are to bring her back, since you were the one who took her out. If you do that, you are pardoned. It is up to you to show if you are worthy of His Excellency's merciful clemency. No harm will come to Mrs. Van de Velde, you have the president's word on that, and by now she may already have in her possession a letter from him proving the truth of what I say. What is required from her is information. Simple things like phone calls made and received, letters, dinner guests, they can reveal much about what we need to know. We are in the process of weeding out the Muthongo elements who are hiding in government positions, and also of finding out which of the smiling-faced foreigners have planned to stab the Kenyan people in the back. She being the wife of Jon Van de Velde, she will have known the identities of some of these people. That is all we require of her. Otherwise she will be permitted to live a normal life here in her own country. You should also urge her to come with the child, because the very thing she feared when she left here could well happen there in Europe. Under the circumstances the boy would be safer here. In these times one cannot tell how trusted a friend really is."

"Where's my lawyer?"

"He is not privy to this information. All this must be kept secret. For her safety, nobody other than necessary should know."

"It could be that she's safer if she just stays put. Just by removing herself from the situation."

Neither of the men bothered to comment on that.

"What if I refuse?"

"You can expect at least ten, maybe as much as twenty years in prison."

"For what? Plotting to take over the government?"

"In addition to the conspiracy charges against you, human trafficking would be included, a separate offense."

"Human trafficking?"

"You smuggled a young woman and a child into a dubious country. That is a fact, regardless of your purpose."

"Can I have some time to think about it?"

The man looked at his watch. "About fifty hours. If you don't get on the plane the day after tomorrow, the offer is rescinded."

The short guy took back the letter and returned it to the manila envelope, which he placed back in his attaché case, subsequently closing it with the snapping of the clasps.

"If you decide to go," said the tall guy, obviously the one in charge, "please inform us as early as possible. You will need to receive further instructions along the way. Here is the number to call."

He was handed a card that had only a telephone number, in a block bold font. No name, address, or anything, just the number.

"You call, then merely say 'yes' or 'no'."

After that statement they left abruptly. The cell door clanged shut to leave Loomis alone with his thoughts.

This was a tough one.

The little devil on his left shoulder told him to take the deal. *You would be together again, with your woman and child; the alternative would be ten years, but probably more, in prison. You like it here in prison?*

The little angel on his right shoulder told him that Amonee's decision was perilous, not only for her, but also for the child. *She is not being rational. She is only doing this out of her love for you. You must be strong. You should do the thinking for the both of you. You should refuse.*

The little devil countered strongly. *That is correct. You are the one to do the thinking. When you meet her in London, just forbid her to come back to Kenya. Simple.*

The little angel contradicted this wholeheartedly. *You know her, know the kind of person she is. She would not go back on her word to the president, and not even you would be able to stop her.*

So make the obvious choice, the little devil advocated.

What is the obvious choice? Loomis asked.

The little angel could only say, *I don't honestly know.*

* * *

In the morning of the next day, Loomis called the guard from behind the door.

"Nini? What??" the guard asked fiercely.

"I need to make a phone call."

LONDON OCTOBER 6 1983

There it was, London, the whole of the city summed up in a view from an airplane window. Flight KQ 132 from Nairobi-Rome-Frankfurt was circling in. He looked for landmarks: the ribbon of the Thames, Tower Bridge, Big Ben...the no-smoking light flashed on, then came the sound of the landing gear emerging from beneath the wings. Nine o'clock Greenwich Mean Time, and in two minutes the DC-10 would touch down, ending what had seemed the longest flight he had ever been on. He had talked to no one during the past twelve hours, knowing there had to be Special Branch officers on board keeping a watch on him. But out of the many African passengers, he could not tell which of them they might be. Then again, there was no reason to think the agents were African; a good number of Europeans and Asians were also in the employ of the Special Branch; it could be anyone.

The jet passed over a motorway, so close he could read the license plates of the vehicles. Trees flashed by and then – the openness of the airfield – the jolting contact between the wheels and the ground – the engines roaring in retrograde – Heathrow!

The plane taxied to the music of a syrupy instrumental until it parked itself at one of the gates. There followed the usual mass-release of seat belts, the fumbling for hand luggage, and the lumbering shuffle off the plane. Loomis had no suitcases to collect, so he went straight to the Immigration queues. The lines were long, but they moved rather continuously, the procedure for most of the people in front of him being quite brief.

Questions came, and answers followed. From Kenya, a few days only, one thousand two hundred dollars, Loomis succinctly replied to the official questions. In just twenty minutes from the time he alighted from the plane he was out of the airport and into a cool, grey, London day.

It was bone-chilling cold; he'd have to buy a coat or jacket somewhere. He headed right away for a taxi.

"Where to?" the driver asked.

"The city."

"Which end?"

"Take me to a small hotel with a low profile, but one that's in a decent neighborhood," Loomis told him, getting in.

"Right. Lexham Gardens? You know it? Lot of small, clean, inexpensive lodgings. Between Kensington High Street and Earl's Court," the driver informed him, pulling out of the terminal.

"Fine." Loomis noticed the driver spoke with an East Anglia accent, pronouncing 'gardens' as gaadens and 'Earl's' as 'ales'.

The taxicab cruised along the M4 while he stared out at the suburban scenery, attempting to calm the butterflies in his stomach. Tomorrow. Tomorrow he would meet her. He'd have to get through the afternoon and a whole night just waiting. He turned his head to look through the back window, thinking that perhaps the black sedan right behind them might be following them. Stupid. This was a motorway into the city, of course everyone was going in the same direction. Still, he was nervous.

"You're lightly dressed for this weather," the driver observed, noting that his passenger wore only a short-sleeved shirt and no outerwear. "Where'd you come from?"

"I a...I just came from...Rome...it was pretty warm down there."

"Must have been a short trip. I see you don't have much luggage."

"Yeah, well...I left in a hurry...went for a funeral...a cousin died."

"Oh, sorry." The taxi driver paused, changing lanes. "But you're a Yank, aren't ya? I can tell by the way you speak."

"Canadian." Loomis couldn't shake his feelings of paranoia, and thought it wise not to answer any more questions. "Say, listen, if I fall asleep, wake me up when we get there." He hoped the cabbie got the message.

* * *

The grey surface of the Thames, rippled with foamy white wavelets, elicited images of dirty, days-old snow on the New York streets of his childhood. Loomis peered out at the river, elbows propped on the railing, the wind tousling his hair, waiting anxiously for one o'clock. That's when she said she would come. He could hardly believe he was here, in London, on the Embankment, standing before Cleopatra's Needle, minutes away from seeing Amonee in the flesh. His eyes followed a small barge as it scudded by. He unrolled the newspaper he was clutching – the Observer – and read the story again: 'KENYAN GOVERNMENT RELEASES AMERICAN DETAINEE'.

It was supposed to be a secret; now the whole world knew. He read the byline: Scott Richardson, AP, Nairobi. Where did that parasite get that info? It wouldn't have been Geoff.

"Some secret," he muttered bitterly. With his fingers he carefully tore out the news item, folded it, and put it in his pocket. It would join his collection.

The chilly, raw breezes off the river stung his face so he turned around – and there she was! Walking towards him! Draped in a maxi-length overcoat, holding the hand of the capped and jacketed little boy who tottered at her side, she took several steps more before halting in front of him.

They stood rooted, gazing concertedly at one another. Amonee's hair had grown into a thin cover over her scalp; the Turkana braidlets were gone. The ebony oval of her face wore an expression of calm sobriety, but flickers of the acute emotions she was bridling inside her were betrayed by a flutter in her dark brown eyes. She let go of the boy's hand and slowly approached him, stopping one pace away. "Hello," she said softly.

He drank in her image before he responded. "Hello."

Each raised their hands gently, and mutually caressed the other's face for some seconds, still intently eying one another as if to assure themselves that the other was real, when Loomis, with the force of his passion, abruptly hugged her. She buried her head in his shoulder and wept while tears welled out of his own eyes.

"We're going back and we'll finish this business and that will be the end of it. Then we're going to have a normal, happy life together." He said it with a tone that guaranteed he would make sure of it.

"Budee! Momee, budee!" exclaimed the two-year-old, pointing to a seagull perched on the railing.

Amonee composed herself and smiled demurely, glancing at her son. "He really has a thing for birds." Then, looking up at Loomis, "Oh, Daryl! I love you so much it hurts." She fell against him, embracing him tightly.

"I love you too," he said. They kissed each other frantically, moistening their cheeks and noses with their tears.

"Budee, budee!"

"I think our son is going to be an ornithologist," he said, laughing. "Let's give him a treat and hang out with the pigeons in Trafalgar Square. C'mon," he urged, slipping his arm through hers.

They walked there. It was a comforting relief to be strolling in the safety of a big cosmopolitan city, so far away from official inquiries, furtive police, and political intrigues; elated just to lose themselves among mothers in down jackets pushing baby prams, past white collar, business-suited executives absorbed in their appointments, aside elderly citizens in tweed overcoats and peaked caps; lollipop-red, double-decker buses and woolly Rastafarians; punky kids with green and blue hair, shoppers shuttling to and from the stores; all of which made them feel like two ordinary contented people cozily wedged inside the city's bustle.

At Trafalgar Square the little boy fed popcorn to the pigeons while Amonee and Loomis sat on a bench bringing each other up to date on what they had been through. She described how her husband Jon had accepted it all: no protests, no threats, no condemnations, only a rancorous silence. She praised the understanding and cooperation of the Kenyan High Commission, through which all communication had been made, while Loomis in turn answered her tearful questions, earnestly assuring her that he had been well-treated in prison, and exaggerating the courtroom heroics of Geoffrey Wanyonyi. They debated over whether or not the long, laborious journey through the Turkana desert and the flight to Europe had been for naught. "Perhaps not," he told her. After all, it had brought her case to the attention of the president, and possibly that added a layer of protection.

At four o'clock it was getting dark, and Loomis opted for their departure.

"I've got us a room in a tiny hotel where no one can disturb us. How does that sound?"

"Anywhere with you would be lovely."

* * *

On the Green Line they wallowed in the shielding cover of the early-rush-hour crowd, unnoticeable other than as a racially mixed couple heading home with their young son. They disembarked at Earl's Court station and walked the fifteen minutes to the Orion Hotel.

The hotel was more like a boarding house, with only eight rooms on two floors, two on each side of a small hallway. The hotel lobby was more like a small parlor, and when the couple entered there was no one except for the person sitting in the one of the three stately plush chairs, his face hidden by the newspaper he was reading, a small travel bag parked near his feet. No one was behind the reception counter.

"Hello, Yusuf!" Loomis called out.

The Orion Hotel being a small enterprise; the Moroccan Yusuf had many other duties besides manning the reception counter: making the continental breakfast, checking stock of the toilet paper and other required sundries for the rooms, and so on.

"Oh, Mr. Loomis, I see your wife, she has come," Yusuf noted as he emerged from the stock room just behind the reception area.

"Yes, and she's very tired, not to mention our boy."

"Oh, sorry, sorry." Yusuf had a tendency to be overly apologetic, especially over things that weren't his fault. "Here you go, room number 4, right?"

"*Shukran*," Loomis thanked him in Arabic, accepting the keys. "Amonee, this is Yusuf, but everybody around here calls him Joe. He's a student at the London School of Economics."

"Nice to meet you."

"Very nice to meet you."

"See you later, Joe." Loomis led them to their room, a bit under-sized for a double, although economically occupied by a pair of twin beds, a miniature table together with two chairs, and a television set mounted on a rolling console. He helped the boy off with his jacket while Amonee hung her coat up in the closet. Then they embraced once again.

The man in the reception area folded his newspaper up and approached Yusuf behind the counter. "Hi, I see that Room 5 is vacant. Can I have that one please?"

"Oh yes, sorry, sorry to keep you waiting," Yusuf replied, signing in the man and handing him his room key.

Inside their room, Loomis announced, "I'm changing my vocation. I'm going to be a farmer. No more work out in the bush for me. I'll be a homebody from now on. How would you like to be a farmer's wife?"

"I'd be a street cleaner's wife if the street cleaner were you."

They kissed to celebrate her declaration. "I want so much for everything to be alright," she said.

"It will."

The little boy hung on her dress and tugged, whining and moaning. "Mommee, Mommeeee! Eeeeee!" He raised his arms in supplication, indicating his longing to be held.

"He's tired," she noted, picking him up.

Outside, next door, the heavy-shouldered blond man carrying the small travel bag stood in front of room number 5, looked furtively up and down the narrow hallway, and inserted his key into the lock.

"Maybe he's hungry," Loomis remarked, regarding the child.

She sat down on one of the twin beds with the boy in her arms, the latter still making half-hearted grunts of complaint. "No, he usually has his nap at this time." She stretched the child out on the bed and took off his shoes, then reposed beside him. Making room for Loomis, she patted the bed. "Come," she beckoned.

"Not a bad idea. I'm still suffering from jet lag, God!" He lay down next to her as she made a little more room for him.

After flinging his coat on one of the twin beds, the blond-haired man crawled under the one opposite, still clutching the travel bag.

"So what do you reckon, Mrs. Loomis? We grow a few acres of maize, all kinds of beans, maybe have a couple of hybrid dairy cows. And definitely goats."

"And chickens. Can't have an African home without a few chickens rummaging around outside."

"Right, let's not forget the chickens. What about some pigs?"

"Only one, as a pet."

"You mean to keep like a dog? Okay, and we can have real dogs as well."

"Look, he's asleep already," she announced, nodding towards the slumbering child. "I know when my son is tired."

In Room 5, the blond man meticulously placed the fusing element, checking the circuit as he did so, and then scrutinized the timer.

"And what will you be doing while I'm farming?" Loomis asked, back in Room 4.

Amonee feigned an expression of having been slighted. "I can help you! In fact I'll most likely have to teach you. I'm surely more experienced than someone who was brought up in New York City. And then there is our son to raise. That's work too."

"Hey, I know, you can start a school for orphans."

She smiled, entertained by his runaway enthusiasm. "You're serious, aren't you?"

"Sure, why not? We can do anything if we put our minds to it."

In the past he had been contracted by many – the IRA, the Red Brigade, even the Palestinians – his anonymity being one of his greater assets, keeping him much in demand. Of these people he knew nothing, except that they paid well.

"Before you get too carried away, you must know I don't have any land," she said. "Traditionally all my father's land goes to my brothers."

"No problem. We'll buy a shamba in Ukambani. Plenty of land there, a bit dry though. But we can sink a borehole. Might as well take advantage of my past vocation."

In the other room, the blond man crawled out from under the bed, grabbed his coat, and made for the door, shutting it gently behind him, taking his now-empty travel bag, and departed hastily from the room without locking it.

"I'm hungry," Loomis said, after a pause in their ramblings.

"I don't feel like going out again."

"No, neither do I really. Let's do this. I'll go quickly to a takeaway place, fish and chips or something, and we'll eat in the room."

"No, don't go away," she coyly objected.

"Just a few minutes. Then I can come back and relax with you. Meanwhile you can have first crack at the shower." He sat up and put on his shoes.

"Please don't be long."

"I won't. I'll be right back." He stood up and grabbed the windbreaker he had purchased in a small shop in the morning. "Do you have any preferences?" he asked her.

"Anything. Oh, and some...milk."

"Milk. Right." He took the keys and opened the door. "Lock the door and don't open it for anyone, not even Yusuf. Be back in ten minutes," he promised.

Out on the streets London was dark and damp and the street-lights were haloed with subtle rainbow rings. Loomis buttoned his windbreaker up to his neck as he strode towards Cromwell Drive.

The four-lane avenue was busy with the cars of commuters and he had to wait for the traffic signal to change before he was able to cross. In the vicinity of Earl's Court, the little street he was walking on bloomed in the neon of a multitude of snack shops and tiny restaurants. As he passed each one he interrogated himself on what he would like to eat. *Chinese? No, probably take too long. McDonald's? Fuck that!* He stopped in front of a little Indo-Arab place. Through the window he could see a tray full of triangular-shaped savories – samosas! He entered and went up to the swarthy-faced, curly-haired, Asian behind the counter. "Samosas please."

"How many?"

"Uh...let me have..." Loomis quickly calculated in his head, "fifteen."

"Fifteen?"

Loomis leaned over the counter and said in a low voice, as if revealing a secret, "I've got a family to feed." He gave the Indian a conspiring wink.

The man smiled. "Very good. Fifteen." He proceeded to deposit the samosas in a paper bag.

"Oh, and, a, do you have any milk?"

"Over there," the Indian told him, pointing to a showcase fridge in the corner.

The items collected and paid for, Loomis left the shop and went back out into the nippy night air. Just as he was once again waiting to cross Cromwell Drive, he thought he saw a flash of light and then came a sound like thunder.

"What was that?" he wondered aloud. He thought of gas-leak explosions and nervously hurried across the big avenue against the traffic light, scurrying in front of the beeping oncoming traffic. He quickened his pace as he reached the pavement, then, like a sudden blow, he was seized with a most profound dread. Dropping the bag of samosas, he broke into a run.

"AMONEE!" he screamed.

He sprinted along the sidewalk, fighting off the obdurate voices of doom in his head, voices mercilessly shouting out irrevocable disaster, which he refused to listen to.

"AMONEE!" he screamed.

Running, he saw the smoke. Running, he saw the small crowd.

"AMONEE!" he screamed.

The startled onlookers, gawking in awe, formed a human barricade. Glass, timber, and shards of brick were splayed across the whole street and on the damaged marquee of the Orion Hotel, it was only the R and an O which remained.

Loomis bulldozed his way through the assemblage of shocked spectators. "AMONEE!" he screamed.

Clear of the mob, he stopped short, wide-eyed with horror at the smoke billowing from the gaping hole where the entrance used to be, his body trembling with terror. He slapped his thighs, "NO, OH GOD, NO!" He beat his chest and screamed so hard he could feel the insides of his throat tearing apart. The crowd watched, stunned, as he made for the fiery building.

"HEY, STOP HIM!" someone yelled. Several youths ran out after him. A teenager in a leather jacket tripped him up and then, falling himself, attempted to grab a hold of Loomis's legs, as they both hit the ground. Loomis tried to break loose by rolling over and clawing at the concrete steps.

"LET ME DIE WITH THEM! I SHOULD DIE WITH THEM!" He freed himself and made another dash towards the burning hotel but the others had already caught up to him. Loomis went wild, his swinging arms injuring some of the people restraining him.

"GRAB HIS ARMS!"

He got a strange feeling of leaving his body and looking down at himself, as if the body convulsing with grief was not his own, as if all this was happening to someone else, not him. In the midst of his seizure mournful voices called to him from the past, first in the distance, then drawing closer, becoming louder, the sounds of chanting, wailing, whistles and keening ululations – the Teso funeral song. Cascading dolefully in his head, engulfing him, it was the last thing he remembered before falling unconscious in the arms of the men who were holding him.

EPILOGUE

Dr. Tessa Thorpe rose from her chair and sat on the edge of her patient's bed. After three months of regular sessions, she felt there was no undue risk in doing that. Three months of sessions in this same, antiseptic, bare, whitewashed room. It had been realized some time ago that Loomis knew nothing more than what Interpol already knew concerning the perpetrators of the attack. Her continuation on the case was solely to get him back on his feet.

"Daryl, even though I know you don't want it, maybe even dread it, I'm going to recommend that you be discharged."

He just nodded his head compliantly.

"I know that you're still debilitated by a great sense of loss, but you're not alone in this. Millions of people all over the world are stricken by long-lasting grief, and they're not committed to mental institutions. They cope. You have to cope."

At this pronouncement, he did not stir.

She leaned over to the lamp-less night table and grabbed her black portfolio briefcase that she used for her documents. After fumbling through it, she produced the two photographs that were taken in Uhuru Park.

"Here, take these."

He stretched his arm to receive the two photos, looking at the one on top despondently, before shuffling to the second one.

Tessa did something that she had made a rule never to do with patients. She became human, compassionate, and worst of all, prose-lytizing. "I understand your feelings of ending your life, but that would be self-defeating. Your wife and child live through you. Your memory preserves them. For that reason alone, you have an obligation to keep living, however much it hurts."

He nodded his head in sober agreement. "I'm sorry for what I did," he said.

"I know. But you have to move on from guilt. It's been long

enough." She put her hand on his shoulder. "Goodbye, Daryl."

"Goodbye, Tessa."

She got up, clutching her briefcase, and walked towards the door. She opened it, then turned around. "I'll arrange to have outpatient sessions at my office. If you want."

He bowed his head in concurrence.

Then she left the room.

Walking briskly toward the exit stairway, Tessa could not, as she usually did, shut out the case of Daryl Loomis from her mind. And worse still, she applied it to herself. She was now grateful, even relieved, that her life did not involve romantic entanglements full of intense emotions. But these thoughts caused an unexpected response. A sob erupted from her throat without warning, and her eyes moistened.

"We're all sorry for what we do," she uttered to herself, without knowing why.

Tessa Thorpe and Daryl Loomis will be back in *Played*, a psychological political thriller.

At Roundfire we publish great stories. We lean towards the spiritual and thought-provoking. But whether it's literary or popular, a gentle tale or a pulsating thriller, the connecting theme in all Roundfire fiction titles is that once you pick them up you won't want to put them down.